The Identicals

KU-488-707

34 4124 0013 3336

Also by Elin Hilderbrand

Winter Storms
Here's to Us
Christmas on Nantucket
The Rumour
Winter Street
The Matchmaker
Beautiful Day
Summerland
Silver Girl
The Island
The Castaways
A Summer Affair
Barefoot
The Love Season
The Blue Bistro
Summer People
Nantucket Nights
The Beach Club

About the Author

Elin Hilderbrand has a twin brother who is not a bestselling novelist. She does her best writing on the beaches of Nantucket as well as on the charming streets of Beacon Hill, in Boston. She has three magical children who beg her not to sing along to the radio or dance in public. *The Identicals* is her nineteenth novel.

You can visit Elin's website at www.elinhilderbrand.net, follow her on Twitter @elinhilderbrand or find out more on her Facebook page www.facebook.com/ElinHilderbrand.

The Identicals

Elin Hilderbrand

HODDER &
STOUGHTON

First published in the USA in 2017 by Little, Brown and Company
A division of Hachette Book Group, Inc.

First published in Great Britain in 2017 by Hodder & Stoughton
An Hachette UK company

1

Copyright © Elin Hilderbrand 2017

The right of Elin Hilderbrand to be identified as the Author of the Work has been asserted by her in accordance with the Copyright, Designs and Patents Act 1988.

All rights reserved. No part of this publication may be reproduced, stored in a retrieval system, or transmitted, in any form or by any means without the prior written permission of the publisher, nor be otherwise circulated in any form of binding or cover other than that in which it is published and without a similar condition being imposed on the subsequent purchaser.

All characters in this publication are fictitious and any resemblance to real persons, living or dead is purely coincidental.

A CIP catalogue record for this title is available from the British Library

Trade Paperback ISBN 978 1 473 61123 8
Ebook ISBN 978 1 473 61124 5

Printed and bound by Clays Ltd, St Ives plc

Hodder & Stoughton policy is to use papers that are natural, renewable and recyclable products and made from wood grown in sustainable forests. The logging and manufacturing processes are expected to conform to the environmental regulations of the country of origin.

Hodder & Stoughton Ltd
Carmelite House
50 Victoria Embankment
London EC4Y 0DZ

www.hodder.co.uk

For Eric, Randy, Heather, and Doug
Together we stand

The Identicals

NANTUCKET

Like thousands of other erudite, discerning people, you've decided to spend your summer vacation on an island off the coast of Massachusetts. You want postcard beaches. You want to swim, sail, and surf in Yankee-blue waters. You want to eat clam chowder and lobster rolls, and you want those dishes served to you by someone who calls them *chowdah* and *lobstah.* You want to ride in a Jeep with the top down, your golden retriever, named Charles Emerson Winchester III, riding shotgun. You want to live the dream. You want an American summer.

But wait! You're torn. Should you choose Nantucket... or Martha's Vineyard? And does it really matter? Aren't the islands *pretty much the same?*

We chuckle and smirk at the assumption, shared by so many. Possibly you're not familiar with the bumper sticker (a bestseller at the Hub on Main Street and proudly displayed on the vehicles of nearly every islander of distinction, including the director of the Nantucket Island Chamber of Commerce) that reads: GOD MADE THE VINEYARD... BUT HE LIVES ON NANTUCKET.

If you're not swayed by that kind of shameless propaganda, then consider the vital statistics:

Nantucket Island

Settled: 1659
Original inhabitants: Wampanoag Indians
Distance from Hyannis: 30 miles
Area: 45 square miles
Population: 11,000 year-round; 50,000 summer
Number of towns: 1
Famous residents: Prefer not to be named

Martha's Vineyard

Settled: 1642 (We say: "Age before beauty")
Original inhabitants: Wampanoag Indians
Distance from Woods Hole: 11 miles (We say: "It's practically the mainland!")
Area: 100 square miles (We say: "Twice as big")
Population: 16,535 year-round; 100,000 summer (We say: "Twice as many")
Number of towns: 6 (We are speechless [!!!]—and can someone please tell us what is up with Chappaquiddick?)
Famous residents: Meg Ryan, Lady Gaga, Skip Gates, Vernon Jordan, Carly Simon, James Taylor, and... John Belushi, deceased and buried off South Road (They have Bluto; we say: "So what?")

Is there any part of Martha's Vineyard that can compete with our cobblestone streets or the stately perfection of the Three Bricks, the homes that whale-oil merchant Joseph Starbuck built for his three sons between 1837 and 1840? Does the Vineyard have an enclave of tiny rose-covered cottages—as whimsical as dollhouses—as we do in the picturesque village of 'Sconset? Does "MVY" have a protected arm of golden-sand beach, home to piping plovers and a colony of seals, as our northernmost tip, Great Point, does? Does it have a sweeping vista like the one offered across Sesachacha Pond toward the peppermint stick of Sankaty Head Lighthouse? Does it have a dive bar as glamorously gritty as the Chicken Box, where one can hear Grace Potter one week and Trombone Shorty the next? You might not want to get us started on the superiority of our restaurants. If it were our last night on earth, who among us could choose between the cheeseburger with garlic fries from the Languedoc Bistro and the seared-scallop taco with red cabbage slaw from Millie's?

We understand how you might confuse those of us here with our compatriots there—after all, our region is lumped together as the Cape and the islands—but we are two distinct nations, each with its own ways, its own means, its own traditions, histories, and secrets, and its own web of gossip and scandal. Think of the two islands as you would a set of twins. Outwardly, we look alike, but beneath the surface…we are individuals.

MARTHA'S VINEYARD

There is a bumper sticker—a bestseller, according to the owner of Alley's General Store—that reads: GOD MADE NANTUCKET, BUT HE LIVES ON THE VINEYARD. Some of us would have edited that bumper sticker to say BUT HE LIVES IN CHILMARK—because who wants to be lumped in with the honky-tonk shenanigans happening down island?

However, in the interest of keeping this a foreign war and not a civil one, let's celebrate the reasons we're superior to Nantucket. The Vineyard has diversity—of races, of opinions, of terrain. We have the Methodist campground, with its colorful gingerbread houses; the Tabernacle; Ocean Park; Inkwell Beach; Donovan's Reef, home of the Dirty Banana—and that's only in Oak Bluffs! We have dozens of family farms that harvest an abundance of organic produce; we have the Jaws Bridge and the cliffs of Aquinnah; we have East Chop, West Chop, the Katama airstrip, and a neighbor in Edgartown who keeps llamas on his front lawn. We have Chappaquiddick, which is a lot more than just the place where Teddy Kennedy may or may not have driven Mary Jo Kopechne to her death off the Dike Bridge. After all, there is a Japanese garden on Chappy! And if we let the air in our Jeep tires down to eleven pounds and pay two hundred dollars for a sticker, we can enjoy the wild, windswept beauty of Cape Poge.

We have rolling hills, deciduous trees, and low stone walls. We have Menemsha, the best fishing village in the civilized world, where one can get the freshest seafood, the creamiest chowder, and the crispiest, most succulent fried whole-belly clams. Have you never heard of the Bite? Larsen's? The Home Port? These are iconic spots; these are legends.

We have the best celebrations: Illumination Night, the Ag Fair, the August fireworks. We aren't sure what anyone celebrates on Nantucket other than being able to land a plane successfully at the airport despite the pea-soup fog or finally being able to find the correct shade of dusty pink on a pair of dress pants.

But what really makes the Vineyard special is the people.

The Vineyard boasts a large and active population of middle- and upper-class African Americans. We have Brazilian churches. We also have celebrities, but you would never recognize half of them because they have to wait in line at "Back Door Doughnuts" and sit in traffic at Five Corners in Vineyard Haven just like everyone else.

Most of us have only been to Nantucket for one reason: the Island Cup. We won't say anything about the football game itself, because no one likes a braggart, but every time we visit to cheer on our high school players, we can't help wondering how our fellow islanders can bear to live on such a flat, barren, and foggy rock so far out to sea.

Still, there is a connection between us that's hard to refute. Geologists suspect that as recently as twenty-three thousand years ago, Martha's Vineyard, Nantucket, and Cape Cod were all part of one landmass. It might be easier to think of us as sisters—twins, even—birthed by the same mother. We like to think of Martha's Vineyard as the favorite.

But then, of course, Nantucket likes to think of herself as the favorite.

MARTHA'S VINEYARD: HARPER

Reed Zimmer isn't on call at 7:00 p.m. on Friday, June 16, when Harper Frost's father, Billy, draws his final breath. Dr. Zimmer is at a picnic at Lambert's Cove with his wife's family; apparently they hold the same party every year at the start of summer—bonfire, potato salad, chicken blackening on the portable Weber grill. Sadie Zimmer's brother, Franklin Phelps, is one of the Vineyard's favorite guitar players—Harper always goes to hear him when he's playing at the Ritz—and Harper imagines Dr. Zimmer, his feet buried in the cold sand, singing along with Franklin to "Wagon Wheel."

Harper is still at her father's bedside when she sends Dr. Zimmer a text. It says: *Billy is gone.* She imagines his shock followed by his guilt; he promised Harper it wouldn't happen tonight. He told her that Billy still had time.

"Check in on him as usual," Dr. Zimmer had said that afternoon when he rose from Harper's bed, the white sheets tangled from their lovemaking. "But feel free to enjoy your weekend." He had looked out her window at the lilac bush, which overnight, it seemed, had exploded into a show-offy bloom. "I can't believe it's all starting again. Another summer."

Feel free to enjoy your weekend? Harper had thought. She hated when Reed talked to her as though she were merely his patient's daughter, a virtual stranger—but isn't she a stranger to him, in a way? Reed only sees Harper when she's sitting by her father's hospital bed or when they're making love in her duplex. They don't go on dates; they have never bumped into each other at Cronig's; Reed claims he has never noticed her driving the Rooster delivery truck, even when she waves at him like a woman drowning. Harper and Reed have been sleeping together only since October, and so she isn't sure what 'another summer' means to him. Today offered the first clue: his wife's parents, the elder Phelpses, are now in residence at their house in Katama, recently arrived back from Vero Beach. There will be family obligations, such as this picnic, when it will seem as though Reed is living on another planet.

Harper waits a few moments before texting anyone else. Her father is right here, but he's gone. His face is slack; it looks *vacated,* like a house where there's no one home. Billy died while Harper was talking to him about Dustin Pedroia of the Red Sox; he took one great shuddering breath, then another, then he looked right into Harper's eyes, into her heart, into her soul, and said, "I'm sorry, kiddo." And that was it. Harper put her ear to his chest. The machine issued its sustained beep. Calling the game. Over.

Reed doesn't text back. Harper tries to remember if there is cell reception at Lambert's Cove. She is always making excuses for him, because of the three men now remaining in her life, he's the one she's in love with.

She sends the same text—*Billy is gone*—to Sergeant Drew Truman of the Edgartown Police Department. Harper and Drew have been dating for three weeks. He asked her out while they were both on the Chappy ferry, and Harper thought, *Why not?* Drew Truman belongs to one of the most prominent African American families in Oak Bluffs. His mother, Yvonne Truman, served as a selectman for more than ten years. She is one of the five Snyder sisters, all of whom own brightly colored, impeccably maintained gingerbread cottages facing Ocean Park. Harper remembered Drew back when he was a high school athlete featured every week in the *Vineyard Gazette* sports pages. He then went to college and the police academy before coming home to Dukes County to serve and protect.

Harper had thought that dating someone new might ameliorate the agony of seeing a married man. She and Drew have gone out six times: they've eaten Mexican food at Sharky's four times (it's Drew's favorite, for reasons Harper can't quite comprehend), they had lunch once at the Katama airstrip diner, and their most recent date was a "fancy" night out at the Seafood Shanty—surf and turf, water views, singing waiters. Harper knows that Drew expected sex at the end of the night, but Harper has been able to hold him off thus far, citing her dying father as the reason she can't be intimate.

Drew is keen to introduce Harper to his mother, his brother, his brother's wife, his nieces and nephews, his aunties, his cousins, his cousins' children—the whole extended Snyder-Truman family—but this, too, is a step Harper isn't ready to take. Part of her does yearn to be taken in, fussed and clucked over, cooked for, admired and petted, even argued with and looked askance at because her skin is white. In short, there is appeal in being "official" with Drew. But the harsh reality remains: Harper loves Reed and only Reed.

Harper sighs. Drew is working the beat tonight. He makes double time on weekends, but with all the bozos out drinking too much and enjoying the first days of the summer season, is it worth it? He'll go on thirty calls, she bets, and twenty-seven of them will be drunk and disorderlies and three will be accidents involving taxi drivers who haven't learned their way around yet.

The third man remaining in Harper's life is her precious, damaged friend Brendan Donegal, who is exiled over on Chappy. Harper wants to let Brendan know that Billy has died, but Brendan can't manage texting anymore. Like twenty-six killer wasps, the alphabet swarms him. He uses his phone only to tell the time.

Nothing from Dr. Zimmer. Will Harper be forced to call? She calls Dr. Zimmer all the time because she has had many legitimate questions about her father's condition—liver failure, kidney failure, congestive heart failure. Billy Frost's end has been a series of failures.

Surely no one will fault Harper for calling Reed *now,* after her father has *died.* But she has an uncomfortable premonition. She waits.

Billy Frost is dead at the age of seventy-three. Harper takes a stab at writing his obituary in her mind as the nurses come in to clean him up and prepare him for the fun-filled ride to the morgue. *William O'Shaughnessy Frost, master electrician and avid Red Sox fan, died last night at Martha's Vineyard Hospital, in Oak Bluffs. He is survived by his daughter Harper Frost.*

And...his daughter Tabitha Frost...and his granddaughter, Ainsley Cruise...and his ex-wife, Eleanor Roxie-Frost, all of Nantucket, Massachusetts. What will surprise people the most? Harper wonders. That Billy has a daughter identical to but completely different from the cute screw-up who delivers packages for Rooster Express? Or that Billy used to be married to the famous Boston fashion designer Eleanor Roxie-Frost, more commonly known as ERF? Or will the shocker be that the other half of Billy's family lives on the rival island—that fancy, upscale haven for billionaires? Harper's twin sister, Tabitha, hasn't set foot on Martha's Vineyard in fourteen years, and Harper's mother, Eleanor, hasn't been here since her honeymoon, in 1968. Harper's niece, Ainsley, has *never* been here. Billy had been sad about that; when he wanted to see Ainsley, he had to go to Nantucket, which he did, religiously, every August.

You sure you don't want to come with me? he used to ask Harper.

I'm sure, Harper would say. *Tabitha doesn't want me there.*

When will you girls learn? Billy would reply, and Harper would mouth along with him. *Family is family.*

Family is *family,* Harper thinks. That's the problem.

Nothing back from Reed. Harper imagines him eating pie. Reed's wife, Sadie, is famous for her pies; her mother used to have a stand along the side of the road, and Sadie has capitalized on that artisanal pie-making endeavor and turned it into a gold mine. She rents a small commercial kitchen and storefront in Vineyard Haven—it's a scant mile from Harper's duplex—and cranks out the pies: strawberry-rhubarb, blueberry-peach, lobster pot. A lobster pot pie costs forty-two dollars. Harper knows this because, near the end of his life, Billy Frost became a fan. One of his female admirers (and there were many) dropped off a lobster pot pie all warm and fragrant and filled with claw and knuckle meat in a thick sherry cream sauce under golden pastry, and Billy declared that he had died and, against all expectations, gone to heaven. When Billy got really bad but could still eat, Harper had felt it her duty to buy him a lobster pot pie. She had entered the shop—the Upper Crust—with trepidation, knowing she was most likely going to come face-to-face with her lover's wife for the first time.

Harper was forearmed, but seeing Sadie had come as a shock. She was far shorter than Harper had expected; her head barely cleared the top of the pie case. Her hair was cut short like a boy's, and her eyes bulged, giving her the expression of a cartoon character perpetually caught by surprise.

Sadie didn't seem to have any idea who Harper was. She displayed no wariness, just a pleasant smile that revealed a gap between her two front teeth. Harper knew that some men found a gap like that sexy, although Harper never understood the attraction. If her own teeth had looked like that, she would have beat it straight to the orthodontist.

"Can I help you?" Sadie had asked.

"My father is dying," Harper blurted out.

Sadie's eyes popped a little more.

"He wants a lobster pot pie," Harper said. "It's the one thing he's been asking for. Mrs. Tobias dropped one off last week for him, and he can't stop talking about it."

"Mrs. Tobias is an excellent customer," Sadie said. She tilted her head. "Is your father Billy *Frost,* by any chance?"

"Yes," Harper said. She felt like she was on a roller coaster, cresting, cresting...

"Mrs. Tobias told me he was sick. You know, he installed some light fixtures for me when I first opened this shop. He was the only electrician who was willing to do it. Everyone else said I had to call the contractor who had wired it back when it was a scented-candle place, but that guy had long ago gone to jail."

"Buttons," Harper said, almost involuntarily. Billy had absorbed much of Buttons Jones's business when Buttons was indicted for tax evasion.

Sadie retrieved a lobster pot pie hot from the oven. For a second, Harper thought the pie would be free of charge, a gift for a man who had long ago done Sadie Zimmer a solid.

"That'll be forty-two dollars," Sadie said.

* * *

Harper has a hard time imagining Reed and Sadie together at home. She knows which house is theirs—it's in West Tisbury, near the Field Gallery—but she's never been inside. She can more easily imagine the Zimmers sitting side by side in the sand in front of the fire at Lambert's Cove. Maybe Sadie has a beautiful singing voice, whereas Harper—although she loves to sing at the top of her lungs in the Rooster Express delivery truck—can't carry a tune. It isn't a competition, Harper knows, not in a column-of-pros-and-cons way. Love is a mystery.

One of Billy's nurses, Dee, pokes her head into the room. "How you holding up?"

Harper tries to nod—*Okay*—but all she can do is stare. "I can't reach Dr. Zimmer," she says, then she worries that she has just given it all away. "I mean, I know he's not on call, but I thought I should tell him. Billy was his favorite patient."

Dee gives Harper an indulgent smile, and Harper nearly expects her to say that all Dr. Zimmer's patients are his favorites; that is the wonder of Dr. Zimmer. Then Harper worries that Dee is waiting for her to vacate the room; after all, she is no longer a paying customer.

But instead Dee says, "You were good to him, Harper. In some ways, you'll probably find this is a blessing."

A blessing? Harper thinks angrily. She wants to tell Dee to go eat some more cake, but then she wonders if maybe Dee is right. For the past ten months, Harper's entire existence has consisted of worrying that Billy was going to die. Now that he's gone, she is, in a way, free. There is nothing else to worry about. But she is left with a heavy mantle of grief, sadness so intense and piercing it should have another name. Since her parents' divorce, when she was seventeen, Billy has been "her" parent. He was her friend, her hero, her unfailing ally, her everyday companion. She could not have dreamed up a better father—and now he's gone.

Gone.

Harper wipes away her tears, sucks in a sustaining breath, and says, like the brave soldier Billy believed her to be, "Onward."

"Atta girl," Dee says. "I'll go fetch Billy's things."

Onward: as per Billy's wishes, his body will be cremated, and his memorial reception will be held at the Farm Neck Golf Club. Once Harper sells Billy's house, she will be able to quit her job at Rooster Express, a desperation job she got three years ago when Jude fired her from Garden Goddesses following the Joey Bowen catastrophe. And then what will Harper do? She could, in theory, start her own landscaping company. She's sure the clients still ask for her, and not just because she used to mow their lawns in a bikini top. She is a nice person and a good person, despite circumstantial evidence to the contrary.

Dee reappears with paperwork for Harper to sign and a large Ziploc bag containing Billy's clothes and belongings, including the gold 1954 Omega watch he inherited from his own father, which was the possession he had treasured the most. Billy Frost had come to Martha's Vineyard in 1995, left flat broke by his divorce from Eleanor, and he had floundered, Harper knew, just as she had that same year as a freshman at Tulane. Billy had scavenged work as an electrical contractor, picking up scraps and leftovers from people like Buttons Jones.

He had befriended the guys who cut down trees and moved houses and insulated crawl spaces; he befriended the fishermen and first mates, the transients and junkies who hung out at the Wharf pub and who, when they were flush, bothered Carmen, the bartender at Coop DeVille.

But Billy always wore his watch, the gold Omega, and this had set him apart.

What will Harper do with the watch? She has no one to pass it on to.

Tabitha has Ainsley, but what does a sixteen-year-old girl want with a gold 1954 Omega? Harper thinks of Ainsley's father, Wyatt. Billy had been fond of Wyatt, but can Harper ever suggest that Wyatt take the watch? No.

Tabitha is a toothache that can't be ignored for another second. Six weeks earlier, when Billy got really bad, Harper copied Tabitha's cell number out of Billy's contacts and, with the help of half a dozen Amity Island ales and three shots of Jägermeister, left Tabitha a voice mail informing her that if she wanted to see Billy one last time before he died, she had better do it soon. Tabitha had never responded—no surprise there. Harper wishes she had called Tabitha while sober, because she fears she slurred her words in the message, making it that much easier to disregard and delete.

Billy's death warrants another phone call, but Harper is too angry to conduct one civilly. Did Tabitha deign to listen to the message? Did she come visit? Has she set foot on the Vineyard even once since the death of her son, Julian, fourteen years ago? She has not. Nantucket is 11.2 miles away, so it certainly hasn't been an issue of proximity.

Harper sends Tabitha the same text. *Billy is gone.* And

then, once safely inside her Bronco, Harper breaks down and calls Dr. Zimmer.

The phone rings six times, then he answers, voice hushed. Harper imagines he has stepped away from the bonfire and is standing in the shadows.

He says, "I'm sorry, Harper. I thought there was more time. Weeks."

What kind of doctor is he? She wants to believe him incompetent or hate him, but she can't. Reed gives everything he has to his patients. He stays late to do rounds; he never rushes; he is thoughtful, consistent, kind, clear. Not once in ten months did Harper ever feel like he wanted or needed to be someplace else; Billy might have been his only patient. Dr. Zimmer would, on occasion, show up with a surprise or treat for Billy—the *Sports Illustrated* swimsuit issue; an arrowhead he'd discovered on a hike; a box of Stoner Food from Enchanted Chocolates, which he knew Billy loved (and technically wasn't allowed to have). Reed Zimmer was like a doctor from TV, but better because he was real. He was both handsome and human. Sometimes he had bags under his eyes from staying up all night; sometimes he had scruff on his face or mussed hair. Sometimes he showed up wearing jeans and a gray T-shirt under his white coat. How could Harper have done anything but fall in love with him?

"Come to me," she says.

"Not tonight. I..." His voice breaks off, and Harper imagines Sadie snatching the phone from his hand. Harper has harbored a sense of foreboding since she woke up that morning. She feels like her Siberian husky, Fish, when his ears prick: that dog can hear a mouse fart three miles away. "I have to stay here with my family."

It isn't your *family,* Harper wants to point out. *It's Sadie's family.*

"My family just died," Harper says.

Reed is quiet—whether out of guilt or because he's distracted Harper isn't sure.

"Have you called your sister?" he asks. "Or your mother?"

My mother? Harper thinks. *Ha!* If Harper calls Eleanor to say that Billy has died, her mother will sniff or cough in response. Maybe. There was a time, during the heavy shelling of the divorce, when all Eleanor had wanted was for Billy to drop dead. At her most gracious, she might say, *I'm sorry for your loss, darling, but with all that smoking, Billy really had it coming.*

Eleanor hadn't always felt that way, of course. Once upon a time, Eleanor Roxie-Frost and Billy Frost were a dynamic, magnetic couple—Eleanor a prominent fashion designer, Billy the owner of Frost Electrical Contractors, Inc. They lived on Beacon Hill in a house they inherited from Eleanor's parents, and there they raised identical twin girls. They did things properly: they attended Church of the Advent one Sunday a month as well as on Christmas and Easter, like good Episcopalians. They sent the twins to Winsor, the private all-girls school where both Eleanor and Eleanor's mother had gone. Billy and Eleanor attended parties at the Park Plaza, the Museum of Fine Arts, and the Harvard Club. At social events, they were photographed so often that they developed a trademark stance: Eleanor would beam at the camera while Billy snaked an arm around her waist and kissed her cheek. They were Boston's sweethearts; the city adored them.

Ultimately, Harper supposes, it was success that ruined them. Eleanor's dresses became so popular that she was able to open a three-story eponymous boutique on Newbury Street.

For nearly two years, Eleanor was at the building night and day, overseeing renovations and designs. A photograph of Eleanor wearing a pencil skirt, stiletto heels, and a hard hat, giving the camera a working girl's come-hither look, appeared in *Women's Wear Daily*. That had been the first thing to set Billy off.

"Your mother," Billy said, holding the photograph up for display over the breakfast table, "is only happy when she's one hundred percent in control."

The real issue, the twins soon learned, was that Eleanor hadn't hired Billy's company to do the electrical work on her boutique. She refused to do so on principle; she said she felt that working together would ruin their marriage.

"That's a bunch of baloney," Billy said. "Your mother is a secret snob. She doesn't want the fancy photographers capturing a picture of her working-class husband. She has always thought she married beneath her."

There were loud fights that year, Harper remembers. Billy accused Eleanor of abandoning her family for the store; Eleanor resented what she called Billy's foot on her throat. Why didn't he want her to succeed? He'd known from the first night he met her that she'd wanted a career.

Billy decided that the only way to get Eleanor to stay home was for him to go out more. He started spending three and four nights a week at the Eire Pub in Dorchester with a group of men Eleanor characterized as thugs. Billy's friends were no better than Whitey Bulger and the Winter Hill gang, she said.

Au contraire, Billy said, his French accent impeccable even after he'd had six or seven whiskeys, thanks to the many years he'd spent living with Eleanor. These friends of his from Southie were aboveboard. They were encouraging Billy to run for city council.

Over my dead body, Eleanor said.

I should be so lucky, Billy said.

Billy and Eleanor divorced the summer before the twins left for their respective colleges. The twins were seventeen, still minors—and with Tabitha heading to Bennington and Harper to Tulane it would be four years at least until the girls were financially independent. It had been Eleanor's idea to split the girls—one would be Eleanor's financial responsibility and live with her during summer vacation, and the other twin would go with Billy. Then, on holidays, the girls would switch parents. What Eleanor could not abide was the thought of split time—both girls with one parent or the other, their possessions traveling between the households in a suitcase. It was unseemly, Eleanor said.

What Harper realizes now is that her mother was terrified of being alone. Eleanor's parents had died; her sister, Flossie, had moved to Florida. Eleanor had no friends, only business associates.

What Eleanor did not bank on, however, was that both girls wanted to go with Billy. When they finally summoned the courage to announce this, Eleanor laughed dismissively and said, "All girls prefer their fathers. That's a known fact. I certainly preferred mine. But Billy can't afford both of you, so I'm afraid one of you is coming with me. I don't care which one of you it is, because unlike the two of you, I don't play favorites. I love you both the same. The two of you work it out between yourselves, please. By morning."

There followed one of the most agonizing nights of Harper's life—an hours-long session of whispered pleading, debating, and bargaining, then finally an out-and-out fight with her sister. Harper argued that she had always been a smidge closer to

Billy—she was the athletic one, and she was the one who liked the Red Sox! Tabitha argued that she had been named for Billy's mother, whereas Harper had inherited the maiden name of Eleanor's mother, Vivian Harper Roxie, who was formidable indeed. Therefore, Tabitha said, Harper should go with Eleanor and Tabitha should go with Billy. It had unspooled like that until finally the girls—just short of coming to actual blows—decided to settle the dispute the way they had been settling disputes for seventeen and a half years: by shooting rock, paper, scissors.

It was a solution Billy had taught them. He claimed that any argument in the world could be solved by rock, paper, scissors. No need for fistfights, lawyers, or war, in Billy's opinion: all you needed was a hand and an understanding of the basic rules—scissors cut paper, rock smashes scissors, paper covers rock.

And then if you don't like the outcome, Billy would say, *you simply ask for the best of three.*

In determining who would go with Billy, Tabitha shot rock and Harper shot paper. Harper won.

Tabitha accused her of cheating.

Cheating how? Harper had said. *By reading your mind?* But she let Tabitha "simply ask" for the best of three. Again, Tabitha shot rock and Harper shot paper. Harper won.

She was going with Billy.

It was fair to say that Harper's relationship with Tabitha had never been the same after that. For a handful of years, they remained civil, but they were no longer friends. Billy left Boston altogether. He bought a house on Daggett Avenue in Vineyard Haven, while Eleanor stayed in the gracious four-story town house on Pinckney Street. Then, when Eleanor sold her shoe line to Steve Madden—a deal her attorney had advised her to delay until after the divorce—she bought a second home, on Nantucket.

The girls stayed with "their" parent every summer, and, as per Eleanor's mandate, each traveled to visit the other parent during the holidays. Harper used to imagine their ferries bouncing over each other's wakes and the contrails of their planes crisscrossing in the sky.

There had been one chance for the twins to reunite, and that was after Tabitha gave birth to her second child—a son, Julian—three months prematurely. Tabitha needed help, and Harper swooped in to save the day...but things had gone catastrophically wrong. Julian died, and Tabitha had seen fit to blame Harper—not only for Julian's death but also for winning at rock, paper, scissors and for causing every single other misery of her adult years.

You ruin everything, Tabitha had said. *Everything is your fault.*

That was fourteen years ago, and the twins have barely spoken since.

Harper realizes that Reed is waiting for her to respond. She doesn't like thinking about her sister or her mother, because this is what happens: it feels like someone has blindfolded and gagged her.

"I texted Tabitha," Harper says. "She'll tell my mother, I suppose."

"Good," Reed says. "Listen, I'm sorry, but I have to go."

"So you won't meet me?" Harper asks. "You're going to make me call Drew?" This is a desperate, dirty thing to say. Harper told Reed that she has started dating Sergeant Drew Truman of the Edgartown Police Department, and it bothers Reed. Drew has the advantages of youth and a policeman's physique and bachelorhood and his large extended family—and he's a nice guy besides. Sergeant Truman and Dr. Zimmer know each other because of heroin overdoses. Drew has administered Narcan three times in the past year, after which he has taken the addicts directly to the hospital, where they were placed in Dr. Zimmer's care.

"Don't call Drew, please," Reed says. "Just go home. Curl up with Fish."

"Fish is a *dog,* Reed, not a person." Harper says. "Billy just *died* in the middle of my reading off Pedroia's stats. What you're asking me isn't fair, and you know it."

"I'll come in the morning," Reed says.

"Tonight," Harper says.

"Fine, tonight," he says. "But late. Midnight. And not to your house—that's too dangerous. I'll meet you in the parking lot at Lucy Vincent beach."

"Do you think *that's* safe?" Harper asks. Before Reed was comfortable coming to her duplex, they used to meet in the back parking lot of the ice rink after hours. It would be deserted this time of year for certain, whereas the beach… "It's nearly summer, Reed. There are people everywhere."

"I realize this," he says. "But I'm not driving down island." He must realize how unkind that sounds, because he adds, "That's the best I can do if it has to be tonight."

"It has to be tonight," Harper says. "Lucy Vincent at midnight."

"For five minutes, so I can give you a kiss and tell you everything is going to be fine," he says.

"Is it?" she says.

"Yes," he says.

Harper goes home briefly to let Fish out. He is a dog, not a person, yet he's standing by the front door waiting for her even though, more often than not these days, he sleeps on his Orvis bed and barely turns his head when Harper comes in. But today he's right there, paws on her thighs, licking her face, giving her all the love he can. He knows. This brings Harper to tears. Her dog knows Billy died, but she feels the need to deliver the news herself. She grabs Fish by the muzzle and looks into his glacier-blue eyes and says, "Pops is gone, bub." He keens and rubs his flank against Harper's leg, and she has to practically push him out the door to her front yard, where he pees on the biggest hydrangea bush on the property. Then he comes trotting back into the kitchen, where Harper says, "Lamb tonight, in honor of Pops." But Fish doesn't snarf down his food, as he normally does; instead he looks up at Harper, as if for permission. "Go ahead," she says. And with something like mournful dignity, Fish lowers his head to the bowl.

When Harper leaves the house, she drives to Our Market to grab a six-pack of Amity Island ale and three nips of Jägermeister. The cashier, Robyn, has known Harper for twenty years, but Robyn is a close friend of Jude's, so Harper is always wary and reserved.

"You want a bag?" Robyn asks.

"Please," Harper says.

Maybe Robyn has heard the news about Billy already, because she throws a Milk-Bone for Fish into the bag for free.

It's eight thirty, and the sun has just set. Harper prefers winter, when it gets dark at three thirty and is pitch black by the time she finishes her shift. The summer sun reveals too much.

Harper opens one of the beers using the metal end of her seat belt and chugs half of it, then she upends one of the nips of Jäger into her mouth. Her mother would be appalled.

Harper should have taken Middle Road, because State Road brings her right by Jude's house, where Harper sees cars and trucks lining the street on either side of the Garden Goddesses sign. It's Jude's annual start-of-summer party for her staff. She has a pig roast and makes cornbread and green-apple slaw from scratch, and there's a big galvanized tub filled with beer. Jude's partner, Stella, makes mudslides in the blender and everyone listens to Jack Johnson and the newbies think, *Wow, what a great place to work!* Only the returning employees know that this is the last day they'll have off until Labor Day, when Jude throws a second party, with lobsters.

Harper hits the gas. She can't get past Jude's property fast enough.

Siren. Lights. Harper checks her rearview.

Police. She hisses and looks at the open container next to her, but there's no time to dispose of it and no place to hide it. She puts her blinker on and pulls over.

This is the last thing she needs. Her reputation has already been shredded, sullied, and stomped upon with steel-toed boots. Three years earlier, Harper was arrested for doing "a favor" for a man named Joey Bowen, whom she knew only casually; he was a frequent patron at Dahlia's, where Harper waitressed one night a week. The "favor" was to deliver a package to the son of one of Jude's landscaping clients, the Monacos; Harper was scheduled to mow the lawn and weed the beds at the Monaco house the following day. All she had to do was hide the package in her wheelbarrow beneath the mulch and fertilizer and bring it to the house. The Monaco son would come outside to collect it. Harper was supposed to park the wheelbarrow outside the side door and turn her back—and for this, Joey Bowen would pay her three thousand dollars. Harper realized she was probably delivering drugs, but the offer was too tempting to turn down; she needed the money. At that point, she was still living in Billy's house. She wanted a place of her own, but the Vineyard was expensive, and it was hard to get ahead.

Little did Harper know that the state police and FBI had been watching the Monaco house for weeks, waiting for this particular delivery. When the son grabbed the package, agents hopped over the fence, dropped out of trees, and came charging across the lawn. The kid got cuffed, and so did Harper.

During the interrogation, Harper explained to the police that this was the one and only time she had ever delivered anything for anybody. Joey Bowen was a customer at the restaurant where she worked, she said. They informed her that Joey Bowen was wanted for drug trafficking from the Upper Cape all the way down to New Bedford.

Harper spent eighteen hours in lockup until Billy found her an attorney. She was released, receiving only six months' probation, but she lost her job, both at Garden Goddesses and at Dahlia's. Jude Hogan openly despises Harper for tainting her landscaping business. The other people who hate Harper are a scarier but far less visible lot—the people who used to buy their drugs from Joey.

But the worst thing, perhaps, was that the Monacos' next-door neighbor was a woman named Ann-Lane Crenshaw, who also happened to be Eleanor Roxie-Frost's college roommate. Eleanor heard about Harper's arrest immediately, and she no doubt shared the appalling news with Tabitha. How could Harper not suddenly feel like the blackest of sheep?

Anyone else would have left the Vineyard. It's a testimony to how pathetic Harper is that she has stayed.

She has nowhere else to go.

And her father is here. Was here.

Tears arrive unbidden. Her father has just died. She'll just tell the officer that. Play the sympathy card.

She puts down her window. She has pulled over about a hundred yards beyond Jude's property line; she dreads *anyone* from that party seeing her.

"Hey, baby."

She looks up. It's Drew.

"What?" she says. She checks her rearview. It's an Edgartown police car, not a car from West Tisbury. She sinks back in her seat while relief drains through to her feet. "Did you really have to pull me over?"

"You're so beautiful you're breaking the law," he says. He leans in her window to kiss her. "Plus you were speeding."

"I was?" she says.

"Why are you all the way out here?" he asks. "I've been trailing you since I saw you leaving Our Market."

"You have?" she says. Drew is a little stalkerish by nature. Possibly he suspects she's keeping a secret. "Don't you have work?"

"I'm on break until nine," Drew says. "I was driving out to meet you at the hospital, actually, when I saw your car." He eyes the beer. "You'll want to be careful with that."

"I'm going to drive to Aquinnah, clear my head," she says. "It's sweet that you're worried about me, but like I said on the phone, I think I just need to be alone."

Drew nods. She's a sucker for him in his uniform. He's so handsome, so upright, such a relentless do-gooder. Why can't she be in love with Drew?

"The aunties are making you a pot of lobster stew," he says. "I'll bring it by tomorrow."

"You told them about Billy already?" Harper asks.

"I called my mother to let her know," Drew says. "Wanda and Mavis were over, helping her end beans, so they overheard. Wanda left right away to start the stew. It's their automatic response to death—a pot of something warm and comforting so you don't forget to eat and waste away to skin and bones."

"They don't have to go to the trouble," Harper says. "They don't even know me."

"They know I like you," Drew says. He bends in for another kiss. "That's all that matters."

Harper smiles and puts up her window.

At midnight, Harper is mostly asleep in the front seat of her Bronco, five of the beers and two of the nips consumed, plus she stopped at Alley's General Store for a jar of their bread-and-butter pickles—her dinner. (The aunties are right to be concerned.) There has been no one in the parking lot since nine forty-five, when a bunch of high school kids came off the beach. Harper is relieved: Lucy Vincent is still perfectly safe.

Reed pulls in at twelve o'clock on the dot; he's nothing if not prompt. Harper brings her seat back up and gets out. He said five minutes, and Harper knows that's what she'll get—no more, no less. He shuts off the engine of his Lexus, climbs out, and jogs over to her. He holds out his arms, and she collapses against him.

"He's gone," she says. "I'm never going to see him again. That's the thing, I guess, the inconceivable thing."

Reed squeezes her tighter. He's a doctor. Dealing with death is part of his job—not every day, but often enough.

He says, "We're all going to die, Harper. Billy's end was peaceful. He had the person he loved most in the world right there with him, reading off Pedroia's stats. What a way to go."

Harper raises her face, and their lips meet. Reed's lips are warm; kissing him lights her on fire all the time, but tonight, because she is ragged from crying, the desire she feels is raw and overpowering. He responds to her, opening his mouth and searching out her tongue, pressing his lower body against hers. He moves his mouth to just under Harper's ear. His hands are all over her. They're going to have sex. Harper can't believe it. He must have had a couple of beers at the family picnic and maybe a Scotch once he got home, since he's not on call this weekend. He's looser than normal, nearly reckless. His hands travel inside her blouse; he unhooks the front clasp of her bra. He plays with her nipples, then bends his head down and sucks her left nipple until she groans. She can't stand it. She strokes the front of his jeans.

He frees a hand to unzip himself, and Harper reaches for the car door.

"No," he says. "Outside."

"Outside?" she says. Is this Reed? Reed Zimmer? He doesn't even bother with protection, something he is fanatical about; he simply thrusts inside her. Harper's back is pressed up against the door of the Bronco, and it's at that second that Harper sees headlights. Passing, she thinks. But no: a car is turning into the parking lot. It's approaching. Harper struggles to disengage, but Reed doesn't notice the lights or the sound of the engine. He's too intent on his rhythm, and his eyes are closed. He finishes with a grunt and a shudder, a soft cry uttered against Harper's neck.

Harper pushes him away, but it's too late. A car door slams, and a woman is shouting, screaming, shrieking. "Reed! Reed! Reed!"

It's Sadie.

NANTUCKET: TABITHA

She has been invited to a cocktail party on the *Belle,* a seventy-seven-foot wooden motor yacht built in 1929 that is now used for entertaining by members of the Westmoor Club. This evening's soiree is being thrown by people Tabitha barely knows, and it's still rather chilly to be out on the harbor, but ever since Tabitha broke up with Ramsay, she has been desperate to get out of the house.

Ramsay will be sitting at the bar at the Straight Wharf, waiting for Caylee to finish her shift. Tabitha was the one to break things off, yet Ramsay has rebounded far more quickly—

instantly, in fact. For the three years Tabitha and Ramsay dated, Tabitha teased him about wanting someone younger, which he denied. And yet Caylee—a name fit for a chew toy as far as Tabitha is concerned—is only twenty-two.

When Tabitha was twenty-two, she was roundly pregnant. She had never had a chance to spend a summer bartending or get a tattoo; she never had the opportunity to break away from her mother's fashion empire and pursue her own passions—real estate, architecture, interior design. And then when she was twenty-five, she endured a tragedy from which she still hasn't recovered. Ramsay knew about Julian, and he knew it was a void that could never be filled—or so Tabitha had thought. But on a frigid night this past February, when they had both been sober—and there wasn't even alcohol to blame—Ramsay had said, *The only way to put your sadness behind you is to start fresh. Let's have a baby.*

There had been no point in responding. He didn't get it. He would never get it, Tabitha realized. She gave him the "we want different things" talk, and two days later, he moved out.

The party isn't bad. The host and hostess are from Tallahassee, so by nature they find New England brisk. Hence they've provided a pile of cashmere wraps in optimistic summertime hues—cantaloupe, fuchsia, aquamarine—for the female guests on the boat to borrow. There is an endless supply of very cold Laurent-Perrier rosé and a piped-in sound track of Sinatra and Dean Martin that Tabitha just loves. Because she had no youth, she has adopted the tastes of her mother, Eleanor. Eleanor is a woman of refinement by anyone's standards, but she is seventy-one years old, and at times Tabitha fears that she has not only skipped her own youth but her middle age as well and landed squarely in the era of hip replacements and hearing aids.

While Ramsay was packing up his things to leave, he delivered a speech in which he enumerated every one of Tabitha's flaws.

She is egregiously snobby. She is uptight. She panders to the whims and wishes of her mother; she has spent her entire adult life in the woman's shadow. She has been a tireless handmaiden in service to Eleanor Roxie-Frost Designs, LLC, yet the boutique on Nantucket *loses money every year!* Tabitha has no business sense; she has run the store into the ground. Ramsay himself had lent her forty thousand dollars so that she might expand the store's inventory beyond the ERF label. "And don't forget, you still owe me that money," Ramsay said.

"I know," Tabitha responded, although she was pretty sure Ramsay understood that with a child to send to college, it would take her a very long time to pay him back.

As his parting shot, Ramsay had said, "It's a good thing you don't want any more children," he said. "You're a piss-poor mother, Tabitha."

She knew he was angry and hurt and heartbroken, but the unbuffered cruelty of this statement forced her to respond, "How dare you?"

He said, "Maybe with me gone, you can get your daughter under control."

The food on the boat is delicious—lamb lollipops, lobster-corn cakes, gougères, deviled eggs. Tabitha helps herself judiciously—Ramsay was kind enough not to mention the fifteen pounds she's gained over the past three years—as she scans the crowd for eligible men to talk to. Ramsay wasn't wrong about her lack of business sense. What she needs, more than anything, is to either hit the lottery or find a sugar daddy.

Pickings on the boat are slim. All the men are older and seem well off, but they're also married—and most of them are from Tallahassee, which rules them out immediately.

Tabitha has the bartender fill her glass of champagne, then she heads out to the bow of the boat alone. They are just rounding Brant Point Light, coming upon a vista so magnificent it takes Tabitha's breath away despite the hundreds of times she's seen it. She leans her elbows on the railing and holds her champagne out with both hands. She closes her eyes.

She is *not* a piss-poor parent. Ainsley is merely at a trying age, and she is rebellious by nature. But if you were to strip Tabitha down to her starkest, most honest thoughts, the ones she would never dare share with another soul, she would admit that where Ainsley is concerned, she has created a monster. After Julian died, Tabitha poured all her energy into raising Ainsley. She was a helicopter parent—a second-generation helicopter parent—controlling Ainsley's every move the way Eleanor had controlled hers. But when Ainsley grew up, she did it fast. Ainsley was a runaway mustang, and Tabitha felt the reins slipping through her hands. The way Tabitha chose to keep Ainsley close was to aid and abet her in her quest to be the most popular, most sophisticated child at Nantucket High School. *Tabitha* bought the makeup and the two-hundred-dollar jeans; *Tabitha* extended the curfew. The fact that Ainsley is now such a powder keg is nobody's fault but Tabitha's.

Being out on the ocean always brings up these thoughts. Tabitha should have stayed on land.

Suddenly there's a man standing next to her. He's wearing a uniform.

He offers his hand. "I'm Peter," he says. "The captain."

"Tabitha Frost," she says. "If you're the captain, then who's driving the boat?"

Peter laughs. "My first mate. I asked him to take over for a second so I could come down here to chat with you. Would you like to help me steer this beauty?"

As they stand side by side at the ship's wheel—any time a crew member happens to wander in, Peter sends him off to fetch Tabitha more champagne or another plate of hors d'oeuvres—he unreels his life story. Coast Guard at nineteen, married by twenty-two, two boys (named PJ and Kyle), divorced by age thirty, ex-wife number 1 lives in Houston.

Tabitha wonders how many ex-wives there are in total. The music, she can hear, has changed to Top 40—the stuff Ainsley listens to when she's in a good mood—and Tabitha envisions the champagne going to everyone's head and the Tallahasseeans contorting their bodies in awkward, embarrassing ways that approximate dancing.

"Go on," she says to Captain Peter.

Married again at age thirty-two. The daughter from that marriage is a shooting star, nineteen years old and a sophomore at Northwestern; ex-wife number 2, the mother, runs a glamorous campground on the Upper Peninsula of Michigan.

Then, at age thirty-five, Peter had a bit of a midlife crisis.

He moved to Maui, captained a whale-watching ship for ten years, lived with a local girl named Lupalai, and had another couple of kids—a boy and a girl, ages fourteen and eleven—although he and Lupalai never married. He sends checks, he says, but he hasn't seen the kids since he moved east five years ago. He has been the captain of the *Belle* for five summer seasons, and in the winter, he goes down to the Bahamas and runs a bareboat charter.

"I just celebrated my fiftieth birthday in April," he says. "How about you?"

"I'm thirty-nine," Tabitha says.

Captain Peter laughs. "All women are supposed to say that, I guess."

"No," Tabitha says. "I actually am thirty-nine. I turn forty in December."

"Oh," the captain says. He's caught by surprise, and Tabitha's spirit flags. She looks older; she acts older. She's wearing a white linen shift with an obi belt. It's the cornerstone of her mother's collection and has been for thirty years; it's called the Roxie. It's meant to convey a classic timelessness, and while it may certainly do that, it is neither youthful nor sexy. Tabitha should have worn the Haute Hippie sequined miniskirt with the hot-pink Milly blouse, but she had worried that would make her look like she was trying too hard. Instead she looks like she's headed to the early bird special before making a fourth for bridge.

The captain says something, but Tabitha doesn't hear him.

"I'm sorry?"

"Would you like to go get a drink after we dock? I'm about to turn this old gal around now, so you'll have to go down to the deck."

Tabitha tugs on her obi. She feels pursued and dismissed at

the same time. Does she want to go for a drink with the captain? She's not sure. It's obvious he's bad news. He probably preys on every halfway decent-looking woman who boards the *Belle.* He's a fifty-year-old man who still plays the seasonal back-and-forth game. He either rents a cottage somewhere on island or he lives in employee housing provided by the Westmoor Club. He likely doesn't own any real estate; he may drive a small pickup truck. That kind of life is okay until one turns... Tabitha randomly picks the age of twenty-eight. After twenty-eight, it's time to grow up. And how many children does Captain Peter have to support? Tabitha lost count. Four? Five? If Eleanor were here, she would veto Captain Peter immediately. Eleanor had disapproved of Wyatt because Wyatt was a housepainter, and Eleanor wanted Tabitha to marry a professional man—a lawyer or someone in private equity. Now that Wyatt owns a painting contracting business that covers the entire Cape and the South Shore from Plymouth to Braintree, Eleanor is more favorably disposed toward him. She adores Ramsay, who works for his family's insurance business on Main Street. Ramsay wears a tie to work, and his family belongs to the Nantucket Yacht Club.

This guy, Captain Peter, isn't the kind of guy Tabitha would ever hook up with. He's the kind of guy... *Harper* would hook up with! Harper has no standards. Harper's bar—for everything in life—isn't just low; it's lying on the ground.

Tabitha should say thank you but no thank you.

"Have you ever lost anyone?" she asks.

"Lost anyone?" Peter says. He seems confused and anxious to get back up to the controls.

"We can talk about it later," Tabitha says. "I'd love to go for a drink."

* * *

As they're walking to the Nautilus, Tabitha regrets her decision. She has a text on her phone from Ainsley that says: *When are you coming home?* Ainsley has been grounded for a week after taking Tabitha's FJ40 for a joyride in the middle of the night without permission and, more egregiously, without having a license. Tabitha discovered the transgression the previous Sunday morning when she had gotten in her car to go to a sunrise yoga class. The gas tank was empty, and the interior reeked of cigarettes. Tabitha had woken Ainsley up and demanded a confession, which Ainsley had handed over without a fuss.

"Yes, I took the car. I drove to Emma's."

Emma's!

Tabitha and Ainsley live in the carriage house behind Eleanor's grand home on Cliff Road, and Ainsley's friend Emma—whose photo should appear in the dictionary next to the phrase *bad influence*—lives at the end of Jonathan Way in Tom Nevers, which is just about as far away as two points can get on Nantucket. Tabitha had shuddered, imagining Ainsley having an accident in the FJ40 while she was driving unlicensed. What if she had hit someone? What if she had *killed* someone? Tabitha would have been sued, and Eleanor would have been sued. The business would have been sued, their livelihood destroyed. And yet Ainsley displayed no guilt. Tabitha had snapped Ainsley's phone up off the nightstand. *That* had gotten Ainsley's attention. She was up and out of bed in a flash, chasing Tabitha through the house, trying to wrest the phone from her mother's grip. She had scratched Tabitha's face in her frenzy, and Tabitha had been so incredulous—struck, basically, by her own child—that she had dropped the phone, and Ainsley had reclaimed it.

"I need this," Ainsley said. "You may be happy to have no social life, but that won't work for me."

"Oh, it *won't?*" Tabitha said lamely. She touched the scratch on her face and looked at the smear of blood on her finger. "Well, too bad. You're grounded."

"Ha!" Ainsley said. "I'd like to know how you plan on keeping me in the house."

Tabitha had been infuriated, but she also recognized her own impotence. How *would* she stop Ainsley from walking out the door? Tabitha could cut off her allowance, but Emma had a steady source of income from her father, Dutch, who ran the restaurant at the airport and was never home, thus resorting to "cash parenting." Emma would lend or give Ainsley money for cigarettes or weed or beer or whatever else they were buying to enhance their evening hours.

"If you set foot out this door, I'll have your cell phone service suspended," Tabitha said. "You'll have your physical phone but no signal—no texting, no calls, no Snapchat, no Internet. And I'll change the password on the Wi-Fi here at the house."

Ainsley had narrowed her eyes skeptically. "You would never do that."

Tabitha had recalled Ramsay's "piss-poor parenting" comment.

"Watch me," she said.

Ainsley had then brokered a bargain. She would stay home for a week as long as she was allowed to keep her phone service.

Fine. Tonight, Friday, is the last night of the grounding—thank God. Ainsley has been verbally abusive and surly all week. She eats whatever she wants but never carries a dish to the sink. God forbid she make her bed. Tabitha has had to ask the housekeeper, Felipa, to work at the carriage house for three extra hours this week to clean up after Ainsley, and Tabitha is just waiting for Eleanor to call and give Tabitha a hard time about adding to Felipa's load.

Tabitha texts Ainsley back: *Home late.*

Immediately Ainsley responds: *What's late? Midnight?*

Yes, Tabitha texts back. Her daughter thinks she has no social life—ha! *Midnight at the earliest.*

Then Tabitha worries that maybe Ainsley is lonely. She grew up afraid of the dark; this fear developed right after Julian died. And Tabitha never gave her another sibling to keep her company.

Tabitha always had a companion growing up: Harper.

Weird, Tabitha thinks. Harper has popped into her mind twice in the past hour. When is the last time *that* happened?

And then even *weirder*—weird bordering on sorcery—Tabitha's phone pings, and Tabitha (although knowing it's rude to keep texting when she's on a sort-of date but thinking it's a response from Ainsley) checks her phone. It's a text that is identified only as *Vineyard Haven, MA.* It's Harper.

"There someplace else you need to be?" Captain Peter asks.

"No," Tabitha says. She tucks her phone into her clutch. She'll read the text later.

Tabitha picked Nautilus because it's a place she never went with Ramsay, and what she needs, more than anything, is a fresh start. She has heard only good things about the restaurant—artisanal cocktails, inventive food—and she has always wanted to try it, so why not tonight?

Nautilus is crowded, and the scene is young. Captain Peter hesitates before they enter. "You sure this is where you want to go?" He seems almost...intimidated, which is not an attractive trait. Tabitha feels her temperature being dialed down from lukewarm to cool. She nearly resorts to asking, "Well, where do *you* want to go?" But she doesn't want to stand outside hemming and hawing, and she does *not* want to end up at the Anglers' Club.

"Yes," she says, "here." And she leads him inside.

The music is loud, and the twentysomethings and thirtysomethings are hooting and hollering and ordering drinks at the bar. Tabitha is still a thirtysomething, she reminds herself. She approaches the hostess. "Table for two?"

The hostess says, "Ninety-minute wait for a table. You're welcome to try your luck at the bar."

Tabitha strolls to the bar, holding her chin up, scanning for seats. There is one empty seat half hidden among a throng of people. Tabitha wiggles her way in and claims it; she sets her clutch confidently on the bar as if planting a flag and turns to see if Captain Peter has followed her. He has, but he looks miserable, as if she were leading him on a leash.

She beams at the bartender, determined to make this work. "Menu?" she says.

A menu appears. Tabitha peruses it. Normally she orders a vodka gimlet or a glass of rosé, but come to think of it, those are drinks that Ramsay introduced her to. Before Ramsay, she drank a Mount Gay and tonic if she wanted a cocktail, or red wine with dinner, because that was what Eleanor drank.

Tonight she will have something called the Nauti Dog. She

hands the menu to Peter and points at the drink. "I'll have one of these."

He whistles. "Fifteen bucks?"

Tabitha closes her eyes, dialing down from cool to cold. She's okay with the fact that Peter isn't wealthy, but she can't handle anyone who complains about the price of a drink.

Peter says, "I'll just have a beer. A Cisco." He hands the menu back to Tabitha.

Is *she* supposed to order? she wonders. She is closer to the bar than Peter is, but Peter is the man. Peter invited *her* for drinks. She turns back to him. He raises his eyebrows expectantly, as if he has never seen her before, then says, "I'm going out front to have a cigarette. Be right back."

A cigarette, Tabitha thinks. It's the final nail in the coffin for this date. She gets the bartender's attention — cute guy, bearded, smiley—and orders the drinks. When he brings them—the Nauti Dog a glorious deep red color, thanks to the Campari and the freshly squeezed grapefruit juice—Peter is still outside. Which leaves Tabitha to pay. She forks over twenty-five bucks. The bartender gives her change, and she says, "Keep it."

"Thanks, bae," he says, and he gives her another smile, looking into her eyes.

Bae, not *ma'am.* She loves him for this. Could she date the bartender? Tabitha wonders as she takes a sip of her drink. He *might* be thirty. Maybe. Is that too young? Tabitha tries to imagine Eleanor's reaction when Tabitha announces she is dating a twenty-nine-year-old bartender from Nautilus. Tabitha would have to explain it for what it is: a rebound from Ramsay.

But no matter the circumstances, Tabitha doesn't sleep with bartenders. Harper does.

Tabitha wonders about the text from Vineyard Haven.

Tabitha and Harper have barely spoken since the horrible weeks following Julian's death, fourteen years earlier.

Then Tabitha remembers the voice mail from five or six weeks back, also from Vineyard Haven. It was Harper, saying that their father, Billy, was having trouble with his kidneys and had to go to the hospital. Tabitha had meant to call Billy, but the news had come at a busy time—she was having the carpet in the boutique replaced and trying to finish up all the summer buying—and then Tabitha hadn't heard anything else, so she'd assumed the problem had cleared up.

Tabitha is tempted to pull her phone out to see what Harper wants, but there is nothing more pathetic in the world, in Tabitha's opinion, than a woman alone at a bar checking her phone.

She takes a long swill off her drink, and when the bartender swings back by, she says, "What's your name?"

"Zack," he says.

Zack: probably he's younger than she thought. Zack is a name that became popular in the nineties.

She turns around to see what's become of Captain Peter, but the crowd is thick and she can't locate him in it. The couple next to Tabitha stands up, and Tabitha wonders if she should snag one of the stools for Captain Peter, but before she has a chance to do so, another couple sits down.

Tabitha blinks. It's Ramsay and Caylee.

Ramsay grins. "What luck."

Caylee swivels around. She smiles at Tabitha. "I'm sorry. Were you saving this seat for someone?"

She is so pretty, her teeth white and straight, her hair long and shiny, tucked behind one ear. But it's her skin that Tabitha really envies. If she could go back in time and change one thing it would be this: she would have worn sunscreen. Lots of it.

"Yeah," Ramsay says. "Who's the beer for?"

His voice is so familiar, his wicked smirk so easy to interpret, that it's as though Caylee unwittingly inserted herself between a long-married couple. Ramsay is the ideal life partner for Tabitha in nearly every way. But there are deal breakers. It's not only that he wants a child. It's also that he has never lost anyone, and he's incapable of understanding the depth and intensity of Tabitha's emotions. There are things that activate her Julian anxiety: Julian's birthday, obviously, and the day of his death, but also babies and boys who are now the age that Julian would have been. Fourteen. Ramsay was impatient with Tabitha's emotional lows as they related to Julian; the more she tried to talk it through and make him understand, the more he urged her to "get over it" and "move on."

That Tabitha is now so unhappy without Ramsay has come as a surprise. That she is fiendishly jealous of Caylee—honestly, Tabitha would like to cut her—is a shock.

"That's my date's," she says. "Captain Peter." She wants the title to make him sound like a figure of authority, but it comes across as goofy. She might as well have said *Captain Crunch* or *Captain Kangaroo*.

"Guy wearing a white uniform like Merrill Stubing's?" Ramsay says. "I just saw him out front. He left."

"He *left?*" Tabitha says. *Have you ever lost anyone?* she thinks. She has now lost Captain Peter, but she feels only a wave of relief. Thank God he's gone! If only this news hadn't been reported by her ex-boyfriend, she would be a very happy woman indeed.

She picks up Captain Peter's beer and drinks the entire thing in one pull. She has, officially, turned into her twin sister.

Caylee looks impressed, Ramsay surprised. Tabitha hides her burp behind a cupped hand.

"I'm out," she says, grabbing her clutch and blowing a kiss to young Zack. "You two have fun."

"Tabitha," Ramsay says.

Tabitha looks at him. He loves her; she can see it written all over his face. But love isn't enough.

"Good night," she says, and she heads for the door.

Tabitha can hear the music, feel the music—hell, she can practically taste the music—from two houses away. It's rap or whatever kids call rap these days, but there are fewer tricky lyrics and a heavier bass line. When Tabitha pulls into the driveway, the music is so loud that the walls of the house seem to expand and contract. It looks like the house is breathing.

Or maybe that's the effect of the Nauti Dog.

Then Tabitha sees the cars. One is the black Range Rover that overindulged, unparented Emma drives, and the other is a white pickup that Teddy—Ainsley's boyfriend—drives.

Tabitha gets out of her car and steadies herself with a hand on the hood. How has Eleanor not heard the music? She really is going deaf. It's so loud Tabitha can't believe the neighbors haven't called the police.

She opens the door into a miasma of pot smoke.

This is just not possible, she thinks.

But of course it *is* possible; Ainsley is sixteen. She is grounded, and what she will no doubt say is that she hasn't left the house. She didn't ask if she could have friends over, because if she had asked, Tabitha would have said absolutely not. But because Ainsley *didn't* ask and Tabitha didn't say no, Ainsley will argue that she is not technically breaking any rules.

Tabitha kicks off her kitten heels. The layout of the carriage house is upside down; the bedrooms are on the ground floor, the living space upstairs. Oh, how Tabitha would love to slip into her room, take an Ambien, and go to bed. She doesn't have the energy to deal with this.

You're a piss-poor parent, she hears Ramsay say.

Then she hears something else. A hollow thocking noise. Thock thock thock. Thock thock thock.

No, Tabitha thinks.

She ascends the stairs stealthily, thinking she would like to appraise the situation before anyone realizes she's home. She grips the handrail as the *thock*ing continues, then stops, then starts again. The song ends. There are a few seconds of silence during which Tabitha freezes. Then Meghan Trainor starts singing that song from the previous summer: "My name is no..." Tabitha congratulates herself for recognizing her daughter's music, then she thinks: *My* name is no. *No no no no no no no.*

She peers between the spindles of the banister at the top of the stairs to see at least a dozen kids smoking cigarettes, smoking weed, drinking cans of PBR, and, yes—the source of that sickening sound—kids playing *beer pong* on her Stephen Swift table.

"No," Tabitha says. She steps into the room and wonders which transgression to address first. She wants to turn off the music, but she is drawn over to the beautiful table, her prize piece of furniture. She grabs the paddle out of the young man's hand on his backswing, and he is so stunned that he accidentally knocks over one of the cups of beer on the table. An amber lake spreads across the sumptuous polished cherry.

"Whoa," he says. It's Ainsley's friend BC. He's cute, dark-haired, wearing a T-shirt from Young's Bicycle Shop. Tabitha has the urge to beat him with the paddle.

She races to the kitchen for a towel, and she finds Ainsley's phone hooked up to the iPod dock. Tabitha yanks it off, and the music stops. Tabitha is so angry that she dumps Ainsley's phone into one of the cups of beer on the kitchen counter.

Someone from the living room calls out, "Music!"

Another voice says, "Her mom is home."

"Yes," Tabitha says. "Her mom *is* home."

"Hey, Tabitha," Emma says when Tabitha comes back into the living room to mop up the beer. Emma is slit-eyed, high as a kite, sitting on the Gervin—Tabitha's excellent turquoise tweed midcentury-style sofa—between two boys.

"Emma," Tabitha says. Tabitha hates that Emma calls her by her first name, but back when Ainsley was small, Tabitha had been so young that she couldn't fathom being called Ms. Frost, and she had never married Wyatt, so she wasn't able to use the name Mrs. Cruise. Eleanor had always insisted that Tabitha's and Harper's friends call her Mrs. Roxie-Frost, which was another reason why Tabitha didn't want to call herself Ms. Frost. It was so pointlessly formal! But what Tabitha realizes now is that a title inspires respect. If Tabitha had long ago trained Emma and Ainsley's other friends to call her Ms. Frost, maybe they would have thought twice before playing beer pong on her dining-room table and infusing the tweed of her sofa with the smell of marijuana smoke.

"Emma," Tabitha says. "Where is Ainsley?"

"Um?" Emma says.

Then Tabitha figures it out: she's downstairs with Teddy.

Tabitha surveys the mess. The other kids are standing in a posture of tense observation, waiting to see how she'll react. *Friend or foe?* they must be wondering. Will Tabitha be the cool mom or will she call their parents?

She wants to order them all out of the house. She wants them *gone.* But the specter of a lawsuit lingers. Emma is not okay to drive.

"Is anyone here sober?" Tabitha asks. She herself isn't sober, not by a long shot. She had four glasses of champagne on the *Belle,* then the Nauti Dog and Captain Peter's beer. She can't offer to drive any of these kids home. So what does *that* mean? They'll spend the night? Unthinkable. She'll have to call the parents.

"I'm sober," a voice says. Tabitha turns: it's Candace Beasley. Tabitha nearly smiles. Ainsley and Candace were friends years and years ago—best, best friends. Until one day—in middle school, if Tabitha remembers correctly—they weren't. Ainsley had grown up and moved on to snarkier, faster girls like Emma. Candace's mother, Stephanie, had been a great friend of Tabitha's, but they drifted apart when the girls did. Part of this was circumstance; part was by design. Tabitha felt extremely uncomfortable when she bumped into Steph at the grocery store or the dry cleaner and Steph said, *Candace really misses Ainsley.* How was Tabitha to respond to that? She tried, *They're girls. Their moods change like the weather. I'm sure they'll be close again before we know it.*

And look! Candace is here at the party! And she is sober! Of course she's sober; she has been raised with love, attention, and, most important, boundaries. She's obedient by nature. She and her mother have the kind of relationship in which they're best friends but Candace still knows who's boss.

"Candace," Tabitha says. "Hi." Just looking at Candace, with her grosgrain-ribbon headband and her coltish legs, makes Tabitha feel, like ten thousand straight pins to the heart, the ways she has failed as a parent. "Can you make sure nobody leaves, please? I need to find Ainsley."

Candace nods; her expression tells Tabitha that she is used to being the responsible one among her peers. Is it wrong to treat Candace as a second adult? Probably, but Tabitha can't fret about that now. She races down the stairs.

The door to Ainsley's room is open, putting her unmade rat's nest of a bed on display along with the piles of clothes—many of them Eleanor Roxie-Frost originals—strewn all over the floor. At first Tabitha thinks Ainsley has run away, and Tabitha panics. Then Tabitha notices the closed door of her own bedroom. She tries the knob: locked.

No, Tabitha thinks. This is *not* happening.

She pounds on the door with the flat of her hand. "Ainsley!" she screams. "Ainsley!" She places her ear against the door. She can't tell if she hears rustling or if the noise is simply her brain scrambling for purchase. Would it not be bad enough if Ainsley and Teddy were having sex in *Ainsley's* room? Does it have to be the horror show of them screwing in *Tabitha's* room? In Tabitha's *bed,* which hasn't been used for carnal purposes since Valentine's Day, which was the last time Tabitha slept with Ramsay?

She pounds again, then the door opens, and Tabitha nearly slaps her hand against Teddy's face.

"Ms. Frost," he says in his country-and-western-star accent. He looks shocked. "I thought you were Emma."

Teddy is bare-chested, but he has jeans on, and Tabitha can see the waistband of his boxers sticking out of the top of his jeans. His red hair is messy, and he's flushed. He has clearly just had his way with Tabitha's daughter, but Tabitha can't hate him. Teddy is sweet; Teddy is polite—she notices that *he* called her Ms. Frost—and Teddy is the victim of some pretty tough circumstances. He and his parents lived in Oklahoma City, but there was a fire at the Nestlé Purina factory, and Teddy's father, a captain with the OCFD, was killed.

That is why Tabitha likes Teddy: Teddy has lost someone.

Teddy's mother subsequently fell apart and tried to take her own life. She is now at a psychiatric hospital in Tulsa, and Teddy was shipped to his only other living relative—his father's brother, Graham Elquot, who is a scalloper here on Nantucket. In the summertime, when scalloping season is suspended, Graham works as a raw bar shucker for all the fancy cocktail parties. Tabitha saw him in action over Memorial Day weekend at the Figawi tent, but she didn't have the courage to introduce herself as Ainsley's mother.

Behind Teddy, the room is shadowy.

"Get your clothes on, Teddy," Tabitha says. "Are you sober?"

"Yes, ma'am," Teddy says, and Tabitha believes him.

"I want you to drive some kids home. You take half, and Candace will take half."

Teddy nods.

"Send Ainsley out, please," Tabitha says.

Her daughter emerges thirty seconds later wearing a vintage Janet Russo sundress of Tabitha's. She has had sex in Tabitha's bed, raided Tabitha's closet, and turned the living room into a Jersey Shore arcade. Tabitha worries that Ainsley will be defiant, but she looks ashamed. Actually that might be overstating it. She looks mildly contrite.

"You said midnight at the earliest," Ainsley says. "I planned on having everyone out and everything cleaned up by then."

"As if *that* makes it okay," Tabitha says.

"Please," Ainsley says. "Please don't be a buzzkill."

Candace takes half the kids—including Emma—home in Emma's Range Rover, and Teddy takes the rest of the kids home in his uncle's truck. Tabitha tells Ainsley she's not going to bed until the upstairs is spotless. There are rings on the Stephen Swift table that will never come out.

"Do you have any idea how much money this table cost me?" Tabitha asks. Then, before Ainsley can answer, she says, "Twenty thousand dollars."

"Do you ever listen to yourself, Tabitha?" Ainsley says. "You are so materialistic."

Do you ever listen to yours*elf?* Tabitha thinks. *You sound like a privileged, entitled snot.*

"Do not," Tabitha says, "call me that."

"Why not?" Ainsley says. "Emma calls her father by his first name."

"It shouldn't be your aspiration to be like Emma," Tabitha says. "That girl is bad news. Always has been, always will be."

"Always has been, always will be," Ainsley says in a high, mocking tone. "You're so judgmental."

Tabitha is about to say that she's supposed to be judgmental where Ainsley is concerned, because how else will Ainsley figure out what's acceptable behavior and what's not? But this will no doubt end up sparking angry responses, coming one after another like an endless string of firecrackers.

Tabitha lets it go.

They get the table returned to its usual place, moving it together, which feels sort of okay—thirty seconds of a common goal. Tabitha empties the ashtrays and tosses out the roaches. She and Ainsley throw the beer cans in the recycling pile.

"So," Ainsley says. "You came home early. How was your night?"

Oh, how Tabitha would love to change the tenor of the evening by sinking into the Gervin and telling her daughter about her night—the party on the *Belle,* meeting the captain, going to Nautilus, bumping into Ramsay. But Tabitha recognizes Ainsley's words for what they are: a strategy. Ainsley has never once asked Tabitha about her night. Ainsley is painfully self-absorbed. Ainsley asking now is Ainsley wanting to butter Tabitha up so that Tabitha forgets she's supposed to punish Ainsley.

It doesn't matter how Tabitha fields the question, because at that moment Ainsley finds the cup in the kitchen that contains her submerged phone. The scream could shatter glass.

Tabitha feels a childish sense of triumph. *Gotcha,* she thinks.

Later, when Tabitha is lying in Ainsley's bed—she isn't about to sleep in her own bed after what happened—and Tabitha is wondering just whose flawed genes her daughter inherited, she remembers Harper's text. She checks her phone. It is now 12:15 a.m., the hour she was expected home.

She clicks on *Vineyard Haven, MA.*

The text says: *Billy is gone.*

AINSLEY

They are going to Martha's Vineyard.

Billy is dead. Billy is the only grandfather Ainsley has ever known, because her father's father, Wyatt senior, died before Ainsley was born.

Ainsley, Tabitha, and Ainsley's grandmother, Eleanor, take the fast ferry from Nantucket to Oak Bluffs. While standing in line, Ainsley accidentally refers to it as Oaks Bluff, and she is reprimanded by a woman even older than Grammie who is standing behind her. This woman puts a hand on Ainsley's shoulder and says, "One tree, many bluffs. Or, more likely, one kind of tree, many bluffs."

"Whatever," Ainsley says.

Eleanor pipes up. "One needs to know."

Ainsley nearly rolls her eyes in her mother's direction until she remembers that she hates her mother. Tabitha intentionally destroyed Ainsley's phone, and thus Ainsley has no way to get hold of anyone—not Emma, not Teddy. Her mother kept her in the house all weekend, even though it was beautiful weather. Her mother didn't go to yoga class and, even more shocking, didn't go to check on things at the boutique.

Ainsley had said, "You can go into the store for a few hours, Tabitha. I'm not going to *go* anywhere." (This was a barefaced lie. As soon as Tabitha pulled out of the driveway, Ainsley intended to ride her bike to Teddy's.)

Tabitha said, "Grammie is going in for me."

"Grammie?" Ainsley said. Eleanor is a *designer.* She is an artist and a genius, but she has not, to Ainsley's knowledge, ever gone into the boutique to manage or supervise. That has always been Tabitha's job.

"Yes," Tabitha said. She had given Ainsley her fakest smile. "I'm staying here with you."

Spending two days shut up in the house without a phone had been a living hell. Because Billy had died, Tabitha spent most of the time mooning around. She pulled out old photo albums—all photo albums were old, Ainsley knew, but these were *really* old—displaying pictures of her mother and Aunt Harper when they were babies. Tabitha had encouraged Ainsley to join her on the sofa, which smelled like marijuana smoke and probably would forever, a fact that secretly pleased Ainsley. Tabitha had said, "You should see these. These are pictures from when we were a whole family. Your grandparents are married, and Harper and I are wearing matching outfits."

Ainsley did not deign to respond. Her mother could ground her, and her mother could drown her phone, but her mother could not make her speak.

Ainsley spent the majority of her time in lockdown worrying. Ainsley and Teddy had planned on going to dinner at the

Jetties, where, it was rumored, G. Love was going to play a surprise set. They had heard this from Teddy's uncle Graham, who would be shucking oysters and clams at the raw bar. With Ainsley grounded, Teddy might offer to take Emma to the Jetties instead. As Ainsley lay in bed watching reruns of *Chopped* on TV, Emma and Teddy might be drunk and swaying together in the crush of people energized by G. Love's magical appearance. They might kiss. Emma is a thrill seeker without morals; she would think nothing of stealing Ainsley's boyfriend. Ainsley wants to hate Emma, but she can't, so Ainsley hates Tabitha.

Tabitha had started drinking wine at five o'clock—the expensive Nicolas-Jay Pinot Noir, from the Willamette Valley in Oregon, that she used to drink before Ramsay put her on rosé. Tabitha had then asked Ainsley if *she* wanted a glass.

Ainsley had thrown her mother a look of contempt. What mixed messages she was sending! The whole reason Ainsley was under house arrest was because she had been drinking (and smoking weed and turning the living room into a frat house), and what does Tabitha do? Offer Ainsley a glass of wine. Ainsley was so agitated about the Emma-Teddy scenario forming in her mind that she could have *used* a drink. But three years earlier, when Ainsley was first experimenting with alcohol, she had consumed a bottle and a half of the Nicolas-Jay Pinot Noir. It was delicious, she'd thought initially—like a rich, plummy juice. But shortly afterward, she'd started puking purple. She would never drink red wine again.

Tabitha passed out by nine, and Ainsley would have sneaked out at that point, except that Eleanor had been alerted to her granddaughter's escapades, and an alarm had been activated that would sound if anyone broke the threshold of the driveway in either direction. There would be no coming or going that night.

Ainsley had ended up paging through the photo albums by herself, and she had to admit it *was* fascinating. There were clippings of Billy and Eleanor on the society pages of the *Boston Globe*—in every photo, Billy leaned in to kiss Eleanor's cheek while she gave the camera a brilliant smile. They looked pretty much in love to Ainsley. There was another photo in the album that showed Eleanor, enormously pregnant—the size of a hippo, really—draped in a yellow dress that might also have been a pup tent. Billy wore square wire-framed glasses and white bell-bottoms and a white patent leather belt, and he held up two fingers over Eleanor's shoulder. So . . . this was the day they found out they were having twins. The dates were stamped onto all the photos, and this one said: OCTOBER 10, 1977. Ainsley felt like she knew that Grammie didn't discover she was having twins until very late in the pregnancy, and now she sees it was only six or eight weeks before the twins were born.

This is what baffles Ainsley about the olden days, before technology: people didn't *know* anything. There were no ultrasounds to tell Grammie she was having two babies instead of one. There was no Internet. How did anyone know *anything* without the Internet? Really, Ainsley can't figure that one out. And there were no cell phones. How did a person live without a cell phone? Ainsley was doing it right now, and it was very stressful. She might have logged on to her laptop and checked Facebook or Instagram to see if Emma had posted anything about going to the Jetties with Teddy, but Tabitha had changed the Wi-Fi password, just as she'd promised.

Most of the rest of the pictures were of her mother and

Aunt Harper. They looked exactly alike: there was no possibility of telling them apart, and Ainsley wondered if when they were babies their identities had been switched, then switched again—maybe switched infinite times—until the day they were old enough to speak and say their names out loud. Then whoever they happened to be that day stuck. Eleanor always dressed them in matching outfits that she made herself, using her turquoise Singer sewing machine (which she still had and always claimed she was going to donate to the Smithsonian). There were green gingham jumpers with giraffes appliquéd on the front; there were pink party dresses with borders of purple sequins at the bottom; there were black velvet dresses at Christmas. Who put two-year-olds in black? Ainsley wondered.

Only Eleanor. It was well documented that Eleanor Roxie-Frost got her big break in fashion when Diana Vreeland happened across the twins wearing yellow linen shifts during a playground outing on Boston Common in 1980. Those dresses were miniature versions of what would become the Roxie. It had been in the era of women's lib, and Eleanor Roxie-Frost became a textbook case. She went from being a stay-at-home mother of twins designing clothes for her daughters and herself to a fashion-design sensation featured in *Vogue* nearly every month. When the twins were in high school, Eleanor found retail space on Newbury Street and opened her flagship store there. The store had been a good thing and a bad thing, because Eleanor became so busy being a famous fashion designer that something in her life had to go. That something was Billy. Ainsley's grandparents got divorced, a fact that Ainsley always found embarrassing. Around half of her friends' parents were divorced, but grandparents were meant to stay together until they keeled over from being so old.

Even stranger and more unsettling was that, after the divorce, Aunt Harper had gone with Billy and Tabitha had stayed with Eleanor, a custody agreement that seemed to have been borrowed from *The Parent Trap.* The Frost family had split right down the middle, like one of these photographs torn in half—Billy holding one twin, Eleanor the other.

When Ainsley had gone to replace the photo album, she came across a tattered envelope wedged between two other books on the shelf. The envelope had an important, secret look, so Ainsley pulled it free. Inside was a plastic hospital bracelet bearing the inscription JULIAN WYATT CRUISE 5-28-03. It was her baby brother's bracelet. Also in the envelope were three snapshots: one of a teensy-tiny Julian at the hospital enclosed in what looked like a plastic display case with tubes and wires running from his mouth, nose, chest, and feet. The second was a photograph of Tabitha holding Julian in two hands. Really, he was no bigger than a submarine sandwich; he had only weighed one pound and ten ounces when he was born, she knew. The third photo was of Tabitha, Wyatt, Ainsley, and Julian all together in a house Ainsley didn't recognize, although they were sitting on the dark brown leather sofa that had predated the turquoise-tweed Gervin. Julian was free of wires, and he was a little bigger, maybe the size of a bag of flour. Ainsley was a pudgy-faced toddler with barely enough hair to make pigtails. But the real shocker was how young Ainsley's parents looked. There were seniors at Nantucket High School who looked older than Tabitha and Wyatt did in that picture. Both of them were smiling—laughing, even—as though the photographer had just said something funny. Who took the picture? Ainsley wondered. Not Eleanor, certainly; she didn't believe in joking around.

Ainsley scrutinized the photo for another moment. It was the only photograph of her nuclear family that she had ever seen. She knew why it was hidden away: Tabitha found the loss of Julian, and maybe the loss of Wyatt, too painful. Ainsley was grateful that Tabitha hadn't kept Julian's death certificate or anything morbid like that. The hospital bracelet was jarring enough. Ainsley returned everything back to the envelope, then the envelope back to its hiding spot between the two books on the shelf. She turned to check on her mother, who was still snoring softly on the sofa. She resisted the urge to kiss her mother's forehead, although she did gently nudge Tabitha awake.

"Hey," Ainsley said. "It's time to go to bed now, Mama." And like a dutiful child, Tabitha had risen and followed Ainsley down the stairs.

Now it's Monday, and Ainsley should be at school, where she finally might discover what had happened during the remainder of everyone's weekend. Maybe she hasn't been the only one to get punished; maybe the unthinkable happened and Emma has been grounded as well—although Ainsley doesn't think so, because it had been Emma's father, Dutch, who provided the weed and the beer for the party. He had actually asked Emma if she wanted any *coke* (not the drink, he said, wink, wink), but Emma had used common sense and said no, thank you. Ainsley had really liked Dutch until she heard that; now she questions his ethics. To provide beer and weed to your sixteen-year-old daughter makes you not only a "cool" parent but also kind of a criminal. To offer coke makes you only a criminal.

Ainsley wonders if Teddy got into any trouble and decides the answer is also no. Graham is an uncle. The whole parenting thing was thrust at him because his brother died fighting a fire and his sister-in-law, Teddy's mother, is a suicidal depressed anorexic back in Oklahoma. Graham is only now mastering the basics: food on the table three times a day, making sure Teddy gets to school and sports practice on time—he's a star at baseball, which is big in Oklahoma, whereas lacrosse is big in Nantucket—make sure he's doing his homework, take him to get his driver's license, give him chores so he learns responsibility. This summer Teddy is going to work as a bellhop at the boutique hotel 21 Broad. Teddy is so grateful for Graham's steadying presence in his life that he doesn't like doing anything that might land him in trouble. He did borrow Graham's truck and say he was going on a date with Ainsley, and Graham did hand him forty bucks, which Teddy gave to BC to buy cups and vodka. But Teddy didn't smoke or drink anything. He only came to the party to be with Ainsley.

Candace Beasley probably got in trouble. This time last year, Ainsley would never have invited Candace to a party. Candace and Ainsley had been best friends when they were little girls. They had the same teachers, participated in the same activities; in fourth grade, when Tabitha took Ainsley to Los Angeles for spring break, Candace came along. They rode the Ferris wheel on the Santa Monica Pier together; they ordered room service in their suite at Shutters on the Beach while Tabitha went to the bar to conduct business meetings. They went to the spa and got their nails painted the same color.

They used to pretend they were sisters. They used to pretend, at Ainsley's insistence, that they were not only sisters but also twins.

But there had been some essential difference between Ainsley and Candace, and it concerned the way they were being raised. Ainsley—because she spent so much time with her mother and grandmother—was always encouraged to act older than she was. She accompanied Tabitha and Eleanor to the Galley for lunch and, when they were in Boston, to tea at the Four Seasons. Ainsley had been allowed to stay home by herself during the day starting when she was eight years old. She could use the microwave to make popcorn and then melt extra butter; she was allowed to watch *Gossip Girl.* She had a triple-decker pink aluminum case filled with makeup that Tabitha had bought her. Once when Candace had been over for the afternoon—on what Candace's mother, Stephanie, still called a playdate—Candace had gone downstairs made up with foundation, powder, blush, eyeliner, eye shadow, mascara, and lipstick, and Stephanie had screamed as though Candace were missing a limb. She had yanked Candace into the powder room and scrubbed her face right there and then with one of the blue soaps shaped like a scallop shell that nobody ever used.

Tabitha had laughed and said, "Don't you think you're overreacting? They're little girls playing dress-up."

Stephanie had said, "You can let your daughter walk around looking like a prostitute, but I'm not going to."

Tabitha had shrugged the comment off, but it had taken root in Ainsley. She knew Stephanie thought there was something inappropriate about the way Ainsley was being raised. Candace, also an only child, was being raised like a baby. She had ten thousand rules to abide by: four bites of everything on her plate (including broccoli and lima beans), PBS Kids and Disney Channel only (no Nickelodeon of any kind), bedtime at eight o'clock, even on weekends, teeth brushing *and* flossing, and a schedule of chores that earned Candace a dollar a week, deposited into her college fund.

Ainsley found much in Candace's house to admire: the meals were homemade and delicious; Stephanie and her husband, Stu, said a nice short grace before eating and then kissed each other; the bath towels were fluffy; the sheets on Candace's bed were always crisp and neatly made; and always, Stephanie would read to them before bed.

Tabitha, by contrast, watched every morsel that Ainsley put in her mouth, forbidding doughnuts, pancakes, and baked potatoes. Ainsley had learned the term *empty calorie* by third grade. Tabitha dressed Ainsley in smaller versions of her grandmother's designs, dresses that would have fetched five hundred dollars or more on eBay. She gave Ainsley lessons in how to walk in high heels and how to throw French phrases into everyday conversation. *À tout à l'heure!* Probably Ainsley's fondest memory of growing up is coming home from school, drinking Coke Zero on the sofa with Tabitha, and paging through the new issue of *Vogue* with Tabitha covering the captions with her hand and quizzing Ainsley on the designers.

Once Ainsley got to middle school, she was able to turn the unorthodox way she'd been raised to her advantage. She was the coolest person in sixth grade: the prettiest, the most developed, and the best dressed by far. Candace had cried on the first day because she got lost changing classes and missed their fifth-grade teacher, Mr. Bonaventura. Like countless middle school girls before her, Ainsley secured her position as queen bee by stepping on the people below her, and her favorite rung had been Candace.

Stephanie had changed her tune over the course of that year. She called Tabitha incessantly, hoping to "get the girls together."

"I'm not sure what happened," Stephanie said. "I think they had some kind of falling-out. But I'm sure it can be fixed, right?"

Through middle school and into high school, Candace had sought Ainsley's attention and approval, but to no avail. Ainsley didn't say hello, didn't acknowledge Candace's presence in the hallway, in the cafeteria, in the classroom. Ainsley became friends with Emma Marlowe, and they had their disciples—BC, Maggie, Anna, and... Teddy.

But just this past spring, something happened with Candace. Her father's online hotel-booking business had been bought up by Orbitz, and suddenly the family was very well off. Stephanie and Stu took Candace to Aspen to ski in February and to Saint Barts in April—and, while they were away, Candace had acquired a set of sophisticated habits. She had, apparently, slept with the son of a sheikh in Aspen, drunk Dom Pérignon at lunch with her parents at a place called Nikki Beach in Saint Barts, and started smoking clove cigarettes. Over the course of a few short months, Candace had become cool, so Ainsley—out of fear of being overthrown more than anything else—had invited Candace to her house for the party.

Candace might have exaggerated her vacation exploits, because at the party she was the only person other than Teddy able to drive when Tabitha got home. Tabitha had given Candace the keys to Emma's Range Rover. Emma might be angry at Ainsley for that, and no one is more intimidating when angry than Emma. Ainsley has no way of knowing what's going on in her world without her phone.

* * *

The ferry is nearing land, and Tabitha goes to stand at the window. Ainsley refuses to join her, but she cranes her neck. There's an expansive green park to the left with a white gazebo in the middle.

Ainsley touches her grandmother's arm. "Have you ever been to the Vineyard?"

"Not since my honeymoon," Eleanor says. "Your grandfather and I traveled to both Nantucket and Martha's Vineyard on a motor yacht my father chartered for us. I'm sure you can guess that I preferred one island and Billy the other. This was Billy's place."

Ainsley processes this. Eleanor and Billy not only split up their possessions, their money, and their twins, they also split up the islands—Nantucket for Eleanor, the Vineyard for Billy.

"Has my mother ever been here?" Ainsley asks.

"Oh, certainly," Eleanor says. "Back before..."

"Before what?" Ainsley asks.

"Before everything happened," Eleanor says. "I believe the last time she came to visit Billy here was when she was pregnant."

"With me?" Ainsley says. "Or with Julian?"

"Who can remember?" Eleanor says. She waves a hand laden with rings. Eleanor is seventy-one years old and the most elegant woman Ainsley knows. She has traveled to Paris and Milan and Shanghai and Bombay and Marrakech and Sydney and Rome and Tokyo. She has boutiques in Nantucket and Palm Beach. The Nantucket store closes in the winter; the Palm Beach store closes in the summer. Eleanor's flagship store, on Newbury Street, shut down for good last year because of declining sales. Ainsley suspects her grandmother's designs are becoming dated.

Ainsley is shocked that her mother and grandmother are even attending Billy's memorial reception. (It's not a funeral. Billy has been cremated, and his ashes will be kept in an urn.) Ainsley saw the photos of Eleanor and Billy together in the album, but for as long as Ainsley can remember, there has been a Hatfield-and-McCoy-type feud between the two halves of the family. Tabitha hates Harper for reasons Ainsley isn't privy to, and she assumes that Eleanor hated Billy as well. She would ask Eleanor, but she's too intimidated.

Tabitha turns to Ainsley. "Oak Bluffs has this thing called the Methodist campground," she says. "It's all these different-colored gingerbread houses, and in the center is the Tabernacle, which is a large outdoor church-type thing."

"It sounds like a cult," Eleanor says.

"Oh, dear God," Tabitha says, looking at the people who have amassed on the dock to await the ferry's arrival. "There she is."

Ainsley sees her mother's double standing in the crowd. The sight is so surreal that Ainsley turns to look at her mother to make sure she is standing right there, then she looks back in the crowd at Aunt Harper. Aunt Harper wears her hair just as her mother does—long, heavy, and dark—but of course her clothes are different. Tabitha wears the Roxie—the linen shift with the obi—in black and a pair of black patent leather Manolo Blahnik pumps that she normally reserves for the city. Aunt Harper is wearing a pair of black pants that looks like something a waitress at a Red

Lobster might wear and some kind of black lace shell that Ainsley—who has developed a pretty sharp eye when it comes to other people's poor fashion choices—suspects came off the sale rack at Banana Republic. The top and pants don't make sense together—the pants utilitarian, the shell dressy—and black lace, according to Eleanor, always references *lingerie,* which makes it inappropriate for a funeral or memorial reception. Despite Aunt Harper's pitiful outfit—or perhaps because of it—Ainsley's heart is captured. Aunt Harper is the underdog here, the first one Ainsley has found herself rooting for in sixteen and a half years.

Harper looks very tense as Eleanor, Tabitha, and Ainsley—in that order—step off the ramp.

"Hello, Mommy," Harper says.

Eleanor takes an appraising look at her daughter. "Hello, darling," Eleanor says. She leans forward to air-kiss Harper's cheek, then she takes the lace material of Harper's top between her fingers. "Where did you get *this?*"

"I don't know," Harper says. "At the store? I'm roasting in it." When she plucks the top away from her body, Ainsley notices that her aunt is wearing her grandfather's gold watch.

Evidently so does Eleanor, because she says, "I can't believe your father managed to keep that watch out of hock. He left it to you?"

"He did," Harper says.

"Be certain to follow his example and hold on to it no matter what circumstances you find yourself in," Eleanor says. "That watch is valuable. It belonged to his father, Dr. Richard Frost. It was Billy's prize possession."

"I realize this, Mommy," Harper says. "I'm saving it for when Ainsley has a son." She looks past Tabitha to Ainsley. "Hello, Ainsley."

Ainsley hasn't seen her aunt in three years. Somehow Ainsley had been allowed to go with Billy to Fenway, and Aunt Harper had been there. Four years before *that,* when Ainsley was nine, she had gone to the Cape with Billy, and they met Harper for lunch in Woods Hole. So this is only the third time Ainsley can remember seeing her aunt, yet Ainsley feels comfortable rushing into her aunt's arms and, inexplicably, starting to cry. "I loved Gramps," she says.

"He loved you," Harper says. She gives Ainsley a hug that feels more maternal than any hug she has ever received from Tabitha.

When Ainsley pulls away, she watches her mother and aunt face each other. The moment is so awkward, so *awful,* that Ainsley's insides twist. *Hug each other,* she thinks. Her mother hates Harper, but is the opposite true?

"Tabitha," Harper says.

"Harper," Tabitha says.

They do not move toward each other, and in fact it feels like the air between them is thrumming with bad energy. It's like they're two magnets with the same poles, repelling each other.

"All right, then," Eleanor says, clearly already weary of the reunion. "Shall we go?"

Ainsley is delighted to see that Aunt Harper drives a vintage navy-blue Bronco that has been impeccably restored. Since

Ainsley has been dating Teddy, she has logged in a lot of hours watching *Barrett-Jackson Live.*

"Is this a sixty-eight?" Ainsley asks.

"It is!" Harper says. "Good eye."

"I thought you were hiring a car," Eleanor says.

"Martha's Vineyard Executive Transport was booked," Harper says. "I assure you, I did call them. I'm sorry, Mommy, but you'll have to slum it."

"Sit up front, Mother," Tabitha says. "Ainsley and I will squeeze in the back."

Ainsley doesn't want to squeeze in anywhere with Tabitha, but she obliges because her grandmother is a senior citizen and belongs up front.

The back of the car is basically a Dumpster for coffee cups, old issues of the *Vineyard Gazette,* greasy paper bags that look and smell like they might contain half of a week-old tuna-fish sandwich, chew toys, and empty airline-size bottles of Jägermeister. Tabitha tries to wrap up all the junk in a sheet of newspaper just so she can find a place to put her feet in their eight-hundred-dollar shoes. The backseat has a sheet over it, but the floor is covered with dog hair.

"Do you have a dog?" Ainsley says. She has been asking Tabitha for a dog ever since she could talk.

"Fish," Harper says.

"You have a fish?" Ainsley says.

"A dog named Fish," Harper says. "He's a Siberian husky."

"That's certainly an odd name," Eleanor says. "It sounds like something your father would dream up. You always were exactly like Billy."

"I'd love to give you a tour of the island—" Harper says.

"I want a tour!" Ainsley says. She had sort of been dreading this day, but already the payoff has been tremendous. Her mother's and grandmother's obvious misery has cheered Ainsley up.

"—but we really don't have time," Harper says. "The reception starts at noon, and your ferry back is at—"

"Not soon enough," Tabitha murmurs.

"Four o'clock," Eleanor says. "But I feel we should return to the dock no later than three fifteen, don't you, Pony?"

"If not earlier," Tabitha says.

Harper snorts. "She still calls you Pony?"

"Who is *she?*" Eleanor asks. "The cat's mother?"

Harper catches Ainsley's eye in the rearview mirror. "You know the story behind that nickname, right?"

"Please don't," Tabitha says.

"Mom wanted a pony," Ainsley says.

"Your mother not only wanted a pony, your mother also *became* a pony," Harper says. "For most of third grade. Ponytail, brown shetland sweater, brown corduroys. She neighed and whinnied. She trotted, cantered, and galloped. She did everything shy of eating hay. The way people were able to tell us apart that year was that your mother acted like a horse and I didn't."

"I remember it differently," Tabitha says.

"We must leave the reception at three o'clock sharp," Eleanor says. "You needn't worry about driving us. I'll happily pay for a taxi."

Ainsley looks out the window, trying to take it all in. There's a pond, a bridge, a field. It looks like Nantucket, but it's not Nantucket.

"Six towns," Harper is saying. "Seventeen thousand year-round residents. The greatest ice cream in the world at Mad Martha's."

"You've never tasted the ice cream at the Juice Bar," Ainsley says. "Or have you? Have you ever been to Nantucket, Aunt Harper?"

"I have," Harper says. "But not in a long, long time."

"Who's going to be at this reception?" Tabitha asks.

"I'm not sure," Harper says. "Daddy wanted this, not me. But an announcement went up on Islanders Talk and my Facebook page, so..."

"So mostly Billy's friends or mostly your friends?" Tabitha asks.

"Daddy's."

"Do you have any friends?" Tabitha asks.

"Mama!" Ainsley says, forgetting that she's not speaking to Tabitha.

"I have friends," Harper says.

"I'm not talking about the men you're screwing," Tabitha says.

"Tabitha!" Ainsley says, more to get her mother's attention than to be disrespectful.

"I'm surprised anyone talks to you after that... that... *drug bust,*" Eleanor says. "I still can't get over a daughter of mine... arrested! Your grandparents are rolling over in their graves, I assure you."

"What do you know about it, Mommy?" Harper says. "Honestly, what do you *know* about it?"

"Ann-Lane told me everything," Eleanor says. "You do realize she lives right next door to the family whose child you corrupted, don't you? She said the state police were there and the FBI."

The FBI? Ainsley thinks. Her aunt is way more interesting than Ainsley realized.

"I didn't corrupt any child," Harper says. "The 'child' in question was already plenty corrupted when I encountered him. Ann-Lane can stick a Pop-Tart up her ass. And I can assure you she will not be at this reception. Unless you invited her. Did you invite her?"

"No," Eleanor says.

"Who is Ann-Lane?" Ainsley asks.

"A busybody," Harper says.

"My roommate," Eleanor says. "From Pine Manor."

There is a loaded silence, during which Harper's driving becomes markedly more aggressive. She honks her horn and flips people off. By way of explanation she says, "It's so early in the season that the taxi drivers don't know where they're going. They're accidents waiting to happen."

"So," Tabitha says, leaning forward. "Are you seeing anyone?"

"You haven't said boo to me in fourteen years," Harper says. "And now you want me to answer personal questions?" She puts on her turn signal and makes a left down a long driveway bordered on both sides by white fencing. The sign says: FARM NECK GOLF CLUB. PRIVATE.

"We're here," Harper says. She seeks Ainsley's eyes out in the mirror again. "This was your grandfather's favorite place on the island. Farm Neck."

"This is private?" Eleanor asks.

"Yes, Mommy."

"How did your father manage to get in?"

"He knew people. Unfortunately, you can't pass the membership on. This died with Billy, but we get to use it one last time."

"I didn't even know Gramps golfed," Ainsley says.

"He was an abominable golfer," Eleanor says. "He downright embarrassed himself at the country club with my father in 1968, the summer we were married."

"He was a better drinker than a golfer," Harper says. "I'll agree with you there. Made him popular in a foursome. Everyone could beat him, and he told good stories at the clubhouse."

"Please don't glorify alcohol consumption in front of my daughter," Tabitha says.

Ainsley rolls her eyes.

Harper parks the Bronco, then hurries around to help Eleanor out. When they are all standing in the parking lot, Harper holds her arms akimbo. She looks off balance, like she might topple over. "Welcome to Farm Neck," Harper says.

The grounds of the club are pretty. There's a line of golf carts, some with bags of clubs in the back, and there's a putting green by the front entrance. The air smells like cut grass and french fries. Ainsley marvels that Billy managed to belong to a private club when she knows that both Eleanor and Tabitha have been languishing on the list at the Nantucket Yacht Club for nearly a decade.

"Obama played here," Harper says. "And Clinton."

"I wouldn't advertise that," Eleanor says.

The reception is being held in a tent off the side of the clubhouse, and although it's a much smaller affair than Ainsley anticipated, it's still very nice. The tent is decorated with white lanterns and potted plants; there are high-top tables scattered throughout, and a waitress holds a tray of champagne flutes filled to the brim, greeting people as they walk in. There's an easel holding a picture of Ainsley's grandfather in his later years, after he'd lost his wire-rimmed glasses and his white patent leather belt. In this photo, he's on a boat. He wears a visor, his face is tan and weather-beaten, and he's holding up a striped bass. Above the photograph, it says: REMEMBERING WILLIAM O'SHAUGHNESSY FROST, APRIL 13, 1944–JUNE 16, 2017. There's a table beneath the easel on which rest blank name tags and a Sharpie marker.

"Are we doing name tags?" Ainsley asks her mother.

"Heavens, no," Tabitha says. She lifts a flute of champagne off the tray. "Hello, gorgeous."

The waitress seems to think Tabitha is speaking to her instead of to the champagne. "Harper?" she says. "I don't think I've ever seen you wear heels before."

"I'm not Harper," Tabitha says. "I'm her twin sister, Tabitha."

"Seriously?" the waitress says.

Ainsley picks up a name tag and writes: BILLY'S GRAND-DAUGHTER, but she doesn't leave enough room for *granddaughter,* so she has to crumple it up and start over. She affixes the name tag to the front of her black Milly butterfly-sleeve dress. The tent is hot; she's going to melt. She wishes she'd worn something more summery, but Tabitha and Eleanor had insisted on black. They are the only people who dressed up. Everyone else is in regular daytime clothes. There is a group of men in golf shirts, a couple of middle-aged women in slacks and comfortable shoes, and a frosted-blond woman of "a certain age" wearing a Lilly Pulitzer sundress and sandals.

Harper is over in the far corner of the tent talking to a policeman, and for a second Ainsley wonders if her aunt is in trouble. But then Ainsley sees tender gestures. First the officer touches Harper's cheek, then the two of them start kissing. If

Eleanor sees them, she'll have a conniption fit; she deplores public displays of affection, and although Eleanor isn't blatantly racist, she is old-fashioned. She calls black people Negroes, no matter how many times both Ainsley and Tabitha have informed her that the term is not acceptable. Will Eleanor care that Harper is kissing a black policeman in front of the assembled guests? Was *that* the reason Harper deflected Tabitha's question about whether she was seeing anyone?

Eleanor and Tabitha are busy signing the guest book, each with a glass of champagne in hand, and they don't notice Harper and the policeman going gangbusters in the corner.

Ainsley misses Teddy. She feels a dull pain—like her heart has a cramp—when she thinks about Teddy with Emma.

Finally Harper pulls away. The policeman strolls out of the tent past Ainsley, close enough for her to hear the static of his walkie-talkie and smell his aftershave. He's cute. He's *young,* possibly closer to Ainsley's age than her aunt's. *Go, Aunt Harper!* Ainsley thinks. Tabitha broke up with Ramsay, which is another reason Ainsley hates her mother. She brought Ramsay into Ainsley's life, encouraged her to love him—and Ainsley did love Ramsay very much—then she gave him the boot. Now Tabitha jokes about taking a younger lover. She jokes about the guy who teaches surfing lessons at Cisco Beach and about Mr. Bly, Ainsley's chemistry teacher. Every time Tabitha brings it up, Ainsley thinks: *Ew.* But thinking about her aunt dating a policeman does not inspire the same distaste.

Tabitha could never catch or keep a guy that young and hot, Ainsley thinks, despite the fact that she and Harper are identical twins. Tabitha is too stuck up and absolutely no fun.

Harper speaks to the gentlemen in golf shirts. She says something that makes them laugh, then she approaches Ainsley.

"Would you like a glass of champagne?" she asks. "I ordered the good stuff. Taittinger. And there are supposed to be finger sandwiches and sliders. I kept it Waspy for your grandmother's sake. No spring rolls, no quesadillas."

"Nothing with any actual flavor," Ainsley says. She gives Harper a conspiratorial smile. It's so bizarre—her mother's face on a much nicer, cooler person. "So was that guy, the policeman, your boyfriend?"

Harper's expression changes. She looks anxious, like she's been caught. "Boyfriend?" she says. "You mean Drew?"

"I'm sorry," Ainsley says. "It's none of my business."

Harper takes a long look at Ainsley, as if she's trying to see inside her somehow. "I wish I could go back to your age," she says. "Start over. I'd do things differently."

Ainsley nods. "I'd love some champagne," she says. "And I'll even eat pale triangular sandwiches. I'm starving. We didn't have breakfast."

Harper says, "Just take a flute of champagne, and if anyone gives you trouble, tell them your grandfather wrote it into his will that you're not only allowed to drink champagne at his memorial, you're also supposed to."

Ainsley nods, knowing full well that this explanation will *not* work with her mother or grandmother.

"I'm going to check on things back in the kitchen," Harper says. "Cut some crusts off myself if I have to."

Harper leaves the tent, and Ainsley feels abandoned. She sees her grandmother and mother standing off to the side, holding their champagne flutes in front of them as they would hold crosses in the presence of vampires. They aren't speaking to each other or to anyone else. God forbid they actually engage with Billy's friends. Why did they even bother coming?

Ainsley grabs a flute of champagne from the waitress's tray and heads over to the men in golf shirts. "Hello," she says. "I'm Ainsley, Billy's granddaughter."

Ainsley drinks that flute of champagne, then Smitty, the ringleader among Billy's golfing buddies, procures her another. The champagne goes right to her head on an empty stomach, but she doesn't care; she kind of likes it. She is a celebrity here, at least among these men and all the people Smitty introduces her to, such as the woman in the Lilly Pulitzer shift, presented to Ainsley—with a nudge and a wink that make Ainsley think she should pay special attention—as Mrs. Tobias.

"I loved your grandpa," Mrs. Tobias says. "He was a dreamboat."

Mrs. Tobias is very tan. She's somewhere in her midfifties, which is too old to pull off the kind of sundress she's wearing—it's best suited for someone Ainsley's age—and her frosted blond hair is styled like Rachel's from *Friends.* But she's pretty. She's a heck of a lot younger and sexier and more attractive than Eleanor, although she lacks Eleanor's elegance and grace.

Dreamboat, Ainsley thinks. Was this her grandfather's girlfriend? Or maybe just his paramour? What to make of the name Mrs. Tobias? Where, if anywhere, is Mr. Tobias?

But before Ainsley can formulate the kind of probing questions that will yield more specifics, her attention is snagged by something happening over by the entrance. The tent has filled up with people, and servers are now passing trays of hors d'oeuvres—shrimp cocktail, radish sandwiches, pigs in a blanket—so it's hard to see, plus Ainsley's vision is hazy, thanks to the champagne. But she hears a woman shouting.

"Where is she? Where *is* she?"

The voice carries over the polite cocktail party chatter, and soon heads turn and voices are hushed. Ainsley sees a couple enter the tent, the woman petite, with very short hair and bug eyes, and a man in a suit and tie, following her, reaching for her arm, trying to quiet her down.

Who is this? Ainsley wonders, and at the same time, Mrs. Tobias murmurs, "Oh, shit. Here it comes."

Here *what* comes? Ainsley's eyes widen in wonder, then shock, as the bug-eyed woman approaches Tabitha and Eleanor.

"You!" she says. The person she seems to be addressing is Tabitha.

Wha...? Ainsley thinks. She sees Aunt Harper enter the tent just as the bug-eyed woman throws a full flute of champagne all over the front of Tabitha's black Roxie dress, and then, with a whip-quick motion, slaps Tabitha across the face.

The sound of the slap reverberates through the tent. The crowd gasps, then goes silent.

HARPER

She understands the timing is bad: her father's memorial reception is held only three days after Sadie catches her and Reed together in the parking lot of Lucy Vincent. Three days is long enough for the rumor to spread but not long enough for people to forget about it and move on.

She considered canceling the memorial reception, but Billy had wanted only one thing, and it was a farewell party at Farm Neck. And besides, in a text sent late Sunday night—when Harper was lying facedown in bed, determined never to rise again—Reed said that he'd managed to calm Sadie down. He *said* he'd convinced her that what she saw wasn't Reed and Harper screwing but rather Reed embracing Harper in an attempt to comfort her after the death of her father. Yes, he understood it seemed odd and, possibly, unprofessional—meeting a patient's family member at midnight in the parking lot of Lucy Vincent Beach, but that was why they loved the Vineyard, right? Because it was a close-knit community where people genuinely cared for one another, and Reed had a long-established history of going above and beyond the call of duty for his patients. Sadie should also remember that she'd had a lot to drink at the barbecue at Lambert's Cove—a lot—and therefore she couldn't trust anything she thought she'd seen.

She was lucky she hadn't been pulled over.

With these assurances from Reed that Sadie had been neutralized, Harper proceeded with her plan. That Sadie had then, apparently, gone all Nancy Drew on him—checking Reed's phone records and quizzing Dee, Billy's nurse at the hospital, who said that yes, she had been suspicious about an affair all along—came as a surprise to Reed but not to Harper.

Sadie's outburst at the reception had, initially, worked in Harper's favor. It was wildly inappropriate—bursting into a beloved islander's funeral, dousing his daughter in drink, then striking her.

In the seconds after Sadie slapped Tabitha—Tabitha, not Harper, a mistake Harper deeply regretted—Drew had appeared out of nowhere to subdue Mrs. Zimmer. He pried the empty champagne flute from her hand—no one wanted to see any breaking glass—and gently restrained her by holding both wrists.

Sadie spat in Tabitha's general direction. "That woman is an evil bitch."

"That woman," Drew said, "is my girlfriend."

"No," Tabitha said. "Not me. My twin sister." She offered her hand to Drew. "I'm Tabitha."

Harper had been amazed that Pony had been able to regain her composure so shortly after being slapped. Her cheek was a hot, blazing red. It was one benefit of spending so many years with Eleanor, Harper reasoned. Tabitha knew how to take a hit.

Despite Harper's mortification, she had the wherewithal to take the crowd's temperature. The friends and neighbors assembled to mourn the passing of Billy Frost seemed aghast—not at Harper or Tabitha mistaken for Harper—but rather at Sadie Zimmer. The island girl who had made such a success of her mother's pie business was revealed to be a raging psychopath! She had slapped one of Billy Frost's daughters—the wrong daughter, as it turned out, the one who lived on Nantucket. As distressing as the matter had been thirty seconds earlier, now that Mrs. Zimmer had been restrained, people became titillated rather than alarmed.

Billy's friend Smitty turned to Roger Door, who was standing next to him, and said, "This has to be the greatest story from any memorial reception ever."

Roger Door raised a glass. "Leave it to Billy," he said.

But it was Eleanor who had the final word. Oh, how Harper disliked her mother at times, yet she couldn't dispute the fact that Eleanor had the countenance of a queen, a regal bearing, an unassailable authority. She had been raised a Brahmin and remained one to her core. Eleanor approached Sadie and said, "I don't know who you are, but showing up at an event like this to air your personal grievances is nothing short of disgraceful. A man has died and deserves to be remembered fondly and cheerfully, so please take your petty drama elsewhere."

Sadie's bulging eyes narrowed with this reprimand. "Your daughter is a tramp," she said.

"I don't care," Eleanor said. "Please go."

Sadie allowed herself to be escorted from the tent by Reed and Drew. A waiter brought Tabitha an ice pack for her face. Some genius in the clubhouse found a way to pipe in music, and immediately Mozart restored civility to the proceedings. Harper, for a second believing she had survived the worst-case scenario unscathed, helped herself to another glass of champagne.

The slap must have knocked Tabitha into a state of shock, but no sooner did she set her ice pack down on one of the high-tops than she returned to her usual self. She glared at Harper. "What the hell was that?"

Harper regarded her sister. "I liked you better when you were a pony," she said. "Remember how I used to ride on your back?"

"Who was she, Harper?"

Harper debated: lie or tell the truth? Eleanor and Ainsley

were both waiting for an answer as well. Could Harper get away with saying she had no idea?

Suddenly they were approached by Ken Doll, the general manager of Farm Neck. "I'm sorry about that little scene with Mrs. Zimmer," he said. "None of us had any idea she was so agitated. Dr. Zimmer is a member in good standing here. We had no reason to expect any trouble."

"Of course not," Harper said. "It's not your fault."

"Is this your sister?" Ken Doll asked. He offered his hand to Tabitha. "So nice to meet you. Please accept my condolences about your father. The entire staff here at Farm Neck were big Billy Frost fans."

Tabitha gave Ken Doll a patient smile. "My father was one of a kind."

"He was a rapscallion," Eleanor murmured. "An incorrigible hooligan."

"Mommy," Harper said, then she remembered that Eleanor had always been a disaster when drinking champagne.

"Well, anyway, it's a pleasure to meet you..."

"Tabitha," Tabitha said.

Ken Doll gave her a little geisha bow, and Harper thought maybe he was flirting with Tabitha. Would that be such a terrible match? Ken Doll—properly Kenneth Dawe—was recently divorced from Penny Dawe, who worked at the Dukes County courthouse, in Edgartown. Ken Doll was as handsome as his namesake but so fastidious that many Vineyarders thought Ken Doll and Penny had divorced because Ken Doll was gay. But he wasn't gay—he was merely particular about how he looked and presented himself, which was appropriate for the GM of an exclusive golf club. And it also made him a potential match for Tabitha.

But no further words were exchanged. Ken Doll moved off to chat with Smitty, and Tabitha got her verbal machete out and held it to Harper's neck.

"Mrs. Zimmer? *Dr.* Zimmer? Were you sleeping with Billy's *doctor?* His *married* doctor?"

Harper said, "I think you'd better go."

"Yes," Eleanor said. "For once, Pony, I agree with your sister."

At six o'clock that evening, when Harper pulls her Bronco up to her duplex and unloads the bakery boxes filled with leftover tea sandwiches, she understands that there will be backlash.

Drew is sitting on her front step in street clothes—jeans, a blue chambray shirt, and navy espadrilles that he wears despite the ribbing he receives from the other officers and from Harper. He is also wearing the face of dejection.

"You were sleeping with Dr. Zimmer?" he asks.

"No," Harper says automatically.

"Dr. Zimmer is such a great guy. I love that guy. I look up to that guy. He's a hero of mine. He wanted to work with me on a drug awareness program in the middle school because he agreed with me that we have to reach kids while they're at their most impressionable."

"Drew," Harper says. She steps around him, opens her front door, and carries the bakery boxes to the kitchen, with Fish in hot pursuit. Fish has never met a bakery box he didn't like; Billy used to buy a dozen doughnuts and give a third of them to the dog. The white powdered-sugar variety is his favorite.

"These are sandwiches," Harper says. She tosses Fish one made from egg salad and watercress, which he devours, then a radish-and-butter sandwich, which he sniffs, then leaves on the floor. "Yeah. I don't blame you."

Drew stays on the front porch.

No, Harper thinks. Whatever is going to transpire here will *not* happen in full view of the street.

"Come in, please," she says.

"I tried calling your cell phone," he says. "I called seventeen times and left eleven messages because I want to know if what Mrs. Zimmer was accusing Dr. Zimmer of is true."

Harper's mind wanders, as it tends to do when she is hearing something unpleasant. She sings off-key, "I saw her today at the reception, a glass of wine in her hand..."

Drew says, "She said you were having an affair with Dr. Zimmer. She said she has proof."

Harper's insides freeze with fear. Proof?

Harper pulls Drew by the arm back to the front door. There's no sign of a vehicle.

"How did you get here?" she asks.

"I had the chief drop me off."

"The chief?" Harper says. "Chief Oberg?"

Drew nods. "When we started dating, he tried to warn me about you. He told me you used to be a coke dealer."

Harper shakes her head. "Not even close."

"But you did *something* wrong."

"If I had, Drew, the last person I would admit it to is you."

"I want you to confess that you were having an affair with Dr. Zimmer."

"No," Harper says. "There was a misunderstanding."

"That's crap."

"Please don't go around talking about what happened at my father's reception," Harper says. "People love to gossip on this island, Drew. Even good, well-meaning people like Chief Oberg."

"Why would Sadie Zimmer act that way if she didn't have proof?" Drew says. "You were having an affair with Dr. Zimmer. You've been lying to me, Harper. I thought we were exclusive. My aunties made lobster stew for you!"

"Please," Harper says. "Please, Drew, do *not* talk about this to your family." She closes her eyes as she imagines Drew's four aunties and his mother, Yvonne—Oak Bluffs' all-time favorite selectman—gathered around the kitchen table with their coffee and their homemade cinnamon rolls, one minute thinking, *Isn't it nice that handsome child Drew found a woman he likes, even if she does live in Vineyard Haven?*, the next minute learning that the woman is a cheat, sleeping with nice, kind Dr. Zimmer, who prescribes their blood pressure medicine, and as it turns out the woman is not only a cheat but also a former criminal, which escaped their previous notice because Joey Bowen only sold drugs to white people. Once the aunties and Yvonne get hold of the story, it will spread like a raging forest fire through the Methodist campground, through their church, through the town administration building, the public library, the hair salon, the Steamship Authority terminal, and finally to the Lookout, where every local person Harper knows likes to go for a drink in the summer. The influence of the Snyder sisters knows no bounds.

"People are going to find out no matter who I tell or don't tell," Drew says. "I'm an officer of the law. I can't date a woman with a reputation like yours. We have to break up."

This pronouncement comes as an unexpected relief.

"Okay," Harper says.

"Okay?" Drew says. "You're just going to let me go?"

"You don't trust me," Harper says. "You believe the talk. There's no hope for a relationship without trust, Drew."

"But—" Drew says.

"I'm too old for you, anyway," Harper says. "Find someone younger. Get married. Have a baby."

"I don't want a baby," Drew says. "I want you."

"Don't second-guess yourself," Harper says. "You're doing the right thing."

"But I think I might be in love with you," Drew says.

"I'll call you a cab," Harper says.

She and Fish eat the rest of the tea sandwiches for dinner, and Harper throws back a six-pack of Amity Island ale. The beer makes her brave, at least temporarily. She turns on her cell phone.

She sees the eleven voice mails from Drew. There is also a voice mail from her boss, Rooster, and a voice mail from a local Vineyard number that Harper suspects is Sadie Zimmer's cell phone. There are seven text messages from Drew and a text from Reed. This last message is the only one she cares about.

It says: *Sadie on a rampage, telling everyone about catching us at Lucy Vincent. I just got a call from Greenie. Pls don't contact me for a while. I'm sorry.*

Harper squeezes her eyes shut. It's over with Drew, and now it's over with Reed. Greenie, Adam Greenfield, is the president of the hospital's board of directors. Uncharted horrors and humiliations lie ahead. How did Harper not understand this three days ago?

Her phone rings, and she thinks: *Reed.* He loves her; of this she is certain. She felt it most keenly in the parking lot. It was more than sex. It was love. Would it be naive of Harper to believe that Reed might leave Sadie for Harper? Reed and Sadie don't have children—they don't even have a dog—so what reason would there be for Reed to stay?

But when Harper checks her display, she sees that the person calling is Tabitha. Harper groans. Nothing from the woman in fourteen years, and now she's blowing Harper up. What are the chances that Pony is calling to check on Harper, see how she's doing, ask if there is anything she can do to help? What are the chances that Tabitha is calling for any reason other than to thank Harper for mucking up her own life so badly that Tabitha became a victim?

Zero chance, Harper decides. She lets the call go to voice mail.

TABITHA

She hopes things will get better once they leave the golf club and are on their way home, but instead things get worse. Once the taxi driver—who doesn't know where he's going and nearly gets into three separate wrecks—delivers them to the ferry, Tabitha and Ainsley go to the office to exchange their tickets so they can take the earlier boat, and Eleanor wanders away like a person with Alzheimer's.

They find Eleanor sidled up to the bar at Coop DeVille,

where she has ordered a glass of champagne (Tabitha assumes that at this establishment, it's prosecco) and is telling the buxom young bartender, Carmen, that she is Billy Frost's widow.

"I knew Billy well," Carmen says. "He came in here all the time. That was his usual stool over there." She points to an empty stool at the far end of the bar, farthest from the dock and closest to the TV.

"Well, then," Eleanor says. "That is where I shall sit."

Ainsley nudges Tabitha. "Grammie is drunk."

Apparently so, Tabitha thinks. Her mother holds her liquor better than anyone Tabitha has ever known, but champagne has always been her Achilles' heel. She loves it, but it gets her blotto. Tabitha only saw her drink one glass, maybe two, at the reception, but Eleanor is sneaky and may have consumed as many as four or five glasses, making this her sixth glass.

"Mother, we have to go," Tabitha says. "The ferry is leaving."

"You have twelve minutes," Carmen says. But even so, she writes out a tab. Five dollars.

Cheap prosecco, Tabitha thinks.

Eleanor continues to drink on the boat. The Hy-Line has upped its food and beverage game over the past couple of years. All the soups and sandwiches are made from scratch, and one can even get a decent-looking cheese-and-fruit platter as well as good wine by the glass or bottle.

"They serve Veuve Clicquot!" Eleanor announces from her place in line.

"Mother, please don't," Tabitha says. She nudges Ainsley. "Can you encourage your grandmother to drink water?"

"I'm not doing your dirty work for you, Tabitha," Ainsley says. "I hate you."

"You *hate* me? Really?"

"You think because Grammie ruined your life that now it's your job to ruin my life," Ainsley says. "Aunt Harper was smart. She went with Gramps. I'm thinking about going to live with Dad for the summer."

Tabitha nearly says, *He doesn't want you.* But that is cruel, primarily because it's true. Wyatt has remarried, sired three sons, ages ten, seven, and four, and lives with his wife, Becky, in a gracious home overlooking Craigville Beach, on the Cape. Becky has a problem with Ainsley. She hates her for no apparent reason other than petty jealousy. She doesn't want Ainsley around the boys, and Wyatt does little in the way of championing his daughter. When he has painting jobs on Nantucket, he will take Ainsley to lunch or dinner. But he never invites Ainsley to the Cape, not even for the weekend.

"Okay," Tabitha says neutrally.

Eleanor sits down next to Tabitha, sips her champagne, then starts to cry. "Your father is gone," she says. "He's dead."

Ainsley leans forward. "Did you love him, Grammie?" She seems genuinely interested.

"With all my heart," Eleanor says. "I met your grandfather on December 22, 1967. He was my cousin Rhonda's date to my parents' annual Christmas party at the country club. Rhonda showed up stoned, and my parents made her leave." Eleanor closes her eyes, and Ainsley can feel her transporting herself to another time, back when people went to parties in horse-drawn carriages. "Your grandfather stayed, and we danced all night."

"That sounds romantic," Ainsley says.

"And you know who else I love?" Eleanor says. "Your aunt Harper. I've missed her desperately."

"Really?" Ainsley says, delighted.

"No," Tabitha says. "That's the champagne talking."

Eleanor reaches across Tabitha to lay a hand on Ainsley's knee. "Here's the secret to all human relationships," she says. "We humans want what we don't have. Harper went with Billy, and I've longed for her ever since."

"Mother!" Tabitha says. "That is simply not true."

"You aren't privy to the secrets of my innermost heart," Eleanor says.

"Aunt Harper is so cool," Ainsley says. "But I'm not talking about how she dresses, obviously."

Eleanor nods. "Her ensemble today was a travesty. I'm going to send her some inventory tomorrow." She turns to Tabitha. "What size are you, dear?"

"I'm a size four, Mother," Tabitha says. "You know I'm a size four."

"I'm going to send Harper twos," Eleanor says. "She looked a little thinner than you."

"It's just that she acts cool," Ainsley says. "She's chill. By which I mean the opposite of uptight."

Tabitha can't believe she's hearing this. Eleanor has been pining for Harper ever since Harper left with Billy? That is revisionist history at its most interesting. Tabitha knows for a fact that Harper used to go visit Eleanor regularly in Boston, although she probably hasn't been since the ghastly drug bust. But still, it's hardly as though they've been kept from each other. The champagne is turning Eleanor into something from *Lady Sings the Blues*. And Ainsley thinks Harper is *chill?*

Harper is *cool?* Did Ainsley miss the part of the reception when the wife of Harper's lover—who also happened to be Billy's doctor—slapped Tabitha across the face, mistakenly believing it was Harper? Is it cool to be called a tramp? It's possible that Ainsley doesn't realize the quagmire Harper got herself into three years ago, delivering *three pounds of cocaine* to a landscaping client. Harper should rightly have gone to prison. They should be going to visit her at Framingham instead of Martha's Vineyard. Would *that* be chill? Ainsley may not realize that her aunt now delivers packages for a living. She didn't get hired by UPS or FedEx because she had no decent references, so instead she works for a local operation called Rooster Express. Billy had shown Tabitha a picture of Harper on his phone: Harper was wearing a red collared shirt and a baseball cap emblazoned with an offensively grinning bird. The job is not chill. It is not cool. Harper's life is a shit show. If Tabitha is the only person here who can see that, then fine.

Tabitha goes to stand by the window and gaze at the water, which is probably a mistake because the feelings of intense self-reflection return. Billy is dead. Everyone assumes that Harper is the only one who feels this loss, but Tabitha is grieving as well. He was her father, too. She wasn't present for his illness; she wasn't at his bedside the way Harper was, but still Tabitha aches. One more person who was related to Julian is dead. During his annual visits to Nantucket, Billy accompanied Tabitha to the cemetery to place flowers on Julian's grave every August 15, the anniversary of the day Julian died. They would bow their heads, and Billy would say a simple prayer and squeeze Tabitha's hand until she thought it would break. "He's with my mother in heaven," Billy would say. "She's taking care of him. You can count on that." Tabitha had never been particularly religious, but the ritual of going to the cemetery with Billy had comforted her as nothing else had.

Have you ever lost anyone? Tabitha has now lost her father.

And Harper, Tabitha admits to herself. Seeing her sister today was a trial. Years of anger and hatred had blanketed the truth, which lay underneath like a sediment, nearly disguised but not quite. Tabitha lost her best friend, her sister, her twin.

Did Tabitha remember the way Harper used to ride on her back when she was a pony? Of course. Tabitha remembers a lot more than that. She remembers their switching classes at Winsor—Tabitha would double up on art, Harper on English. She remembers them both candy-striping at the Brigham, intentionally confusing senile Mrs. Lawton—Tabitha would walk out one door at the same time Harper walked in another—and giving themselves side stitches from laughing so hard. She remembers summer camp at Wyonegonic and how the other girls thought Tabitha and Harper would hate each other, as the twins in *The Parent Trap* did, but they had been best friends, inseparable. They waited together in their bathing caps at the end of the dock before diving into freezing-cold Moose Pond in perfect tandem. They paddled together in the canoe, Tabitha in the stern, Harper in the bow. Tabitha would steer; Harper added power. They lined up side by side in archery, their bows poised exactly the same way.

She remembers rock, paper, scissors and Harper rolling away with Billy, leaving Tabitha behind to suffer through a future of living up to Eleanor's impossibly high standards. Tabitha had waved good-bye, standing on the brick sidewalk in front of the house on Pinckney Street, but Harper hadn't bothered waving back; she had been too busy fiddling with the radio.

Tabitha remembers Harper showing up on Nantucket to help Tabitha take care of Julian.

Tabitha stops herself there.

When they get home, there's a brown box sitting on the front porch of the carriage house. It's Ainsley's new phone, which cost Tabitha seven hundred dollars, making it more punishing to Tabitha than to Ainsley.

"My phone!" Ainsley shrieks, and she jumps out of the FJ40—which *still* smells like cigarettes—while it's moving.

Tabitha slams on the brakes. She tries to remind Ainsley that she is grounded from her phone until Friday. But there will be no taking it away from her now. Or, rather, Tabitha can take it away, but it will no doubt involve a physical fight in which Tabitha may well get struck for the second time. She isn't up for it.

You're right, Ramsay, she thinks. *I'm a piss-poor parent. I crumble like a day-old cookie every time.*

She watches Ainsley disappear into the carriage house with the box. Tabitha continues down the long white-shell driveway to her mother's house, Seamless—a 4,500-square-foot edifice with three floors, six bedrooms, six and a half baths, and a glassed-in porch that perches on the edge of a cliff, offering uninterrupted views of Nantucket Sound. Tabitha has always assumed that someday this house will be hers—as well as the town house on Pinckney Street—although lately Eleanor has been dodgy about money. The ERF boutique on Newbury Street folded the year before, and Eleanor must have sustained a hit to her finances and her ego, although she was predictably stoic about both. Tabitha has always assumed that Eleanor is sitting on a comfortable cushion of cash, but obviously it wasn't enough to save the flagship store. The Nantucket store will be the next to sink—short of a miracle—despite Tabitha's efforts to diversify the inventory. The Palm Beach store is just fine because... well, because the clientele in Palm Beach is old. Older.

"Do you need help getting inside, Mother?" Tabitha asks.

Eleanor inhales dramatically. "You have no idea how today taxed me."

"It taxed all of us," Tabitha says. *I got slapped!* she thinks. *And doused!* Her dress looks pretty good considering—another selling point for the Roxie. It can absorb a full glass of champagne without showing a stain or a wrinkle. "He was my father."

"He was my husband," Eleanor says.

"Ex-husband," Tabitha says. "You were divorced from Billy longer than you were ever married to him."

"I don't expect you to understand," Eleanor says.

"I *don't* understand," Tabitha says. "I find this sudden mourning and this *heartbreak* a little manufactured and more than a little self-serving. Billy lived eleven miles away. Did you ever go to see him? When he was here, on Nantucket, did you ever offer to take him to lunch? Or to invite him inside this house? No! When his name came up, you insulted him. You outgrew Billy long ago. You divorced him, then you forgot about him, Mother. I can't believe you're now telling my daughter that you loved him with all your heart."

"You've never been married, Pony," Eleanor says. She reaches into her purse and pulls out a newspaper clipping. She hands it to Tabitha

"What's this?" Tabitha says. She unfolds the clipping; it's

well worn, softened, and smudged. It's a photograph of Billy and Eleanor, Eleanor smiling as though she's won fifty million dollars in the lottery, Billy kissing her cheek. The caption reads: *Boston Royalty—Fashion designer Eleanor Roxie-Frost and husband, Billy Frost, enjoy an evening out at Locke-Ober to raise funds for the Boston Public Library. Ms. Roxie-Frost wears a gown of her own design.*

Tabitha has seen dozens of such photographs of Billy and Eleanor together, and she always thinks the same thing. *Those were the days, my friend, we thought they'd never end...* but end they did. Still, this photograph prompts Tabitha to acknowledge her mother's sorrow. Eleanor thought to bring this clipping to Billy's memorial reception; it means something to her. Even after all the years of contempt and disregard, she might still have loved him.

Tabitha can't deal with the emotion right now; she is too exhausted. So instead she says, "I don't think I've ever seen that dress." It's a long strapless column of dark silk with a pleated top reminiscent of a Japanese fan.

"I still have it," Eleanor says. "Someday it will go to the Smithsonian."

"I'm sure it will," Tabitha says. "It's very..." She nearly says *pretty,* but *pretty* has never meant anything to Eleanor. "Strong. Makes a statement. Perhaps you should bring it back." She returns the clipping to Eleanor.

"Perhaps I should," Eleanor says. She tucks the clipping into her purse before laboriously getting out of the car. She's less steady on her feet these days, especially when she's wearing heels—slingbacks, at that—and she's had at least half a dozen glasses of champagne. Tabitha should walk her to the door, help her get situated inside—make her a cup of tea, fix her a snack, fetch her a robe.

But no. Tabitha won't do it. Not tonight. She's too angry, and the things Eleanor has said today are too hurtful. Eleanor longs for Harper. Fine. From now on, when Eleanor wants something, she can ask Harper for it. Harper can manage the Nantucket store, maybe sell meth or heroin in addition to the Eleanor Roxie-Frost label. That, at least, would put an end to their cash-flow problems.

"Have a good night, Mother," Tabitha says.

Eleanor makes her wobbly way up the flagstone path toward the steps of the front porch. Tabitha studies the grandness of the house and decides that she will throw a party there in a few weeks, when Eleanor goes to New York to meet with the tailors and ERF manufacturing people. Ha! Tabitha is no better than Ainsley! But really, Eleanor's house is ideal for entertaining—cocktails on the porch, buffet dinner in the dining room, dancing in the living room. Maybe Tabitha will invite Captain Peter. Maybe she'll invite young Zack, the bartender from Nautilus. She will definitely invite Stephanie Beasley now that Ainsley and Candace are friends again. And maybe Teddy's uncle Graham while she's at it.

She needs more friends, she thinks. Ainsley is right. Eleanor has ruined her life.

Eleanor climbs the stairs holding on to the rail. It's like watching paint dry, Tabitha thinks.

She'll invite the Tallahasseeans!

Harper has been conducting an affair with Billy's married doctor. Does no one but Tabitha find this disgusting?

Eleanor reaches the porch and turns around to wave, or maybe not wave, maybe signal, because she is now crying. She steps forward—possibly she wants to apologize to Tabitha or maybe she's left her reading glasses in Tabitha's car—but she misjudges her footing and falls down the porch stairs, landing in a heap at the bottom.

AINSLEY

She is so busy getting her phone up and running that she doesn't know anything is wrong until she hears the ambulance sirens. At first they're distant, and she barely registers them, but then they get closer, and then they're basically on top of her, and she looks out the window and she sees the flashing blue and red lights pull into their driveway. She spies the distant figure of her mother waving the ambulance over in the direction of Grammie's house.

Ainsley dashes out the front door in time to see the paramedics sliding Grammie onto a stretcher and into the back of the ambulance. Tabitha gets in her car, does a doughnut in the driveway, and follows the ambulance out. When she sees Ainsley, she puts down her window.

"Grammie fell. I'm going with her to the hospital. Do you want to come with me or stay here?"

"Stay here," Ainsley says. She feels bad for that choice, but her mother actually looks relieved.

"Does your phone work?"

"Yes."

"I'll call you," Tabitha says. And off she goes.

* * *

Ainsley goes back into the house alone. This is what she's been waiting for since Friday night—to be left alone, with a mode of communication—yet she regrets the answer she gave her mother. She should have gone to the hospital. What if her grandmother *dies?* What if she loses both of her grandparents in the same week?

She waits for her phone to boot up. She's expecting a host of texts and missed calls, but only one text comes in, from Emma, dated Sunday at noon. It says: *Head hurts. Call me.*

That's it? Ainsley thinks. Nothing from Teddy? He doesn't know her phone was drowned, although maybe he guessed. He doesn't know her grandfather died and that she went to the memorial on the Vineyard.

She has been completely out of touch. She assumed he would try to contact her, yet her phone shows nothing. *Did* he go to the Jetties to see G. Love with Emma? Emma complained of a headache at noon on Sunday, but that doesn't mean she didn't rally for a big rager on Sunday night.

Maybe Teddy lost his phone privileges as well. Maybe Uncle Graham finally went to the library and checked out a parenting manual. But somehow Ainsley doesn't think so. Teddy didn't do anything wrong except spend his date money on vodka. Maybe Teddy's mother showed up, fresh out of Brookhaven Hospital in Tulsa, and took Teddy back to Oklahoma with her. This is what would happen in a Charles Dickens novel; Ainsley has been paying enough attention in English class to know this much.

Ainsley calls Teddy. When he answers, he sounds weary. "Hey, Ainsley."

"Teddy?" she says. "My mom sunk my phone on Saturday night, which is why I haven't called. And then we found out on Sunday morning that my grandfather died, but I still had no way to reach you. I missed school today because we went to the memorial reception on the Vineyard. I just got back, and my new phone was here, so that's good news, but the bad news is that my grandmother got drunk at the reception and fell down. An ambulance came, and now she and my mother are at the hospital. I'm here alone." She swallows. "Can you come over?" She's asking not because she wants to have sex but rather because she could really use some companionship, a friend. Her mother doesn't *want* her at the hospital, and can Ainsley blame her? On the ferry, Ainsley told Tabitha she hated her. "Please, Teddy?"

"Ainsley," Teddy says. "I've got something to tell you."

Ainsley understands how her mother must have felt earlier that afternoon: struck out of the blue for no discernible reason.

"I want to break up," Teddy said.

"What?" Ainsley says. "Why?"

"Why?" Teddy says.

"Why?" Ainsley says. "Is it Emma? Did you take Emma with you to see G. Love at the Jetties?"

"I didn't go to the Jetties, and G. Love never showed anyway," Teddy says. "And this has nothing to do with Emma. I like someone else."

Ainsley sucks in her breath. "Someone *else?*" she says. "Who?"

"Candace," Teddy says. "I like Candace."

Candace? Ainsley thinks. *Candace Beasley? Measley Beasley?* Ainsley thinks Teddy must be kidding, but then he launches into a monologue about how he needs positive influences in his life. He can't get caught up with the drinking and the smoking. If he gets in trouble and Graham kicks him out, he's looking at foster care or a group home. Candace is an A student and an altar girl at Saint Mary's. She and Teddy were the only ones at Ainsley's party who stayed sober. Teddy called her on Sunday, and they met for a walk on the beach. They talked. He tried to kiss her, but she wouldn't let him until he'd properly broken up with Ainsley.

"She doesn't want to hurt you," Teddy says. "She doesn't want you to be able to say she stole me from you, because it isn't like that."

Ainsley is speechless. She is stuck back on the phrase *positive influences.* Isn't *Ainsley* a positive influence? Was she not the one who befriended Teddy when he first arrived on Nantucket? He could have been an outcast, a weird loner from Oklahoma, but Ainsley had introduced him to all her friends. She had included him. And then soon afterward, once they started dating, she had given him her virginity. She understands that he doesn't want to mess up and get in trouble. He doesn't have to drink or smoke; she has never pressured him to do so.

Maybe Ainsley isn't on the honor roll. Maybe Ainsley isn't an *altar girl* at *Saint Mary's*—her mother never had her baptized, much less confirmed—but she has a heart, and her heart loves Teddy.

Candace Beasley! *Backstabber,* Ainsley thinks. She will destroy Candace Beasley. She will destroy Candace and Teddy together. They can be good people, but they will be alone.

Ainsley recognizes those last few thoughts as those of an

evil, vengeful person—which is exactly what pushed Teddy away. Ainsley takes a deep breath. "I'm sure she doesn't want to hurt me. Candace and I used to be best friends, then we drifted apart. When I invited her over on Saturday, it was because I wanted to try to get close to her again."

"That's what she told me," Teddy says. "She also told me that you and Emma have been pretty mean to her."

"We have been," Ainsley admits. *And now she's exacting her revenge.* "I'm sure you guys will be happy together. Happier than you and I were. I wish you the best."

"Ainsley—" Teddy says.

"Good-bye, Ted," Ainsley says, and she hangs up.

Ainsley stares at her phone for a few seconds. She's proud of herself for not kirking out; she handled herself exactly as her grandmother might have.

But wow, she hurts. Tears sting her eyes. She's upset about Teddy and Candace, she's worried about her grandmother, and she is so, so sad about Billy. The only good thing that has happened is that she got to see Aunt Harper, but even that visit was cut short.

Ainsley picks up her phone to call Emma. But Emma isn't good at commiseration; she doesn't know how to be comforting or supportive. Neither do BC and Maggie and Anna. Ainsley has chosen friends who are too cool for any kind of genuine human emotion.

Should she call her father? Ask him if maybe she can spend the summer on the Cape? She could work as a nanny for her half brothers. Right now she's supposed to put in forty hours a week at the ERF boutique, but Ainsley would love to tell her mother she's found a better job. Tabitha probably doesn't want Ainsley to work at the boutique anyway. If Ainsley goes to the Cape, Tabitha will be able to hire someone reliable and competent, someone she will be able to trust rather than doubt.

What does it say when your own mother doesn't believe in you?

Ainsley dials her father's number, but after six rings it goes to his voice mail. Ainsley hangs up. She's not sure whether Tabitha has told Wyatt about Ainsley stealing the car and throwing the party, but if she has then it's safe to say a summer on the Cape is out of the question. Becky, Ainsley's stepmother—or, more accurately, Wyatt's wife—hates Ainsley. She doesn't allow Ainsley within five feet of the boys.

Ainsley's phone rings. It's her mother.

"Grammie broke her hip," Tabitha says.

Ainsley exhales. "But she's okay otherwise? She's alive?"

"She's alive, but the break is bad, and they're flying her to Boston on the MedFlight helicopter. I have to fly to Boston, too. I would have you come with me, but I don't want you to miss any more school. So...what do you think? Can you stay home by yourself tonight? There's cash in the tea tin if you want to order a pizza for dinner, or there's a hunk of low-fat Gouda in the deli drawer. No rice crackers, though. We finished those up last night."

"Will you be home tomorrow?" Ainsley asks.

"I'm not sure, sweetheart, but I have to go with your grandmother. She doesn't have anyone else. Please, *please* just be good until I get back. Do your homework, take the bus to school. No smoking, no drinking, no parties—okay?"

"Okay," Ainsley says. "I promise."

* * *

She hangs up. Broken hip: not the worst news, but still serious; Ainsley gets that. Why do old people always break their hips? It's like a thing.

So now Ainsley has the house to herself—overnight and maybe longer. Three hours ago, this was exactly what Ainsley dreamed of, but right now... well, she feels more miserable than she has in all her life.

HARPER

When she wakes up the morning after Billy's memorial reception, the answer is clear: she has to leave the Vineyard.

Harper's phone continued to blow up the night before, to the point where she wished her phone would actually *blow up.* There were texts from Drew and from an unfamiliar number, which turned out to be Drew's cousin Jethro, the son of Wanda, the aunt who made the stew. Harper deletes these texts without reading them. She feels anew the shame of three years earlier. What had she learned then? The Vineyard is a great place to live... until you screw up. Being part of a community means you have a responsibility to behave, to obey the laws, to act like a decent human being. And when you don't, you let everyone else in the community down.

There was a text from the other Rooster Express driver, a former addict named Adele, that said, *Is it true????* There was, most frighteningly, a text from Jude, Harper's former employer. Harper wasn't sure why she even kept Jude's contact information in her phone; they had agreed never to communicate again. Harper stupidly thought that maybe Jude had heard about Billy's death and decided to reach out. But the text said: *SCUM.*

After that, Harper was determined to flush her phone down the toilet, but then a text came in from Rooster, her boss, and Harper thought it might have been a change to her work schedule. The text said: *Listen to your voice mail, please, Harper. Or just call me back.*

Harper sighed, then played her voice mail. "Hi, Harper. It's Rooster. Sorry I missed Billy's reception. I was in the weeds with you taking the day off. I heard some pretty weird shit went down at the golf club, and it sounds like maybe you have some personal issues you need to work out. So anyway, I'm relieving you of your delivery duties for the foreseeable future. Sorry about that, Harper."

Harper replayed the message because she couldn't understand what he was trying to tell her. Relieving her of her delivery duties for the foreseeable future? Was he *firing* her? Yes, it seemed he was.

There was also a voice mail from Tabitha. It had come in at two thirty in the morning. Harper hadn't listened to it, because how much abuse, really, was she expected to take?

Reed gone.

Drew gone.

Her job gone.

She has to leave. Where she'll go is less of a concern than the steps she needs to take to wrap up her life here.

She has to go over to Chappy to see Brendan, but that will need to wait.

She has to pay Ken Doll at the golf club, as the reception was far from free, but she'll deal with Ken Doll by e-mail because by now he's probably heard the reason for Sadie Zimmer's outrageous behavior. It was justified: Harper had been sleeping with her husband, the wonderful member in good standing, the island's favorite doctor, a man as squeaky clean as Marcus Welby, MD—Dr. Reed Zimmer.

No, Harper thinks. Sadie's behavior was *not* justified. Showing up at Billy's memorial to slap Harper in front of the assembled guests—unacceptable. And why is *Harper* the only one being held accountable for the infidelity? *She* isn't married. She isn't betraying anyone at home. Well, okay, she was betraying Drew. He thinks they agreed to be exclusive, but they've only been dating for *three weeks.* They haven't even slept together, and Harper knows the word *exclusive* never crossed her lips. But why isn't anyone vilifying *Reed?* Why is it *Harper* who is cast as the evil seductress? Does it go all the way back to Nathaniel Hawthorne? Yes, she supposes it does.

The house. She has to sell Billy's house—and fast. She needs a real estate agent. Is there anyone left on the Vineyard who might still speak to her?

She snaps her fingers. Polly.

Polly Childs has been through this. Back when she was a sales associate at Shipshape Real Estate, she slept with her boss, Brock, while Brock and Polly were married to other people.

Both marriages broke up, and Polly took a trip to Ethiopia, where she traced her ancestry back to the royal family—at least, that was the rumor—and did some humanitarian work. When she returned to the Vineyard, she had reinvented herself enough to get a job at Up-Island Real Estate, where her African princess self proceeded to make a killing. She immediately sold a harborfront home in Edgartown to the famous talk-show host Sundae Stewart. This had been major Vineyard news! It was made even bigger when Polly and Sundae were caught fooling around in the master bedroom suite by Sundae's actress lover, Cassandra K. The public relations frenzy had been insane *on a national level*—the supermarket tabloids, TMZ. For a full celebrity-gossip news cycle—nine days—Polly Childs's name was mentioned everywhere you looked.

Harper would have locked herself in a car and driven off Dike Bridge—but Polly had held her head high. Harper had seen her in the produce section of Cronig's that week, and in an attempt at normalcy Harper had asked Polly the best way to tell if a pineapple is ripe. Polly had informed Harper in a normal, cheerful voice that if a whole pineapple gives off a sweet fragrance, it's ready to eat.

Harper calls Polly and says, "Polly, it's Harper Frost. I'm looking to sell my father's house. I need to get off this island."

There is silence from Polly, and Harper thinks that maybe even Polly Childs is unwilling to do business with her, for she's certain that Polly has already heard the rumors. The real estate offices are hotbeds of gossip. If Polly can't help, then Harper has truly sifted down to join the caste of untouchables.

Finally Polly says, "I know the house. Daggett Avenue? I'll meet you there in fifteen minutes."

* * *

Polly arrives first, as Harper had to feed Fish and let him out, then change her clothes—she had fallen asleep in the black outfit she wore to the reception—and brush her teeth and wash her face in an attempt to make herself look respectable. Harper is wearing white denim shorts, a pale blue golf shirt that used to belong to Billy before Harper requisitioned it for gardening purposes, a Red Sox hat, and her father's watch. She is the world's most underwhelming mistress.

Polly, by comparison, is wearing... well, here Harper blinks. She's wearing one of Harper's mother's designs—the Roxie—in amethyst purple, a color that makes her skin look like polished bronze. Harper knows nothing about fashion, but she would know her mother's dress, that dress, anywhere—it's a linen shift with an obi. Obis were a fashion statement made popular by geisha girls in Japan. Eleanor's entire empire is based on reworking a symbol of female subservience and turning it into something empowering.

"I like your dress," Harper says.

"I like your watch," Polly says. "Stylish. Makes a statement. I should get a man's watch."

"It was my father's," Harper says.

"You have my condolences," Polly says. "I heard I missed meeting your mother yesterday by a minute or two. I went to Farm Neck for a late lunch."

"That's not all you missed," Harper says.

Polly smiles in an inscrutable way. Now would be the time for Polly to say something encouraging, maybe dust off the old chestnut about the man who sees his friend down in a hole and jumps into the hole with him because he's been there before and knows the way out. Polly clearly found *her* way out—she looks fantastic! Harper wonders if she's still seeing Sundae Stewart. Sundae and Cassandra K. have split, that much has been well documented—at which point Polly vaporized from the story. Maybe Harper doesn't have to leave; maybe she can ride this out. But then she thinks of Jude's text: *SCUM*. Scum—like you find in a ring around the bathroom sink or like peanut butter that has collected inside the lid of the jar. Harper has to go.

"Anyway, here it is," Harper says, pointing to the house. It's only now that she thinks to worry about the state of things inside. Harper has been here periodically to grab things for Billy, but no one has been in to clean, and the weather has warmed up considerably, but Harper hadn't thought to open any windows. So when she unlocks the door and she and Polly step inside, they are both assaulted by a wave of stale, hot, foul-smelling air.

Polly keeps her game face on. Surely this isn't the worst house she's seen on the island. Right?

"Your father was a smoker?" Polly asks.

"Pack a day," she says. "Hence the congestive heart failure at age seventy-three."

"Did he have a dog?" Polly asks.

"No," Harper says. "No dog." Technically this is true, but Fish was over here all the time, and Billy had no rules, so Fish used to lie across the sofa like a fat pasha. Polly can probably smell him, and although huskies aren't known as shedders, Fish still leaves hair wherever he goes.

Harper knows that Polly will not approve of the wall-to-wall carpeting, but Billy was adamant that he liked the feel of it under his feet. *Much friendlier than wood floors,* he said. Harper is sure Polly will also not approve of the recliner or the clunky old coffee table reclaimed from the dump or the *Jaws* poster hanging on the wall in the powder room. Billy had been inordinately proud that the movie was filmed on the Vineyard. If Harper closes her eyes, she can hear Billy's voice, clear as day: *You're gonna need a bigger boat.*

Harper says, "I'll give you the grand tour." She leads Polly through the living room into the dining room, where the table is covered with old onion lamps, broken fixtures, wires, cords, outlet covers, bulbs of various shapes and sizes, and a pile of unpaid invoices.

Harper will have to deal with what's owed, referring Billy's current customers elsewhere and dismantling the business. It might be a good thing she got fired.

The dining room has four tall, skinny windows that look out onto the backyard, which is a nice size but completely unkempt—woods and unmowed grass, in the midst of which is a patch of overgrown vegetable garden. Billy had allowed Harper to put it in back when she was still working for Jude, and in the first season they harvested zucchini, cucumbers, cherry tomatoes, and one enormous misshapen pumpkin that won honorable mention at the Ag Fair.

"Windows," Polly says, like a toddler learning new words. "Yard."

They head into the kitchen, which Harper knows is the weak link. It features peeling linoleum floors, stained Formica countertops, and particleboard cabinets, several of which are loose on their hinges. With a stranger standing next to her, Harper can see how terribly the house presents, but she never gave it any thought because it was what it was: Billy's house. The fridge is a hundred years old, but it kept Billy's beer cold. Billy would rather have eaten takeout from the Home Port every night than spend money on renovating the kitchen. But the kitchen looks so bad that Harper feels she should apologize.

"Needs work," Polly says with a rise of her perfectly plucked eyebrows. "Rest of the house?"

They wander through the three bedrooms upstairs, including the lavender bedroom that belonged to Harper before she finally moved out a week after her thirty-seventh birthday. They peek in the two underwhelming bathrooms—the tile floors are fine, but the sinks and tubs and toilets are outdated. And one of the bathrooms is Billy's and still has a can of shaving cream on the sink, along with his green comb. The green comb had been Billy's since the beginning of time. It probably cost him five cents at a drugstore on Charles Street in Boston in 1978, but it's so deeply ingrained in Harper's mind as *Billy's comb* that it's as if his beating heart is there on the bathroom counter. Harper struggles not to lose her composure in front of Polly Childs.

They peer into the shallow linen closet, then into the deeper closet that holds the washer and dryer.

"Laundry," Polly says. "Good."

"Well, yeah," Harper says. The house is an eyesore, she understands this anew, but at least they aren't hanging out at the Laundromat every Saturday.

Polly turns to Harper and says, "Listen. I'm not going to bullshit you."

Harper nods. "Good." Although really, she could use a little candy coating, a little pie in the sky.

"You have two options," Polly says. "We sell this as a teardown, lot only. Listings in Vineyard Haven have taken a nosedive lately. This town can't decide what it wants to be. And Daggett Avenue is...meh. So it would be listing at six, closing at half a mil."

"Oh," Harper says. This is far less than she anticipated. "The other option?"

"You gut it. New kitchen, obviously, new bathrooms. The whole house needs a new coat of paint. You pull up the carpet, restore those wood floors, buy new furniture, every stick, and hire a landscaper. If you pour a hundred twenty-five, hundred fifty into this place, I would list it at one point one, and you walk with a million bucks, guaranteed."

Harper stares at Polly's feet. She's wearing Jack Rogers sandals, the same color purple as her Roxie, and her toenails match as well. How does she do it? Harper wonders. How, with all she's been through, does she keep on keeping on?

"Can I sleep on it?" she asks.

"Absolutely," Polly says. "Call me tomorrow."

Harper drives home slowly, and all the while, her phone buzzes. It's Drew calling. What did he not understand about their last conversation? They went on six dates, and now the relationship is over. The phone rings again, and Harper thinks, *That's it!* She's going to throw the phone out the window, then back up over it. She checks the display: *Nantucket, MA.* It's not Tabitha's phone, but maybe it's the landline. Maybe her mother's landline. Despite Harper's conflicting emotions, she needs to talk to someone with taste and good business sense about Billy's house. She answers.

"Hello?"

"Aunt Harper?"

It's Ainsley.

"Grammie fell and broke her hip. Mom's with her in Boston

at the hospital, and I'm here on Nantucket by myself. I was wondering... well... is there any way you can come over?"

"Come over?" Harper says. She's not sure what Ainsley means. "To Nantucket, you mean?"

"Yes," Ainsley says. "Can you please?"

Harper is taken hostage by the novelty of the situation: someone is seeking out her company. But then reality intercedes. "What does your mother think about this?" she asks.

"She says it's totally fine," Ainsley says. "She would appreciate your help."

There is no way this is true. Tabitha could be bleeding out in a school of great white sharks and she wouldn't appreciate Harper's help. But then Harper remembers the voice mail that came in at two thirty in the morning. She hasn't bothered listening to it, but maybe it is indeed Tabitha, asking for help.

"Really?" Harper says.

"Really," Ainsley says.

TABITHA

The break is bad, and after Eleanor is seen by Dr. Karabinis, the orthopedist at Mass General who specializes in geriatric hip breaks, it is determined that Eleanor will need surgery. There is no one to operate tonight, so they've stabilized the leg, managed Eleanor's pain, and they will operate in the morning. Recovery takes six to eight weeks and involves bed rest and physical therapy. Thankfully, Eleanor is knocked out and can't argue with her treatment plan, though argue she will—eventually.

Tabitha accepts this news stoically, although inside her is a three-ring circus of despair, angst, and resentment. Eleanor is, essentially, out of commission, and not only that, she's going to need help. Hiring a live-in nurse comes to mind, although Eleanor is finicky about strangers and will, no doubt, want Tabitha to serve as the nurse. A live-in nurse is also expensive, probably more than a thousand dollars a day, seven thousand dollars a week, thirty thousand dollars a month, adding up to a grand total of forty-five to sixty thousand dollars, depending on how quickly Eleanor heals. Eleanor may have that kind of cash lying around, but if she does have it, she won't want to spend it—at the end of the day, there's no one more frugal than a Yankee WASP—and if she doesn't have it, that's even worse news.

Tabitha will have to live in Boston this summer with her mother. But if Tabitha does that, who will run the Nantucket store during its peak season? They can't close the store; they owe eighty thousand in rent. There's the manager, Meghan, who is perfectly capable, but she's eight months pregnant. First babies are often late, so Tabitha had hoped to make it through the Fourth of July weekend, during which time Meghan would teach Ainsley everything she knows and Ainsley would take Meghan's place with Tabitha right there overseeing.

Ainsley. If Tabitha moves to Boston for six or eight weeks, what will happen to Ainsley? She's too young to stay by herself; she would burn the carriage house down and turn Eleanor's house into an opium den. Tabitha shudders as she imagines the Snapchat photos: Ainsley and Emma in string bikinis pounding cans of Coors Light, doing bong hits, modeling Tabitha's entire wardrobe. It might even get worse—nude photos, cocaine, older men. No: Ainsley can't stay alone.

But Ainsley will refuse to come to Boston—of this Tabitha is certain. Would Wyatt agree to have her live with him on the Cape? That might work, except Tabitha *really* needs Ainsley to work at the store.

If Tabitha were still with Ramsay, there would be no problem. Ramsay would have stayed with Ainsley and kept her in line. He would have had her reading Ayn Rand; he would have taught her to make her bed with hospital corners. He would have delivered her to and from work, and then, once the weather grew consistently clement, he would have made her ride her bike. He would have taken her to dinner at the yacht club on Friday nights and made certain she ordered Shirley Temples.

But Ramsay is gone. Ramsay is with Caylee, and even someone as young and freewheeling as Caylee would probably not be okay with her new boyfriend caring for his ex-girlfriend's teenage daughter.

Tabitha can't worry about the summer right now. Right now she has to see Eleanor safely through her surgery. Tabitha will stay in Boston tonight, tomorrow night, and maybe Wednesday night as well. She needs someone to go stay with Ainsley. Whom can she ask? Ramsay is out, which leaves...

Well, the girl has a father. Tabitha calls Wyatt.

"Tabitha?" he says. He sounds surprised, wary; she rarely phones him. Most of their communication about Ainsley is done via e-mail. "Everything okay?"

"Not really," Tabitha says, and she bites her bottom lip.

Like her mother, Tabitha sees no point in dwelling on the past or reflecting on what might have been, but for some reason, hearing Wyatt's voice takes her back. She's twenty-two years old, and he's a year older, standing on a ladder painting the trim on the next-door neighbor's house. Tabitha has wandered over to the Colemans' yard to gather up Blaise Pascal, Eleanor's dachshund, who has run off. Wyatt is wearing wraparound Oakleys and a Cornell University visor. His brown hair has flecks of white paint in it.

"Do you go to Cornell?" Tabitha asks.

"Nah," he says. "This is my roommate's."

Tabitha knew right then what she should do: ask this guy to give his roommate Tabitha's number. But Wyatt is cute, and Tabitha doesn't want to offend him.

Wyatt smiles. "You live next door, right? I've noticed you walking your dog. If you're not busy later, the Radiators are playing at the Muse. I have an extra ticket."

"I'd love to go," Tabitha says.

That's the thing about relationships, Tabitha thinks. They start innocently, based on shared interests, hormones, and the prospect of fun. She and Wyatt go to see the Radiators at the Muse. They dance and drink cheap draft beer; they kiss in the front seat of Wyatt's Jeep in front of Steamboat Pizza. They have sex for the first time three days later on the tiny harborfront beach in front of Sayle's Seafood—on top of an overturned kayak. Wyatt doesn't have an Ivy League education or a college education of any kind. Painting houses, smoking weed, and seeing bands are the ways he spends his time. He has no ambitions, but Tabitha convinces herself it doesn't matter. No matter where this relationship goes, it will end on Labor Day.

They become boyfriend and girlfriend and drive out to see the sun set in Madaket and go to bonfires with the guys Wyatt paints with and go to the Dreamland theater to see *Armageddon* on the one day that it rains. When Tabitha leaves for Boston to start working for her mother, she stands at the railing of the ferry waving a fond adieu to Wyatt, and she marvels at what a storybook summer romance she has just enjoyed.

A week later she will discover that she is pregnant. When Tabitha tells Eleanor, she expects her mother will insist she and Wyatt get married, but Eleanor does just the opposite. She doesn't think Wyatt is good enough for Tabitha to marry. She says, "Don't make..." But then she trails off, leaving Tabitha to finish the thought. *Don't make the same mistake I did.* Tabitha is incensed by this; she is sick of Eleanor's innate sense of superiority just because Eleanor's father was a bank president and her mother a miserable matron of Beacon Hill. Tabitha nearly marries Wyatt out of spite. But in her heart, Tabitha knows she doesn't love him enough to stay married forever, and she will *not* get divorced, as Eleanor and Billy did. Not ever.

"Is it Ainsley?" Wyatt asks. "Is she in jail? Did she run off and elope? Did she OD?"

Tabitha laughs, though, sadly, none of those guesses is out of the question. "Ainsley is fine. Or sort of. So... I should have told you this earlier: my father died."

"And I should have called you earlier," Wyatt says. "Because I saw your sister's post on Facebook."

"You're friends with my sister on Facebook?" Tabitha says. "Tell me you're kidding."

"Tabitha, stop."

Tabitha has a lot of old hurt inside her, and this man knows how to tap into it.

"You're right," she says. "You should have called. He's your daughter's grandfather."

"*You* should have told me," Wyatt says. "I shouldn't have had to find out on social media." He huffs. "Listen: I'm sorry about Billy. He was a great guy. Whenever I had jobs on the Vineyard, I met him for lunch."

"You met my father for lunch?" she says. "I'm sure you saw Harper while you were at it."

"Tabitha, stop."

Stop, she thinks. Pursuing this particular strain of conversation will lead to no good. Tabitha takes a sustaining breath. "I can't begin to explain what happened at the memorial reception, so all I'll say is that my mother drank too much, and when we got home to Nantucket, she fell down the front steps of her house and broke her hip."

"Oh, jeez," Wyatt says.

"And so now I'm in Boston and she's having surgery tomorrow and I won't be able to get home until Wednesday night at the earliest and I'm wondering if you might be able to go over to the island and keep an eye on Ainsley."

"Wow," Wyatt says, and Tabitha immediately knows what's coming.

I wish I could, she mouths.

"I wish I could," he says. "But I have a project in Orleans that's on deadline, and Carpenter has pinkeye, so our house is kind of on lockdown."

"I wasn't suggesting Ainsley go there," Tabitha says. "I know Becky doesn't like her."

"Becky likes her just fine," Wyatt says in a combative tone. "But I have three kids, Tabitha."

"You have *four* kids," Tabitha says. *You* had *five kids,* she thinks. She wonders how often Wyatt thinks about Julian. "And one of them needs you."

"Don't be this way, Tabitha, please."

"You're her father," Tabitha says. "Act like it for once."

"Good-bye, Tabitha," Wyatt says, and he hangs up, leaving Tabitha to watch his name vanish from her cell-phone screen. She supposes that asking Wyatt to take Ainsley for the summer is out of the question.

Whom else can Tabitha call? The next person who comes to mind is Stephanie Beasley. Candace had been at that party, which is both good news and bad news. It's good news because apparently Ainsley and Candace are friends again, and it's bad news because if Stephanie has found out about the details of the party, she will never let Ainsley stay there. Tabitha *has* to ask. She will *not* have Ainsley staying with Emma Marlowe and her father. Tabitha imagines more Snapchat photos: Ainsley and Emma and Dutch all doing shots of Jack Daniel's and snorting lines of cocaine off the granite countertops in the kitchen, Ainsley in lingerie, sitting on Dutch's lap. No!

Tabitha is too emotionally spent to have a reunion phone call with Stephanie, so she sends a text: *Hey, stranger! My mother broke her hip. I'm in Boston at MGH, and Ainsley is at home on Nantucket. Is there ANY way I could impose on you and Stu and ask you to take Ainsley in for 2–3 nights? I know it's an enormous favor out of the blue but I'm desperate. I'll make it up to you. Thanks xo.*

She's a coward, sending a text. They're talking about the well-being of Tabitha's only child. Tabitha hates herself. She should have called. Yes, it would have been awkward—it's easily been four years since Tabitha and Steph have had any kind of meaningful conversation—but sending a text was too casual.

As if to punish Tabitha for her cavalier handling of the situation, her phone pings with a response: *I checked with Candace. She doesn't think having Ainsley here is a good idea. Sorry I couldn't be of more help! xo.*

Oh, sure, Tabitha thinks. *Blame it on the sixteen-year-old.*

In her heart, she knows this is the answer she deserves.

Tabitha will have to call Meghan and ask her to stay at the carriage house. There is simply no one else. Meghan is as big as a house, and her pregnancy has been a trial—she has developed carpal tunnel syndrome *and* gestational diabetes. Her ankles are so swollen that she can't wear shoes, only flip-flops; she has to pee every ten minutes, and when she leaves the other sales associate, Mary Jo, in charge of the store while she goes to the bathroom, something inevitably walks out of the store unpaid for. Mary Jo is seventy-eight years old and myopic. Tabitha has to fire her, but she's worried about getting slapped with a lawsuit for being ageist.

Meghan will watch Ainsley. She is beholden to Tabitha because Tabitha is paying her through her maternity leave despite the fact that she is a seasonal employee. But Meghan won't *want* to do it. All Meghan wants to do when she gets home is eat the low-sugar snacks she's allowed to consume and watch *Ellen.* On the one hand, Tabitha thinks it would be good for Meghan to get some hands-on parenting experience, albeit at the other end of the spectrum. *This is what your child will be like at sixteen if you're very unlucky!* On the other hand, Tabitha knows she should let Meghan enjoy her last two or three weeks of caring for herself and spending quiet time with her husband, Jonathan.

But if not Meghan, then who?

* * *

The next day finds Tabitha in a different waiting room, alternately paging through back issues of *Town & Country* and dozing with her head up against the concrete block wall. Eleanor is expected to be in surgery for a few hours, but Tabitha is afraid if she leaves the hospital something awful will happen. If she stays here and suffers, Eleanor will be fine.

At twelve thirty, Tabitha's phone rings. She checks the display: It's Ainsley. Twelve thirty means Ainsley is at lunch. No doubt she's wondering how much longer she's going to be left an orphan.

"Hi, sweetie," Tabitha says. "I'm trying to find someone to stay with you."

"I called Aunt Harper," Ainsley says. "She can be here tomorrow night and stay for as long as you need her to, but she wants to make sure you're okay with it."

"No," Tabitha says. "Not Harper."

"Just let her come, Tabitha. Mama, I mean—sorry. Please? Please please please? That way you can take care of Grammie and not worry about me. Aunt Harper can stay as long as you need her to. She quit her job."

Quit her job? Tabitha thinks. More likely she got fired. Tabitha doesn't want Harper to be the one to fix things, because Harper never actually fixes things. She only makes things worse. Look at her life. Tabitha caught the doctor's wife's champagne in the face!

And yet having Harper come to watch Ainsley is an answer of sorts. It would allow Tabitha to go back to the town house on Pinckney Street once Eleanor is safely out of surgery to get some much-needed sleep.

But then the memories assault Tabitha: Harper walking into the rental cottage on Prospect Street with a bouquet of wildflowers. Harper singing a song in Julian's tiny ear as she rocked him. The song was "If I Had $1000000" by the Barenaked Ladies; it calmed Julian immediately. It was the only thing that could. Harper making cioppino with clams and mussels, the tomato-rich broth the first real food Tabitha had eaten since Julian's birth.

Harper braiding Tabitha's hair and ironing Tabitha's dress.

A bottle of champagne with their bare feet dangling off the end of Old South Wharf, dinner at 21 Federal, all eyes on the two of them. Dancing in the front row of the Chicken Box to a band that played old U2 songs. Harper's arm crooked around Tabitha's neck as they belted out the lyrics to "With or Without You."

Tabitha can't think any further. It is simply too awful.

"No," Tabitha says to Ainsley now. "I'm sorry, but no. Not your Aunt Harper."

"But Mom—" Ainsley says.

"No," Tabitha says, and she hangs up.

HARPER

Tabitha must be really desperate if, as Ainsley said, she approved of Harper staying with Ainsley for the summer. So Harper packs up just what she will need for the season—clothes, shoes, toiletries, books, computer, one good kitchen knife, her food processor, her cast-iron skillet, leashes, chew toys, rawhides. What else? She is nearly forty years old, but she has acquired very little in the way of material things. Will she need her surf-casting pole or her mountain bike? Doubtful.

Fish follows Harper around as she tucks things in boxes.

"Go lie down," Harper says, pointing to his Orvis bed. But he won't.

"I'm not going to leave you behind," Harper says, and she kisses his snout and rubs his back, his mostly black fur silvered now.

She throws away everything in the fridge and most of what's in the cabinets. What should she do with Billy's ashes? she wonders. She doesn't want to leave them here, in the nearly empty duplex, but taking them off the Vineyard feels wrong as well.

She decides to take them over to Billy's house, where she places the urn on his mantel. Billy's clothes she'll donate, but later. When? When she comes back?

Yes, she decides. She will come back in a few weeks, a month or two, by the end of the summer. For now, she takes Billy's invoices and accounts-payable file; she can work on his paperwork while Ainsley is at school this week.

Before she leaves the house, she snaps a bunch of pictures—every room and the yard, so she has them for posterity. She has decided to sell the house as a teardown, which pains her. As bad as it might have been, it was Billy's. But the idea of a gut renovation—finding talented, available, reasonably priced people to hire, then *managing* them—is simply not an option. Harper has been fired; she has *no income.* She doesn't have the money to pay for a renovation. Billy has around ninety grand in his savings account, but according to Polly Childs, it will cost nearly double that to do the work required. Harper will have to sell the house as is, pay off Billy's mortgage, and split the difference with Tabitha. That part can't be avoided. Harper had taken

Billy to his lawyer in Edgartown, and they went over the terms of the will: everything was to be split down the middle with Tabitha. Mrs. Tobias had served as a witness. If they sell the house as is, they will each walk with a hundred grand, maybe a little more. Would it be nice to sell it for a million and get triple that amount? Sure. But Harper isn't up for the challenge.

Harper wants to see Reed, but she can't call him and she can't text him. She *cannot* walk into the hospital to confront him in person, which is what she has wanted to do since he left the reception.

But Harper does drive through the hospital parking lot; Reed's Lexus is there. It looks the same; nothing about it announces a major upheaval in his life.

What is it like for him at home now? Harper imagines the air is crackling with things unsaid. How has he explained the affair to Sadie? Has he said it was a mistake, a lapse in judgment? Has he blamed Harper, called her a vixen, a temptress? Has he told Sadie he loves Harper? Has he admitted to being torn and confused? And what has he said to Greenie? Reed isn't a demonstrative man. He is serious and discreet; he is a doctor. Being *caught* like this, talked about, discussed as the object of gossip and rumors, must be soul-shredding for him.

Harper blames the whole affair on the Morning Glory Farm market.

In the weeks preceding the visit to the farm, Harper had logged in a lot of hours at the hospital with Billy, back when his problems were treatable. Dr. Zimmer had been the man in charge of Billy's medical care. He explained what was going on with Billy's kidneys, his liver, and his heart. He went over the medications in meticulous detail with Harper. Also, he talked to her about Billy's diet and exercise, what he was allowed to do and what he wasn't. It was all very professional. Only once had he laid a hand on Harper's arm and said, "He's lucky to have a daughter like you."

Harper had responded, "He's been an excellent father to me my entire life. I'm the lucky one."

When Harper bumped into Dr. Zimmer at the counter at the Morning Glory Farm market, she had recognized him but couldn't place him. He was wearing a tight, colorful biking outfit and a helmet and wraparound sunglasses. Harper was standing at the counter, where she was about to order a Morning Glory muffin fresh out of the oven. The market was engulfed in the aroma of cinnamon, raisins, orange zest, and toasted pecans.

"Harper!" Dr. Zimmer had said. He smiled at her, and Harper thought, *Wait a minute. Who is this guy?* Then, an instant later, she figured it out.

"Dr. Zimmer!" She checked out his spandex; he looked like he was wearing the flag of Uganda. "I didn't know you biked."

Dr. Zimmer nodded at his Fuji, leaning up against a tree. "Stress-relieving hobby," he said. "Do you have time for a cup of coffee—my treat?"

"Sure," Harper said. "Thank you." She rarely hung around the Morning Glory because there was too great a chance she would bump into Jude or Jude's partner, Stella, or someone who worked for Jude. And, sadly, Harper didn't have friends she could meet at the farm for coffee and a muffin. She occasionally brought Fish with her for companionship, but Fish always attracted attention because he was so darn good looking, and attention was precisely what Harper wanted to avoid.

To sit with Dr. Zimmer was a good thing, though, she thought. Dr. Zimmer was a revered member of the community, and he would lend Harper respectability by association.

They had sat at the picnic tables under the oaks for the better part of an hour. They started out talking about Billy—Harper confessed that Billy was still smoking one cigarette a day despite the fatwa on tobacco—then they wandered off topic, experimentally at first.

Dr. Zimmer had said, "Do you have siblings? Other family?"

Harper sipped her pumpkin-flavored coffee; this was the first time it had been available since the previous fall. It was a natural question to ask, she supposed, but it put the pleasantness of the encounter at risk.

"I have an identical twin, actually. She and my mother live on Nantucket."

Dr. Zimmer had slapped a hand down on the green painted wood of the picnic table. Like most doctors, he had beautiful hands; he didn't wear a ring, but Harper knew he was married to the woman who owned the pie shop in Vineyard Haven. She had, at least, done that much research. "An identical twin on Nantucket?"

Harper pulled off a chunk of muffin, then opened one of her three foil-wrapped pats of butter. Normally Harper dragged the muffin through the butter, making a mess of the butter and her fingers, but that day, in the polite company of Dr. Zimmer, Harper had used a plastic knife. The muffin was already rich and moist, and adding butter was like dipping jelly beans in icing. "You wouldn't be able to tell us apart."

"Come on."

"I'm serious. We look exactly alike. The teachers at our

school never figured it out. Neither did our camp counselors or our friends. Our own parents. Lots of other people."

"And she lives on Nantucket with your mother. That's crazy, right? You and your father live here, and your identical twin and your mother live on the other island?"

"Crazy," Harper said in agreement.

"Are you close?"

"No," Harper said. "Our parents' divorce drove a wedge between us, then my sister and I had a pretty serious falling-out fourteen years ago now."

"That's too bad," Dr. Zimmer said.

Harper shrugged. "I talk to my mother periodically, although she's tough. Her name is Eleanor Roxie-Frost. Have you ever heard of her?"

"No," Reed said. "Should I have?"

"I guess not," Harper said. "She designs dresses. She's a pretty big deal in the fashion world, or she used to be."

"You're single, right?" Dr. Zimmer asked. "Are you dating anyone?"

Again, Harper shrugged. "I date here and there. I've never been married, no kids. Do you have kids?"

"No, no kids," Dr. Zimmer said. "I want them; my wife doesn't. And to be fair, when we got married I didn't want them, either. Apparently changing one's mind about wanting children isn't allowed..." He let his voice drift off. "What do you do for work?" He was changing the subject. No kids with Mrs. Zimmer was a sore spot.

Harper smiled. He obviously hadn't heard about her involvement with Joey Bowen. "I deliver packages for Rooster Express."

* * *

The next time Harper saw Dr. Zimmer, they were back at the hospital. It was late evening, and Billy had been urinating blood. Dr. Zimmer had him admitted and told Harper she could go home for the night. He was leaving the hospital as well, and he had walked her to her car. It had been the quintessential autumn night, cool but not yet cold, the air smelling of wood smoke and leaves.

"Would you like to go get a drink?" Dr. Zimmer asked.

They went to the Brick Cellar at Atria, a place Harper liked but where she would never go alone. Reed ordered a glass of wine, and Harper followed suit, although she preferred a beer and a shot. Reed—as soon as they got out of their respective cars to go inside, he had insisted Harper call him Reed instead of Dr. Zimmer—said he was hungry, and since Harper could always eat, they ordered a grilled Caesar salad, the lobster tacos, and the peach-blueberry cobbler and shared everything. When Harper groaned over the cobbler—which *was* a rather orgasmic groan, because the cobbler was *so* good—Reed turned to her and said, "You know that's arousing, right?"

That had been the start of things, Harper supposed. Her inadvertent food groan elicited Reed's choice of the word *arousing,* which automatically gave their new friendship a sexual edge.

It had been Reed who ventured there first, not Harper.

They each had another glass of wine, then a glass of some persimmon cordial that the bartender pressed on them—she had received a complimentary bottle from her wine rep and was anxious to be rid of it—and the next thing Harper knew, she and Dr. Zimmer were kissing like teenagers in the backseat of his Lexus. The details were hazy, but Harper knows that she did not invite herself into his car, so he must have enticed her.

It went on like that—clandestine meetings whenever Reed worked late. They would meet by the East Chop Beach Club or in the back parking lot of the ice rink. And then, in the spring, Reed finally agreed it would be safer to meet at her duplex. Three weeks ago, when Harper told Reed she was going on a date with "Sergeant Andrew Truman of the EPD—you know him, right?" Reed had left the hospital to meet her at her duplex in the middle of the day.

He was jealous, he said. He knew it was unfair, but he didn't want Harper to start dating Drew.

She had laughed. *You can't ask me to do that,* she said. *You can't ask me to do anything. You're married.*

Harper stares at the Lexus a few seconds longer. It's a black car, baking in the sun.

Good-bye, Reed, she thinks. Her stomach is hollow and sour. She wants to leave him a note or a sign—a heart drawn in the yellow pollen on his back window—but she can't.

She pulls out of the parking lot and considers driving by the Upper Crust to see if it's open, if Sadie is there. Harper would just as soon believe that Sadie is back at work as that she has hung a sign on the door that reads: CLOSED: HUSBAND CHEATED ON ME. Harper is afraid to drive by the shop; she's afraid that Sadie will see her. She's afraid to drive around the island. She could bump into Dee, Billy's nurse, who sold Harper and Reed out, or she could bump into Franklin Phelps, Sadie's brother, whom Harper had always counted as a friendly acquaintance. She loved going to hear Franklin sing at the Ritz—now she can't show her face in the audience again. She could bump into Drew or Chief Oberg or one of the Snyder sisters, all of whom would know by now that Harper is a faithless catastrophe.

But Harper has to drive through Edgartown—right down Main Street, in fact—to get to the Chappy ferry. There's simply no way around it.

Before this week, Harper had loved Edgartown. There are certainly things to love about the rest of Martha's Vineyard—the low stone walls, the farms, the cliffs of Aquinnah, the wild beauty of Great Rock Bight, the gritty fishiness of Menemsha, the Methodist campground and Tabernacle in Oak Bluffs—but Edgartown is still the crown jewel of the Vineyard, in Harper's mind. Or maybe that's just because of a snobby aesthetic preference she inherited from Eleanor. Edgartown is like Nantucket: it has an architectural integrity and an elegance that Harper finds powerful. The Old Whaling Church and the Daniel Fisher house are like the grandparents of town—old, white, and stately. Harper loves all the clapboard homes with the voluptuous window boxes on North Water Street. Main Street has the best shopping and the restaurants with the most delicious food. Edgartown has the prettiest harborfront and the most picturesque lighthouse.

Edgartown would be a fine place for Eleanor to open a boutique. Harper had long thought this and even suggested it once, but her mother had merely laughed.

Not on Billy's island, she'd said. *That would be the last place I'd pick.*

* * *

Harper lines up for the Chappy ferry. She has to say good-bye to Brendan, not only for her own peace of mind but also because she can't stand to think of him wondering why she's disappeared.

How can Harper explain what exists between her and Brendan Donegal?

Harper had known Brendan when she was younger, in her twenties, and spending every spare moment on South Beach. This was before she worked for Jude. Back in Harper's first days on the Vineyard, she scooped ice cream at Mad Martha's and sold tickets at the Flying Horses carousel. On her days off, she cultivated a group of friends at South Beach—surfers and the girls who loved them. Among this group, Brendan Donegal was legend, the best surfer the Vineyard had seen in fifty years. He had been sponsored by Rip Curl since he was in high school, and although he had traveled all over the world—Oahu, Maui, Tahiti, Sydney, Perth, South Africa—he always spent the month of August at home on South Beach.

He drank and smoked pot at the bonfires. Everyone did.

Harper lost track of Brendan for a bunch of years. They had never been close, never hooked up. Harper had been downright thrilled when Brendan had, one day, wandered into Mad Martha's, ordered a double scoop of shark attack ice cream (vanilla ice cream colored blue, with white chocolate chunks and raspberry swirl, a wonderfully sick joke and very, very popular), and called Harper by name.

He had returned to the Vineyard for good, people said, to establish a surfing school. But shortly thereafter, he had an accident.

He'd been high on something stronger than weed, and he'd gone out in prehurricane swells. The waves were real monsters, although presumably nothing Brendan Donegal couldn't handle.

But the combination of the drugs and the waves got him. People spotting thought he was gone. He was under *forever,* his buddy Spyder said. But then they saw his board pop up, and shortly thereafter Brendan became visible in the washout. Spyder dragged him out and performed CPR; the Edgartown Fire Department showed up seconds later and brought him back from the dead.

It was a tremendous story—until it became clear that Brendan wasn't the same after that. Simple tasks eluded him. He could watch TV but couldn't read. He could ride a bike but couldn't tie his shoes. He could not surf, could not own or operate a surf school. That dream was over.

Thank goodness Brendan's mother, a woman who was only ever referred to as Mrs. Donegal, was wealthy and owned a house on Chappy's East Beach that had a guest cottage where Brendan could live; he went to occupational therapy once a week in Falmouth to try to regain at least part of what he once had.

After Harper got fired by Jude, she was left with nowhere to go during the day. It was autumn, and Harper had wanted to ride her mountain bike, but she feared that one of Jude's work trucks would run her off the road. She couldn't take Fish to Great Rock Bight or take yoga—too public—nor could she drink all day at the Wharf or the Ritz because Joey Bowen still had friends there.

And so, at that confusing and painful time in her life, Harper went to the place many Vineyarders go when they want to get away: Chappaquiddick. She started out by packing up for the day with Fish and heading out to Cape Poge with her surf-casting rod, but the weather soon grew too chilly, at which point Harper sought refuge at Mytoi.

Mytoi, owned and operated by the Trustees of the Reservations, is a full-fledged, beautifully maintained Japanese garden, complete with a koi pond spanned by an arched wooden bridge, a stone sculpture garden, and benches well placed for introspection, even as autumn deepens, even as snow falls in December.

It had been snowing when Harper first saw Brendan there, the snowflakes light and dry, so pretty against the steel-gray sky. Harper had gone to sit on what she thought of as "her" bench, a long red wooden seat with a curved back that overlooks the koi pond and bridge—but someone else was sitting on it. This was the first time Harper had encountered another soul in the garden. Although it was a magical place and, she thought, transformative, it was largely ignored in the off-season. Who was this, then? Harper's first instinct was to leave—the whole point of Mytoi, for her, was solitude—but she approached. And then she saw it was Brendan Donegal.

"Hey," she said. He was far less intimidating since his accident. Not an object of pity, exactly—at least not to Harper. More of an accessible god. He wore a knit cap and a Carhartt work jacket over a flannel shirt; his feet were in sturdy work boots. She wondered if he had tied the laces himself or if he'd had to ask his mother to do it.

"Brendan?" Harper said. "Hi—it's Harper. Harper Frost."

A slow smile spread across Brendan's face. He was still good looking—gorgeous, really—with his light blue eyes and his sandy blond hair kept long and shaggy.

"Harper," he said. "Hi." He patted the spot on the bench next to him.

She knew enough, somehow, not to bombard him with questions, and they sat in silence for a long while as the snow fell and the wind rippled the surface of the pond.

Finally Brendan turned to her. "Why do you come here?"

"To get away," she said. "I made a bad decision, and I lost my job and most of my friends."

"Really?" Brendan said. "Me, too."

When Harper went back to Mytoi the next day, Brendan was there, and Harper sat with him again. The third day it was bitterly cold, and Harper nearly skipped her trip to Chappy, but it had become a ritual of sorts, so she bundled up and went. Brendan was there yet again, but after a few minutes of sitting and shivering side by side on the bench, Brendan stood up and offered Harper his hand.

"We're going," he said.

"Okay," Harper said. "Where?"

"My house," he said. "I'll make you an Irish coffee."

Harper had been hesitant because of Mrs. Donegal. Mrs. Donegal was wealthy and well connected; Harper feared she had heard about Harper's fall from grace. She might have been friends with Jude or one of Jude's clients; it was impossible to comprehend the millions of circuitous routes that gossip traveled on the island.

But it had been fine. The Irish coffee Brendan made was strong and hot, and Harper had two mugs of it. When she was finished with the second, Brendan took her mug and set it in the sink.

"I'm not the same," he said. "I'm not the same as I was."

"It's okay," Harper said. She had no idea if it was okay or what kind of scrambled messages his brain might be transmitting. "I like you the way you are now."

"You do?" he asked.

"Yes," Harper said.

And he had kissed her on the cheek.

They spent time together on Wednesday evenings and Sunday mornings, always meeting at Mytoi, then going back to Brendan's house for Irish coffee. After a few months, Harper introduced Brendan to Fish—dogs weren't allowed at Mytoi, so Fish slept across the backseat of the Bronco in the parking lot—and it was love at first sight. Fish had cuddled up to Brendan immediately, his tail wagging as though he'd found a long-lost friend.

Harper has been going over to see Brendan twice a week for nearly three years. Their relationship has no name; it has depth but no breadth. Harper isn't about to suggest that she and Brendan go to dinner or grab coffee or spend a summer day on Lobsterville Beach. There is only Mytoi and the coffee and a kiss on the cheek when she leaves.

The Chappy ferry is a platform barge that holds three cars and travels the 527 feet that separate Chappaquiddick from the rest of the Vineyard in ninety seconds. Harper prefers the *On Time II* to the *On Time III* because her favorite ferry master, a woman in her seventies named Indira Mayhew, works on the *II*. Indira is as salty as they come, but after three years of Harper's regular Chappy visits—summer and winter, spring and fall—she knows Harper and even grants her a smile or two.

"Missed you last week," Indira says.

Harper feels a swell of tenderness. Perhaps Indira hasn't heard the rumors about her and Dr. Zimmer, or maybe she has but she doesn't connect the name Harper Frost with the brunette in the navy-blue '68 Bronco.

"I missed you, too," Harper says. Then she feels guilty. She missed a visit for the first time ever. She will have to explain it to Brendan, or try to.

A few minutes later, Harper is driving off the barge onto Chappy. Her heart is pounding. If Brendan isn't at Mytoi, she will have to go to his house unannounced, which makes bumping into Mrs. Donegal—something Harper has managed to avoid up to this point except for a few waves from afar—a valid concern. Harper pulls into the parking lot; hers is the only car, but that doesn't mean anything. Brendan walks from home.

Okay, she thinks. *Here goes.*

The gardens are another place altogether now, at the start of summer. The cherry trees are blushing pink; their luscious blooms and fragrance are almost indecent. The ferns have unfurled, and the dell planted with camellias is in its full glory. The pond is full to brimming and nearly overflowing with fat koi. The fish swim with renewed energy, flashing the silver and tangerine of their scales. There are butterflies flitting and a concert of birdsong.

Harper meanders over the newly packed dirt trail around

to her spot, their spot, and she sees Brendan sitting on their bench... with another woman.

What? Harper thinks. She hasn't been here for a week, it's true, but she never thought she'd be replaced.

As she gets closer, she sees the woman is older. It's Brendan's mother. Harper considers turning around and going back to her car, but then Brendan sees her and waves her over.

There is no escaping.

It's okay, Harper thinks. She can do this. Maybe Mrs. Donegal knows who she is and what she's done—but maybe she doesn't. *Smile and the world smiles with you.* That had been one of Billy's favorite sayings.

Harper smiles.

"Hello," she says.

Both Brendan and Mrs. Donegal stand up.

"My mom," Brendan says.

Harper offers her hand. "Mrs. Donegal, it's lovely to finally meet you."

"The pleasure is mine," Mrs. Donegal says. "And please, call me Edie. Brendan has told me so much about you. You've been such a good friend to him in a dark time."

"Oh," Harper says. This is the opposite of what Harper expected. She expected Mrs. Donegal, Edie, to be protective and territorial. Does Edie think that Harper and Brendan have been sleeping together? She hopes not. She doesn't want Edie to see Harper as a woman taking advantage of Brendan but rather as what she is—someone who is attracted to the stillness of Brendan's mind and the gentle nature of his soul. "I've known Brendan for nearly twenty years. We used to hang out together at South Beach." She flails for a second. She and Brendan don't talk about the days when he used to surf. She probably shouldn't bring it up now. "I was happy to reconnect with him."

Edie nods and offers a warm smile. "You've made quite an impression."

At this, Brendan springs to life. He reaches out for Harper's hand. "I thought you were lost," he says. "Lost to me."

Harper's heart cracks. "Lost to you?" she says. She looks him in the eyes; his are a kaleidoscope of blue and gray. "Never. Okay? Never."

"Okay," he says. He holds her gaze for an instant, then stares down at his feet. He's wearing flip-flops. His feet are pale; his toenails need cutting.

"Shall we sit?" Harper asks. "Would that be okay?"

Brendan and Edie settle on the bench, and Harper sits next to Brendan, closer than she might have if they were alone. They're still holding hands, which is also something that never happened before.

"My father died last week," Harper says. She looks at Edie. "He was an electrician here on island. Billy Frost."

"I didn't know him personally," Edie says. "But I knew of him. He was spoken of very highly."

"Thank you," Harper says. Is this true? Billy was known mostly for his carnival-barker presence at the bar, although he also would take a service call at nine o'clock on a Sunday night, making him popular and well loved by his clients. Harper sighs. "In addition to my father dying, my mother broke her hip, so I'm leaving tomorrow for Nantucket." She tries to catch Brendan's eye. "I may be gone for a while."

"A week?" he says.

"Probably longer," Harper says. She envisions being on Nantucket for a week or so, and then, once Tabitha has figured things out, she'll move on, maybe go to Vermont or Maine. She will have to come back at some point to close on her father's house.

"I love Nantucket," Edie says. "We rented a house on the beach at Cisco for three or four summers when Brendan was growing up. Do you remember that, Brendan? That's where you and Sophie learned to surf. On Nantucket, at Cisco Beach."

Slow nod from Brendan.

Edie says, "We bought you a white surfboard with a green stripe down the middle."

"From Indian Summer," Brendan says. "The owner had a dog. A Great Dane."

Edie smiles at Harper. "Yes."

"We drank mudslides at the Atlantic Café," Brendan says.

"Good," Edie says. "You do remember Nantucket."

Brendan turns to Harper. His eyes take on a sharp focus; Harper sees a lucidity. "Come back," he says. "Please."

AINSLEY

She is a sixteen-year-old left to fend for herself.

Make no mistake: Tabitha is far from domestic. She and Ainsley eat takeout or go to restaurants nearly every single night, and when they do stay home, it's cereal or cheese and crackers for dinner. Tabitha never cooks, and Eleanor is even worse—she has never prepared a meal in her life.

Neither does Tabitha clean; she has Felipa for that. Four days a week, Felipa is the "housekeeper" at Eleanor's, but on

Wednesdays, she cleans the carriage house tits to tail. She changes the sheets, does all the laundry, cleans the kitchen—including, once a month, the inside of the nearly empty refrigerator—and she dusts, vacuums, straightens and plumps the pillows, and replaces the vases of fresh flowers.

So on Wednesday when Ainsley gets home from school, the house is clean and quiet, Ainsley's bed has been made up with fresh sheets, and all the clothes strewn across her room have been folded and put into her drawers.

In Ainsley's top drawer is a bag of weed and rolling papers. Ainsley has a ten-page paper about Zora Neale Hurston due in the morning, but she can hardly be expected to worry about her schoolwork when she is dealing with family emergencies *and* a breakup.

She rolls a joint, smokes half of it, then takes the keys to Eleanor's house off the hook in the kitchen and walks down the white-shell driveway to Seamless. It's three thirty, which means Felipa will be in her room watching *Gran Hotel,* the Latino television series she's addicted to. Ainsley eases open the front door and tiptoes into the living room. The house smells like lily of the valley and lemon Pledge; the only sound is the ticking of Eleanor's clocks. There's the grandfather clock, the grandmother clock, two banjo clocks, a beehive clock, and a brass carriage clock on the mantel. Every fifteen minutes, these clocks provide a mini concert of chiming, which Ainsley used to find mesmerizing, but now that she comes into her grandmother's house only on surreptitious missions to steal alcohol, cigarettes (her grandmother keeps a delft-blue cup filled with individual cigarettes on the coffee table, as though it's 1955), or cash (crisp hundreds in an envelope in the secretary), the chiming nearly always gives Ainsley heart palpitations, and the ticking makes her feel like she's walking through the inside of a time bomb. One day, she assumes, she will get caught.

The weed isn't helping with her paranoia. She should leave. But instead she heads for the brass bar cart in the corner. She tucks a bottle of Grey Goose vodka under one arm and a bottle of Bombay Sapphire under the other and leaves the house, only expelling her held breath once she is scurrying back down the driveway.

She makes a drink: vodka, tonic, ice, and a fat wedge of lemon.

By five o'clock, Ainsley is drunk and really, really stoned—she polished off the second half of the joint and didn't even bother opening a window. Her mother has effectively abandoned her, so whatever behavior Ainsley exhibits is Tabitha's fault.

Now Ainsley is ready to take action. At school that day, Emma had been on her like white on rice, asking if she was okay. Apparently a rumor had been circulating through Nantucket High School that Ainsley had been locked in a closet in her house for two days as punishment for throwing the party.

Where did people come up with this stuff? Ainsley wondered.

"No," she said. "I was grounded Saturday and Sunday. Then my grandfather died, so on Monday we had to go to his funeral on the Vineyard."

"Oh," Emma said. She sounded disappointed. "I thought Tabitha finally went postal. I thought she might have broken out the duct tape and the rope."

"No," Ainsley said. "My mother is annoying, but she's not psycho. My grandfather died."

Emma had shrugged. "That's what grandparents do," she said. "They die."

Ainsley had considered telling Emma about the woman who came to the reception and slapped her mother, but Emma can't be trusted with that kind of story. She either wouldn't care or would care too much.

"What's up with you and Teddy?" Emma had asked at lunch. "Did you two fight?" Teddy was, for the first time ever, sitting with the baseball team at lunch instead of with Ainsley and Emma.

"I'll tell you later," Ainsley said. "I don't feel like getting into it now." She looked across the cafeteria at Candace, who today was wearing a pink silk button-down, a pair of white AG Stilts, and nude Tory Burch flats. Her mother, Steph, used to be big into braiding Candace's hair or doing half ponytails, but now Candace wore her hair straight and shiny. It pained Ainsley to admit it, but Candace was pretty. Her clothes were stylish and effortless. Her skin was clear. Her eyes radiated the pureness of her heart.

Except that she had stolen Ainsley's boyfriend.

Now, drunk and stoned and alone, Ainsley calls Emma. "Are you ready to hear what happened?" she asks. Emma isn't good at offering comfort or support—but revenge? Revenge Emma excels at.

Ainsley is sitting in third-period English. Her paper on Zora Neale Hurston's *Their Eyes Were Watching God* is six and a half pages long instead of ten. It is poorly written, repetitive, and untethered to the text because Ainsley didn't read a single page of the book. She had tried the night before, but the dialogue is written in the southern vernacular, which might as well be a foreign language.

Candace and Teddy are both in Ainsley's English class. Ainsley is sure that they have turned in ten-page papers using appropriately annotated selections from the book to back up their thesis statements and have probably also supported their arguments with quotations from Alice Walker, Toni Morrison, and Angela Davis, the way Mr. Duncombe suggested. Candace and Teddy don't speak, they don't even look at each other, but Ashley can see the pearlescent waves of true love shimmering between them. She only has to suffer this particular hell for a few moments, however. Before Mr. Duncombe can even start in on how important the literary voices of the marginalized are, the intercom buzzes. Ainsley sucks in a breath. Ms. Kerr asks for Candace Beasley to be sent down to the office.

By lunchtime, it's all over the school: a nearly full bottle of Bombay Sapphire and a baggie holding what appeared to be cocaine residue were found in Candace Beasley's locker.

"Wow," Maggie says as she and Ainsley move along the salad bar. "I remember when Candace was a total goody-goody. Don't you?"

Ainsley shrugs. "I do. But people change."

"Most of the time it's the good kids you have to watch out for," Emma says. "They're *so* good that one day they just *snap* and become really, really bad."

"She's facing a possible three-day suspension," Maggie says. "Her parents came in and everything."

Three-day suspension, Ainsley thinks. She has three days to get Teddy back.

"I'm surprised she's not facing legal action," Emma says. "I mean, alcohol is one thing—but cocaine?"

"She says it isn't hers," Maggie says. "She told Dr. Bentz someone must have planted it in her locker."

"That would be what I would say if I were her," Emma says. " 'Wasn't me; someone planted it.' She didn't ask my advice, but if she had, that would have been my suggestion."

"Still, how would someone else get into her locker?" Ainsley says. "Unless she gave someone the combination. The last person who had that locker graduated, like, two years ago. And they're impossible to break into."

"Impossible," Maggie says in agreement.

Ainsley is both buoyed and terrified for the rest of the school day. The news about Candace is everywhere: the school is on fire with it. Candace Beasley, a straight-A student and an altar girl at Saint Mary's, brought a bottle of gin and maybe also cocaine to school. It's so outlandish that Ainsley expects to be yanked out of class at any moment. But Emma had promised Ainsley that the plan was foolproof. Back in November, Emma had been tardy for school for the fifth time, which required her to meet with the principal, Dr. Bentz. She was asked to wait in the room outside his office by herself until Dr. Bentz returned from a Rotary Club breakfast. There was a fire drill; the school emptied out, but Emma stayed put. That was when she started snooping. She found teacher evaluations (boring), ninth-grade MCAS scores (boring), and the combinations for every locker in the school. The list of combinations she kept.

So infiltrating Candace's locker was easy. Ainsley was the one who had left an anonymous note for the school nurse saying there was a "rumor" going around that Candace Beasley had been bringing "hard drugs" to school and telling people it was for "medicinal purposes." The school nurse, Mrs. Pineada, was fanatical about preventing student drinking and drug use. A search of Candace Beasley's locker had immediately followed. Bam.

As Ainsley is leaving school, someone grabs her arm. It's Teddy.

"Ainsley," he says, "I need you."

Ainsley practically falls into his arms. She must be in love with him. How else can she explain the searing pain in her heart, the longing, the fervent desire for simple affection—a kiss on the cheek, a squeeze of the hand? Ainsley loves his blue eyes, his freckles, the way his red hair curls under his ball cap, the hollow at the base of his neck.

I need you. This is what Ainsley wants to hear, right? And yet she feels insidiously guilty about what she and Emma have done to Candace. Ainsley should have won Teddy back by cleaning up her act and showing him that she can be good. But she had followed Emma down the dark path, as always. They had made Candace look bad. It felt like tripping Candace up in a footrace instead of simply running faster.

"What's up?" Ainsley asks. She decided in history class

that the best tack with Teddy is to play dumb. Or if not *dumb*—he wouldn't believe that Ainsley hadn't *heard* about Candace—then at least calm and unemotional. If Candace Beasley has been caught with booze and drugs, what concern is it of Ainsley's?

"Can you come to the cubby?" Teddy asks. "Do you have time?"

The cubby is a secluded nook on the back side of the school building. It's shielded from the playing fields by the parked school buses and the Dumpster used by the wood shop. It isn't romantic, but it is private, and couples who don't have cars frequent the cubby before school, after school, and during school. Allegra Pancik and Brick Llewellyn purportedly had sex in the cubby during morning announcements a few years earlier—the stuff of high school legend.

Ainsley follows Teddy through the corridors and out the back door of the cafeteria. Jasmine Miyagi, the queen bee of the freshman class, tries to stop Ainsley. She probably wants to gossip about Candace, but Ainsley waves her off. Nobody thinks anything about seeing Ainsley and Teddy together because nobody other than Ainsley, Teddy, Candace, and Emma know they've broken up.

Teddy is three strides ahead of Ainsley. She had thought maybe he would walk alongside her, maybe hold her hand.

They get to the cubby, find it empty. Teddy checks in all directions to make sure the coast is clear, which is standard operating procedure when using the cubby for intimate purposes. Ainsley can't wait to kiss him.

But suddenly he slams her up against the shingles of the building. Her head smacks hard. Teddy's hands are around her throat. His eyes are blue fire, and his voice drops to a scary whisper.

"It was you," he says.

"No," she blurts.

"It was you. I know it was you. And Emma, that little tart. She lifted the cocaine bag from her father's jeans pocket after he came home from work, and you stole the gin from your grandmother's bar cart."

Ainsley blinks. He's exactly right.

"I know you, Ainsley," Teddy says. "I know your tricks, and I know Emma's tricks. I've spent all year with you. I've waited outside while you lifted booze from your grandmother's house. I've been inside your grandmother's house. I've *seen* the Bombay Sapphire. The coke was probably Emma's idea. You probably resisted at first, but then she talked you into it the way she talks you into everything."

Every sentence he speaks is truer than the last, but Ainsley can't give that away. She clamps her fingers, like bracelets, around his wrists.

"Get your hands off my neck," she says. "You're scaring me." Teddy's mother is in a mental hospital. Ostensibly her state of mind was affected by his father's death at the cat-food factory, but what if mental illness runs in the family and Teddy is not actually the greatest guy Ainsley has ever met but rather some kind of maniac who is going to strangle her here behind the high school?

"You're scared now?" Teddy says. "Just wait." He lets go of her neck, but she's even more intimidated. "I'm going to Dr. Bentz in the morning. That gives you time to turn yourself in this afternoon."

A part of Ainsley does want to turn herself in. She will cry to Dr. Bentz, admit her wrongdoing, tell him the gin was hers but not the coke. She'll explain her broken heart, her grandfather dying, her grandmother breaking her hip, her mother leaving her alone for days. If she needs to, she will hark all the way back to losing her baby brother. She was only two, she doesn't remember him, but that doesn't mean she wasn't affected when he died. Her mother was forever changed: when Tabitha looks at Ainsley even now, she sees Julian's ghost. (This may sound like a stretch, but how does Ainsley know it isn't true? Her life, she is certain, would be better if Julian had lived.) Dr. Bentz is famous around school for being evolved, in tune with the careening emotions of teenagers. He has a record of being lenient with students who admit their wrongdoing, but what he can't stand... is a liar.

To admit the truth, however, means to turn in Emma. Can Ainsley betray her best friend? No, she can't. Emma only swiped her father's empty baggie of cocaine in order to help Ainsley get back at Candace. It was Emma who took the risk of placing the incriminating evidence in Candace's locker; someone could easily have seen her.

Ainsley realizes that what she wants most—a chance at recapturing Teddy's affections—is lost to her either way. By trying to destroy Candace, she has made Candace into a heroine.

So now Ainsley's choices are between bad and worse. She chooses bad; she calls Teddy's bluff.

"You sound like a hillbilly who came East and watched too much *Gossip Girl,*" Ainsley says. "This is Nantucket. People don't plant alcohol and drugs in other people's lockers on the off chance they'll get suspended, Teddy. You can tell Mr. Bentz your conspiracy theory, but it'll sound like something you saw on Netflix. I already told you: I like Candace. You two make a cute couple. I wish you only the best." Ainsley tries to force sincerity into these last sentences, but still they feel flaccid.

Teddy pauses, however. He may know her, yet she also knows him. He's unsure now.

"Fine," he says.

Ainsley has no idea what "fine" means: he's going to Mr. Bentz or he isn't? However, asking him to clarify seems dangerous.

"Fine," Ainsley says, and she walks off with the manner of a girl who has nothing to fear.

Emma has already left school, and although Ainsley knows she is probably just down the street at Cumberland Farms hanging out with BC and Maggie, smoking weed and devouring three slices of cardboard pepperoni, Ainsley decides to walk home. She needs to think.

She never meant to be a bad kid; she only wanted to be a cool kid. When she really lets herself think about it, she can't *believe* what she and Emma have done. It's shameful, and it's dangerous. They're going to get caught. Of course they're going to get caught. They are going to be the ones to get suspended... or worse. And Dutch will likely get in trouble, too, because the cocaine was his.

Going to college might be in jeopardy. What will her mother think? What will her father think? Her stepmother, Becky, will be proved right: Ainsley is a bad seed, a terrible role model. She should not be allowed around her half brothers.

With each car that passes as she walks, Ainsley turns, hoping it's Emma in the Range Rover. Or that it's Teddy in his uncle's truck. But all the cars are unfamiliar. The summer people are here; no one recognizes her.

In the driveway of the carriage house, Ainsley sees a navy-blue Bronco. She blinks. Aunt Harper's car.

She came! Ainsley feels a rush of elation and relief. *Aunt Harper came!* But her joy is chased by a panicky fear. She told Aunt Harper that Tabitha was fine with her coming, but that was a big fat lie.

Tabitha is still in Boston with Eleanor. When Ainsley spoke to her mother at lunchtime, Tabitha hadn't disclosed when—or if—she was coming home. Tabitha said she was sending Meghan over to check on Ainsley. Ainsley is just going to have to tell Aunt Harper the truth: Tabitha doesn't want her there. Maybe Aunt Harper won't care. Maybe Aunt Harper will stay anyway.

Ainsley opens the door and is immediately greeted by a Siberian husky with eyes the color of glacial ice. A dog—Aunt Harper's dog—is *in the house!* Again, Ainsley is both thrilled and extremely uneasy. Ainsley has wanted a dog since the beginning of time, but Tabitha always said no. Eleanor once had a dachshund, but it ate shoes, and they had to give him away.

"Hello? Ainsley, is that you?"

Aunt Harper peers down over the stair banister. The house smells *delicious*—like sautéed onions and bacon. Ainsley can't remember the house ever smelling so good before.

"Hi," she says shyly. It's still surreal to see her mother peering down on her, only now her mother is smiling, friendly, happy to see her. Only now her mother isn't her mother. "You brought the dog? You're cooking?"

"That's Fish," Harper says. "Where I go, he goes. He's a very good boy. And for dinner, I'm making my famous pasta carbonara. Your grandfather loved it. And salad and garlic bread. We'll eat around seven. Is that all right? I figured that would give you a chance to do some homework. And I brewed some iced tea. It looks like you and your mom drink a lot of Coke Zero, but you know that stuff will kill you, right?"

"Right," Ainsley says. Her stomach is now growling. When is the last time she ate? A few radishes and green beans from the salad bar at lunch, but before that? Dinner the night before had been half a bag of cheddar SunChips. She ascends the stairs to find her aunt filling a glass with ice, then tea, then squeezing a wedge of lemon into it; the drink could be on the cover of a magazine. Ainsley sucks the whole thing down, and Harper laughs. "Thirsty?"

"I walked home from school," Ainsley says. "My ride cut out."

Harper pours another glass of tea, then pulls out a jar of mixed nuts and a container of marinated mozzarella balls. "Snack?"

Ainsley's eyes fill with tears. Someone is here, taking care of her. Someone loves her. Ainsley reaches for a pecan, blinking her eyes, then she quickly wipes away the tear that falls. Harper must see it, however, because she holds open her arms. "Give me a hug," she says. "It's good to see you."

Ainsley goes down to her room. She doesn't have any homework, but finals start in a few days. It would be wise to buckle down, pull some good grades out of her ass to end the year, but all Ainsley can think about is Candace. Since Candace has gotten suspended, will she even be able to take finals? Ainsley checks her phone, afraid of what she might find, but there's nothing. She's tempted to call Emma and tell her what Teddy said. Maybe she can convince Emma that turning themselves in is the best course of action.

Emma will never agree. They will fight. It will end badly, and Ainsley is too exhausted for another scene. She lies back on her bed. From out of nowhere, a smile crosses her face. Aunt Harper is here.

HARPER

She can't get over the sense of exhilaration that fills her when she drives her Bronco off the ferry onto Nantucket. She hasn't been here in fourteen years, but even so, everything is basically the same: Young's Bicycle Shop, the Juice Bar, Steamboat Pizza.

But by far the best thing about Nantucket is that here, *nobody knows her!* There is no one to avoid, no one to be scared of.

She drives to the house from memory, making a wrong turn only once before turning into the white-shell driveway of 776 Cliff Road. It's as stunning as ever. There are hundred-year-old trees and a verdant lawn, hydrangeas on the verge of exploding into bloom, neatly trimmed boxwood hedges, and window boxes on both houses. The window boxes have mandevilla trellised in the back going up in spires. Between the spires are bursts of Whirling Butterfly gaura, thick, silvery Provence lavender, and Fairy roses. Fountains of Silver Falls dichondra and hot-pink million bells spill out over the edges, and tucked into the crannies are dark leaves of ipomoea and sprays of Diamond Frost euphorbia. This is an extravagant combination not unlike those at the estate Jude used to privately call the floral whorehouse, which she charged seven hundred and fifty dollars per container to plant and maintain.

Harper parks at the carriage house and, finding it unlocked, lets herself in.

The house smells like Evening in Paris, the scent Eleanor wore all through their childhood. Harper supposes that Tabitha must now wear it, because she is slowly but surely turning into Eleanor. The carriage house is upside down—three bedrooms and two baths on the entry floor, then stairs that lead up to the living space. Fish goes nuts with the cornucopia of new smells; he is in and out of every bedroom, his tail slamming against the door frames.

Harper identifies Tabitha's room—all-white bed, fifty million pillows in different sizes, and a bolster the size of a fallen tree. She probably still sleeps on top of the covers, because getting underneath them messes up the sheets, and somewhere within the logic of Tabitha's brain, it is better to *have* crisp, clean sheets than to enjoy sleeping in them.

Whatever.

Ainsley's room is the one that smells like pot and has a highball glass filled with—Harper takes a tiny sip—*vodka* on the dresser. Okay! Harper dumps the glass in the bathroom sink and throws her duffel bag in the third bedroom, which appears to be a catchall. There's a bed with a full-size mattress and a coverlet that Harper remembers from... from... wow... the cottage on Prospect Street. It's white matelassé, yellowed now.

There is a desk covered with shelter magazines—*Domino, House Beautiful, Traditional Home, Architectural Digest.* (Someone is an interior designer wannabe. Ainsley? *Tabitha?*) There's a Windsor chair at the desk, but aside from that, nothing else. Plenty of room for the dog bed.

Upstairs is more formal—a gorgeous cherry dining table with six low-armed chairs around it and a tall bouquet of fresh delphiniums in the center; there's a turquoise tweed sofa with swanky 1960s curves, above which hangs a rectangular mirror. There is a TV on a glass-and-acrylic console and dressmaker's dummy in the corner wearing the Roxie in lime green, which initially gives Harper a fright. She thinks, for an instant, that it's Tabitha.

The kitchen is beautifully outfitted and well equipped, but it's too clean—never-used clean.

Shame, she thinks. What she could have done these last fourteen years with a kitchen like this.

Fish comes to bury his snout in her crotch, a sign that he approves.

"Well, good," Harper says, scratching his ears. "Just don't get used to it. Six days. Seven at the most."

Harper finds the grocery store. It's a Stop & Shop, and Harper feels a pang of longing for Cronig's and the Reliable Market, which is really reliable only for being expensive.

As Harper is climbing out of her Bronco, she feels a hand on her arm.

"Tabitha?"

Harper looks up to see a very handsome, clean-cut man in a shirt and tie and horn-rimmed glasses. He looks like Superman before he's Superman. He looks like Clark Kent.

"I'm not—"

"Did you get a new *car?*" Clark Kent asks. He gasps when he sees Fish asleep across the back. "Did you get a *dog?*"

The look of utter shock on Clark Kent's face is enough to make Harper laugh. She nearly plays along. How many times in their early life did one twin pretend to be the other? A twister, they called it, short for "twin sister." No one could tell them apart.

No one.

Harper nearly says, *Yeah, I traded in for this old clunker. Can you believe it?* What does Tabitha drive? Harper wonders. A red Mercedes convertible, as sleek as a woman's shoe? *And I got a dog. I figured I needed one more pressing responsibility.*

But Harper can't do it to this guy. She grins. "I'm not Tabitha."

"Tabitha," Clark Kent says, "I know the other night was awkward, and I'm sorry—"

Harper is, naturally, dying to hear about Tabitha's awkward night, but she interrupts because to let him continue only to satisfy her wanton curiosity seems cruel. She's on Nantucket, it's a fresh start, and she's going to be nice. "I'm Harper Frost, Tabitha's twin sister."

"Her..." Clark Kent fish-mouths as he searches for words.

"Her twin sister. I live on Martha's Vineyard."

Clark Kent nods once. "She told me about you."

"Well, that's something," Harper says. "We haven't communicated much in the past decade and a half, but last week our father died..."

Clark Kent's eyes widen.

"...and on Monday evening, our mother fell down and broke her hip."

Here Clark Kent gasps. "Eleanor?"

Harper tilts her head. "How do you know my sister?"

Clark Kent straightens up and offers Harper his hand. "I'm being terribly rude. I'm sorry. My name is Ramsay Striker. I'm...or I was...well, I lived with your sister...Tabitha...I dated Tabitha for four years, lived with her for three. We broke up in February."

"Ah," Harper says. She studies the guy: tall, successful looking, well dressed. Tabitha's type, or what Harper has always pictured as Tabitha's type, although the only *real* boyfriend of Tabitha's that Harper has ever met is Wyatt, who was *not* Tabitha's type. Which is one reason—of many, she supposes—that it didn't work out between them.

Harper would like to pin Ramsay Striker to a board like a butterfly specimen and ask him ten thousand questions.

As if reading Harper's mind, Ramsay Striker checks his watch. "Do you want to go grab a drink?" he asks.

It's the lunch hour, and places will be crowded, Ramsay says, so he suggests "the brewery" because Harper can bring her dog.

Brilliant, Harper thinks. Ramsay is thoughtful. And, as it turns out, the brewery—CISCO BREWERS, the sign says—is the perfect laid-back place to go on a mild, sunny afternoon.

Harper loves Nantucket already!

The brewery features a large brick patio surrounded by rustic farm buildings. One building sells beer, another sells wine, and yet another sells spirits. Perched on a stool with a golden retriever at his feet is a long-haired guy playing the guitar. There are a few dozen people sitting at picnic tables, drinking and eating guacamole and chips or oysters from the food trucks.

Ramsay and Harper choose an empty picnic table, and Ramsay says, "How does a beer and a lobster roll sound?"

Harper loves a man who instinctively knows what a particular moment calls for. "Like heaven," she says.

Harper limits herself to two beers and just a sip of the third because she still has to go to the store and make it back to the carriage house before Ainsley gets home from school. She has told Ramsay about herself and Tabitha growing up—all the way to the divorce and the family divided between two islands.

Ramsay says, "So why the rift between you and Tabitha?"

Why the rift? So many reasons, starting with that fateful game of rock, paper, scissors. Harper tries, for the ten thousandth time, to imagine what would have happened if Tabitha had chosen scissors instead of rock. It would have been hellish to watch Tabitha roll away with Billy while Harper was trapped with Eleanor in the mausoleum on Pinckney Street. The furniture in that house was all two hundred years old—heavy, dark, and ornate with brocade upholstery and velvet drapes; the library was filled with dusty books, and oil portraits of their creepy Roxie ancestors hung on the walls. Would she have hated Tabitha? Yes, she supposes she would have. But she wouldn't have become Eleanor's disciple. That had been Tabitha's willful choice.

Other things had happened to Tabitha that had been beyond her control.

Julian.

Harper is *not* going there.

She realizes that information has only been flowing one

way during this lunch. Ramsay hasn't divulged anything about his relationship with Tabitha, and they're running out of time. It's already two o'clock.

"How are you able to do this?" Harper asks.

"This?"

"Take a two-hour brewery lunch."

"Oh." Ramsay laughs and nudges his glasses up his nose. "My name is on the door. Family business on Main Street. Insurance."

"Why did my sister let you go?" she asks.

"Wow," Ramsay says. "Nice reversal."

"Thank you." Harper smiles at him. "I don't know why I'm assuming it was she who broke up with you. It might have been you—"

"No, it was Tabitha," Ramsay says. But he doesn't seem inclined to add anything more, and Harper takes the hint.

She says, "This has been really fun. Thank you for lunch. But I have to go. I'm pretty sure Ainsley gets home from school between three and three thirty."

"She does," Ramsay says. "Assuming she's not staying for detention."

"Detention?" Harper says. "Is Ainsley a bad kid?"

"She's a great kid," Ramsay says. "But she's been given no boundaries, so she pretty much does whatever she wants."

"No boundaries?" Harper says.

"None," Ramsay says. He holds up his palms in a gesture of surrender. "It'll be good for her to have a different authority figure."

"I'm only staying six days," Harper says. "Seven at the most."

"Give her all the love you can," Ramsay says. "And some from me as well. Tell her I miss her."

* * *

At seven o'clock, Harper calls Ainsley to the table, and Ainsley approaches with wide eyes.

"Wow," she says. "This is the first time we've ever used the table this way."

"What way?" Harper asks.

"Like, for eating," Harper says.

Harper tries not to let the surprise show on her face. "Really?"

"We go out," Ainsley says. "Or we eat Thai food standing at the counter. Or cereal in front of the TV."

"Oh," Harper says.

"My mother is very busy," Ainsley says.

Harper has lit the candles and filled the Waterford goblets with ice water. "Cheers," she says.

Ainsley lifts her glass. Her hand is trembling.

"Are you okay?" Harper asks.

Ainsley nods, but she doesn't meet Harper's eyes. Is she stoned? Harper wonders. Has she been throwing back vodka shots in her bedroom?

"Ainsley?"

"This is pretty," Ainsley says, indicating the candles, the tablecloth and china, the silver, the wide shallow bowls filled with pasta and salad, the basket of bread. "Thank you."

She seems on the verge of tears, and a lump presents in Harper's throat. But Harper sensed this, didn't she, at Billy's memorial reception? Ultimately that's why Harper agreed to come. Tabitha treats Ainsley like another adult, which was how Eleanor treated both Tabitha and Harper. They were never allowed to cry or whine; they weren't cuddled or indulged; they weren't allowed to be *children.* They hadn't been *mothered.* Tabitha had rebelled the year she turned into a pony, and Harper...well, Harper had rebelled later, she supposes.

And now, Tabitha is doing the same thing with Ainsley. She doesn't cook for the girl, and Harper would bet she doesn't kiss her good night. She doesn't nurture, when even the toughest, most badass child requires a little nurturing.

Harper fixes Ainsley a plate of food, then a plate for herself.

"Eat," she says. "Eat."

After Ainsley has cleared her plate, wiping up the last of the sauce with a piece of bread, she falls back in her chair. "That was really yum."

"I'm glad you liked it," Harper says. She rests her elbow on the table, chin in her hand. "We were so busy eating that I neglected to ask about you. How's school? Do you have a boyfriend?"

Just like that, the tears start, and the story falls out: *Had a boyfriend, Teddy, new kid this year from Oklahoma, everything fine until this party I threw here last weekend. He decided he doesn't want me, he wants Candace Beasley. Candace was my friend then not my friend then almost my friend again until she stole Teddy.*

"Oh, honey," Harper says. She holds out a hand, and Ainsley takes it and squeezes. *It's a story as old as time,* Harper thinks. *I love you; you love somebody else.* For the first time since she got to Nantucket, she thinks of Sadie Zimmer and

Drew, the people she has wronged. Then she thinks of Reed. He is an ether surrounding her. Harper's love for him is her atmosphere; she's always thinking of him, even when she's trying not to think of him.

"But that's not the worst thing," Ainsley says. She's all snotted up, so Harper rises to fetch some tissues. Her poor niece is suffering from teenage angst, trying to make sense of an unfair world. Oh, how Harper had hated growing up! No matter what she has gone through recently, it has been ameliorated by the adult knowledge that regardless of how bad things get, she will survive.

"What is the worst thing?" Harper asks. She hands Ainsley a box of tissues and sits down, scooting her chair closer. Fish, sensing people anxiety, plops down at Harper's feet.

"My best friend?" Ainsley says. "Her name is Emma..."

There's a noise. A slamming door. A voice, amped up with anger. "Ainsley?"

Ainsley's eyes widen, and she leaps to her feet, knocking over her Waterford goblet, which snaps where the cup meets the stem, a clean decapitation. Harper inwardly curses—Tabitha will blame *her* for that, no doubt—but Ainsley doesn't even seem to notice.

"Mom?" she says. Her voice contains what sounds like terror.

Tabitha is clicking up the stairs; Harper can hear her stilettos on the hardwood. She wonders if the unthinkable has happened and Eleanor has died. But it quickly becomes apparent from the set of Tabitha's mouth and the smoke coming out of her ears that the problem isn't Eleanor. It's Harper.

"What the *hell* are you doing here?" Tabitha asks.

TABITHA

What bothers her most is how cozy they look. The Stephen Swift table is set with china, silver, and the Waterford goblets that were a wedding present to Eleanor and Billy. The candles are lit, dripping wax down the Georg Jensen candlesticks.

Harper has cooked a meal. The air still smells of toasted bread, garlic, onions, *bacon*. Tabitha's stomach rumbles. At the hospital it was coffee and crackers from the vending machine, and back at the hotel, it was wine and microwave popcorn.

Two of the chairs are pulled close together. Tabitha imagines her daughter and her sister sharing confidences. Tabitha had preferred seeing the table used for beer pong.

"I specifically told you that she wasn't allowed here, Ainsley," Tabitha says.

"*She?*" Harper says. "Who is *she*—the cat's mother?"

"You," Tabitha says.

"Ainsley asked me to come," Harper says. "She assured me she had your blessing."

"She lied," Tabitha says. She turns her gaze on her daughter. Ainsley looks younger than she has in years. Her face is clean of makeup, her pale hair pulled back in a slack ponytail. "Again."

"Hey, now," Harper says. "Take it easy."

"Take it easy?" Tabitha says. "This is *my* house. Don't you dare tell me to take it easy."

"I'm sorry I lied," Ainsley says. "I wanted Aunt Harper to come. I needed someone to watch me. I needed family."

"Family?" Tabitha says.

"You *abandoned* me!" Ainsley says. "I'm sixteen years old, not eighteen, not twenty-five. You just can't leave me alone for days."

"But look," Tabitha says. "You lived."

"Aunt Harper cooked for me. She bought groceries. She brewed iced tea because Coke Zero is poison."

"It's not poison," Tabitha says.

"It is, though," Harper says.

When Tabitha looks at Harper, she catches a glimpse of fur at her feet. She barely stifles a scream. "Is that your *dog?* Your dog is in *my house?*"

The dog lifts its head, seemingly in response. Tabitha sees the intelligent face and the clear cerulean eyes of a husky.

"This is Fish," Harper says. "Fish, meet my sister, Pony."

Fish studies Tabitha in a way that's unsettling, almost as if the dog is human. The dog turns to look at Harper, then back at Tabitha.

He notices the resemblance, Tabitha thinks. She nearly smiles, but she stops herself. She doesn't want a dog in her house. Even a beautiful dog like this one.

"I want you out in the morning," Tabitha says to Harper. "I told you never to come back here."

"I thought we got past that," Harper says.

"I was civil to you on the Vineyard," Tabitha says. "Civil, despite the fact that I got drenched and humiliated. We have your poor decision making to thank for that. I can be civil to you for an afternoon, Harper, but that is a far cry from allowing you to live in my house and care for my child."

"Are you back, then?" Ainsley asks.

"Yes," Tabitha says, but her cheeks burn with the lie. She only came back to grab her things and check on her daughter;

she has a ferry reservation back to the mainland in the morning. Eleanor needs her; there is no one else. Tabitha called Eleanor's younger sister, Flossie, in Palm Beach, but was informed that Flossie was on a cruise in the Greek islands. Tabitha will be in Boston through the weekend at least, maybe longer. She called Meghan to see if she could come stay with Ainsley, but Meghan, showing an unusual amount of backbone, said she would rather not. Tabitha called Wyatt again—no answer—and then she called and left a pleading message with Stephanie Beasley.

Part of Tabitha considers just letting Harper stay.

"I met a friend of yours today," Harper says. "We had lunch. Ramsay Striker?"

Tabitha's mouth drops open. "You had lunch with Ramsay?"

"At the brewery," Harper says. "He thinks it's a good idea that I stay with Ainsley."

Ramsay thinks it's a good idea. *You're a piss-poor parent, Tabitha.*

Against her will, Tabitha remembers the bouquet of wildflowers; she recalls skimming the cool water of the harbor with her toes. She remembers Harper's hot, boozy breath as she sang. *I can't live with or without you.*

"Forget tomorrow," Tabitha says. "I want you out tonight. Pack your bags."

"Mom!" Ainsley says.

"It's okay," Harper says. She lifts the bowl of salad from the table.

"Do not," Tabitha says. "Do *not* touch my things."

"I want *you* to leave," Ainsley says. "I wish Aunt Harper were my mother instead of you."

"Ainsley," Harper says.

Tabitha knows she is acting abominably. She wishes she had the capacity to forgive her sister and to celebrate her sister and daughter's forging of this new bond. But Tabitha can't get past twenty-two years of sour history—Harper has had it *so* easy, living with Billy—or past what happened the night that Julian died.

Tabitha's phone rings. It's Stephanie Beasley.

Tabitha snaps back to the present moment; she feels a cool wave of relief. Stephanie will watch Ainsley. This is the solution Tabitha was hoping for.

"Hello?" Tabitha says as she moves into the living room. Incredibly, the dog gets to his feet and trots after her. "Stephanie?"

"Tabitha," Stephanie says. "Your daughter..."

"What?" Tabitha says. She sits on the sofa and, in spite of herself, reaches out to stroke the snowy white fur at Fish's throat.

"Your daughter is a monster," Stephanie says.

Tabitha continues to rub Fish's coat even as the ugly accusations spin out of Stephanie. *Bottle of Bombay Sapphire and a Baggie containing cocaine residue planted in Candace's locker. Planted by Ainsley Cruise and Emma Marlowe. The girls were taking revenge because of what happened between Teddy and Candace.*

"I'm sorry?" Tabitha says. "It sounds to me like your daughter is trying to deflect the blame. She may have gotten in over her head, Stephanie. Ainsley can't be the automatic scapegoat here. Surely you see how unreasonable that is."

"Unreasonable?" Stephanie says. "You've been away, and

your daughter has been left *without any adult supervision.* I'm sure she waltzed right over to your mother's house and strolled out with the gin. Then she and her evil little friend planted it in Candace's locker."

Tabitha closes her eyes. If she goes over to Eleanor's house and checks the bar cart, will she find the Bombay Sapphire missing?

Of course she will.

She revisits what Stephanie said a few seconds ago. *The girls were taking revenge because of what happened between Teddy and Candace.* Teddy and Candace are together now, so soon after Tabitha found Ainsley and Teddy together in her bedroom? Ouch.

Stephanie says, "You'll be hearing from Dr. Bentz tomorrow."

Tabitha doesn't respond. She simply ends the call.

When she reenters the kitchen, she sees that Ainsley and Harper are clearing the table. Tabitha watches the two of them moving in concert. It's like watching herself—the mother she always wanted to be, the mother she would have been if Julian had lived—with her beloved teenage daughter.

"Stay," Tabitha says. Her voice is stern, and Fish, who has followed at Tabitha's heels, dutifully sits and gazes up at her. To Harper, Tabitha says, "I have to go back to Boston in the morning. Eleanor needs me."

"Why don't *I* go take care of Eleanor?" Harper asks. "You stay here with Ainsley."

Tabitha considers this. She recalls Eleanor weeping about

Harper after Billy's memorial service; Eleanor, like Ainsley, is sick of Tabitha. But Tabitha didn't put in years and years with Eleanor and the business only to be replaced by Harper at the end. There will be a payoff: Tabitha will inherit the empire. And even if that empire is diminished, Eleanor still owns a mighty fortune in real estate: the house here, the house on Pinckney Street. Tabitha will not relinquish her claim to that.

"Eleanor is my responsibility," Tabitha says. "We both know that."

"Don't sound so put-upon," Harper says. "I've spent the last ten months caring for Billy."

Tabitha scoffs. "Sleeping with his doctor."

"*Caring* for Billy," Harper says. "Feeding him, bathing him, driving him around, getting him to and from his doctor's appointments, making sure he wasn't smoking too many cigarettes or drinking Jamo on the sly. And now I have to deal with selling Billy's house, and once I do that, you and I are splitting the proceeds, as per Billy's will."

This is news to Tabitha. Her wheels start to turn. *Proceeds* sounds like unexpected income, the windfall she so desperately needs. "Wait a minute," she says. "What's the deal with the house, exactly? How much are we talking about?"

"I had a broker come look at it. She said we can either renovate it or sell it as a teardown. I am *not* going to renovate. It'll cost too much and take too much time, and the contractors on the Vineyard pride themselves on being unavailable. As a teardown, she says we can list it at six hundred and settle for half a million."

"Teardown?" Tabitha says. "Is it really that bad?"

"It's really that bad," Harper says. "Which you would know if you had ever come to visit."

Tabitha accepts that barb in silence. She clears her throat. "Is there a mortgage?"

"Mortgage of two sixty-nine," Harper says. "Six percent of the sales price goes to the Realtor, and there will be other closing costs. If we do absolutely nothing to the house, we will each walk with a *hundred grand*."

A hundred grand: Harper makes this sound like a king's ransom. And maybe to her it is; she couldn't be making more than twenty bucks an hour at her delivery job. But for Tabitha, a hundred grand won't even scratch the surface. Once she pays Ramsay back the forty thousand she owes him, that leaves sixty, which will be eaten up by Ainsley's first year of college. Selling it as a teardown is Harper's preference because that's the quick, easy way out.

"How much if we renovate?" Tabitha asks.

"Moot point," Harper says. "We aren't renovating."

"Just tell me what she said, please."

Harper sighs. "She said she would list it an one point one if it's a quality job, but the place has to be gutted. And I'm sorry, but that is *not* happening. I don't have any savings. Billy has ninety grand in the bank but probably less than that because I still have to pay the golf club for the blasted reception. Polly said a renovation would cost a hundred and fifty. That means I would have to go to the bank for a loan or borrow money from Mommy, and I am *not* doing that—"

"Mother doesn't have it," Tabitha says. "Even if she did, she wouldn't lend it to you for Billy's house."

"It doesn't matter," Harper says. "We're selling it as a teardown, Pony."

Tabitha lets use of the odious nickname slide because she's busy doing the math. If they sink one fifty into Billy's house and sell it for a million, they would both walk with more than three hundred grand.

Ainsley says, "Aunt Harper should stay here, and you should go to the Vineyard, Mom. Haven't you always said it's your dream to renovate a house?"

"Grammie's house," Tabitha says. She has long yearned to be given permission and an unlimited budget to redo Eleanor's house on Pinckney Street—but needless to say, neither has been granted. "I said that about the house on Beacon Hill."

"Do Gramps's house instead," Ainsley says. "You'd be good at it."

Harper turns on Ainsley. "No. We aren't renovating. Whose side are you on, anyway?"

Ainsley frowns. "I want you to stay," she says.

Ainsley's suggestion is completely outrageous, yet something about it appeals. If Tabitha can reach Flossie or get Eleanor to pay out for a private nurse, she would be free to work on Billy's house, which is something she would profoundly enjoy. With Tabitha's eye and a little elbow grease, they'll make three times the money. How can Harper argue with that?

While Tabitha is handling the renovation, Harper can stay here and deal with the fallout of Ainsley's behavior *and* Harper can work at the boutique. The boutique is going to go belly-up at the end of the summer—Tabitha has done everything within her power to resuscitate it, but to no avail—so why not let Harper take the blame for its demise?

Is it too cruel to let Harper take over the sinking ship that is Tabitha's life?

She remembers the sting of cold champagne in her face, then the slap.

The wildflowers. The Chicken Box. "With or Without You."

Julian, dead.

"Once I get Mother settled . . . *if* I get Mother settled, I'll go over to the Vineyard and take a look," Tabitha says. "I'll handle the Realtor and the sale, and you can stay here with Ainsley. But there are conditions."

"Such as?" Harper says.

"Your first responsibility is my daughter," Tabitha says. "I'm going to call the school secretary in the morning and let them know that you're in charge for the remainder of the school year. There are only a few days left, but if there are any issues, you'll get the call."

Harper nods.

"Will there be any issues?" Tabitha asks Ainsley.

Ainsley looks at her feet. "No."

"Ainsley?"

"No," Ainsley says.

Tabitha closes her eyes for an instant. She is so tired, so *weary,* that she could fall asleep standing up. *You're a piss-poor parent, Tabitha.* She wonders if her real motivation in agreeing to this plan is just an unwillingness to deal with Ainsley's bullshit.

Maybe, yes. And the feeling, apparently, is mutual. Ainsley's eyes are shining with hope. She wants her aunt.

Be careful what you wish for, Tabitha thinks.

"Your second responsibility is the ERF boutique on Candle Street," Tabitha says. "Meghan is going to have her baby soon. She'll show you the ropes tomorrow, and both of you will have to put in a lot of work. I can do the buying remotely, but you'll be in charge of tracking the orders, getting them out on the floor, accounting for inventory, ringing up sales, and going to the bank each morning with the deposits. In addition to hand-selling, of course. You'll have Mary Jo to help."

"She's blind," Ainsley says.

"Myopic," Tabitha says.

"I can handle it," Harper says.

"Yes," Tabitha says, and the part of her that has long wanted revenge on her sister is placated. There is no way her sister can handle it. "I'm sure you can."

HARPER

Her alarm goes off at six thirty the next morning, and Harper's feet hit the ground with a sense of purpose. Fish is already waiting by the bedroom door, wagging his tail.

In the distance, Harper hears the wail of the ferry's foghorn. Tabitha is on that boat with her car. She is gone. Harper is in charge.

"Take care of the daughter," Harper says to Fish. "Then mind the store."

After Harper lets Fish out, she heads upstairs to find the coffee brewed and a handwritten set of instructions written out, along with an envelope containing fifteen hundred-dollar bills.

Harper reads through the instructions, marveling at how Tabitha can be nearly forty years old yet her handwriting is still the same as it was when she was a ten-year-old girl and won the fourth-grade penmanship award.

Harper, the note says, *please follow these basic instructions.*

Harper finds herself grateful for guidelines. She is both elated and terrified at the previous day's turn of events. She is going to spend the next few weeks—or longer?—in Nantucket caring for her sixteen-year-old niece, which is something she knows exactly nothing about.

> *1. Ainsley: No drinking. No drugs. Infraction = Loss of phone for one week. NO EXCUSES.*
> *2. Felipa comes on Wednesdays to clean. Felipa lives in the basement of Eleanor's house, and she will know if you are over there* <u>*SNOOPING*</u>.

The words are capitalized and underlined, as if Harper's snooping were a given. Tabitha thinks Harper is a cheat, a liar, *and* a thief.

Numbers 3 through 6 are about the store: the address, the security code, the numbers of the maintenance man, the landlord, Meghan, Mary Jo, the police department, the fire department.

> *7. Dress yourself from present inventory. Pick six outfits (one MUST be the Roxie) and cycle through. Write down the exact items you take. One pair of shoes only. This store is a direct reflection of the Eleanor Roxie-Frost brand. Don't mess this up.*

Harper gets an immediate case of the hot pricklies. She knows the Nantucket boutique carries brands other than Eleanor Roxie-Frost, but these other brands will still be too fussy and feminine for Harper, and she is going to have to wear the blasted Roxie at least one day a week.

She has a succession of nauseating memories: her confirmation at Church of the Advent, her ninth-grade dance, her prom. Her adolescence was pockmarked with events for which she had to dress up. Tabitha had loved it. Tabitha had worn dresses and skirts *voluntarily*.

Harper will worry about the store later. For now she will focus on the daughter.

She raps lightly on Ainsley's door. There is no answer. She knocks again a little louder, which elicits a groan. Harper cracks open the door.

"Time to get up," Harper says.

"I'm sick," Ainsley says. "I have a migraine."

Harper nearly laughs. It's startling the way ailments, either real or perceived, pass down through the generations. For Eleanor, every headache was a "migraine" and required a cool, dark bedroom for three hours, followed by a double espresso and a double gin martini.

"Get up," Harper says.

"Seriously, I get them," Ainsley says. "I can't move. My vision gets all splotchy, and I feel nauseated. I'm staying home today."

"You're going to school today," Harper says. She snaps her fingers twice, and Fish leaps onto the bed and starts barking. Ainsley groans again and extends a foot to the floor.

While Ainsley is getting showered, Harper makes her famous scrambled eggs—famous to her and Billy, anyway. Harper uses double yolks, half-and-half, and a handful of shredded Cheddar. She cooks the eggs slowly over low heat until they are deep golden and creamy.

Harper makes a plate for Ainsley with a piece of lightly buttered rye toast, but Ainsley pushes the dish away. "I don't eat breakfast."

"You do today," Harper says.

"I thought you were cool," Ainsley says. Her voice has a ragged, snotty edge, and Harper wants to growl the way Fish does whenever Harper pulls out the grooming brush.

"I am cool," Harper says. "But if you think I'm going to let you do whatever you want this summer, you are sorely mistaken."

"Mom let me do pretty much anything," Ainsley says.

"Well, no offense, but that strategy doesn't seem to be working," Harper says. "I found the vodka in your bedroom yesterday, and I'm sure if I poke around, I'll find weed."

Ainsley sneers. "I'll save you the trouble. It's in my top drawer."

Harper stares. "Eat the eggs."

Reluctantly, Ainsley takes a bite. She nods. "They're good. What do they have, like, ten thousand calories per bite?"

"Pretty much," Harper says, and the teenager grants her a smile.

Rocky start, Harper thinks, but according to Billy's watch, she and Ainsley and Fish climb into the Bronco on time. Harper delivers Ainsley to the front door of the school before the bell.

"Have a good day," Harper says.

"Fat chance," Ainsley says.

"Do you want me to come pick you up?" Harper asks. "You're done at two thirty?"

"I get a ride home with my friend Emma most days," Ainsley says. "I'll text you if I need a ride." She climbs out of the car, tosses her hair, and strolls toward the front door. She is so pretty and so confident. How is this possible at sixteen? She is wearing skinny jeans, ballet flats, and a white cotton tunic embroidered with violets. Her hair is pulled off to the side in a messy braid, which adds a relaxed air to her very rigid posture. Her shoulders are set as if she's expecting an attack.

It's only as Harper pulls away that she recalls their conversation at dinner. Ainsley's boyfriend, Teddy, has been stolen away by a friend of hers—but not Emma. Someone else. Ainsley did mention Emma, but Harper can't remember in what context.

Fish climbs up to the front seat, resuming his usual post as copilot.

"Well, the first days are the hardest days, don't you worry anymore," Harper sings off-key. She reaches out to rub the back of Fish's neck, wondering how long it will be until she knows the ins and outs of Ainsley's personal dramas. At least she remembered that the boyfriend's name was Teddy. And now she knows that Emma gives Ainsley a ride home.

Harper's phone rings in the console. She doesn't answer because she suspects it's Tabitha calling to make sure Harper got Ainsley to school on time. But when Harper gets back to the carriage house and checks her phone, she sees the missed call is from Rooster.

Harper sighs. She had thought for a moment that she had successfully escaped her life on the Vineyard. She lets Fish out of the car.

"Go," she says. "But stay out of trouble."

Fish trots off to check out the grassy terrain of Eleanor's front yard.

Harper stays in the car, contemplating the phone in her lap. She pictures Rooster, so called because of his bright red hair styled up into a cockscomb, slumped over his desk, wearing his Ray-Ban Wayfarers inside because he is hungover.

Why is Rooster calling? Maybe he wants her to come back to work. Maybe he has been unable to find anyone to replace her. It takes a very long time to learn all the little dirt roads in all the towns. It doesn't make any sense to hire a college kid, because by the time he or she finally figures out how to do the job effectively, the summer will be over. Also, a spotless driving record is required—finding people with no speeding tickets, no accidents, and no DUIs is more difficult than one might imagine. Yes, Harper decides, Rooster is definitely calling to offer her her job back. He probably thinks she's desperate for it, but he would be wrong. Turning him down will be a gratifying way to start her day. She calls Rooster back.

"Harper," he says. He hits both syllables in a way that makes them sound like spikes. Harper has always liked her name for its Waspy androgyny, but it's not soft or feminine. That name went to her sister.

"Wally," Harper says, trying to lighten things up. Rooster's real name is Wallace. "What's up?"

"The rumors keep a-comin'," Rooster says. "I heard a real doozy yesterday. Are you sitting down?"

She's still in the Bronco, still belted in, which seems appropriate. *They can't hurt me,* she thinks—all those Vineyarders who are so bored with their own lives that they have to titillate themselves by parsing Harper Frost's questionable decisions.

"I don't want to know," Harper says. She means it: how will it help to know what people are saying? When the news broke about Harper's association with Joey Bowen, she had tirelessly tracked who had said what to whom. She had written it all down on a piece of poster board and drew lines to connect people until the thing looked like a spiderweb. Harper had then set out to do damage control, calling all the principal rumor spreaders to explain her side of the story, which had led to secondary and tertiary rumors that fanned the fires of people's interest and kept the gossip alive. It was a miracle Harper hadn't ended up in jail with Joey Bowen.

From the distance of three years, Harper can see that what she should have done when the news broke was...nothing. She should have let people talk, then lose interest. It had been a one-time incident. What she'd done had been wrong—really, really wrong from Jude's perspective—but Harper had been a very small cog in a far-reaching, well-oiled drug-selling machine. She had merely been guilty of delivering a package. It had ended up being three pounds of cocaine, but for all Harper knew, it was three pounds of potato salad.

"Just listen," Rooster says. "I think you'll get a kick out of it."

"I won't get a kick out of it," Harper says. "It's my *life,* Rooster."

"Everyone knows you were having an affair with Dr. Zimmer," Rooster says. "That was last week's news. This week's news is that you're also sleeping with the messed-up surfer on Chappy."

Harper groans. "Brendan Donegal? He's a *friend* of mine, Rooster. I'm still allowed to have friends, right?"

"I'm your friend," Rooster says. "That's why I'm telling you this."

"You're not my friend, Rooster. You're my boss. And you're not my boss, you're my ex-boss."

"Then guess what I heard? I heard that Sadie Zimmer *left* Dr. Zimmer."

Harper bites her tongue. *Sadie left?* This is something

Harper hasn't considered: instead of Reed leaving Sadie, Sadie might leave Reed.

"But then I heard she didn't leave, *he* left. Dr. Zimmer took a leave of absence from the hospital."

A leave of absence from the hospital? Harper thinks. She closes her eyes.

"*Then* I heard that you were gone and nobody knew where you went and no one knew where Dr. Zimmer went, so people are thinking the two of you are on the lam somewhere, like in *Natural Born Killers,* except not murdering anyone. Or maybe you are leaving bodies in your wake. Nothing would surprise me at this point, Harper, because the stories keep piling up like cars in a highway crash. So anyway, I'm glad you answered your phone. I have your final paycheck. Where would you like me to send it?"

She says nothing. There's no doubt in her mind that Reed's "leave of absence" was forced upon him by Adam Greenfield; there's no way Reed would ever abandon his patients of his own volition. But he left the *Vineyard?* Where is he? Is he out in America looking for her?

"Harper?" Rooster says.

"I'm here," Harper says.

"Where's here?" Rooster says. "Where do you want me to send your check?"

She hates that people are now talking about her and Brendan. She shudders at the thought of Mrs. Donegal somehow hearing the rumor.

"Harper?" Rooster says.

She doesn't want to tell Rooster where she is. The check is for six hundred and thirty-two dollars or thereabouts, too much to ignore, but she doesn't want anyone to know she's on Nantucket. She doesn't want Sadie finding out, or Drew, or

Drew's aunties, or anyone else. Nantucket is, in so many ways, the perfect place to hide right in plain sight.

"Send it to my PO box," Harper says. "Number 1888, Vineyard Haven."

"So you're here, then?" Rooster asks. "You're on island?"

Before she can confirm or deny, there's a beeping noise. It's her call waiting. The number is unfamiliar, but underneath the number it says: *Nantucket, MA.* Harper disconnects Rooster without explanation, without good-bye. Let him think she's in a place with poor reception—the Andes Mountains, the Yukon. It's the only way.

"Hello?" Harper says.

"Ms. Frost?" a man's voice says. "This is Dr. Bentz. I'm the principal at Nantucket High School. I'm going to need you to come in right away."

AINSLEY

Ms. Kerr doesn't contact the classroom over the intercom. Instead she and Dr. Bentz show up at the door of Ainsley's American history class *in person.*

"Ainsley," Ms. Kerr says. "Come with us, please."

A murmur goes through the classroom, and Dr. Bentz offers a game-show-host smile. "Don't let us interrupt your learning about Prohibition," he says. "It was put in place for a reason."

Ainsley grabs her bag and slips past Dr. Bentz into the hallway.

* * *

Gathered in Dr. Bentz's office are Emma and her father, Dutch; Candace, Stephanie, and Stu Beasley; and Tabitha. No, not Tabitha—Aunt Harper. Ainsley burps and tastes the eggs Harper made her for breakfast.

She tries to catch Emma's eye. They are close enough as friends to be able to agree upon a strategy without speaking. But Emma's face is cast down at the table. Dutch looks pissed. His shaved head is ruddy with aggravation, and his tattooed arms are locked across his chest. Candace looks wounded, her parents solemn. Only Aunt Harper appears sanguine. When she sees Ainsley, she offers a shrug—she has no idea why they are here—and a consoling smile.

The smile brings tears to Ainsley's eyes.

Dr. Bentz takes the last seat at the table. He seems present and engaged but studiously unperturbed. He loves conflict resolution, Ainsley knows. A poster of Jimmy Carter hangs in his office.

"Emma, Ainsley," Dr. Bentz says. "We invited you here with your parents and/or guardian today to see what either of you knows about a bottle of Bombay Sapphire gin and a baggie containing cocaine residue left in Candace Beasley's locker."

Ainsley says, "I know nothing about it. I mean, I *heard* Candace was caught with alcohol and drugs in her locker, but that's it."

Dr. Bentz studies Ainsley as though he intends to paint her portrait from memory. "You're *sure* about that, Ainsley?"

Ainsley scrutinizes Dr. Bentz right back. He has an oversize head, a walrus mustache, and glasses that make his eyes appear large and gelatinous. Dr. Bentz is so thoroughly a principal that Ainsley has a hard time imagining him outside the school. She knows that he lives in 'Sconset in a home owned by his wife's parents and that in the summer, when his in-laws are in residence, he goes salmon fishing on the Copper River, in Alaska. Ainsley feels sorry for Dr. Bentz because he doesn't get to enjoy Nantucket summers; he must like his job a lot, because why else would he accept such a raw deal?

Before Ainsley can respond with a calm, metered *Yes, I'm very sure*—Ainsley has spent the last year making lies sound like the truth—Emma speaks up.

"It was all Ainsley's idea," Emma says. "Candace stole Teddy away from her, and Ainsley wanted revenge." Shrug from Emma. " 'Hell hath no fury like a woman scorned...' That's a direct quote from William Shakespeare."

Dr. Bentz clears his throat. "Actually, it's the other William. William *Congreve.* And the quotation, Miss Marlowe, is 'Heav'n has no rage, like love to hatred turn'd, nor hell a fury, like a woman scorn'd.' "

Emma gives Dr. Bentz an indulgent smile, though Ainsley knows she would like to tell him to go pound. "Same difference!" she says, then she pauses for effect. "Back to my story. Ainsley stole the gin from her grandmother's house, and the cocaine packet she got from Felipa's boyfriend. Felipa is the housekeeper, from *Mexico.* Then Ainsley begged me to sneak both things into Candace's locker."

Ainsley feels a zing, like she's been hit in the face at close range by a rubber band. "What?"

Dr. Bentz silences Ainsley with a hand. "And how, Emma, did *you* gain access to Candace's locker?"

"She gave me the combination a few weeks ago," Emma says. "I forgot my chemistry textbook at home, and Candace lent me hers as a favor so that I could finish that day's assignments. I wrote down the combination."

Dr. Bentz turns to Candace. "Is this true? You gave Miss Marlowe your combination?"

Candace nods, and Ainsley is so incensed—Emma and Candace are in *cahoots*—that she blurts out, "No, Emma. You stole the combination of *everyone's* locker from the office during a fire drill in the fall."

"I gave Emma my combination," Candace says in confirmation.

Ainsley is silenced. She feels her aunt's hand on her back. Harper leans in. "Just tell the truth," Harper whispers. "It's okay, whatever it is."

"I stole the gin from my grandmother's house," Ainsley says. "But it was Emma's idea, not mine, to plant it in Candace's locker. Emma stole the locker combination of every student in the school from this office in November. She's the one who brought in the cocaine packet. My housekeeper doesn't have a boyfriend. Emma took the cocaine from her father's jeans."

At this, Dutch Marlowe stands up and roars. "Watch who you're accusing, young lady!"

Everyone at the table, including Dr. Bentz and Stu Beasley, recoils. In these peace talks, Dutch is the renegade nation.

"Watch how you speak to Ainsley," Aunt Harper says. Now she, too, is on her feet. "Your defensiveness tells me that you're probably guilty, and your demeanor is consistent with someone who abuses cocaine."

"Shut up, Tabitha, you stuck-up bitch," Dutch says. "Why don't you have your mommy call her lawyer?"

"Now, now, Mr. Marlowe," Dr. Bentz says. "There will be no name-calling."

"It was Ainsley's idea, pure and simple," Emma says. "I was wrong to agree to such a cruel plan, but Ainsley and I have been friends a long time..." Here Emma starts to cry, and Ainsley's eyes grow wide at the sight. In the five years that they've been hanging out together, Emma has never grown weepy, much less shed a tear—not even when discussing her mother, who moved to Florida when Emma was in kindergarten and never returned. "And so I just went along with it, even though I knew it was wrong."

"It was *your* idea," Ainsley says. "You pulled that cocaine packet out of your front jeans pocket yesterday before school."

"I've heard enough!" Dutch says. He glares at Harper. "You tell your daughter to stop accusing people of things they didn't do!"

Dr. Bentz touches the knot of his tie. "What we have established thus far is that neither the alcohol nor the packet with the cocaine residue in it belonged to Miss Beasley."

"Correct," Stephanie Beasley says. Her hair is in a loose bun, and she's wearing a gauzy sundress, looking pretty and natural and every bit like half of the kindest, most solid parental unit in all the world. Stephanie gives Ainsley a pained look. "I don't know what Candace ever did to you. But you spent years making her life miserable, culminating in this regrettable stunt. The astonishing thing to me is that you thought you could get away with it. Because you've never been held accountable for any of the atrocious things you've done or said to people. And that"—here she looks at Harper—"is *your* fault, Tabitha."

"I'm not..." Harper says, but then, apparently thinking better of it, shuts her mouth.

"This is my aunt," Ainsley says. "Not my mother."

Everyone at the table stares at Ainsley as if she has two heads.

"This letter, left at the nurse's office," Dr. Bentz says, pulling it out and setting it in front of Ainsley. "You wrote this? Saying that you'd *heard* Candace Beasley had alcohol and drugs in her locker?"

Ainsley looks at the typed paper. She had misspelled alcohol (*alcohal*) on purpose to make it seem like someone less intelligent than she wrote it. Her grades aren't stellar, but at least she can spell. She doesn't know if she should admit to the letter. Can they check it for fingerprints or check the ink type against her computer at home?

"Yes," she says.

Dutch checks his watch. "Can we go?" he says. "I have a restaurant to run."

"Yes," Dr. Bentz says. "Everyone may go except for Ainsley and her guardian. I'll handle things from here. Thank you for coming."

It's worse than the Salem witch trials, Ainsley thinks. Worse than Galileo or Joan of Arc. She, Ainsley Cruise, has been *framed*. She is so flustered at the failure of Dr. Bentz to see past Emma's bullshit and Dutch's intimidation tactics that she can't find the words to speak in her own defense.

"I'm giving you a three-day suspension," Dr. Bentz tells Ainsley. "However, you will serve it in school, and you will take your exams. That's a kindness from me. I'm well within my rights to assign you an out-of-school suspension and let you take zeros. Do you understand?"

Ainsley opens her mouth to speak. *It was Emma's idea, not*

mine. The baggie of cocaine was Emma's contribution. She encouraged me to steal the gin. She said this was the only way to teach Candace a lesson—not only for stealing Teddy but also for trying to be popular, like us. Emma stole the locker combinations right out of Ms. Kerr's filing cabinets during a fire drill.

But it won't do any good because Ainsley started out with a lie. She lost all credibility, and there's no getting it back.

She nods. Aunt Harper's hand is still on her back, steadying her.

"I'm very sorry about this," Harper says.

"It's Ainsley who should be sorry," Dr. Bentz says. "While serving your suspension I expect a written apology to Candace and her parents and one to Emma as well for leading her down a wayward path."

Ainsley swallows. "Okay," she says.

She has to start serving her suspension immediately. She is taken to a room in the interior of the school that she didn't even know existed. She is being chaperoned by a teacher named Ms. Brudie, whose sex had remained a mystery for most of tenth grade. "Ms." indicated female, but her appearance (crew cut, men's polo shirts, flat-front khakis) said otherwise. Understanding of her job at the school had also been hazy. Now Ainsley understands that Ms. Brudie deals with discipline problems—serious discipline problems—one-on-one.

Ms. Brudie takes Ainsley's phone and hands her a stack of loose-leaf paper. "Apology letters," she says. Her voice is surprisingly delicate and feminine. "Then you may study."

"What about lunch?" Ainsley asks. "What about the bathroom?"

"You'll have a chance to get your lunch and eat it here," Ms. Brudie says. "You get one five-minute bathroom break."

The suspension room has no windows except for one in the door the size of an airport paperback. There is a desk and a chair; the walls are cinder block painted institutional beige.

It's jail, and no sooner does Ms. Brudie shut the door—she will be sitting right outside—than Ainsley starts to cry. The loose-leaf paper on the table in front of her catches tears dingy with mascara, like so many sooty raindrops.

When she is allowed to go to the cafeteria—only long enough to stand in line and get her food, with Ms. Brudie as an escort—Ainsley declines. She can't bear the idea of what people will say to her or about her. By now, news of her reversal of fortune will be everywhere. It's possible—likely, even—that her friends have defended her and possibly even spoken to teachers and the administration in protest. It won't do any good, but it makes Ainsley feel a little better when she imagines it.

The bathroom, however, can't be avoided. Ainsley waits until the last possible minute, but then she *has* to go. She stands and taps on the door. There isn't a clock in the room, so Ainsley has no idea what time it is; all she knows is that it is after lunch.

Ms. Brudie sets down her book—she's reading Dostoyevsky, which must be a joke or a prop—and writes Ainsley a pass for the bathroom. "You have five minutes before I come hunting you down," Ms. Brudie says. "Use the bathroom outside room one-oh-seven. It's the closest."

She won't lie: when she is in the hallway alone, Ainsley feels like running away. Out the door of the school, all the way home, never to return. She will be a tenth-grade high school dropout. She wends her way out of the dimly lit corridors to the main part of the school and finds a clock. It's only 12:50; there's still an hour and a half to go. Ainsley hurries to the girls' room across from room 107, then she realizes that room 107 is her chem class. She looks in the open door of the classroom—they're in lab—and catches Emma's eye. Ainsley doesn't know what she expects. An apology, some sign of contrition or desperation. Maybe Dutch *forced* Emma to say what she did; maybe he threatened to send her to a convent or even hurt her. But what Emma does is unexpected.

She gives Ainsley the finger.

TABITHA

Eleanor is a demanding and finicky patient. After she is released from the hospital, she and Tabitha repair to the town house on Pinckney Street, a place Tabitha had adored growing up but that now feels stale and glum. The house has a layer of dust throughout; there is a lavish bouquet in the niche in the entryway—a weekly delivery from Winston's for as long as Tabitha can remember—that has died and browned to a crisp.

"Mother," Tabitha says, "we need to bring Felipa up here with us. I won't be your nurse *and* your maid."

Eleanor sniffs.

"Or we can hire someone new," Tabitha says.

"Heavens, no," Eleanor says. "I can't have a complete stranger seeing me like this."

This is also Eleanor's excuse for not hiring a nurse.

"I'll call Felipa," Tabitha says. "She'll be here tomorrow."

Eleanor has an actual bell—an antique she inherited from her great-grandmother, who was a member of Boston society and a friend of Isabella Stewart Gardner—that she rings when she wants Tabitha to adjust her pillows or find *Law & Order* on the TV (Eleanor loves *Law & Order,* which is convenient, as the show pretty much plays twenty-four hours a day). Tabitha brings Eleanor fresh ice water, portions out her pain meds, and makes three trips a day to the Paramount on Charles Street—breakfast, lunch, and dinner. Tabitha would complain about this, but it gives her a chance to get outside. It's June, and the city is experiencing the most beautiful days of the year. The Common is lush and leafy. New mothers are out with their baby carriages, and there are skateboarders and bikers and joggers with their sinewy muscles; college girls in Ray-Bans and ponytails bob along, talking on their phones: *like like like.* Carefree. When Tabitha goes to fetch lunch for Eleanor, she ambles through the Boston Public Garden; she can always blame the delay on the Paramount's perpetual line. The garden is in full bloom—iris, peonies, roses. The pond is clear and clean, and the swan boats paddle along with barely a ripple.

Tabitha's childhood here had been storybook in many ways. Eleanor had taken Tabitha and Harper to the Boston Ballet to see *The Nutcracker,* to the Museum of Fine Arts to see the Renoir exhibition, and Billy had season tickets at Fenway. As a family, they had a regular table at Marliave on Friday nights because Eleanor loved the Welsh rabbit; they brunched on Sundays at Harvest in Cambridge. Tabitha first got drunk at a party in Grays Hall after the Head of the Charles regatta her sophomore year in high school and late that night puked at the feet of the John Harvard statue.

Her Boston pedigree is impeccable in its details, but after so many years on Nantucket, she now feels like a visitor—and, under present circumstances, a captive.

But she has no choice. She must care for Eleanor. When Harper calls with the news of Ainsley's suspension, however, Tabitha announces she's returning home.

"Please don't," Harper says. "It won't change anything. Ainsley is experiencing some pretty wicked backlash from her friends at school, and unfortunately this is my area of expertise. Being ostracized."

Tabitha is ashamed at how relieved she feels at being let off the hook. She is livid at Ainsley—she hates thinking that her daughter is capable of an act so stupid and cruel—but neither can she bear to think of Ainsley suffering at the hands of the other kids. She sends Ainsley a text.

Tabitha: *You okay?*

Ainsley: *What do you care?*

Tabitha: *I'm still your mother.*

Ainsley: *So?*

Tabitha: *So I love you.*

Ainsley: *Whatever, Tabitha.*

Tabitha reads this exchange over again and again until tears blur her eyes. She wants to go back to Nantucket and shake her daughter—or hug her. But she tells herself that the way to be the best parent right now is to stay away. If Tabitha were to walk in the house and take back the reins, Ainsley would do something even more destructive than she's already done. Tabitha is sure of it.

Deliverance shortly arrives in the person of Tabitha's aunt Flossie, Eleanor's sister, from Palm Beach.

Flossie is a firecracker. She's eight years younger than Eleanor, but she looks and acts like she's Tabitha's age. She is a self-declared trophy wife, married to an eighty-five-year-old descendant of Henry Flagler. She plays tennis, she shops, she lunches, and, in the winters, she works three days a week at the Eleanor Roxie-Frost boutique on Worth Avenue.

When Flossie arrives at the town house on Pinckney Street, she apologizes for not coming sooner. "I was on a cruise when you called, and then when I got home, I still didn't want to come. Boston is depressing, and my sister is a bitch on her best day. But then I thought about you. No one should be subjected to Eleanor like this. You've done enough, Pony." She makes a shooing motion with her hand. "I hereby set you free."

Tabitha goes up to her room to pack her things to go home—but then she remembers that she and Harper have a deal.

The thought is not unappealing: she will go to the Vineyard.

HARPER

Meghan is the most miserable pregnant person Harper has ever seen. It doesn't help that the island has been experiencing record high temperatures and that Meghan is four days past due. And yet still the poor creature comes to work at the boutique—because the boutique has air-conditioning and her house does not. She also wants to make sure Harper and Ainsley learn everything about the store before she goes into labor. Harper gets the feeling Meghan is saying a permanent good-bye; she has the giddy air of escape. But maybe that's just the hormones.

The Nantucket boutique is different from the Palm Beach store because, in addition to selling the Eleanor Roxie-Frost label, it sells Milly, Tibi, DVF, Nanette Lepore, Parker, Alice and Olivia, and Rebecca Taylor.

"This was Tabitha's idea, and she really had to push your mother to do it," Meghan confides. "I think Tabitha was growing weary of all ERF all the time."

"Tell me about it," Harper says. Working at the boutique is part of the deal, she knows, but she is, quite possibly, the least qualified woman in America to do so. In the twenty years she's lived on the Vineyard, she has spent a sum total of two or three minutes thinking about what to wear. Now, as she browses the racks and shelves of dresses and skirts, pants, blouses, summer-weight sweaters, halter tops, shorts, blazers, sandals, belts, scarves, and the impulse-buy display of lacy thong underwear and stick-on bras, she sees that maybe she has missed out. The prints, the silks, the sequins, the feathers—it's all alluring, sexy, chic.

"I'm going to be frank with you," Meghan says. Meghan's dishwater blond hair is pulled back in a sweaty bun, and her pale face is puffed like a marshmallow. Her fingers and ankles are swollen. She is wearing a stretch maternity dress in kelly green, which makes her look like a vegetable—a pea or a brussels sprout. "This store has a bad reputation."

"How so?" Harper says.

"People think we're snooty," Meghan says. "Because we *are* snooty. Your mother and your sister train us to sniff out who's buying big and who's not, and we are to treat the customers accordingly. Tabitha doesn't like browsers, and she positively hates tryer-oners."

Ainsley nods emphatically. "She complains about them all the time. The people who try on eight or nine different outfits but buy nothing."

"There are a couple of people she's banned from the store," Meghan says.

Harper laughs. "Is that even legal?"

"No," Ainsley and Meghan say together.

Meghan says, "She doesn't let men go into the dressing rooms because one time a couple had oral sex in there."

"The girl was loud. Everyone heard," Ainsley says.

"Good God," Harper says.

"Men have to stay in this part of the store," Meghan says. She points to two leather wing chairs over by the three-way mirror. "These are the appraising chairs."

"Or they can stand," Ainsley says. "But not within peeking distance of the dressing rooms."

"Classical music only," Meghan says. "I tried Billie Holiday one day..."

"Mom blew her stack," Ainsley says.

"There *is* one piece of good news," Meghan says. Then she places her hands under her prodigious belly and groans. "Braxton Hicks."

"Oh, dear," Harper says. Harper is getting a funny feeling about Meghan. She's like a champagne cork about to pop.

"The good news is that Mary Jo's son and daughter-in-law have finally intervened. They're moving her to a retirement community in Maryland, closer to them."

"Thank God," Ainsley says.

"So you get to hire someone new!" Meghan says.

"Or we can just do it ourselves," Harper says.

Meghan groans again. "You can't possibly do it yourselves," she says. "You'll lose your mind—I guarantee it. Place an ad and find someone with retail expertise. It doesn't have to be in fashion. Someone responsible but relaxed, firm but friendly. That's what this store needs to become—relaxed and friendly. A place where you're welcomed and remembered and talked to pleasantly, even if you do come in wearing culottes with Skechers. It's up to you guys to change the reputation of the Eleanor Roxie-Frost boutique on Nantucket. Before it goes under."

"Under?" Harper says.

"Sales stink," Meghan says. "That's another thing Tabitha seems to have her head in the sand about. This store has been losing money for years."

For the first time in practically ever, Harper feels a pang of sympathy for her mother and sister. In so many ways, they are their own worst enemies. It looks like it's up to her and Ainsley to rescue the store. She can just picture Tabitha and Eleanor shuddering at this thought.

"I'll give it a shot," she says.

* * *

It's nearly the end of school. Ainsley has only one half day left, which she is already pressuring Harper to let her skip.

"Don't you like the last day?" Harper asks. "Don't you all sign one another's yearbooks?"

Ainsley looks at her feet. She's wearing a pair of fancy flip-flops decorated with faux jewels—red, turquoise, yellow. The baubles look like gumballs. Harper was excited to see that Tabitha carries more flip-flops like this—Mystique sandals—in the boutique. Harper is going to get a tortoise-shell pair and wear them all summer long.

"Ainsley?"

"What?" Ainsley says. Each day after school she has been more somber and withdrawn than the day before. There have been no rides home with Emma or other friends. Just now, in the shop, she was the most lively she's been since her trip to the principal's office. "The half day is pointless. It has something to do with state mandates. No one is going to be *teaching*. I'd rather be at the boutique."

"Let me think about it," Harper says. She squints as she steps out of the cool, fragrant boutique onto the bright, busy street. She misses Edgartown, the Vineyard in general, Reed.

Reed is *gone?* Harper has done a gut check every day since Rooster told her this. Does she believe Reed has left the Vineyard, and, if so, where did he go? *Is* he looking for Harper? If he were looking for Harper, where would *he* go? Where would he think *she'd* gone?

The circular reasoning addles her.

He would never guess Nantucket. He knows Tabitha lives here, and he knows Harper and Tabitha don't speak.

Furthermore, Vineyarders don't go to Nantucket and vice versa. It's like some weird law: you pick one island or the other.

Harper likes caring for Ainsley because it limits the time she has to dwell on such things. "Let's get ice cream."

"Pharmacy," Ainsley says. "Not the Juice Bar. Kids from school will be at the Juice Bar."

"Pharmacy it is, then," Harper says.

A bell jingles as they walk in the door of the Nantucket Pharmacy. It's that kind of charming, old-fashioned place. There's a Formica lunch counter with vinyl-and-chrome stools. Ainsley and Harper take seats. There's a man in a shirt and tie sitting at the end of the counter eating a thick tuna-salad sandwich on pumpernickel bread.

"Hey, you!" Ainsley says.

"Hey, Trouble!" The man rises from his seat, and Harper realizes it's Ramsay, whom she had lunch with the week before. He scoops up Ainsley and hugs her tightly. Ainsley rests her head on Ramsay's chest and locks her arms behind his back. They are slow to part, and when they do, Harper sees that Ainsley's eyes are misty.

She comes right out and confesses. "I got suspended." Then she starts to cry.

Ramsay gathers her up again, shushes her, plants a kiss in the part of her hair. "I see growth," he says. "Because six months ago, you would have treated getting suspended like no big deal, maybe even like a badge of honor. Now at least you know better."

"Hello, Ramsay," Harper says.

Ramsay releases Ainsley and extends a hand to Harper. “It’s still eerie to me,” he says. “You two look exactly alike.”

Ainsley wipes her face with a paper napkin, leans across the counter, and orders a chocolate frappé. “What would you like?” Ainsley asks Harper.

Harper eyes Ramsay’s plate. “Bag of chips,” she says. “I prefer salty to sweet.”

“That would have been a dead giveaway,” Ramsay says. “Tabitha loves her sweets.”

“When she eats,” Ainsley says.

“When she eats,” Ramsay concedes.

A yellow bag of Lay’s appears in Harper’s hands. “Don’t let us keep you from your lunch,” she says. She checks the clock; it’s four thirty. “Or your dinner.”

“Lunch,” Ramsay says. “I’ve been working too hard.”

“Aunt Harper and I are going to start working at the boutique,” Ainsley says. “Mary Jo is moving to Maryland, so we get to hire someone new.”

“Wow,” Ramsay says. “I was certain Mary Jo would meet her peaceful end while refolding folded sweaters.”

“Do you know anyone who’s looking for a job?” Harper asks.

“I do, actually,” Ramsay says. He adjusts his glasses. “Let me take your cell number.”

“Okay,” Harper says. She gives him the number, which he programs into his phone, then she wonders if it’s okay to have given her number to Tabitha’s ex-boyfriend. “Who should I be on the lookout for?”

Ramsay clears his throat. “Her name is Caylee,” he says. “Caylee Keohane. She was bartending at the Straight Wharf, but she lost her job last week. I know she’s pretty desperate for something else.”

"Lost her job? Why?" Harper says.

"Some jerk grabbed her ass, and she dumped a drink in his lap," Ramsay says. "Management blamed her."

"Wait a minute," Ainsley says. "Is this the girl you're dating?"

"Was," Ramsay says. "We parted ways." He gives Harper a look. "Ultimately, she was too young."

"Have her call me," Harper says. She wonders if she can possibly hire Ramsay's ex-girlfriend to work at Tabitha's boutique. The longer she stays here, the more trouble she gets in. She waves at Ramsay. "No promises, but send me her info and I'll schedule an interview."

It will be interesting, anyway, to meet the woman Ramsay chose to replace Tabitha.

"Maybe we can hang out some weekend," Ramsay says. "You, me, and Ainsley. We could pack a picnic and go to the beach at Ram Pasture. Someone has to show you the island."

"That's a lovely offer," Harper says. "But we have to work."

"How about a week from Sunday?" Ramsay says. "The boutique will be closed. Day of rest and all that."

"I don't know," Harper says.

"Please?" Ainsley says. "Let's do it."

"Don't you want to hang out with your friends?" Harper asks.

Ainsley's face darkens. "Not really."

"Okay," Harper says to Ramsay. "That sounds like fun. Thank you."

On the way home, Ainsley sips her frappé in silence.

"I'm not sure about interviewing Ramsay's ex-girlfriend," Harper says. "Much less hiring her."

"Do it," Ainsley says. "Mom will flip. She was, like, *so* jealous when Ramsay started dating her. She's young. Like, just a few years older than me."

"What do you think about going to the beach with Ramsay next Sunday?" Harper says. "Is that something you want to do? We could blow him off and just go you and me and Fish instead. Fish is fun at the beach."

"I want Ramsay to come," Ainsley says. "Mom and I always went to the beach with Ramsay on Sundays before. I think I need some consistency in my life."

Harper laughs, though she's still not quite comfortable with the beach plans. When Harper and Tabitha were growing up, lots of people thought they were interchangeable. They looked exactly alike, so therefore they *were* exactly alike. But Ramsay isn't that simple, is he? He realizes that Harper isn't Tabitha, not at all. She has different proclivities and aversions, different passions, a different life philosophy. If he doesn't realize it now, he'll figure it out soon enough.

Harper is so consumed with these thoughts as they turn into the driveway and get out of the car that she doesn't notice the front of the carriage house until Ainsley screams. And once Ainsley screams, Fish starts barking from inside.

The front door, the porch, and the flagstone walk have been bombarded with raw eggs, probably four or five dozen of them. In the hot sun, it smells like a sulfurous fart.

Harper nearly gags, but she holds herself in check in front of Ainsley.

Sadie, she thinks. Sadie has found her here. In blue sidewalk chalk on the flagstone, it says: YOU SUCK EGGS.

Ainsley sees it and squawks.

"Emma," she says. "This was Emma. And Candace, too, maybe."

Harper closes her eyes. Of course it wasn't Sadie Zimmer. For the first time in her life, Harper understands what it feels like to be a parent: she wants to take every bullet; she wants to protect Ainsley from every insult and affront. Harper can handle an egging. But Ainsley races into the house, sobbing, her sparkling flip-flops crunching on the broken shells and sliding through the albumen slime.

Harper closes her eyes and sends a brief prayer for strength to the universe. Then the smell gets to her, and she vomits in the bushes.

At the beginning of the week, Harper interviews Caylee alone at a place called the Lemon Press on Centre Street, which Caylee suggested. The Lemon Press has Mocha Joe's coffee and an organic menu. Harper doesn't enjoy food that is aggressively healthy, but she has to admit that the offerings look delicious. Caylee has ordered an iced jasmine tea and an assortment of avocado toasts—some with radishes, some with heirloom tomatoes, some with hard-boiled egg. Unfortunately, at the sight of the egg, Harper feels queasy, hot, and dizzy. She orders a hot water with lemon.

Caylee is young—too young for Ramsay—and pretty in a wholesome way: long dark hair, big blue eyes, and a crooked nose that keeps her from being too beautiful. She has a tattoo of a pink ribbon on the inside of her wrist, and initially Harper thinks, *Uh-oh, tattoo,* but when Caylee sees Harper looking at it, she says, "I lost my mother to breast cancer three years ago."

Harper feels herself misting up. "I just lost my father," she says. "It's hard."

Caylee reaches a hand across the table and squeezes Harper's forearm.

"You're hired," Harper says. She doesn't care if Tabitha objects. Caylee is going to work at the boutique. Caylee has a fresh energy, and she looks great in all the clothes. She is bubbly and fun, she needs a job, and she can work whenever Harper schedules her to work—the more hours the better. She doesn't have any actual retail experience, but she spent all last summer and the first part of this summer bartending at the Straight Wharf, so her people skills and customer service are on point. Also, and possibly most important, she has friends—lots of friends, many of them girls from privileged families with unlimited discretionary income. Others work in the service industry on Nantucket, making hundreds of dollars in tips per night, and they just might need a new outfit for their days off.

When Caylee takes a tour of the store and picks out her six outfits, each one cuter than the last, she says, "I promise you—my friends have no idea you carry lines like Milly and Rebecca Taylor. They think it's just ERF, which is what our mothers wear. We have to get the word out. We have to have a party."

They plan the party for Friday, despite Meghan saying, "I'm going on the record. Tabitha would *not* allow a party in here. Never mind Eleanor."

"We need to lighten things up," Harper says. "We need a new image."

"We need *customers,*" Ainsley says. She, even more than Harper, has fallen under Caylee's spell. Caylee is kind and solicitous, sort of like an older sister. Harper understands the attraction. Ainsley needs a friend, especially since the egging. But Harper worries that Caylee is just a little bit too old. She's twenty-two, and her friends go to the bars at night—Cru, Nautilus, the Boarding House, the Chicken Box.

Harper has done her damnedest to keep an eye on Ainsley without seeming overbearing. There is always a glass next to Ainsley's bed, and Harper checks at every opportunity to make sure it contains water and not vodka. She sniffs Ainsley's bottles of Vitaminwater as well. So far so good.

Caylee posts news of the party on her Facebook page—when she announces that she has 1,100 "friends," Harper gasps—and sends it to a Nantucket news and social website called Mahon About Town as well as to a super-hot blog called Nantucket BlACKbook.

When Harper expresses doubt—she feels like they should send out proper invitations or place an ad in the newspaper—Caylee laughs.

"Everything is social media these days," she says. "You're just going to have to trust me."

They do their best to transform the space. They dim the lights on the enormous crystal chandelier. Why Tabitha insists on bright light when it's full sunshine outside is beyond Harper; possibly it's a concession to Eleanor's failing eyesight. They clear the sweaters from the pedestal table in the center of the room—the food will go there—and set up a bar over by the appraisal chairs.

"Spillage," Meghan says. "There's a reason why no decent store in America allows food or drink. People spill. They don't mean to, but they do. Tabitha had this carpet replaced this spring. I happen to know it cost eighteen thousand dollars."

Harper looks down at the carpet. It's a dull silver, the color of nickels. It matches the oyster-colored walls in its understated solemnity, but the silver, pewter, and gray palette screams *old age.*

"I don't care," Harper says.

The party is to be a happy hour from 4:00 to 5:30. Caylee, the bartender, makes a Foxy Roxie punch—vodka, champagne, mango nectar, and cranberry. (*Cranberry,* Harper thinks. *Sure to leave a stain.*)

Harper has prepared big bowls of truffled popcorn, a lavish crudités tray with three kinds of dip, and tiny avocado toasts like the ones from Lemon Press, only smaller. Harper wonders if they shouldn't have more food, since they're serving alcohol, but Caylee points out that no one wants to eat a lot before trying on clothes and that feeling a little buzzed always leads people to spend money.

Caylee and Ainsley's playlist includes: Rihanna, Beyoncé, Adele, Norah Jones, Alison Krauss, Miranda Lambert, Diana Krall, Gwen Stefani—and, as the token male, Prince.

Harper plans to have Fish on a leash by the front door, hoping he will be the store's best ambassador. There isn't a human alive who doesn't love a husky.

At quarter to four, Harper is so nervous that she feels dizzy, and she has to sit in the cool dark of the storeroom with her head between her knees. She hasn't thrown a party in recent memory other than at Billy's memorial reception—and that, of course, was an unmitigated disaster. Harper is positive no one will come. People will pass by on their way to more glamorous and fun venues, only peeking in to see Harper (wearing the Roxie because she feels obliged to, although she chose the cherry-bomb red version, which has far more sex appeal than the others), Ainsley (looking young and chaste in a white Nanette Lepore eyelet sundress), and Meghan (in a stretchy amethyst T-shirt dress that they don't even sell at the store, but it's now the only thing that fits her). The passersby will catch a whiff of desperation, of trying too hard, of a failing attempt to change the image of ERF, an image so indelible as to be chiseled in cold stone.

But . . . they will also see Caylee in white AG Stilts, a brightly patterned off-the-shoulder Rebecca Taylor blouse, and a great pair of wedge sandals, her long hair loose and flowing with one tiny braid off to the side for whimsy . . . and all of them will want to be just like her: beautiful, smiling, carefree.

Maybe Caylee can save them.

When Caylee hands Harper a cup of the punch, she takes a sip, but her stomach rears up in protest; it's probably best she stay sober anyway. She joins Ainsley and Meghan in pouring herself a cup of sparkling water. At five minutes to four, Harper ties a navy bandanna around Fish's neck and puts out the balloons. Caylee turns up the music.

Meghan drops her head into her hands with a groan, and Harper knows she's thinking about what Tabitha would say if she were here.

But, Harper thinks as she sips her water, *Tabitha isn't here.*

By quarter after four, there are twenty-five people in the store, half of them either trying on clothes or waiting for a dressing room. And people keep pouring in. Caylee is handing out punch left and right while Ainsley does the hand-selling.

"You want the sophistication of an LBD, but you're a redhead, so you should try forest green," Ainsley says. She holds up a silky slip dress that is actually an ERF style Eleanor designed right after her divorce. Meghan told Harper that she and Tabitha have nicknamed the dress the Midlife Crisis. It's popular with newly single women and women who have just discovered a husband's infidelity. ("Tabitha knows how to spot these women in an instant," Meghan said. "I'm sure she does," Harper said.)

Now Meghan is behind the cash register ringing up sales, and with each transaction she grows incrementally less morose. "This is working," she says. "I can't believe it."

People keep coming. Some of them are friends of Caylee's—they shriek when they see her, hug her, and announce how much they miss her at the Straight Wharf ("The new guy is such a dud. He needs more cowbell!"). They tell her how much they love her top, her pants, her shoes.

"We sell them all here," Caylee says.

The crowd begets a bigger crowd; everyone wants to be where the action is. Fish gamely accepts pats on his head and rubs on his back. His tail, curled up and over his hindquarters like a plume, wags for every new customer. He loves the spotlight. Someone feeds him a handful of popcorn; someone else slips him an avocado toast. He'll be sick later, of this Harper is certain, but his appeal is undeniable. Joan Osborne sings "Midnight Train to Georgia," and some of the women sing along.

"Great party!" a man's voice says. Harper spins around; it's Ramsay. He's dressed like a Kennedy cousin, as always: blue striped shirt turned back neatly at the cuffs; navy tie printed with beach balls; khakis; Gucci loafers without socks. He grins. "I've never seen the store this crowded. Ever. Not even close." He looks over Harper's shoulder at Meghan. "What do you say, Meg? Maximum number of shoppers at one time before today: five?"

"Four," Meghan says. "And even those instances I can count on one hand."

"Well, it's all thanks to Caylee," Harper says. "Thank you for suggesting her. This party was her idea, and as you can see she's the belle of the ball." Together Harper and Ramsay look upon the cluster of beautiful young ladies surrounding Caylee in obvious worship. Harper feels a twinge of jealousy—not for herself but for Tabitha. Even if Tabitha was the one who broke up with Ramsay, it couldn't have been easy to see him start dating someone as young and magnetic as Caylee.

"Caylee is a good kid," Ramsay says. Both his tone of voice and his gaze are avuncular. "I thought it would be a playboy fantasy, dating someone who's twenty-two. Plus, I wanted to piss off your sister..."

"Yeah," Harper says.

"But it was more like babysitting. She cries when she's drunk."

"Doesn't everyone?" Harper says.

"And I had to explain things," Ramsay says. "She didn't know who Van Morrison was. She didn't know who *Bob Dole* was. And why would she? She was an infant when he ran for president."

"Right," Harper says, thinking of Drew—poor Drew, who had professed his love for her and changed his Facebook status to "in a relationship." "Well, this boutique needs her youthful energy, her fresh ideas."

"I'm glad it's working out," Ramsay says. "I just stopped by to lend my support and to remind you about the beach on Sunday. I'll swing by at noon to pick you and Ainsley up."

"Oh," Harper says. She still feels uneasy about the beach date, but she can't come up with an excuse that will get her out of it. "Okay."

Ramsay blows Ainsley a kiss on his way out. "See you Sunday."

Ramsay isn't the only man at the party. As they move into the five o'clock hour, all kinds of men wander in. Some of them are servers at restaurants, already wearing white shirts and black aprons knotted at their waists, but there are also guys just off fishing boats and off the golf course. There's a clean-cut kid in a shirt and tie who looks like he stepped out of Ramsay's office. These men shyly accept punch from Caylee, then self-consciously browse for something they might buy for their girlfriends. Most are clueless. *What size should I get?* They hold up a skirt in a size 14, shoes in a 5½. Ainsley tries to help, as does Caylee—she knows some of these guys and their significant others—and Meghan facilitates the impulse buys at the register. They start out with a huge glass jar filled with

Hanky Panky lace thongs; Meghan sells at least one pair to every single man who walks out of the store.

Prince sings "Kiss." A collective hoot goes up, and women start to dance. Ainsley races over to the iPod and starts to DJ. Soon the store looks like South Beach at three in the morning.

Meghan's eyes widen. "This keeps getting more and more surreal."

Ainsley appears happy, and Harper feels a sense of accomplishment. Tabitha and Eleanor may take umbrage with the party, they may claim that Harper is cheapening the ERF brand with frivolity and fun, but neither of them can argue with the expression on Ainsley's face.

Just as Harper is congratulating herself, however, the smile falls from Ainsley's lips as fast as a jumper falls off a bridge. Harper follows her eyes to the front door. Two girls have just walked in, arms linked. One is dark-haired, one strawberry blond—both of them, like Ainsley, look way older than they probably are. The dark-haired one reaches out eagerly for a cup of punch, but Caylee lifts the punch beyond the girl's reach. "Sorry, but I have to see ID."

"At a free party?" the dark-haired girl says. "A free party at a tired old-lady boutique?"

Harper is about to march over and take care of the little hellcat, but Ainsley steps forward.

"Emma," she says. "Candace."

"Hey, Ainsley!" Emma says, in a voice of mock surprise. "We came to get a dress for Candace. Teddy is taking her out for dinner tonight."

Ainsley nods, and Harper sees the brave set of her jaw. *Hold steady,* Harper thinks. *You can do this.*

"Where are you going?" Ainsley asks.

Candace shrugs. "Ventuno."

"Nice," Ainsley says.

"He sent her flowers today," Emma says. "He wants her to wear one in her hair tonight. Isn't that the most romantic thing you've ever heard?"

Ainsley's eyes harden, and—whoa!—Harper gets a chill. In that instant, Ainsley looks exactly like Tabitha. Harper knows what's coming: *Fuck you, Emma.*

Go ahead, Harper thinks. *Say it.*

But before Ainsley can speak, there is a shriek, loud enough to rise above "Hollaback Girl." The sound puts an instantaneous end to the dancing. It came from Meghan. She is standing with her legs akimbo, and water gushes out of her onto the sumptuous silver-gray carpeting of the ERF boutique.

"My water broke!" she cries. "The baby is coming!"

TABITHA

She can't believe the freedom she feels when she drives off the ferry in Oak Bluffs. For the first time in a long, long time, Tabitha doesn't have to take care of anyone—not her mother, not her daughter. She can do whatever *she* wants. She can be her own person. It's completely novel.

Harper, of course, has lived like this for years and years. She had Billy—but Billy was nothing like Eleanor. He didn't make demands or requests or assumptions; he didn't hold impossibly high expectations. Harper has had it so easy.

Tabitha drives down Circuit Avenue in Oak Bluffs, past a place called the Ritz that advertises LIVE MUSIC TONIGHT and emits the mouthwatering smell of char-grilled burgers.

Burgers. Live music. Tabitha will drop her things off at Billy's and come back to the Ritz for dinner. Even thinking about this makes her feel like a new person.

Billy's house really is bad. It reeks of cigarettes and dog—Tabitha shudders, imagining Fish peeing and shedding all over the carriage house—and the whole thing is shabby, stale, outdated, and ugly. Billy always made a good living, but he never invested any of it in his domicile. The furniture would be at home circled around a hobo campfire. The recliner—ugh! The kitchen—ick!

Tabitha is nothing if not organized. She wanders the first floor, making notes about what she would do if Harper agrees: pull up carpet, refinish floors, gut kitchen (despite the fact that she doesn't cook, it has always been Tabitha's dream to renovate a kitchen), paint everything, get a new toilet and sink for the powder room, buy new light fixtures (it looks as though Billy has salvaged only the most hideous fixtures from his twenty years on this island and installed them in his own house), and order brand-new furniture. (Houzz! Wayfair! One Kings Lane! Tabitha has scoured these websites late into the night for years, dreaming of the imaginary rooms she would someday curate.)

Upstairs, she appraises the bedrooms—her father's and the lavender room that used to be Harper's; the Hootie & the Blowfish poster is still on the wall. The third bedroom, Tabitha's old room, still has the god-awful beige wall-to-wall carpeting, but the walls have been painted light blue. What color was it when Tabitha used to stay here so long ago? She doesn't remember. The window over the neatly made full-size bed looks out on the backyard. At this time of day, the room is the recipient of bountiful golden sunlight. Billy could easily have used it as his office instead of the dining table downstairs. Or, as in other homes, the room might have held an underutilized piece of exercise equipment or cast-off furniture. But it's clean and empty except for the bed, as though it has been waiting for her to come back.

She closes her eyes, and tears leak out. *I'm here, Daddy,* she thinks. *I'm here now.*

Tabitha did some research: Billy's bank account holds ninety-two thousand dollars. To do what she envisions, she will have to use all that and tap into her own reserves. This is a little scary, considering that Ainsley is heading to college in two years, but Tabitha will pay herself back out of the proceeds from the sale, and, since she's doing all the work, she will pay herself a salary. All she needs is for Harper to agree. Harper is against renovating because Harper is timid and unimaginative. She doesn't understand what Tabitha is capable of.

Before she heads out for dinner, Tabitha realizes that she needs to call Ainsley and Harper and tell them she's here.

Ainsley doesn't answer her cell phone, and neither does Harper. Well, that makes sense. The boutique stays open late on Friday nights, and they should both be at work. She calls the boutique, but no one answers. Tabitha puzzles over this and gets a bad feeling. Then, a second later, Meghan calls from her cell phone. She is in the storage room—Tabitha can tell just by the way her voice reverberates off the concrete floors.

"Tabitha?" Meghan says.

"Can I talk to my daughter, please?" Tabitha says. "Or my sister?"

"Um," Meghan says. "They're busy."

"Busy?" Tabitha says. She assumes this is a euphemism for *They cut out of work early so they could have cocktails at the Gazebo.* She starts to tremble with anger and frustration. She should never have left Ainsley in Harper's care.

"They're with customers," Meghan says.

"Both of them?" Tabitha says.

"Both of them," Meghan says. "We're slammed right now."

"Slammed?" Tabitha says. This sounds like a snow job. In all the years she has been running the boutique, she would never have described it as slammed. It's not a slammed kind of place, despite Tabitha's efforts to diversify the inventory. The ERF boutique is similar to the art galleries in town; it's for interested and serious buyers only. And Eleanor refuses to put anything on sale. *Sale* means "dirty" in French, and that's exactly what Eleanor thinks of the word. It's dirty. Every ERF piece evokes a classic timelessness, a quality that should never be discounted. Every once in a while, a group of well-heeled women will come in off someone's enormous yacht and indulge in competitive shopping, but that kind of behavior pretty much petered out when the economy failed in 2008. "So you're telling me that they're both there but that they're too busy to come to the phone?"

"That's what I'm telling you," Meghan says. "And I was in the middle of helping someone as well when you called the store line." She pauses, and Tabitha thinks she hears music, voices; she hears a dog bark. A dog? Surely she's mistaken. "So I'd better hang up..."

"Okay," Tabitha says. She is still suspicious, but her stomach is rumbling, and she's thinking about the burgers and live music in her future. She should ask about Meghan's pregnancy, but she doesn't want the answer to ruin her night. As long as Meghan is in charge, Tabitha doesn't have to worry that there's a dog in the store or that merchandise has been put on sale or that any other protocols are being broken. Once Meghan goes into labor, it will be another story. "Have one of them call me as soon as she's free, please. Either. Both."

"You got it," Meghan says. She sounds eager to end the call.

Tabitha stares at her phone. Should she worry about the store? she wonders. She probably should, but she doesn't want to. She's off to the Ritz.

Going out by herself in a strange town is an unfamiliar experience, but rather than being self-conscious, Tabitha is energized. She has tried to dress down—white AG Stilts and a pink-and-orange Trina Turk halter top—and she put her hair in a ponytail and went light on the makeup in an attempt to convey that this is no big deal.

From the outside, the Ritz Café looks like a dive. Does Tabitha care? Is she going to be a snob about the establishment? No. She enters with a smile fastened securely to her face, her best accessory.

The bar is dark and smoky and completely mobbed. Tabitha nearly turns around—back to the safety of her FJ40, back to Vineyard Haven, back to Billy's house. And then tomorrow, back to Nantucket. But she hears the strum of a guitar, and she turns to see a guy in jeans and a Mocha Mott's T-shirt sitting on a stool behind a microphone. The blackboard behind him says: THE VINEYARD'S OWN FRANKLIN PHELPS. The Vineyard's own Franklin Phelps is around Tabitha's age and incredibly hot. He has dark shaggy hair and big brown eyes, and he rests his guitar casually over one knee. When the Vineyard's own Franklin Phelps sees Tabitha, he waves, and she thinks, *He knows me!*

But then she gets it.

Franklin starts playing "Carolina in My Mind," by James Taylor, and a cheer goes up.

There's a seat at the bar, despite the crowd. Tabitha sits and smiles at the bartender, a young woman with clear eyes and a friendly smile.

"Hey, Harper," she says. "Long time no see! You want a beer and a shot?"

Tabitha opens her mouth to correct the young lady. *I'm not Harper.* But the bar is loud, and this girl actually seems to like Harper, so Tabitha sees no harm in nodding. Beer and a shot? Sure! Tabitha has never had a beer and a shot in all her life. Maybe she's been missing out.

The drinks appear—a tall golden pilsner glass full of beer with a neat half inch of foam and a shot of some purplish-brown liquid. Tabitha lifts the shot glass for a discreet sniff.

Dear God: Jägermeister.

She throws it back, trying not to cry, and chases it with a long draught of her beer. Her chest instantly warms. The Vineyard's own Franklin Phelps segues into "Wild World" by Cat Stevens, which is a particular favorite of Tabitha's, and she lets out a little fan shriek. She is so embarrassed that such a noise came from her mouth that she drinks more of her beer.

So this, she thinks, *is what it's like to be Harper.*

A man sits next to her at the bar. He's tall and good-looking in a wealthy-jerk kind of way. He's wearing a pressed red-and-white gingham shirt turned back at the cuffs and a golf visor printed with the name of some bank, even though it's dark outside.

He says, "What's up, pretty lady?"

Tabitha rolls her eyes.

"You look like a tourist," Visor Man says. He signals the bartender, and a gin and tonic lands in front of him. He takes most of the drink in one swallow. "Are you a tourist? Don't tell me: let me guess. You're from New Canaan, right? Or no, wait: Greenwich!"

Tabitha takes offense. If anyone looks like a tourist, or at least not like a local, it's this guy. He's wearing an Audemars Piguet watch with a black lizard strap, which Tabitha knows costs five figures. He has a way about him that broadcasts a lifetime of privilege, private schools, and money, money, money.

"Neither," Tabitha says. "I live on Nantucket."

Visor Man throws his head back and laughs. "What a coincidence!" he says.

She cocks an eyebrow at him. Coincidence? Does she know this guy?

"I'm the man from Nantucket!" he says. Tabitha closes her eyes and hopes that when she opens them again, this jerk will be gone. But...he remains. There is also, however, a second shot of Jägermeister, which has materialized out of nowhere. She throws it back without hesitation.

"I've been to Nantucket, you know," Visor Man says. "I've been to the Chicken Box. You ever been there? Great bar, live music, but no chicken. Not one piece of chicken."

When the music stops, the noise of the crowd gets louder. Tabitha would like to get this guy off her shoulder; he's drunk. But he is, at least, someone to talk to, so she'll give him the benefit of the doubt for thirty seconds longer. "I haven't been to the Box in a long time," she says. She peers over the bar into the kitchen. Is anyone working back there? "Do you happen to know if I can still order a burger? I'm starving."

Visor Man is absolutely not listening to her. "Where's your husband?"

"I'm not married," Tabitha says.

"You're divorced?" Visor Man asks. "Did you come out to the Vineyard with your big fat alimony check looking for some action?"

That's it, Tabitha thinks. She's done. This guy is such a jackass that he makes Captain Peter look like a catch. Where are all the nice, normal men? she wonders. The ones with interesting jobs, smart senses of humor, and compassionate, kind hearts? *They're at home,* she thinks. With their wives and their well-behaved children. They're certainly not out at a bar like this, looking to pick up someone like her. She needs to meet someone during the day. She should take up sailing, maybe—or golf.

She needs to break free of Visor Man posthaste, but the bar is crowded and there's nowhere else to go. Then Tabitha feels a hand on her shoulder. She turns to see Franklin Phelps holding his guitar by the neck as though it were a strangled goose.

"Harper," he says. "I thought maybe you'd gone for good."

Visor Man slams back the rest of his drink and gets to his feet, swaying like a tree in the breeze. "Hey, I was talking to the tourist."

"Back off, pal," Franklin Phelps says. He elbows Visor Man out of the way and takes his stool. Then he beckons to Friendly Bartender Girl and says, "Caroline, can I get a Guinness, shot of Jameson, please?"

Beer and a shot, Tabitha says to herself. For a brief moment, she feels like she's starting to figure things out.

Visor Man squares his shoulders. "I was sitting there."

"Go home, bud," Franklin says. "You're drunk."

"Are you the husband?" Visor Man says. He looks at Tabitha with the eyes of a wild killer. "Or are you just banging her?"

In an instant, Franklin Phelps is on his feet. He launches Visor Man across the bar so that he collides in a tangle with the mike stand and Franklin's stool. Visor Man doesn't even try to get up.

"That's Tripp Malcolm," Caroline, the bartender, says. "He owns that big fat house at the end of Tea Lane."

"I could not"—here Franklin Phelps takes a sip of Guinness, winks at Tabitha, and throws back his whiskey shot—"care less. I do not pander to the summer money."

Tripp Malcolm gets to his feet and charges Franklin like a bull. Franklin grabs his beer and moves deftly out of the way so that Tripp slams into the bar, where he breaks a glass.

"That's it! You're out, Tripp!" Caroline says. She shakes her head at Franklin and Tabitha. "I don't pander to the summer money, either."

Franklin points to Tabitha. "Put Harper's drinks on my tab, Caroline. We're leaving."

* * *

Tabitha wakes up at three in the morning in an unfamiliar bedroom . . . next to Franklin Phelps.

This is happening, Tabitha thinks. She squeezes Franklin's bicep, and he stirs and reaches an arm around to cup her ass. She throws her leg over his. This is happening!

He raises her chin and kisses her. "I've never wanted anyone like this before."

She would love to believe this is true. It's certainly true for her. Sex with Wyatt was fun for exactly eight weeks—then Tabitha got pregnant. After she split from Wyatt, Tabitha dated Monroe, who was the son of one of Eleanor's friends. He was elegant and appropriate and had a stick up his ass; he wouldn't initiate sex unless they had both just showered. That pretty much said it all.

And sex with Ramsay was fine for a while, but then it became exhausting both physically and emotionally. Ramsay had wanted, so badly, to please her. He had done everything short of handing her a survey afterward. Did she like it better on top or on bottom? On her stomach? Lights on or off? How did she feel about massage oil? Were her orgasms more or less intense than the ones she'd had on Thursday? Because to him it sounded like she'd been more into it on Thursday. Also, Ramsay didn't like to have sex after they'd been drinking, because he'd read that alcohol dulled women's nerve endings and he didn't want her to have a subpar experience—or, God forbid, one she couldn't fully remember. *Are you kidding me?* Tabitha thought. What was the point of going out drinking if you weren't going to enjoy some off-the-wall sex afterward?

Alcohol consumption lowered inhibitions; *that* was the time to try the things that might have embarrassed you when you were sober. But Ramsay hadn't seen it that way.

Tabitha doesn't kiss Franklin so much as taste him, and then, soon after, devour him. He's alive—sweaty, salty, strong. His fingers press into her arms, most likely leaving bruises; his mouth opens on her neck in a place that sends nearly painful waves of ecstasy through her. When his fingertips find her nipples, she groans. Nothing has ever felt this good—the sweet longing, the strain of not screaming, not swearing, not striking out. She locks her legs around him. For the first time ever, Tabitha indulges her animal instincts. She is a woman, Franklin is a man, they are coupling, it's natural, it's nature. How has sex never struck her this way before? It had been something to enjoy or endure, but it had never been a revelation.

Until now. Franklin.

This is happening.

She barely knows him, but that doesn't matter. They fit. They lock together like two pieces of a puzzle. Tabitha rides him up and down until she cries out and he cries out, his hands clenching her waist. She falls on top of him, exhausted.

He says, "You are the most breathtaking woman I have ever seen."

She laughs. "What about my sister? She looks exactly like me."

"You're so different from Harper," he says. "More elegant, more pulled together, more graceful. It's funny, because now I can see how distinctive you are."

"Yeah, right," Tabitha says. It wasn't until they stepped out onto Circuit Avenue that Tabitha confessed she wasn't Harper but rather her twin sister.

Ahh, Franklin had said. *I heard there was a twin.*

I'm Tabitha Frost, she said. *Sorry to disappoint you.*

That was when Franklin reached for her hand. *Are you kidding me?* he said. *That's the best news I've heard all night.*

Now Franklin grabs her chin. "I would never have gone home with Harper. You need to know that. I was friends with her..."

"Was?" Tabitha says.

"Was? Am, I guess. I don't know. She made some questionable choices..."

"She was sleeping with our father's doctor," Tabitha says.

"Reed Zimmer," Franklin says quietly.

"You know about that?" Tabitha says. "Everyone on the Vineyard knows about that?"

"Pretty much," Franklin says.

"I'm not Harper," Tabitha whispers.

"I know," Franklin says. "I can tell." He starts to sing "Here Comes the Sun" by the Beatles. His voice is so clear and true that Tabitha is nearly encouraged to sing along. She *does* sing along, and the moment is so incredibly romantic that Tabitha allows herself to believe that she sounds okay. When they are finished—*doo do doo do*—she rests her head on his chest, and he rubs her shoulder.

"You know what?" she says.

"What?" he says.

"I'm starving."

"Stay right there," he says.

It's the best meal she's ever had at four in the morning, maybe the best meal she's ever had, period: a pastrami-and-Swiss sandwich with tangy bread-and-butter pickles and horseradish mustard on Portuguese bread that Franklin has griddled until the bread turned golden brown and the Swiss melted and the whole thing became a gorgeous, gooey mess. They eat their sandwiches in bed, and Franklin pops open two icy Cokes, the first sip of which is so crisp and snappy it makes Tabitha's eyes water.

The sandwich is ridiculously delicious. "You can really cook," she says with her mouth full. She's grateful her mother can't see her in this moment, for many reasons. She pops a pickle that has fallen onto the sheet in her mouth. "So who *are* you?"

Franklin George Phelps: he has one sister, Sadie, eighteen months younger. His parents, Al and Lydia Phelps, are still married. They live in a house out in Katama, a house his father inherited from his own parents, who used it as a summer cottage. Al and Lydia winterized the house and raised Franklin and Sadie there. Al was the principal of Martha's Vineyard Regional High School for thirty-five years, and Lydia baked pies. Now they go to Vero Beach in the winter.

"It's amazing everyone on the Vineyard isn't bipolar," Franklin says. "This island is one place in the summer and another in the winter."

"Same with Nantucket," Tabitha says. She often wonders if this isn't the cause of Ainsley's troubles. The winter is quiet and boring. It's too cold to go outside, but there is nothing to do inside. Everything closes down; everyone leaves. Then in the summer, there is too much to do and not enough time to cram it all in. Tabitha works all the time, and there are social commitments nearly every night. The people who come to Nantucket are wealthy and privileged, even the kids. Especially the kids! They have access to their parents' boats; they have access to their parents' pills. Girls like Ainsley and Emma struggle to keep up, Tabitha knows.

Franklin managed better than most kids, he says. He played tight end on the football team and sang in a garage band with three guys in his class.

"You must have been quite a stud," Tabitha says. She feels jealous of all the girls she is sure he's bedded. Probably every desirable girl on the Vineyard. Tabitha is so enthralled that she can't think of another man with the appeal of Franklin Phelps—not Clooney, not Pitt, not Downey junior.

"I had a girlfriend," Franklin says. "Same girlfriend from seventh grade until halfway through junior year in college. Patti Prescott." He exhales, and Tabitha recognizes the sound of ancient pain.

Tabitha sets their empty plates on the dresser and climbs under the comforter. "What happened to Patti?"

"She was brilliant," Franklin says. "She went to Williams. But…she came home halfway through her junior year. I was doing a semester in London. I knew she was battling depression, because she couldn't get out of bed some days. I would call her from a pay phone, but I could only talk for a few minutes. Her parents sent her to a shrink, then the shrink put her on meds, and they thought she was getting better."

Tabitha pulls the covers up to her chin. *Have you ever lost anyone?*

"She killed herself in her parents' garage," Franklin says. "Carbon monoxide poisoning."

"Oh, no," Tabitha says. "I am so sorry."

"It was tough," Franklin says. "I carried guilt about it for a long time."

"Guilt?" Tabitha asks. "Why?"

"I should have come home," he says. "I should have come home and saved her. But I didn't. I was too busy drinking pints at the Flask in Hampstead, playing rugby, and singing for money in Regent's Park. I think her parents hold me responsible. It's a small island; everyone here knows me. I think a bunch of people hold me responsible."

"No," Tabitha says. "Certainly not."

"It's okay," Franklin says. "The rumor mill is part of the island, and the island is my home. I love it here." He kisses her until she feels dizzy. *This is happening.*

When she wakes up, it is bright daylight, and Franklin is gone.

"Hello?" Tabitha says experimentally. The door to the bathroom is open; Tabitha can see Franklin's toothbrush in a glass by the sink. She didn't have a chance or the wherewithal to check the place out when they walked in the night before, but she's relieved to see only one toothbrush. He's a bachelor, as he said. *Did* he say that? Or did she assume? She checks the nightstand: the sandwich plates are gone.

Tabitha gets out of bed and finds her clothes—her white pants are flung over a chair, the Trina Turk halter is a puddle of crumpled silk on the floor. Tabitha can honestly say she has never done this before: slept with a nearly complete stranger—okay, a complete stranger—and then woken up in said complete stranger's house forced to put on her clothes from the night before and find her way home.

Where is she?

She peers out the window and sees her FJ40 on the street. *Yes!* she thinks. She remembers that Franklin offered to drive it back here.

Once she's dressed, she creeps down the stairs. "Hello?" she says. The house is quiet. She tiptoes through the living room past a moss-green velvet sofa with coordinating throw pillows in various textures and patterns. A woman's touch? she wonders. In the kitchen, she finds a pot of coffee brewed, her clutch purse (thank God!), and a note. The note says: *Had to go to work. Thanks for a great night! xo*

Tabitha sets the note down and checks through her purse for her wallet and phone. Both accounted for.

She reads the note again. *Had to go to work.* Where does Franklin work? Did he tell her? Does he have a job other than playing the guitar? He did a semester abroad in London, but did he say what he was studying? She didn't see what he drove. Was there a car or truck in the driveway when they got here? She has no idea. There must have been, otherwise how did he get to work?

Thanks for a great night! Well, it *was* a great night, but something about him thanking her feels yucky. There is no mention of getting together again, and he did not leave his number.

She has to admit she's crushed.

It was a one-night stand, she tells herself. Just because it ranked as one of the best nights of her life doesn't mean he felt the same. Men don't take dalliances like this seriously.

But what about that thing he said? *I've never wanted anyone like this before.* He probably says that to all the women he brings home. Why wouldn't he? It's a very effective line. What about calling her breathtaking? What about the sandwich? Does he make pastrami sandwiches from heaven for all his conquests? Are there other conquests? He's a *singer* at a *bar*—of course there are other conquests!

What about telling Tabitha the story of Patti Prescott? He gave her a peek into his sweet, soft heart. That was a real, adult conversation; it was *intimate.*

Tabitha can't believe he didn't leave his number or ask for her number. She can't believe how much she cares. Probably Franklin thinks she's the kind of woman who does this all the time. It's no big deal to him. Why should it be a big deal to her? She needs to shake it off.

She pours herself a cup of coffee. There is a speckled ceramic pitcher of cream set out, and the sugar bowl is full. She feels like searching through the refrigerator and his cabinets. She wants to peruse all the photographs on the living-room shelves, see pictures of his family, maybe even of Patti Prescott. But if she's never going to see him again, what's the point?

She takes a sip of coffee, then abandons the cup on the counter. When he sees it, he'll be forced to think of her. She's tempted to leave her number, but that feels too forward, and she doesn't want to spend the next few days wondering if he's going to call.

It's a small island, she reasons. If he wants to see her, he'll find a way.

When she gets back to Billy's house, she realizes she never heard from either Ainsley or Harper. It's only twenty after nine, and the boutique doesn't open until ten, so no one will be at the store just yet. Tabitha doesn't quite trust either Harper or Ainsley to tell her the truth about exactly what's going on, so Tabitha calls Meghan's cell phone.

Meghan answers after five rings, sounding very, very groggy. "Hello?"

"Meghan?" Tabitha says. "It's me. Are you okay?" It seems like she might have woken Meghan up—but today is Saturday, the first of July. The store is open, and Meghan needs to be there.

"I'm fine," Meghan says. She pauses. "I'm a mommy."

"A what?" Tabitha says. Then she gets it. "Oh, my goodness! Did you have the *baby?*"

"Last night at eight o'clock," Meghan says. "A little boy. We named him David Wayne Mitzak. He weighed nine pounds two ounces and measured twenty-three inches long."

Tears unexpectedly gather in Tabitha's eyes. She's so, so happy for Meghan, but she's also thinking of Julian. "I'm thrilled for you, Meghan. Congratulations."

"Thank you," Meghan says. Another pause. "So I assume you heard about the party, then?"

"Party?" Tabitha says. Both her joyous and bittersweet feelings pop like soap bubbles. "What party?"

"Oh, I'm sorry. I thought... I mean, since you didn't know I'd had the baby I figured you were calling because you were upset about the party at the store."

Tabitha blows a breath out through her nose. Her head aches, and she desperately needs a shower, although she doesn't want to wash Franklin's scent off. Has she ever felt that way about a man before? Nope: never. But even her afterglow seems inconsequential when compared to the phrase *party at the store.*

"What party at the store?" she says evenly.

"For the record, I knew you wouldn't approve," Meghan says. "I told them it was a terrible idea, but I got outvoted."

"Outvoted by whom?" Tabitha says. "Harper, Ainsley, and Mary Jo?"

"Mary Jo left the island," Meghan says. "Didn't Harper tell you? Marissa and Scott moved her down to Maryland finally."

Finally, Tabitha thinks. However, this small piece of good news does little to assuage the sense of dread mounting inside her. "Tell me about the party, Meghan."

"The good news is that the party brought a lot of foot traffic into the store," Meghan says. "Like, a *lot* of foot traffic. I rang up over six thousand dollars in sales before my water broke."

"Your water broke at the party?" Tabitha says. "Your water broke in the *store?*"

"On the carpet," Meghan says. "I'm so sorry, Tabitha. Harper said she was calling the carpet cleaners today. Not only because my water broke but also because of spillage."

"Spillage?" Tabitha says. This is, quite possibly, her least favorite word in the English language.

"There was punch," Meghan says. "It was called the Foxy Roxie punch. It had cranberry juice in it."

"Cranberry juice!" Tabitha says. She lowers her voice, remembering that Meghan is in the hospital with an hours-old baby. She doesn't want to upset Meghan and be responsible for souring the woman's breast milk. Tabitha staggers over to Billy's recliner. Despite being as ugly as a hairless rat, it's very comfortable. Tabitha would like the recliner to swallow her up.

"And there was popcorn," Meghan says. Her voice becomes livelier, and Tabitha can tell she's starting to relish her role as tattletale—either that or the hormones are kicking in. Or possibly Meghan has been waiting for the last seven years to deliver this kind of devastating news to Tabitha as payback for any and all of the ways Tabitha and Eleanor might have mistreated her. "And Harper made these avocado toasts with different toppings. They were delicious. And there was music. Loud music. People were dancing. To Beyoncé and Prince."

Tabitha closes her eyes and imagines Ainsley's Snapchat: Harper and Ainsley toasting with cranberry punch before spilling it all over the freakishly expensive carpet, Meghan cramming pieces of avocado toast into her mouth until her water breaks all over the aforementioned carpet, couples doing *God knows what* in the dressing rooms. Women dancing to "Little Red Corvette" and grinding popcorn into the now ruined carpet with their stiletto heels. Tabitha isn't sure why she's so shocked that Harper saw fit to throw a rave in the most hallowed, elegant retail space on Nantucket, among dresses that cost anywhere between seven and fourteen hundred dollars apiece, but she is. It demonstrates an appalling lack of judgment, even for Harper.

Tabitha pushes herself up and out of Billy's recliner. She's so livid she's calm. She scares herself with how calm she is. Her next step is obvious: she needs to hop on the ferry back to Nantucket. She won't tell Meghan this, however, because Meghan might warn Harper, and Tabitha wants to catch Harper by surprise.

She channels her inner Doris Day and feigns a *que será será* attitude. She says, "Well, the good news is we get to hire someone new to replace Mary Jo."

"We already hired someone new," Meghan says, and her voice falters.

"We did?" Tabitha says. "Who?"

"I think you'd better call Harper," Meghan says.

"Who is it, Meghan?" Tabitha asks.

Meghan says, "They're bringing the baby in for me to feed. I'll send you pictures. Thanks for calling, Tabitha. Bye!" She hangs up.

Tabitha stares at her phone as Meghan's name vanishes from her screen. Harper hired someone new, and from the sounds of it, Tabitha won't like who it is. Of course Tabitha won't like who it is! Tabitha needs to go home right this second and take control of the wheel.

The weird thing—no, the truly bizarre and novel thing is... Tabitha doesn't want to. Let Harper ruin the store! Let her face Eleanor's inevitable wrath! Let her defile the entire ERF brand—which their mother started building decades ago, which she sacrificed her marriage to Billy for!

Tabitha doesn't care. Tabitha isn't going to jump in and save the day again. Tabitha isn't going to take yet another slap meant for Harper. Tabitha is going to stay put. After all, she and Harper had a deal. Harper is in charge on Nantucket now, and Tabitha is in charge here on the Vineyard. Harper did what she wanted without consulting Tabitha, and now... well, now Tabitha is going to do likewise. She is going to renovate this house, Harper be damned!

Tabitha looks around the living room, newly energized. She is going to turn this toad into a prince.

AINSLEY

She feels like a traitor and a heel, but on Sunday morning, when Aunt Harper goes to the hospital to give Meghan her baby present—after only two hours in labor, she delivered David Wayne Mitzak—Ainsley claims a migraine.

"I need to sleep," Ainsley says.

Harper gives her a skeptical look.

"Please," Ainsley says. "It's eight o'clock on a Sunday."

"You've known Meghan a lot longer than I have," Harper says.

"She's a bitch," Ainsley says. "Kidding. Give her my love. But who names a baby Wayne, anyway? It's like a name from one of those silent westerns."

Harper shakes her head. "You're not getting out of going to the beach," she says. "Ramsay is coming at noon."

"Fine," Ainsley says. "I'll be ready. I just have to sleep now."

"I'm leaving Fish here to keep an eye on you," Harper says.

Ainsley pulls the quilt up over her head.

* * *

Ainsley waits until Harper is out of the driveway, then she waits an extra seven minutes on the off chance that Harper forgot something. Then Ainsley slips from bed, pulls on shorts, and shuffles into flip-flops. Fish is in fact standing right outside Ainsley's door, but Fish is a dog, not a person; he can't tell on her.

Ainsley slips out the door. Fish barks.

She hurries over to her grandmother's house. Felipa has gone to Boston to be with Grammie, so there is no one to avoid. Ainsley checks the bar cart first. She took the Grey Goose, and it hasn't been replaced. She considers walking with the Mount Gay or the Johnnie Walker Black, but she can't chance Aunt Harper smelling it on her.

And so to the basement Ainsley goes. The clocks chime quarter past the hour; Ainsley inhales the fragrance of her grandmother's Evening in Paris, which is also the perfume her mother wears. It's the scent of her oppressors.

The basement of Seamless is like the basement of a morgue, only instead of dead bodies the space is populated by headless dressmaker dummies, which terrify Ainsley and have done so since she was small. Tabitha keeps one as a conversation piece *in their living room,* despite Ainsley's protests. Ainsley must have had a nightmare at some point about the dummies coming to life or calling out in agony about their missing heads and limbs, because she can't explain her fear away. She knows they are horsehair and Styrofoam, but they remind her of deformed bodies.

Ainsley holds her breath the way she and her friends used to when they drove past one of Nantucket's many cemeteries, and she darts among the dummies to the far wall of the basement, against which Eleanor keeps stacked cases of booze.

A bottle of Grey Goose. Just one bottle, although Ainsley considers taking two. She scurries back toward the stairs while the dummies stand in silent judgment.

Ainsley catches sight of Caylee's tangerine-colored Jeep through the filmy white curtains of Eleanor's front window. Next she sees Caylee herself, wearing the Roxie in emerald green. The Roxie is a matronly dress, but somehow Caylee totally rocks it. She's wearing nude patent leather heels, which make her legs look a mile long. Her hair is straight and shiny, and she's wearing cat's-eye sunglasses.

"Hey!" Ainsley says to Caylee as she steps outside.

Caylee waves and trots through the gravel toward Ainsley in her heels. "Hey, girl!" She sees the bottle of Grey Goose, and her expression darkens. "What are you doing, Ainsley?"

Ainsley holds up the bottle. "Shots," she says. "Kidding. I was going to make a screwdriver. Do you want one? Are you on your way to brunch?" Ainsley knows Caylee has hundreds of friends, all of them fun, and when she's not working, her life is a whirlwind of drinks, dinners, concerts, beach parties, and brunches. Ainsley can't wait to be older.

"I just came from church," Caylee says. She produces a bouquet of hydrangeas from behind her back. "A woman on Main Street was selling these, and I thought of you." She drops the bouquet in what looks like defeat. "I know it sucked for you to have your former friends come into the store like that... but Ainsley, you shouldn't be drinking. You're only sixteen."

Ainsley's mouth falls open. She can't *believe* Caylee isn't being chill about this.

"I'm serious, Ainsley," Caylee says. "Put that bottle back where you found it."

"It's mine," Ainsley says.

"It's not yours," Caylee says. "You just came out of your grandmother's house. Obviously you stole it…"

"I didn't *steal* anything!" Ainsley says. "This is where I live." She swallows; it feels like there's a walnut caught in her throat. "You should probably go. Leave. Get off my property."

"I'll happily go," Caylee says. "But I'm calling Harper to tell her."

"Tell her *what?*" Ainsley says. She raises the bottle in defiance. Honestly, she is so angry, so *indignant,* that she would like to smash it on the ground. "This is mine!"

"Ainsley."

"I thought you were my friend!" Ainsley says. Tears pool in her eyes, although the last thing she wants to do is cry in front of Caylee.

Suddenly Caylee's arms are around her. "Hey," she says. "I am your friend. Which is why I'm going to insist you put the vodka back. I'll go with you."

Ainsley takes a deep breath. She wants to inform Caylee that she can't *insist* Ainsley do anything. Caylee isn't her boss; Caylee isn't her mother, her aunt, or her sister. Caylee shouldn't even be working at the boutique. All Ainsley has to do is call her mother, and Caylee will be fired. But when Ainsley opens her mouth, she starts to sob. She is so upset and so, so heartbroken. Teddy breaking up with her was one thing, but then she got suspended from school—how is that going to look on her transcript?—and her friends betrayed her. Emma and

Candace egged her house! But even so, when the two of them walked into the ERF boutique, Ainsley was pathetic enough to let her hopes rise. There was no doubt the party they had thrown at the boutique was cool. That it might have been cool enough to lure her friends back in wasn't something Ainsley had considered until she saw them stroll through the door. But they had only come to shoot Ainsley between the eyes with a poison dart about Teddy and Candace. Teddy was taking Candace to Ventuno for dinner, a place he had promised to take Ainsley because his uncle Graham's girlfriend, Marcella, waited tables there and would let them order wine. Or maybe that was just Teddy talking big—it probably was, but even if there was no wine there would still be candlelight and beautiful Italian food and Teddy across the table, holding Candace's hand and admiring the flower in her hair.

And on top of all that, Ainsley's mother left, her grandmother left, and her father won't return her calls. Whom is she left with? Aunt Harper and Ramsay, both of whom feel sorry for her, she's certain.

She lets Caylee lead her back up the stairs of her grandmother's house. Caylee waits in the doorway while Ainsley places the Grey Goose on the bar cart. Caylee pulls a tissue out of her clutch and hands it to Ainsley, who wipes her eyes.

"Can you come to Ram Pasture with us later?" Ainsley asks.

"I'm going to Nobadeer with my other friends today," Caylee says. "Besides, I don't think Ramsay would want me on your beach excursion."

"Why not?" Ainsley says. "I thought you guys were still friends."

"We are," Caylee says. "But I think he's interested in your aunt."

"My aunt?" Ainsley says.

"That's the sense I get," Caylee says.

"Oh," Ainsley says. She's not sure what to think about that. She misses Ramsay terribly and would like him back in her life, but it wouldn't be fair if Ramsay started dating Harper. Poor Tabitha! "Well, thank you for these." She sniffs the flowers. "And thanks for stopping by."

"How about we grab breakfast one morning next week?" Caylee says. "I know a great little place. It's kind of a secret."

"Okay," Ainsley says. She's embarrassed by how much the invitation thrills her—but then she worries that Caylee sees her as a charity case, an ostracized teenager without any friends. She could turn Caylee down—she doesn't eat breakfast—but her loneliness gets the better of her. "How about Wednesday?"

HARPER

They decide to take Harper's Bronco to Ram Pasture.

"It's the quintessential beach buggy," Ramsay says. "I will finally be one of the cool kids."

"I wouldn't go that far," Ainsley says.

When they load up the Bronco, Harper feels like she's part of a family. Ramsay is the father figure, Harper the mother, Ainsley the child, Fish the dog. It's a peculiar sensation. Harper is no one's mother, Ramsay is no one's father, and Ainsley is no longer really a child. Fish is, at least, a dog. Maybe because the construct is artificial, it feels fun—like playacting. Ramsay loads up three chairs, half a dozen towels, the Sunday *New York Times,* a brand new Carl Hiaasen novel, and a Frisbee. Just seeing the Frisbee causes Fish to bark.

Harper is in charge of food and drink. She has made grilled-chicken BLTs, a classic picnic macaroni salad she threw together, sliced sugared peaches, and lime sugar cookies. She fills a cooler with lots of cold bottled water.

"And this," Ramsay says, handing her a bottle wrapped in a paper bag.

It's a bottle of Rock Angel rosé. Harper rolls her eyes. "You, too?"

"I thought all chic women liked to drink rosé at the beach. Your sister loves it."

"I'm not my sister," Harper says. "Normally I drink beer, but my stomach has been funny lately." The truth was, she had nearly vomited up her breakfast that morning; she constantly feels dizzy and unsettled, like she's just stepped off a carnival ride.

"Let's just take it," Ramsay says. "Please?"

Harper unsheathes the bottle and plunges it into the icy bath of the cooler. She won't make a big deal about it. Today will be pleasant. Today they will be like a family from a storybook, one without conflicts, one without vices, one without history.

They drive the Bronco out Madaket Road, and Ramsay shows Harper where to turn left. They turn onto the dirt and sand of Barrett Farm Road; it takes them on a winding, slightly bumpy journey over an open plain that reminds Harper of pictures she's seen of the African savanna. This is nothing like the

Vineyard. The Vineyard has hills and trees—both pine forest and lush deciduous stands. Nantucket, by comparison, is flat, with low-lying vegetation that makes it easy to see the blue ribbon of the ocean in the distance. There's a pond on the left and bushes of *Rosa rugosa* with their lovely pink blossoms. She sees a red-tailed hawk circling overhead. Has that hawk ever made the trip eleven miles west to the Vineyard? she wonders.

She misses Reed. The pain is constant, a heartache, a gut ache. He has moved out and stopped working at the hospital. Nobody knows where he is. Is he thinking about Harper? Is he thinking about anything other than Harper? Does Sadie know where he is? Does she call him? Do they talk? Is his leave from the hospital permanent? Has he been fired? If he has been fired, will he work elsewhere, and if so, where will he go?

Is he eating? Drinking? Smoking? Reading? Riding his bike?

Did Harper ruin his life? Does he blame her? That's what she really wants to know. Their relationship—the affair—was a mutual decision, as much his as hers, but Reed may feel he has paid more dearly than she has for their indiscretion.

Harper would like to tell him that she, too, has paid dearly. She lost her job. She shredded what was left of her reputation. But what hurts the most is that she lost him.

She wonders if the relationship would have fallen apart on its own with Billy's death. The circumstances that knit them together would have changed. What would they have had in common?

"You're awfully quiet," Ramsay says, snapping Harper out of her reverie.

She offers him a smile. "Sorry," she says. "Just thinking."

"About?" he asks.

Harper checks the rearview. Ainsley has her face buried in Fish's neck, and she's humming along to the radio.

"The usual," she says.

The beach is stunning—a wide swath of sand that extends in both directions with only a few people visible in the distance. The waves pound the sand, and Fish runs to the water's edge and barks his happiness, his relief. He has missed the ocean.

Ramsay puts up a striped umbrella and sets up the chairs, arranging Harper's out in the sun with two neatly folded towels and a cold bottle of water tucked in the cup holder of the armrest. Ainsley arranges her towel in the sand, then charges in the water, shrieking with delight.

Harper follows suit, diving into an oncoming wave. This is her first swim of the season, and the water is divine. She developed her preference for cold water during all those summers that she and Tabitha spent at Wyonegonic Camp, swimming in Moose Pond. Harper treads water while looking at the horizon. The day is so crystalline that she can just make out the Vineyard in the distance.

Chappy. What she's seeing is the coastline of Chappaquiddick.

Brendan, Drew, and Reed—they're all over there.

She turns back toward shore. Ainsley climbs out of the water, splashing Ramsay as she goes. Ramsay has taken off his glasses; he looks younger, and Harper can easily imagine him in a Boy Scout uniform decorated with the most demanding badges: first aid, citizenship, lifesaving. He squints and waves in her general direction.

* * *

As the day goes by, Harper feels better—more centered, less lost. She and Ramsay settle on the blanket under the umbrella to eat lunch. Ainsley has fallen asleep facedown on her towel, and Harper, in her mother role, covers her back and shoulders with her sarong so she doesn't burn.

The picnic is delicious, if Harper does say so herself.

Ramsay says, "I can't believe what a great cook you are."

Harper laughs. "It's a sandwich."

"Well, your sister has a hard time with cold cereal," he says.

"She is my mother reincarnated," Harper says.

"I realized when you said you were thinking about the usual that I know almost nothing about you," Ramsay says. "Have you ever been married?"

"Never married, no kids," Harper says.

"That's unusual, right?" Ramsay says. "You and Tabitha are almost forty and neither of you ever married?"

"Let's assume it was our parents' fault," Harper says.

"Do you have someone special on the Vineyard?" Ramsay asks.

Harper shrugs. It's too complicated to explain. "It was the right time to get away. I actually can't believe Tabitha allowed me to stay. So she must have needed a break herself."

"She did," Ramsay says. "Explain to me how she can be so uptight and you can be so laid-back. Was it always that way?"

Was it always that way? Tabitha had long been an approval seeker, whereas Harper figured if other people didn't like her, they could buzz off. Harper was, by nature, lazy and easily distracted. She had barely made it through Tulane; Bourbon

Street was simply too alluring. As an adult, it seems, the traits that distinguished the twins from each other had only become exaggerated and solidified—although what, really, did Harper know of Tabitha's life over the past fourteen years? Harper hasn't spent any time with her sister since the week leading up to Julian's death.

Those fraught, frantic days had been the time when Harper had felt closest to her sister. Isn't that true? The fault lines created when Billy and Eleanor divorced had knit themselves back together and nearly healed. Until the final night. After that final night, the relationship ended.

"She lost a child," Harper says. "That changes a person."

"She lets that loss overshadow everything in her life that's good. She does it still. She doesn't open herself up to the possibility of future happiness, real happiness."

"With you, you mean?"

"I wanted to have a baby with her," Ramsay says. "No sooner did I say the words than Tabitha asked me to move out."

Harper nods. She suddenly feels protective of her sister. She understands why Ramsay would want a child, but she also realizes that Tabitha would never have conceded. No way. The topic is too complex and painful to discuss any further, and Harper isn't going to let the day go up in flames. "You know my sister far better than I do. I haven't known her in a long time."

"You never told me what happened between the two of you," Ramsay says. "When I asked you about it at the brewery, you changed the subject."

"For good reason," Harper says. She gets to her feet. "How about a glass of that rosé?"

* * *

The afternoon sun beats down as Harper sips at her glass of wine and Ramsay does the *Times* crossword puzzle in his chair. Harper is lying across the blanket reading *Valley of the Dolls,* a book she found on Tabitha's shelves that has Eleanor's name written in pencil inside the front cover. Harper has never read it, but she knows it was splashy and scandalous in its day, and part of the joy of reading it is imagining Eleanor's shock—and possibly her delight—at the sex and the pills. So many pills!

Ramsay looks up from his puzzle. "Myanmar, to JFK. Five letters."

"Burma," Harper says without looking up.

"Look at you!" Ramsay says.

"You'd never know it, but I had a very expensive education," Harper says. "Winsor, then Tulane."

"Tulane?" Ramsay says. "Impressive."

"Not so impressive," Harper says. "I barely graduated. I pretty much majored in shots at Pat O'Brien's."

"You've never told me what you do for a living," Ramsay says.

"Until recently, I delivered packages for a Mickey Mouse operation called Rooster Express," she says. "Before that, I did it all: ice cream scooper, cocktail waitress, landscaper, drug mule."

Ramsay laughs, and Harper goes back to her book.

When Ramsay fills his glass with the last of the rosé, he settles down on the towel next to Harper. Harper immediately checks on Ainsley; she's still snoring away on her towel. Harper has forgotten how long and deeply teenagers can sleep. Fish is dozing in the shade behind Ramsay's chair.

"I've had enough sun," Ramsay says.

He is too close to Harper. She sits up. "I could actually use some sun, I think."

"You don't have to get up," Ramsay says. He reaches out for her blindly—his glasses are off—and he ends up grabbing her thigh. It takes her by surprise, and she responds by swatting at him. It's meant to be a get-your-hands-off-me swat, but it ends up being more playful than stern. The little bit of wine she's had has gone to her head, and the next thing she knows, she and Ramsay are tussling on the blanket. She tries to wrestle away but finds herself with her hands pinned over her head, Ramsay's face hovering above hers.

"Ramsay," she says. "Don't." She gets purposefully to her feet. Fish barks.

Ramsay holds his hands up. "Whoa," he says. "Talk about mixed signals."

Has she been sending mixed signals? If she has, it has been unintentional. She should never have agreed to come to the beach with Ramsay.

Harper stares at him, at a loss for words. Ramsay is a lovely and authentic person. She loves the buttoned-up order of him, the preppy clothes, the horn-rimmed glasses, his soothing manner, and his earnest desire to help. He is Clark Kent *and* Superman, or he has been until now. Now he's just a man on the make. There is no way Harper is going to let anyone else get close to her, least of all Tabitha's ex-boyfriend.

"You said earlier that you don't know anything about me. And you don't, really. I realize that I look just like Tabitha, and it must be disconcerting to discover that we're so different—opposite, even." She maintains eye contact with Ramsay, though it's hard; his face is about to crumple with dejection. She looks at Ainsley's chest rising and falling with breaths of ocean air, then she watches the encroaching and retreating of the waves. This is not her island. This is someplace she is visiting. Borrowing, even. "I need you to believe me when I say that the last thing I need is another boyfriend."

Ramsay, to his credit, asks the right question. "What *do* you need?"

Harper gives him a small, sad smile. "A friend friend," she says. Fish barks. "A human friend."

"I'm in," Ramsay says.

AINSLEY

She meets Caylee at the corner of Broad and Water Streets at eight thirty in the morning on Wednesday for breakfast. Caylee greets her with an enthusiastic hug and a kiss on the cheek, as though she is a sorority sister or a soul mate, and Ainsley stands up a little straighter.

She worked with Caylee on Monday, and although Caylee had been civil, even pleasant with Ainsley, there had been a distant reserve—or so Ainsley thought: no chatter, no confidences shared. Ainsley worried that Caylee no longer found her worthy of her friendship or tutelage. Ainsley had let her down. How had she so severely misread Caylee? Caylee was a good person in a cool body, whereas Emma Marlowe was a bad person in a cool body. Caylee had just come from church and wanted to stop by with flowers for Ainsley as a gesture of solidarity; she had been wearing the Roxie because it was appropriate for church *and* it was promoting the brand she worked for. Ainsley shudders when she thinks of how disappointed Caylee must have been to see Ainsley holding the vodka—which she had, indeed, *stolen* from Eleanor's house. And then she had told Caylee to get off her property, which is something you say when you're five years old.

Ainsley realizes she needs to clean up her act or she's going to lose everyone close to her. Tuesday was Caylee's day off, and Ainsley worked with Aunt Harper, but on Tuesday night, Ainsley sent Caylee a text that said: *Are we still on for breakfast tomorrow?*

Caylee had responded immediately: *You bet.*

Being "downtown"—and, yes, Ainsley knows that four square blocks of Nantucket hardly qualify as a downtown, but it's what she has grown up with—used to be fun. Now it's a place filled with pitfalls. Ainsley could bump into anyone from school at any moment, which is why she has kept her trajectory simple: home, work, home. She hasn't been into Force Five to try on bikinis; she hasn't shopped for earrings at Jessica Hicks; she hasn't gone to the Juice Bar for ice cream. But when Caylee threads her arm through Ainsley's, it's like protection. Ainsley lets Caylee lead her across Broad Street and up the stairs of a Victorian house.

"Ainsley?"

Ainsley swivels her head around. Teddy is standing on the porch of the house, wearing a uniform of khaki pants and a white polo emblazoned with the name of the property: 21 Broad.

"What are you doing here?"

Wait. Ainsley is discombobulated. Caylee said they were going to some secret place for breakfast, and now they're standing on the front porch of the hotel where Teddy works. It's going to look like she's stalking him. Ainsley takes half a step back, but Caylee holds her fast.

"We've come for breakfast," Caylee says. "I've been invited by the owner."

Teddy looks back and forth between Ainsley and Caylee, clearly confused but maybe also impressed. "Right this way," Teddy says.

In back of the hotel is a charming porch, and set up on long wooden tables is what's called the small plates breakfast. Ainsley hadn't been excited about actually eating, but she's never been anywhere that has a breakfast as enticing as this. There are locally roasted coffees and organic teas, glass pitchers of juice in jewel tones, and a platter of fresh fruit—fat berries and figs and fresh sliced peaches and plums, wedges of watermelon and rings of juicy pineapple. There are two kinds of smoothie—kale and strawberry—and there are freshly made scones with clotted cream and guava jam. There is overnight oatmeal with raisins, nuts, and dried cherries, and there is an elaborate platter of cheeses and meats and smoked fish.

Caylee picks a table in the corner, then she leads Ainsley over to the buffet, and together they start filling their plates.

"This is actually the prettiest breakfast I've ever seen," Ainsley says. "How did you find out about this place?"

"The owner used to come into the Straight Wharf," Caylee says. "He told me about it and invited me to come try it."

"You are so lucky," Ainsley says.

"There were a lot of perks in that job," Caylee says. "I miss it."

Ainsley feels a pang of fear. "But you like the boutique, right?"

"Right," Caylee says.

Ainsley exhales. The worst thing that could happen now is for Caylee to quit the shop and go back to bartending.

"I'm so angry about how I lost my job," Caylee says. "I have a revenge dream about the man who grabbed me. In the dream, I stick a corkscrew in his eye."

"Nice," Ainsley says.

"Would you like coffee?" Caylee asks.

"I'd better not," Ainsley says. Her heart feels like a rock that is skipping across the surface of the water. *Teddy. Teddy. Teddy.* Ainsley thinks about him all the time, but seeing him has jarred her. She had hoped that she had built him up only in her mind and that in person he would seem diminished. The bad news is he's even more appealing in person, and now her longing for him is sharper, which she didn't even think was possible.

"That was a friend of yours out there?" Caylee asks, spearing half a strawberry.

"My old boyfriend. He dates Candace now, the redhead who came into the shop during the party."

"How long did you go out with him?" Caylee asks.

"All of last year," Ainsley says. "He was new. I made friends with him on the first day of school, and by the end of the week he was my boyfriend." It seems like a lifetime ago, but Ainsley can remember how jumped up they had all been by *a new boy in their grade.* Ainsley, Emma, Maggie, probably even Candace—all of them had been excited, and who can blame them? They had all been swimming circles in the cloudy fishbowl that is the Nantucket Public Schools since kindergarten. Over the years they had seen kids come and go, but mostly go. Danny Dalrymple and Charlotte Budd went to boarding school, and Saber Podwats's parents moved to Swampscott because they couldn't afford to live on Nantucket anymore.

Emma had seen Teddy first because they had both driven to school and been assigned spots near each other in the parking lot.

Prepare to be disappointed, Emma had texted. *He looks like a refugee from the dipshit rodeo #everythingbutthespurs.*

As luck would have it, Teddy had been assigned to Ainsley's first-block English class, and before Mr. Duncombe had given them their permanent seats, Teddy had chosen the chair next to Ainsley's. He had been wearing Wrangler jeans, a flannel shirt over a plain white undershirt, cowboy boots, and a cross on a leather strap around his neck.

Everything but the spurs, Ainsley thought. *Dipshit rodeo.* But Teddy wasn't ugly—far from it. He had auburn hair, freckles across his nose, strong shoulders, long legs. The outfit was off-putting, but Ainsley knew better than anyone that new clothes were an easy fix. Put this kid in a Force Five T-shirt and madras shorts and a pair of Reefs, and he would be hot.

He had his jaw set, his green eyes focused forward on the whiteboard, which was blank except for Mr. Duncombe's name and e-mail address. Ainsley remembered the stories she had heard—father dead, mother suicidal then hospitalized, kid shipped two-thirds of the way across the country then thirty miles out to sea. He probably felt like a long-horned steer dropped into a tank of killer whales.

Ainsley tapped the edge of his desk to get his attention. "Hi," she said. "I'm Ainsley Cruise. Welcome to Nantucket High School."

He had given her a slow cowboy smile, filled with relief and gratitude. "Thank you," he said.

* * *

That first week, Ainsley had made welcoming Teddy Elquot her personal mission. She showed him where the wood shop was, she invited him to sit with her in the cafeteria, she introduced him to BC and Maxx Cunningham and Kalik and D-Ray and the other jocks and insisted they be nice to him.

Emma was as skeptical and crude as ever, joking that Ainsley was working off her mandatory community-service hours by being nice to Sheriff Woody Pride. Either that or she was hoping to finally lose her virginity, and wasn't it common knowledge that ranch hands were well hung?

Ainsley ignored Emma's comments—to defend him would only fuel Emma's fire—and she found that she really liked Teddy. The first days of school were still warm, and Teddy had use of his uncle's truck, so Ainsley showed him a different beach each day. By Friday, out on Smith's Point, with the coastline of Tuckernuck close enough for Teddy to throw a baseball at, Ainsley persuaded him to take off his boots and his Wrangler jeans and go for a swim. He had hooted with fear and the cold—although in early September the water was as warm as it got all year—and admitted it was his first time in the ocean.

They sat on a beach towel together afterward, Teddy basking in the late afternoon sun, and he started telling Ainsley things: his father was a hero, a first responder to a huge industrial fire. He had died instantly in a chemical blast. His mother hadn't been particularly stable before the accident, but afterward she lost her mind.

She locked herself in her bedroom for days, Teddy said. *She didn't cook, didn't shop, didn't shower. I finally called nine one one myself. Once my mother had been committed, my father's younger brother reached out. Uncle Graham. He saved me from foster care.*

Uncle Graham was cool, but Teddy wasn't sure about Nantucket.

It's cold-hearted here, Teddy said. *Yankee.*

At home in Oklahoma, he said, there was plentiful sunshine, football, open space—long highways, thousand-acre farms, ten-thousand-acre ranches—barbecue, and good music.

What do you consider good music? Ainsley asked.

He had played her a song called "Head Over Boots" by Jon Pardi, and as the song was ending and the sun setting, he'd kissed her.

They became boyfriend and girlfriend. Ainsley bought him a couple of sweaters from J.Crew and some long-sleeved T-shirts, a pair of new jeans. He traded in his boots for Nikes. Emma allowed him to sit at their lunch table, but she did not fully embrace him. She called him Woody to his face and imitated his accent. Ainsley knew that Emma was jealous, but she couldn't figure out if Emma wanted Teddy for her own or if she didn't like losing Ainsley's time and attention.

Ainsley told Teddy things she had never been comfortable sharing with anyone else—about her parents, their split, her father moving off island and starting a new family, effectively leaving Ainsley to be ruled by a two-woman dictatorship. Ainsley even told Teddy about her brother, Julian, who had been born premature and had, one night, simply stopped breathing, leaving Tabitha an emotional cripple.

Ainsley and Teddy didn't have sex until Thanksgiving.

Ainsley had enjoyed dinner with her mother and grandmother at Ramsay's house with Ramsay's family. Tabitha had been in one of her rare happy-drunk moods, taking Ainsley's face into her hands and calling her honey bear and honey pear. She had been slurring her words, and Ainsley was anxious to get to the driveway, where Teddy idled in Uncle Graham's truck. Teddy and Uncle Graham had gone to the Faregrounds for their Thanksgiving dinner—full-plate turkey and all the trimmings for $19.95, with seconds and thirds included—but now Graham was drinking with his scalloping buddies at the bar, and Teddy had the truck and no curfew.

They had gone to the carriage house and done it in Ainsley's bed. It had hurt a little, but the hurt paled to how wonderful it felt to be that close to Teddy.

All these memories zip through Ainsley's mind as she stares at her fruit salad. She looks up at Caylee, who is mixing dried cherries into her overnight oatmeal with the intensity of a chemist seeking the Nobel Prize. Caylee, she has noticed, isn't afraid of food. She *relishes* eating, yet she remains slender. Such a thing is also possible, like being cool and going to church.

"I have to go to the bathroom," Ainsley says.

"I can't believe you're leaving your scone unprotected," Caylee says. She grins. "Kidding. Go."

Ainsley wanders out to the lobby of the inn, looking for Teddy. There is a stunning young woman with thick dark hair and olive skin and a beauty mark working at the front desk, and Ainsley feels a stab of jealousy. Maybe Teddy has left Candace. Maybe he's dating this young woman now, or maybe he's having an affair with one of the older, attractive divorcées staying at the hotel alone. For someone like Teddy, Ainsley supposes, the possibilities are endless.

Beauty Mark looks up from her computer terminal. "Can I help you?" she asks.

At the same time, Ainsley hears her name. Teddy is galloping down the stairs toward her. Beneath the white polo shirt of his uniform, Ainsley sees the leather strap and, dangling from it, the cross. She knows now that Teddy has been raised Pentecostal. She had always meant to google what that meant, but she never has. Candace probably knows. Maybe it's similar to being Catholic.

"Hey," Ainsley says.

"Hey," Teddy says. He is tan under his freckles, and his hair is a shade lighter, golden glints in the red. He's been in the sun, at the beach, probably with Candace and Emma and BC and Anna and all Ainsley's former friends. The tan makes him look healthy and strong; it's a blessing summer has bestowed upon him. At least Ainsley got to the beach on Sunday with Harper and Ramsay. Maybe she looks like she's glowing, too, although she kind of doubts it. Most of her summer so far has been spent under the fluorescent lights of the boutique or in her bedroom, doing her summer reading. She is going back to school in the fall as one of the truly pathetic kids who actually found time to get it finished before Labor Day weekend.

"I was looking for the ladies' room," she says.

"Who is that woman you're here with?" Teddy asks.

"My friend," Ainsley says. "Caylee."

"Never seen her before," Teddy says. "Is she in *college?*"

"Out of college," Ainsley says. "She used to bartend at the Straight Wharf. Your uncle probably knows her."

"Probably," Teddy says. "So is she, like, your nanny or babysitter, then?"

"No," Ainsley says with a patient smile. "She's just a friend. How is your summer going?"

He shrugs. "Fine, I guess."

"How's Candace?" Ainsley asks. She doesn't mean to ask this; she doesn't want to know. Yes, she does, but she doesn't want him to know that she wants to know. "I heard you took her for dinner at Ventuno."

Teddy's forehead creases the way it used to when he didn't understand the math homework. "I didn't take Candace to Ventuno," he says. "Emma did."

"What?" Ainsley says.

"I don't have the money to take Candace to Ventuno."

"But you have a job."

"I sign my checks over to Graham. He's saving them for my college tuition. But Dutch gives Emma however much money she wants. She took Candace to Ventuno, and they both got really drunk, I guess, then Candace threw up in the street outside the Juice Bar, and I guess Mr. Duncombe was in line with his kids, and he called Candace's parents to come pick her up."

"Oh," Ainsley says. She is vibrating with suppressed glee. Emma, not Teddy, took Candace. The announcement in the boutique was a bluff. The detail about the flower in Candace's hair had been fabricated. And Candace—an altar girl at Saint Mary's—had gotten sick in front of the Juice Bar, and Mr. Duncombe saw her! The only downside to this story is that Ainsley hasn't heard it from anyone else. She is really and truly a social pariah if no one thought to share this news with her. Ainsley warns herself against being too judgmental. If she had stayed on her self-destructive course, she could easily have been the girl puking on the street. But it wasn't her this time.

"You and Candace are still a couple, though, right?" Ainsley says.

Teddy scuffs the toe of his plastic-looking Top-Sider against the wooden floor. "Honestly, I'm not sure. She hangs out with Emma all the time now. They go to the beach together every day. Neither of them has to work. They go to parties with all the summer kids."

"That's what I did last summer with Emma," Ainsley says.

"Yeah," Teddy says. "It's like Candace is you now. The new you."

"If Candace is the new me, then who am I?"

Teddy gives her the slow cowboy smile. Ainsley basks in the warmth of his gaze—he's looking at her the way he used to—and she nearly falls into that golden pond. But no. She will not be such a pushover.

"Ladies' room?" she asks.

Teddy snaps back to his senses. "Behind you," he says.

"Thanks," Ainsley says. "See you around."

When Ainsley returns to the table, Caylee says, "I was about to send a search party."

Ainsley spears a juicy chunk of pineapple. She thinks she handled Teddy pretty well, considering. She didn't tear up or beg him to take her back. She wasn't snotty or disdainful or sarcastic, even when he asked her the offensive question about

Caylee being her babysitter. She had been pleasant, calm, even-tempered. If Candace is the new Ainsley, then maybe Ainsley is now the old Ainsley, the person she had been before meeting Emma.

Ainsley's phone pings.

"Hmm...wonder who that could be," Caylee says, but she sounds like she already knows.

Ainsley checks the display. It's Teddy.

I miss you, the text says. *Can I call you sometime?*

TABITHA

Finding a contractor to work on Billy's house is going to be more challenging than Tabitha imagined. It's not like choosing a dry cleaner or a pizza delivery place. Billy's house doesn't have Wi-Fi—the house is resolutely stuck in 1993—so Tabitha resorts to using the good old Martha's Vineyard phone book, which she finds on the mantel next to the urn containing Billy's ashes. She turns to the back, the business listings, and looks under "General Contractors." There are dozens and dozens of them, and for a moment she is heartened. She doesn't know any of these builders from Adam, so she decides she'll start with AA Vineyard Builders and proceed alphabetically from there.

1. "...waiting list of three years..."
2. "Sorry: we're booked solid for the foreseeable future..."
3. "Is the project inside? I may be able to sub out my New Bedford team in January..."

4. "What's the last name again?" "Frost," Tabitha says. Click.

5. No answer.

6. Voice mail. Tabitha leaves a message.

7. "I'm sorry. We can't take on any new projects at the moment."

8. "Frost, as in Harper Frost, that chick who ratted out Joey Bowen?" Click.

9. "I'll have my husband or his partner call you back by the end of the month at the very latest."

10. "Sorry."

11. "Sorry."

12. "I wish I could say yes, I really do, but I'm just the mother-in-law. My daughter and son-in-law are in Vermont until Labor Day. A lot of builders take the summer off. You might want to call back in September."

13. "This number has been disconnected..."

14. "I'm free, but is the house down island? I refuse to work on any house that's down island. I'm simply not dealing with that traffic every day."

15. "I'm slammed, quite frankly, but I know for a fact that Franklin Phelps is finishing up a house in Katama and is looking for something small right now. He might be able to help you. You got his number?"

Tabitha freezes. "Franklin...Phelps, you say?"

"You got his number?"

"No. I...I'm using the phone book." She runs her fingers down the listings to *P*. She doesn't see...

"The phone book? Lady, I can promise you you will never find a builder using the phone book. You need to know someone. Call Franklin Phelps, tell him TF sent you. Here's his number."

Tabitha writes down the number, then hangs up the phone and stares at the notepad. Franklin is a builder in addition to being a musician. Okay. Franklin could be the answer to her prayers—if she hadn't slept with him. But because she slept with him, because she has honestly not been able to stop thinking about him, she cannot possibly call him.

She decides to abandon the cold calling for the time being and do something productive. She's off to the dump.

She loads up the disgusting rag rugs, the old bathmats, and the mildewed shower curtains. She gets rid of the hideous lamps, stacks of magazines, chipped dishes, Tupperware without tops, the *Jaws* poster that hangs in the powder room, the broken microwave, the dollar-store oil paintings, the plastic place mats and rickety TV trays, the cracked canisters for sugar and flour, both empty. She tosses old batteries and half-empty cans of paint, boxes and boxes of defunct lightbulbs, frayed extension cords, a dented colander, and baking pans that contain the residue of a hundred nights of burned nachos. It's all going.

It's Sunday, and the dump is crowded. It must be mostly locals, because Tabitha immediately picks up on a sense of community. People exude harried good cheer. It's summer, they're busy, there is money to be made, and if they do happen to have the weekend off, they want to get to the beach—but no one is too busy to lend a hand. An old gentleman with white hair and a long white beard, looking like a skinny Santa, sees Tabitha discarding the *Jaws* poster and offers to give her ten bucks for it.

"Oh, please," Tabitha says. "Just take it."

Unloading all the crap out of the back of the car feels good, the same way that flossing her teeth feels good. As Tabitha is getting ready to leave, she notices a woman wearing a mannish crew cut and a pair of really ugly boots step out of a truck that says GARDEN GODDESSES on the side. *Local landscaper,* Tabitha thinks. She remembers what TF told her on the phone: *You have to know someone.*

Okay, Tabitha thinks. Here goes.

"Excuse me," she says. "I'm looking for a general contractor to do a gut renovation on my father's house down island." She squints at the sky. She can't remember: *is* Billy's house down island? She thinks down island is Oak Bluffs and Vineyard Haven, but actually that makes no sense because Chilmark and Aquinnah are south, so maybe *that's* down island? "It's in Tisbury. The house."

The woman stares at Tabitha with undisguised contempt, and Tabitha gets it. She hates nothing more on Nantucket than being asked questions by tourists, or, even worse, brand-new residents. Tabitha always counted her impatience as a personality flaw, but now she sees it's a trait that people on the Vineyard share. There's a certain way things are done here, and if you don't know what it is, then you don't belong.

"A general contractor?" the woman says. "You have got to be kidding me. You'll never find anyone to work for you on this island."

"I know, right?" Tabitha says. "I called fifteen people this morning, and not one of them could do it. I had no idea it would be so difficult. I thought maybe if you had any suggestions..." But the woman gets into her truck, slams the door, and through the open window gives Tabitha the finger.

Tabitha thinks, *Wow, okay.* Vineyarders aren't only impatient, they're also mean! And vulgar! It's only after the truck drives off in a cloud of dust that it dawns on Tabitha that the woman must have thought Tabitha was Harper. She must have been one more person whom Harper pissed off. *You'll never find anyone to work for you on this island.*

I'm not Harper! Tabitha wants to shout.

She's about to cry and thinks that Harper was probably right—they should tear down the house because they will never find anyone available and willing to fix it up. But it has *such* potential; she recognized that as she was clearing it out. There are wide plank heart-pine floors under the crappy carpeting—it was such a find that Tabitha hooted with delight—but the process of pulling up the carpet and the pad and bringing those floors to life is a job that's beyond her modest DIY skills.

She feels a hand on her shoulder and turns to see the skinny Santa who took the *Jaws* poster.

"I happened to overhear your conversation," he says. "My wife and I used a company called Hammer and Claw for a guesthouse we built for our kids and grandkids to use. The principal guy's name is Phelps. Franklin Phelps."

Tabitha nods, knowing she should be surprised—but she doesn't feel at all surprised. Franklin's company is called Hammer and Claw, and this is now the second time this morning he has been recommended.

Tabitha still feels stung by the charming woman from Garden Goddesses—and Tabitha would like to point out that this woman is no one's idea of a goddess—but she gives skinny Santa a smile for the kindness of his input, as unsettling as it is. "Thank you," she says.

* * *

Back at home, Tabitha checks the phone book. She had made it through the alphabet to Haggerty Construction, and the very next listing is Hammer and Claw. Is it a sign? Third time's a charm? Or now that she has been warned this is Franklin's company, should she skip down to Inkwell Beach Builders? She's dying to talk to Franklin, which is an argument only for *not* calling. If she calls, it could easily end badly for her.

Her mother would, no doubt, advise Tabitha not to call. A woman should never pursue a man, in her opinion, although it's a well-documented fact that Eleanor ruthlessly stole Billy Frost from her cousin Rhonda.

And what would Billy say? Tabitha wonders. She eyes the urn containing his ashes. Safe to assume Billy would give advice opposite to Eleanor's. *Nothing's going to happen until you make it happen.*

She's in Billy's house; perhaps that's why his argument is more compelling.

Franklin answers on the first ring. "Yo."

Yo? Tabitha thinks. That's the way Ainsley's friends answer the phone. It's probably not inappropriate, then, that she suddenly feels like a sixteen-year-old trying to pass for an adult.

"Oh, hello," she says, wondering if her acting skills are up to snuff or if she will be completely transparent. "I'm looking for a contractor for my father's house, on Daggett Avenue. My father recently passed away, and I want to do a gut renovation so I can put the house on the market."

"Uh-huh," Franklin says. "How many square feet is the house? And when were you thinking of starting?"

"It's a little over seventeen hundred square feet," Tabitha says. "And I'd like to start as soon as we can. Tomorrow, if possible."

"Tomorrow!" Franklin says. "I can see you're a woman who knows what she wants. It just so happens I'm finishing a project in Katama, and I don't have anything else lined up until fall, so I may be able to squeeze this in, if—and this is a big if—it's not too extensive. I'm going to have to come look at it before I give you an answer."

"Oh," Tabitha says. "Okay. The address is Fifty-Five Forty-Nine Daggett Avenue. When were you thinking of coming over?"

"I'm free right now," Franklin says.

"Okay," Tabitha says.

"I'm sorry, I didn't get your name," Franklin says.

She closes her eyes. "Tabitha," she says. "Tabitha Frost."

Silence. *He's going to hang up,* she thinks.

Then he says, "Tabitha?"

"Yes," she says.

"This is Franklin. Franklin Phelps, from the other night?"

"What?" Tabitha says. "You're kidding! I didn't realize... I'm sorry...the phone book just said Hammer and Claw..."

"Don't apologize, please," Franklin says. "Listen, I'm coming over now, okay? Right this second. Don't go anywhere."

"I won't," she says. "I'll be right—"

But Franklin has hung up. Tabitha runs to find a brush and lipstick.

* * *

She doesn't know what to expect. She's sober; it's daytime; this is a business call. Will it be weird? Will the magic be gone? That's what she hopes for, of course—that the magic is gone, that Franklin Phelps is just another guy, less attractive and not at all appealing under this new set of circumstances.

From the window, she watches him pull up in a big black Dodge pickup, then stride up the walk. He's wearing Carhartt pants and a Black Dog T-shirt that has a rip in the neck. He's the most gorgeous man she's ever seen.

This is bad, very bad. She wants to go crawl under one of the beds with the dust bunnies.

When she opens the door, he stares at her, then he shakes his head. "I'm going to put my pride on the line here. This morning I looked at the ferry schedule to Nantucket."

"You... what?"

"I wanted to go over and find you," Franklin says. "I've been thinking of you, oh... basically nonstop since Friday night."

Tabitha grabs him by the dog on the front of his shirt and pulls him inside.

They make love in the kitchen and nearly pull the countertop free of the wall in the process.

Franklin is behind Tabitha, kissing the back of her neck. "Yeah," he says. "This house needs some work."

* * *

She shows him the pine floors under the carpet, the powder room, the three underwhelming bedrooms upstairs.

"I'm not going to lie to you," Franklin says. "This project is exactly the right size for me to take on. I can get this done in six weeks."

"Six *weeks?*" Tabitha says. She can't believe her reversal of fortune. This morning she had neither Franklin nor a contractor—and now she has both!

"But," Franklin says.

Or not both, she thinks.

He runs his hands through his dark hair. "There are extenuating circumstances," he says.

"What are they?" Tabitha says. *Girlfriend,* she thinks. Or he doesn't want to commit to Tabitha, because what if he doesn't like her as much as he thinks he does?

"I don't want to get into it," he says. "Just let me think about it, okay?"

"Okay," she says.

"What are you doing right now?" he asks.

"Other than trying to find a contractor, you mean?"

"Put your swimsuit on," he says. "And a pair of sneakers. We're going to the beach."

Franklin drives her to a place called Cedar Tree Neck, a nature preserve on a spit of land known as the Fishhook in Vineyard Haven. They walk through a thickly wooded area that offers luxurious shade on a hot day. Through the canopy of trees, bits of brilliant blue sky are visible, and Tabitha hears birdsong. When was the last time Tabitha enjoyed nature? Probably when she was fifteen years old at Camp Wyonegonic. They hike along in silence for a while, holding hands, then they crest a hill and Franklin stops. He takes her face in his hands and kisses her. His face has a day's worth of growth on it, which is so sexy against her face that her knees nearly buckle.

The kissing intensifies. Franklin backs her up against a tree.

"Are we?" she whispers into his mouth. "Here?"

He nods, reaching a hand into the bottom of her bathing suit.

The trail ends at a sandy, boulder-studded beach that cradles a small bay. Franklin lays out two towels, then he shucks off his shorts and races into the water, buck naked.

Tabitha shrieks. She looks both ways down the beach—nobody is around. She hesitates for a moment, wondering if she can go through with it. Swimming naked in a public place isn't something Tabitha Frost does. Tabitha Frost is dignified, her behavior unimpeachable.

Tabitha Frost is uptight, she thinks.

She unties her bikini and goes racing into the water.

The feeling is novel and delicious. The water is soft as it envelops her, all of her; she feels coddled, like a baby in embryonic fluid. And she enjoys the daring of it. For the moments when she is in the water, she is free.

Franklin scoops her up. When he kisses her, he tastes like salt water. She is weightless in his arms.

* * *

Back on her towel on the warm beach, she raises her face bravely to the sun. Her shoulder blades melt into the sand, and she falls asleep.

When she wakes up, the sun is lower in the sky, dappling the surface of the water. Tabitha turns her head to see Franklin on his side, his head propped on his arm, staring at her.

"You are so beautiful," he says.

Her stomach swoops.

This is happening.

Franklin has chosen a place called the Outermost Inn for dinner.

"It's in Aquinnah," he says. "You'll see all of up island on the way."

Tabitha puts on an orange Alexander Wang sundress with skinny straps that crisscross her now tanned back. It's the sexiest thing she owns, and she congratulates herself for deciding to bring it.

Franklin whistles. "Or we can just stay here and I'll eat you for dinner."

As they drive out South Road through Chilmark, Franklin plays the dutiful tour guide and shows Tabitha Beetlebung Corner. A beetle, he explains, is a mallet used to bang bungs—or stoppers—into barrels.

Tabitha laughs. "Thank you for telling me that. It sounds like something that infests your attic."

She loves all the low stone walls and the family farms. "And the cute street signs. Look at that one!" She points to a small wooden sign that says: SHEEP XING.

"Good old Sheep Crossing," Franklin says. The tone of his voice is suddenly arch. "The first cottage after the turn is where my brother-in-law is hiding out."

"Your brother-in-law?" Tabitha says. She tries to remember what Franklin has told her about his family. She isn't good with this kind of thing. The parents—she has lost their names—the father was the high school principal, the mother... she can't remember. Did Franklin mention a brother-in-law? The husband of his sister? His sister's name is... Charlotte? Nope, that's Ramsay's sister.

She waits for him to say more, but he merely shakes his head. "Never mind," he says.

Any awkwardness vanishes as they approach the Outermost Inn. It's set way up over the cliffs of Aquinnah; even from the parking lot, the views over the water are dramatic. Franklin is a perfect gentleman, ushering Tabitha inside, his hand resting lightly on the small of her back. Tabitha thinks briefly of Ramsay—his manners were impeccable, bordering on stuffy—but he never electrified Tabitha with his touch, as Franklin does.

The hostess at the intimate restaurant is roughly Tabitha's age. She has curly blond hair and wears a silk broomstick skirt that reaches to her ankles.

"Franklin!" she says. "Baby doll!"

"Annalisa," Franklin says. He kisses her on the lips, Tabitha notices. Okay, she's jealous. She feels a tightening across her shoulders and tries to fight it. She loves the decor of the inn, the candlelight, the smell of garlic, herbs, roasting meat, butter, good wine. She has only known Franklin for a few days. He has lived here for forty years.

Tabitha smiles at Annalisa, hoping she will not be mistaken for her sister. "Hello," she says. "I'm Tabitha Frost. I live on Nantucket."

"Oh yes, I know," Annalisa says. "The folks at the Steamship Authority send out an alert when someone from 'the other island' broaches our shores."

Franklin squeezes Tabitha's shoulder, and Tabitha manages a smile.

Annalisa sits Franklin and Tabitha at the best table in the house—out on the wide, gracious porch in the corner closest to the water. Franklin selects a bottle of Sancerre and a bottle of Malbec, and he pours Tabitha a glass of each.

They touch glasses, and Franklin shakes his head. "I can't tell you how happy I am that you called me," he says. "Even if it was by accident."

"If you wanted me to call you not by accident, you should have left your number in the note," Tabitha says. "I figured you never wanted to see me again."

"I . . ." Franklin sips his wine and looks off at the horizon, where the sun is sinking into the water. A streak of glorious orange light illuminates his face. "I wasn't sure of the protocol, I guess."

"You can't tell me you don't bring women home all the time," Tabitha says.

"I don't," Franklin says. He gives her an earnest look—could he possibly be telling the truth?—and then he changes the subject. "Tell me about you. I can't believe *you're* single. A gorgeous woman like you on an island with all those millionaires on their yachts."

Tabitha laughs. "Oh, I'm single. I was in a relationship for four years, but we broke up in February."

"Have you ever been married?" Franklin asks.

"No," Tabitha says. "But my first serious boyfriend and I have a child together. A daughter, Ainsley. She's sixteen."

"Sixteen!" Franklin says. "Is that even possible?"

"Possible," Tabitha says. "I had her when I was twenty-three. She was a surprise then...now she's just a handful. A few weeks ago, she threw a party at the house while I was out, and I came home to find the kids playing beer pong on my dining-room table."

Franklin throws his head back and laughs. "Oh come on. You have to admit that's funny," he says.

Is it funny? Tabitha lets herself smile. It's a lot funnier now than it was at the time, that's for certain. "We're enjoying a much-needed break from each other right now. Harper's over there watching her."

"Ah, I see," Franklin says. "You pulled the old switcheroo."

Tabitha wonders how Harper and Ainsley are doing. Maybe they've rolled all the ERF inventory outside for a sidewalk sale. Maybe they've hosted a dog show or are posting their political opinions on a Twitter account under Eleanor's name. Tabitha is so blissed out that she doesn't care.

Their food starts arriving from the kitchen, all dishes

meant to share: a velvety lobster bisque, a lightly dressed salad of microgreens and brightly colored disks that turn out to be crisp, sweet radish, pan-seared lobster with a grapefruit beurre blanc served over savory soft polenta, sirloin au poivre that comes with dauphine potatoes—walnut-size croquettes filled with buttery heaven. Franklin stops between bites and kisses Tabitha lightly on the lips, which incites desire more than a deep kiss might. They don't take any photos; they don't check in or post. This date is like something from another age. Tabitha tries to memorize every detail so she can relive it later.

Dessert is an assortment of treats served on a wooden lazy Susan: a passion-fruit panna cotta, miniature cannoli filled with pistachio cream, lemon blueberry tarts with an almond-ginger crust, toffee blondies topped with coconut fluff.

Tabitha takes a bite of each, then groans because she is so full. She excuses herself for the ladies' room.

When she emerges, Annalisa is standing in the vestibule, seemingly waiting for her.

"I hope you didn't mind my wisecrack about Nantucket," she says. "I was just having fun with you."

Tabitha, loosened by the wine, laughs. "Not a worry."

"I think it's great that Franklin wanted to bring you out here for dinner. He sounded so excited when he called to make the reservation. And he was very clear that he was bringing *Tabitha* Frost, not *Harper* Frost. Because I think we can all agree, if he took your sister out here for dinner, that would be really weird."

"Weird," Tabitha repeats. "Weird because..."

Annalisa swats Tabitha's arm. "Because of everything that just happened. But I'm glad you aren't letting that stand in your way. You two are a regular couple of lovebirds."

* * *

On the way home, Tabitha realizes that she didn't tell Franklin about Julian. She skipped right over him, as if he didn't exist—but if she wants Franklin to know her, then she has to remedy that. She's just not sure how to bring it up.

When Ainsley was eighteen months old, I got pregnant again. But things didn't go as planned. I went into labor at twenty-eight weeks...

Tabitha leans her head back against the car seat and closes her eyes. She'll tell Franklin about Julian another time, she decides. She doesn't want to ruin the magic of their time together.

"There's something I need to talk to you about," Franklin says. He reaches across the console and touches her thigh. "Tabitha."

Tabitha opens her eyes. His voice sounds serious. But only seconds ago she decided she didn't want to talk about anything heavy, deep, or real. She thinks back to the peculiar interaction with Annalisa. *Weird... because of everything that just happened.* Annalisa must have been referring to Harper's affair with Dr. Zimmer; it would indeed be weird if Harper then went on a romantic date with someone else.

"Maybe we should save talking for tomorrow," Tabitha says. "I've had a lot of wine."

"This concerns tomorrow," Franklin says. "I just decided that I'm going to help you with Billy's house."

"You are?" Tabitha says.

"I am," Franklin says. "We can talk about a plan of attack in the morning."

"Are you sure?" Tabitha says. "You seemed hesitant before. You said there were extenuating circumstances."

"There were. There *are.* But I've been mulling it over, and I cannot"—here he squeezes her leg—"and I mean I *cannot* let anyone else on this island work that closely with you. It has to be me. I'm your guy."

She nods, thinking, *I'm completely in love with this person.* Intellectually she knows this isn't possible. You do not *fall in love* with someone you've known for well, basically, a matter of hours. It's called something else—infatuation, which evaporates like dew in the sunshine.

But it feels just like love.

HARPER

Billy Frost had been fond of the phrase *halcyon days,* which was how he liked to describe their Vineyard summers. *These are the halcyon days,* he would say as he steered his Boston Whaler out of the harbor. *All hail the halcyon days of summer!* he would cry out from the wall in Menemsha where he and Harper would watch the sun extinguish itself in the ocean as they waited for their fried clams from Larsen's Fish Market to be ready. Billy had used the phrase so often that Harper had finally looked it up. It originated in Greek mythology. Alcyone, the daughter of Aeolus, lost her husband, Ceyx, in a shipwreck. She drowned herself in the sea, and they were both transformed into halcyon birds, or kingfishers. When Alcyone made a nest on the beach, the waves threatened to sweep it away, so her father, Aeolus, suspended the winds for seven days, known as the halcyon days—the days when storms do not occur.

Days when storms do not occur.

Harper enjoys her own string of halcyon days on Nantucket. At first she doesn't notice anything out of the ordinary, but then it dawns on her: she's happy.

Business at the store is booming. Harper, Ainsley, and Caylee have divided up the schedule so that two of them are always working together at any given time, and they have incorporated the strategies that worked effectively at the party. Fish is stationed outside the store for an hour in the morning and an hour in the afternoon; the rest of the day, he snoozes in the back office or waits for Harper to take him on his walk through town. This daily constitutional always ends at Ramsay's office with a dog treat.

Good music plays in the store now at all times, a carefully curated playlist—90 percent women, 10 percent Prince. And every morning, Caylee posts a photo of herself on social media wearing the "outfit of the day"—dress, skirt or pants, and top and sandals. It never fails: by day's end they have sold out of the outfit in all sizes.

Meghan comes to the store every day with baby David Wayne in his carriage. Harper never holds the baby—she has been afraid of babies since Julian died—but Ainsley and Caylee dance him around the store while Meghan marvels at the previous day's receipts.

"I can't believe how well the store is doing!" she says. "We are up *five hundred percent* so far from last summer."

Ainsley is happier each day. She hasn't made up with any of her friends, but she seems content spending her free time with Harper and with Caylee. She asks for their advice about Teddy.

After she and Caylee bumped into him at breakfast, Teddy texted Ainsley, saying, *I miss you. Can I call you sometime?*

Ainsley hasn't responded to the text, which has led Teddy to send more texts, all of them saying he misses her.

"It's like the only way to get him back is to ignore him," Ainsley says.

"The conundrum of human relationships," Caylee says.

On days when Harper isn't working, she explores the island. She loads Fish into the car and drives up to hike the scenic loop at Squam Swamp. She drives through the moors and swims in the clear green water of Jewel Pond. She packs a picnic and goes to Great Point for the day and climbs to the top of Great Point Light, which even Ainsley and Ramsay, two Nantucket natives, admit they've never done. In the evenings, Harper cooks dinner for Ainsley, and once a week they invite Ramsay over. Harper makes huge composed salads with fresh veggies from Bartlett's Farm and grilled shrimp or scallops from 167; she serves the salads with her famous "frosted garlic bread"—famous to her and Billy, anyway. She makes a chilled Thai cucumber-coconut soup; she makes peach and blueberry hand pies, which leak fruit and sugar everywhere but are delicious nonetheless.

At the end of each day. Harper is more tired than she can remember being in her entire life. She sleeps like a heavy stone resting at the bottom of a pond.

Despite her exhaustion and the fact that alcohol turns her stomach now, she lets Ramsay talk her into having an adult evening at the Pearl. She makes it clear to Ainsley, Caylee—

and especially to Ramsay—that this is *not* a date. It's dinner with a friend.

"At a very sexy bar," Caylee says. "Be careful. The tuna 'martini' sometimes has strange effects on people."

"I need help picking out something to wear," Harper says.

"Why do you care?" Ainsley asks. "If it's not a date."

This is a good question. Harper knows what Ramsay will wear: khakis, a Vineyard Vines tie, a navy blazer. His hair will be parted to the side and hold comb marks. He will be clean-shaven and will have polished the lenses of his glasses. Harper could get away with a Lilly Pulitzer or even with the least suggestive dress ever designed—the Roxie—in petal pink or Barbara Bush blue, but now that she has spent the last few weeks dressing people, she realizes that she has wasted almost forty years wearing... what? Her father's old golf shirts, cutoff shorts, T-shirt dresses from J.Crew, and to "dress up," things off the sale rack at Banana Republic and Ann Taylor Loft—and everything she owns is three sizes too big. It's a revelation to finally own beautiful clothes, feminine clothes, clothes that fit. She wants something fun and distinctive for this dinner. It's her first time going out on Nantucket. She's a different person here. She wants to dress like it.

She loves the Parker brand, but she can't pull off sequins or feathers, and their knit dresses are too casual. She tries on dresses by Nanette Lepore and Rebecca Taylor—but the winner, according to both Caylee and Ainsley, is a white silk Alice and Olivia slip dress with three black lace diamond-shaped inserts running down each side.

Because of her dark hair and her summer tan, the black-and-white combo really pops. Ainsley picks out a black suede choker, and Caylee selects a pair of black patent leather slides with kitten heels, which is as much heel as Harper can handle.

Once dressed, she stands for a moment in front of Tabitha's full-length mirror. She looks good, she thinks—and it has little to do with the dress or the shoes. She is relaxed. She is smiling.

The Pearl *is* a sexy place—swank and stylish. Ramsay has reserved them two corner seats at the white onyx bar. The bar is lit from underneath; it emits an otherworldly glow.

"Two passion-fruit martinis," Ramsay says. Harper nearly protests, but a passion-fruit martini does sound delicious, and she hopes her stomach issue has finally resolved itself.

Harper raises her glass and touches it to Ramsay's. The night is off and running.

Ramsay orders for both of them: duck confit dumplings, the tuna martini with crème fraîche and wasabi tobiko, the sixty-second steak topped with a fried quail egg, the stir-fried salt-and-pepper lobster.

"And another round of martinis!" Ramsay says.

The bartender, a pert and pretty blonde with a posh English accent, gives Ramsay and Harper a smile. "I'm glad to see you two back in here," she says. "I've missed you."

"Oh," Harper says. "I'm not..."

"Thank you, Jo," Ramsay says. "We've missed you, too."

* * *

With the third martini—and three will be it, Harper decides, then she'll switch to water—she can finally talk to Ramsay about the things she's afraid to talk to him about during the daylight hours.

"Do you miss my sister?" Harper asks.

"I do and I don't," Ramsay says. "I'm a fixer by nature. I tried and tried with Tabitha, but I couldn't help her. She wouldn't let me."

Harper nods. "She was born ninety seconds before me. She has always been independent and self-sufficient. Whereas I always needed help."

"So who is your support?" Ramsay asks.

How is Harper to answer that question?

"In recent years, my love life has been complicated," Harper says, and she shakes her head at the understatement. "I had a lover, a married lover."

"Ahh," Ramsay says.

"His name is Reed Zimmer," Harper says. It feels so wonderful to say his name out loud that tears stand in her eyes. "He's a fixer, too. A doctor. He was my father's doctor, so he took care of my father, and by association he took care of me. He has a quiet authority that made me feel safe when I was with him. Which of course was foolish because I was the opposite of safe. He belonged to someone else. His wife, Sadie. And I fell into the trap that all mistresses fall into: I believed Sadie didn't matter. I believed he would leave her for me eventually."

"But he didn't?" Ramsay says.

"Sadie found out about us," Harper says. "She caught us

together on the night my father died, and then a few days later she made a scene at Billy's funeral. Reed sent me a text message asking me not to contact him for a while." Harper stares into the bottom of her martini glass. Truth serum. She *never* talks this much—but then again, whom does she have to confide in? Only Ramsay, here and now. "I heard from other sources that he moved out. I heard he took a leave of absence from the hospital. I don't know where he is or what he's doing. I don't know if he's still on the Vineyard or if he's walking around out in the real world. I don't know if he's looking for me or looking for himself. I feel guilty about what I did to Sadie, but I feel more guilty about what I did to Reed. Because I believe he's a good, true person, and yet somehow I led him astray. I stained his character, shredded his integrity. The night Sadie caught us, I asked him to meet me. He didn't want to, but I begged him."

"Well, your father had just died," Ramsay says. "Right?"'

Harper spins her martini glass. "I mess up whatever I do," she says. "It's like a curse. When our parents divorced, and I got to go with Billy, I thought I'd won some kind of contest. But it turns out I'm a loser, through and through."

"You don't believe that," Ramsay says.

"I do, Tabitha does, and I think even my mother does. And my father, right before he died, turned to me and said, *I'm sorry, kiddo.* At first I wasn't sure what he meant, but I figured it out. He was sorry I was the way I was. He was sorry he couldn't help me."

"Harper, come on," Ramsay says. "You are a beautiful, intelligent woman. Every bit as intriguing as your sister but, if I may say so, way more fun."

"So much fun that I barely graduated from Tulane," Harper

says. "So much fun that while I was cocktail waitressing at this place in Edgartown called Dahlia's, I agreed to deliver a 'package' for a guy everyone knew was a drug dealer. I got arrested, ratted him out, brought down the whole operation."

Ramsay's eyes grew wide behind his glasses. "You're kidding."

"But that's not the worst thing I've ever done," Harper says. "And sleeping with Dr. Zimmer isn't the worst thing, either."

"Do I dare ask?" Ramsay says.

Harper studied him. "Tabitha never told you why we don't speak? She never hinted?"

"Never," Ramsay says. His face is earnest, but Harper can't believe that Tabitha lived with someone for so long and didn't tell him about the night Julian died.

"Well," Harper says. She's not sure what to say. She almost wishes Tabitha had given her version of the story so that Harper could confirm or deny. She drains the last sip of her martini. What she really wants is a shot of Jäger. "Tabitha blames me for Julian's death."

Ramsay shakes his head like he's trying to clear water from his ears. "What?" he says. "Why? Why would she do that?"

But this is beyond Harper's ability to answer. She slides off her bar stool and stares at him, willing him to understand that she did *not* smother Julian with a blanket or drown him in the bathtub or shake him because he wouldn't stop crying. Harper should explain the events of that day, that night—but even now, fourteen years later, it's too painful to revisit.

"Thank you for dinner," she says, and she leaves the restaurant. She turns back once to look at Ramsay. He is sitting, stunned, and makes no move to follow her.

* * *

She walks all the way home in her bare feet—kitten heels be damned—and thinks to herself: *The halcyon days—days when no storms occur—are over.* She can't last a second longer. She pulls out her phone and stares at the screen—it shows a long-ago photo of her and Billy on the boat, with Billy holding up a striped bass—willing herself to let reason rule here. But no, sorry. She calls Reed and is shuttled to his voice mail. She has something to tell him. It's only a hunch, but she can't leave it in a message. She hangs up.

But then, almost immediately, Harper's phone rings. Reed? Or is it Ramsay, just now recovering from his shock? Harper waits for the ringing to stop and the chime to sound indicating a voice mail, then she checks her display.

It's an unfamiliar Vineyard number, exchange 693. She stops in her tracks on the side of Cliff Road. Maybe it's Reed, calling from a landline.

It's a moment or two before Harper can bring herself to listen to the message.

"Harper, hello. This is Edie Donegal, Brendan's mother. I understand you might still be away, but I felt the need to call you. Brendan isn't doing well. I know you care about him, and as much as I don't want to impose, I can't help but ask if you might be able to visit him sometime soon. It's the only thing I can think of that might help. Thank you, Harper. Good night."

Harper's head suddenly feels too heavy to hold up. Brendan. Poor Brendan. And yet in her current state of mind, Harper doesn't believe she can help Brendan. She will only make things worse.

She deletes the message.

She can't take another step. Her stomach roils, and green waves of nausea wash over her. She vomits into the grass on the side of the road.

More than a hunch, she thinks. She knows.

She's pregnant.

NANTUCKET

A stretch of days arrives when the weather is so brutal that it's the only thing people want to talk about. It's eighty-seven degrees at noon—unheard of since the heat wave of 1936. The brick sidewalks of town bake in the sun; the beaches are unbearable. There is no breeze, no clouds, not a second's respite from the punishing heat.

It's too hot to gossip. Nobody can sit still long enough to listen.

But the insurance offices of Striker & McClain are mightily air-conditioned, so much so that every client who walks in sighs with the deliciousness of it.

Percil Ott sinks into the armchair next to the desk of the receptionist, Bonnie Atkinson. Percil tells Bonnie he needs to see Ramsay Striker about a windshield replacement.

"But no hurry," Percil says to Bonnie. "I could sit here all day."

Bonnie rolls her eyes. Percil is a retiree who likes the sound of his own voice. She isn't about to get sucked into his vortex.

"I'll let Ramsay know you're here," Bonnie says.

Ramsay works back in the corner of the office, and Bonnie notices his privacy walls are up, which is unusual. Bonnie has worked at Striker & McClain for twenty-one years, and she can't remember this ever happening before. Intellectually she realizes that privacy panels mean that Ramsay would like privacy, but Bonnie suffers from an acute case of natural curiosity. She peeks through the crack and sees Ramsay intently studying his computer screen. Bonnie's hand flies to her chest. Pornography? She never pegged Ramsay for the pornography type; he's handsome enough to have any woman he wants—look at the twenty-two-year-old bartender he dated for nearly three months! But then Bonnie squares her expectations with reality: *everyone* watches porn. Everyone except Bonnie and her husband, Norm Atkinson. Norm watches reruns of *The Andy Griffith Show.*

"Excuse me, Ramsay," Bonnie says. "Percil Ott is here to see you."

Ramsay startles as if he has indeed been caught at some illicit activity. Over his shoulder, however, Bonnie catches a glimpse of the screen. It's an old article from the *Inquirer and Mirror.*

Ramsay stands and moves aside one of the privacy panels. "Thanks, Bonnie," Ramsay says. "I know Mr. Ott isn't your favorite. I'll handle him." He strides down the hall, leaving Bonnie to stand at the opening of his office.

Most of us may claim that we would never do what Bonnie Atkinson then did, but most of us would be lying. Bonnie steps quickly over to Ramsay's computer and scans the contents of the screen. It's an obituary, she realizes. An obituary for an infant boy, Julian Wyatt Cruise, born May 28, 2003, died August 15, 2003. Bonnie inhales sharply. Not even three months old. The cause of death is stated as "respiratory failure."

Why would Ramsay be interested in *this?* Bonnie wonders. Then she sees the names of the surviving family. *Father: Wyatt Cruise. Mother: Tabitha Frost.*

The other place that is lavishly air-conditioned during the hideous heat wave is the ERF boutique. We understand the rationale: nobody wants to try on clothes when she's sweating, and in weather such as this, all air-conditioned venues are seeing an increase in foot traffic.

At eleven o'clock on the fifth day of unbearable hellfire heat, Caylee Keohane is experiencing a lull in her workday. The store has been empty just long enough for her to wonder: *Is this heat wave a result of global warming?* And is the new president planning on *doing* anything about it?

Caylee is bored. It's Ainsley's day off—she said she was going to stay home, eat ice chips, and binge on *Girls*—and Harper arrived at work in such a foul mood that Caylee suggested she take a long lunch, maybe drive her Bronco out to 40th Pole and go for a swim. Initially Caylee had thought Harper's mood was attributable to the heat, but when she thinks back, she realizes that Harper has been irritable since her non-date date with Ramsay. Did something happen? Did Ramsay make moves on Harper against her wishes, or did he *not* make moves when she wanted him to? Caylee can't ask Harper these questions because she and Harper haven't developed the closeness that Caylee and Ainsley have. Harper is always friendly, always congenial, but she holds personal information in reserve.

As Caylee is cogitating on what might be up with Harper, the door opens, and a dark-haired girl wanders in, holding an iced coffee. The girl looks familiar, but before Caylee can suss out who she is, she has to deal with business.

"I'm sorry," Caylee says, trying to sound genuinely sorry and not merely annoyed—although really, there *is* a sign on the door that says NO FOOD, NO DRINK, NO EXCEPTIONS. "You'll have to leave your coffee outside."

The girl tilts her head and hitches up the strap of what Caylee thinks is a Chloe hobo bag in saddle-tone leather. "When I was here before, there was food *and* drink. What's up with that?"

Then Caylee realizes: this girl with the twenty-five-hundred-dollar bag is Ainsley's friend—or former friend—Emma. Unlike Harper, Ainsley has confided everything about her personal life to Caylee. She told Caylee that she stole gin from her grandmother's house and that Emma planted it in Candace's locker, but then somehow the situation flipped on its head and Emma and Candace ganged up on Ainsley and Ainsley ended up serving a three-day in-school suspension. Then the girls egged her house. It's enough to take Caylee back to the heartache of her own high school days. Kids are cruel because they are jealous or confused or simply badly parented. Ainsley has told Caylee that Emma lives with her father, Dutch, who owns the restaurant at the Nantucket airport. The mother lives somewhere in Florida; apparently Emma never sees her. Caylee feels for any child who has lost a parent to either death or desertion—Caylee's own mother died of breast cancer three years ago, and Caylee misses her every second of every day—but she also suspects that in Emma's case, a lack of a mother has curdled her soul until it's as sour as a glass of expired milk.

"That was a special occasion," Caylee says. "We don't allow food or drink during regular business hours. I'm sorry. You're welcome to finish your coffee outside."

Emma places the cup on the front step. Caylee will bet fifty bucks that she forgets all about it and leaves it for Caylee to throw away.

"Thanks," Caylee says. "Now, can I help you find something?"

"Actually," Emma says, "I'm looking for Ainsley. Is she here?"

"She's not," Caylee says, though certainly that's apparent. The store is deserted. "It's her day off."

"Oh," Emma says. "Lucky her." She takes an ERF dress off the rack—long-sleeved with a floppy bow at the neck, reminiscent of what Dustin Hoffman wore in *Tootsie*—and holds it up against her body. "This is hideous."

Caylee happens to agree, but she isn't about to bond with Emma over taste, nor is she going to let Emma insult the signature brand. "I'll tell Ainsley you stopped in," she says.

Emma sniffs and heads to the part of the boutique that features the other, younger lines. She fingers a black beaded Parker top.

"I have this in white," Emma says.

Caylee smiles blandly. Emma moves to the table where the "littles" are kept—rope belts, scarves, sunglasses, and the jar of lacy thongs. She fingers the scarves, inspects the belts, tries on the sunglasses. Caylee stifles a yawn. Norah Jones sings "Come Away with Me."

Then suddenly Caylee gets an idea.

"I have to use the ladies' room," she says. "I'll be back in a minute."

"Whatevs," Emma says.

Caylee steps into the back office and closes the door firmly with a click. She brings up the store surveillance camera on her phone as she strides with heavy wedge-heeled footsteps down the hallway. Sure enough, Emma Marlowe's head is on a swivel, checking the store for cameras, but the camera Eleanor had installed is designed to look like a sprinkler head. Emma reaches into the glass jar and grabs two lace thongs. She drops the thirty-six dollars' worth of merchandise into her twenty-five-hundred-dollar bag. If it were anyone else, Caylee would have handled the shoplifting herself, but for Emma, Caylee calls the police.

Gotcha, she thinks.

Nobody is surprised to hear that Emma Marlowe has gotten caught stealing. Even the officer who responds, Sergeant Royal DiLeo, is unsurprised. He has busted up every teenage beer party this summer, and Emma, with her snarky, entitled attitude, has been present at them all. People *are* surprised to hear that Dutch Marlowe actually leaves the airport restaurant in order to come to the store and lobby on his daughter's behalf. Little does he know that this unprecedented bit of parental support will backfire. For the second he walks in to the ERF boutique and sees that it's Caylee Keohane who has caught his daughter, he is sorry indeed.

Caylee's eyes shoot streams of green fire at Dutch. "What are *you* doing here?" she asks.

"That's my dad," Emma says.

"Your... your..." Caylee says.

Dutch runs a hand over his shaved head and silently begs the young woman not to disclose how she knows him. It was Dutch Marlowe who grabbed Caylee's perfect peach of an ass, causing her to unload a Jack and Coke in his lap. She had then been fired by Shorty, the manager at the Straight Wharf. Shorty hadn't wanted to fire Caylee. She was a tireless worker with a great personality—a winning combination in the service industry, where so often you get either one or the other—and he was 100 percent sure that Dutch *had* grabbed Caylee's ass. But unfortunately, Shorty had no choice. He was a regular at the Wednesday night poker game at Dutch's house, and he was into Dutch for forty-five hundred dollars.

Dutch, as we all know, is a person with absolutely no conscience, but he had felt guilty about getting Caylee fired. He hadn't meant to pinch her ass, meaning it hadn't been premeditated, but she had been out from behind the bar a lot that night, waving her tush around in those white jeans like a matador waving a red flag in front of a bull. What could Dutch say? He was a man, horny all the time and lonely besides.

But still, he doesn't love the idea of Emma hearing that her father is a lecherous jerk.

Caylee snarls. "Your dad?" she says. She takes a deep breath and prepares to tell Emma the truth about her father, but in the end she just shakes her head. "Why am I not surprised?"

MARTHA'S VINEYARD

The island is so crowded in July that we fear it might tip over—down island will nose-dive, upending Chilmark and Aquinnah. The population hits ninety thousand, then ninety-one thousand.

The steamship sits so low in the water—weighted down with Jeeps, Land Rovers, Hummers—that it reminds us of a pregnant woman after the baby drops. State Beach is parked out by nine in the morning; the Port Hunter has a two-hour wait for a table. The line at the Bite has 111 people in it at five thirty, which increases to 147 people at six thirty. There is an average of fifteen car accidents a day; six of these involve taxis.

And yet who among us hasn't longed for these summer days? Indians and IODs tack and jibe in Edgartown harbor, tennis balls hit the baseline at the Field Club, eliciting our best John McEnroe imitations: *That ball was in! Chalk flew up all over the place!* Daughters of the scions of industry tan their breasts on the shores of Lucy Vincent. Authors come nightly to read at Bunch of Grapes—Charles Bock, Jane Green, Richard Russo. Skip Gates rides his tricycle out to Katama; Keith Richards takes his grandchildren to pick blueberries at the patch off of Middle Road; Noah Mayhew, the reservationist at the Covington, becomes so overwhelmed by calls from demanding and entitled people that he quits and moves to an ashram in Oregon.

Upon hearing this news about her great-nephew, Noah, Indira Mayhew, who has worked as the Chappy ferry master for nearly forty years aboard the *On Time II,* thinks seriously about following suit, although she has never practiced yoga.

With all this happening, how does anyone have time to figure out what's going on at Billy Frost's house? Daggett Avenue is an average, year-round part of Tisbury that falls beneath most people's notice—and from the curb, the house looks the same. If someone had been staking out the street—selling lemonade on the corner or casing the neighborhood with criminal intent—he might have noticed Franklin Phelps's truck driving around the neighborhood, and further snooping would have revealed Franklin's truck parked in Billy's backyard. But no one is staking out the street.

Franklin has been careful to hire subcontractors from off island: the electrician hails from Falmouth, the plumber from Mashpee. These guys don't know who from what as far as Vineyard gossip is concerned; they just come in and do the work. The only person Franklin trusts—and, for this project, *needs*—is Tad Morrissey. Tad is Franklin's right-hand man. He can do anything—tile, plaster, cabinetry—and he does so without complaining. Also, despite being Irish, he's a man of few words. A human vault. Franklin doesn't have to explain the fine print to Tad, but he does it anyway: *My sister cannot find out that we are renovating Billy Frost's house. Do you understand?*

Tad nods with mouth full of nails.

Franklin worries that someone saw him with Tabitha that first night at the Ritz and reported back to Sadie, thinking Tabitha was Harper, but by the following day, when he hadn't heard about it, he figured he was safe. He had been clear with Annalisa at the Outermost Inn: *I'm bringing in Tabitha Frost, Harper's twin sister, and nobody can know.* Franklin has known Annalisa since elementary school. He told her he trusted her with his life, hoping that would be enough to ensure her silence.

A few days after Franklin starts seeing Tabitha and working full-time on her house, he is summoned to his parents' home in Katama for dinner. His mother doesn't use a cell phone or a computer, so she tapes an index card to the front door of his cottage, on Grovedale Road in Oak Bluffs, that says: DINNER MONDAY 6:00 P.M. Franklin is lucky he even sees this minimalist invitation; he has spent every night with Tabitha at Billy's house. He stops at home only to get clothes and, finally, to grab his electric razor.

He sighs. He can't, obviously, take Tabitha to his parents' house for dinner. All hell will break loose.

All hell is going to break loose anyway, he realizes. But he can stave it off a little while longer.

And in fact things at the Phelpses' that evening start out fine. Tabitha accepts the news that Franklin is eating with his parents with equanimity. She says she's going to stay home and paint the powder room a shade of silvery gray called Paul Revere's Ride. Franklin approves: Tabitha's taste is impeccable, which is to say, it matches his own.

The elder Phelpses are in good spirits, as ever. Al Phelps is a favorite with nearly all of us because he was such a dedicated and benevolent principal during his tenure at the high school, and now, in retirement, he runs errands to Shirley's and Mocha Mott's seemingly just so he can spread goodwill. He is famous for buying his former students a cup of coffee. Meanwhile, Lydia is an active member of the Excellent Point book group, and she volunteers each week at the Island Food Pantry.

Both the elder Phelpses embrace their son. Lydia runs a hand over Franklin's now smooth face.

"I'm glad you shaved," she says. "Christine Velman told me she saw you stopped at the Barnes Road intersection and that you were growing a beard."

"No," Franklin says. He shakes his head. If Christine Velman reported back to his mother about the state of his facial hair, how long will it be before someone tells Lydia that Franklin is dating the twin sister of the woman who betrayed Sadie—and, worse, is working on their father's house?

Al Phelps claps his son on the back. "Can I buy you a beer?"

"Please," Franklin says.

Sadie arrives in short order, which is good, Franklin thinks, because it doesn't leave Lydia any time to talk about her. One look at his sister, however, tells Franklin what his mother would have said if she'd had the chance. Sadie has lost at least ten pounds, and she wasn't a very big person to begin with. Her cheeks are sunken; her face, for lack of a better word, looks cadaverous. She keeps her hair very short, but now it looks as if she's taken kitchen shears to it in a fit of grief. There are purplish-red circles under her eyes, and she is shaking.

Franklin's heart sinks. He knows that Sadie has closed the pie shop "until further notice," but he had hoped she would have taken the hiatus to rest and recoup. He had hoped she would rise above her circumstances and maybe even revel in her newfound independence. Reed betrayed her—yes, he did. He cheated on her with the daughter of one of his patients, a woman whose morals were already held in question by most of the island because of her involvement with Joey Bowen.

Franklin has refrained from sharing his opinion with his sister, which is that he doesn't think Harper is a bad person. He has always liked her. She has been a fan of his music; she came to see him every time he played and was the first person to buy his ill-fated CD of original songs. Harper has never been anything but sweet and lovely to him, and he had witnessed firsthand the crap she had to put up with as a cocktail waitress at Dahlia's. Those girls were teased and manhandled and harassed. A chance to quit slinging drinks and do something far easier—if illegal and dangerous—for Joey Bowen must have seemed like an answer of sorts.

Franklin also believes that no affair is ever one partner's fault; it signifies the collapse of the union. This past winter, Franklin stopped by Reed and Sadie's house to get a prescription for a Z-Pak; Franklin had a nasty case of bronchitis that was wreaking havoc with his carpentry and singing. It was a Sunday afternoon: Sadie was at the pie shop, and Reed was home alone, drinking an eighteen-year-old Aberlour, watching the Patriots in the playoffs. He invited Franklin to stay.

He held up his glass. "Aberlour has its own medicinal properties, you know."

After they had each had two glasses—Franklin's with water, Reed's straight—Reed muted the television; the Pats were winning in a blowout. Reed said, "Does your sister ever say if she's happy being married to me?"

The question was as welcome as a bowling ball to the groin. Franklin sucked in a breath and opened his mouth to reassure his brother that yes, his sister was happy. Of course she was happy! Why wouldn't she be happy? It was islandwide opinion that Dr. Reed Zimmer was a *great guy.* Reliable, trustworthy, dedicated. A Martha's Vineyard treasure—a hero, even. But Franklin had, in fact, accidentally overheard Sadie talking to their mother, Lydia, during one of the family dinners Reed hadn't been able to attend because he'd been called into the hospital. Sadie had been venting to Lydia because Reed had suddenly decided he wanted children.

But I won't do it, Sadie had said. *And I will punish him until he takes the words back.*

Franklin had stopped listening at that point. He had sought refuge with his father, who was loath to talk about anything more controversial than local politics.

"I don't know," Franklin said to his brother-in-law. He and Reed had never had a heart-to-heart chat before. He didn't know Reed was capable of it. But of course Reed needed a confidant; everyone did.

"We haven't slept together in over a year," Reed said. He had slugged back his Scotch and poured another two fingers. "And I'm talking sex, but I'm also telling you we now keep different bedrooms. She won't touch me at all, Franklin."

Franklin had been muted by discomfort. The next-to-last thing he wanted to hear about was his sister's sex life; the last thing he wanted to hear about was his parents' sex life. But he put two and two together and deduced that cutting Reed off was Sadie's way of exacting her punishment. Now, Franklin is *not* saying Reed was justified in having an affair. But he isn't sure how Sadie saw that strategy working out to her advantage, other than that it would ensure she wouldn't have a child. At this point, neither does she have a husband.

They sit down to dinner promptly at six. Franklin's mother doesn't believe in a cocktail hour; she claims hors d'oeuvres ruin the appetite. She also has no use for seasonality. It's mid-July, and she has made a pot roast with potatoes and carrots and onions, snowflake rolls from scratch, and an iceberg salad with bottled blue cheese dressing. Franklin has warned his mother that one day the Martha's Vineyard farmer's market police are going to arrest her simply for serving iceberg lettuce. But Lydia feels no shame.

Franklin sweats his way through the meal in more ways than one. All he can do is hope that his mother made pie for dessert— peach or triple berry. He pictures Tabitha rolling Paul Revere's Ride onto the powder-room walls, a few specks of paint dotting her nose. She had told him, right before he left, that Wyatt, her children's father, was a professional housepainter and had long ago taught her how to tape off a room. The thunderbolt of jealousy Franklin experienced nearly caused him to pass out.

It was only on the way to his parents' house that he thought, *Children?* He has only heard about the daughter, Ainsley.

"So," Sadie says, contributing to conversation for the first time. "Where are you working these days, Frankie?" The childhood nickname is a playful touch. Maybe she's not as damaged as she looks. But even so, Franklin can't own up to the truth. He harbors the naive belief that if he just lets some more time pass, Sadie's mind-set will improve, and she won't care when he tells her he's seeing Tabitha Frost.

And the word *seeing* doesn't begin to convey how he feels. He's gobsmacked. He's neck-deep in emotion for the woman.

"Cuttyhunk," he says nonchalantly.

"Really?" she says. Her tone is indecipherable. Is she calling his bluff or merely impressed?

"Really," he says.

"So you're using the boat, then?" she asks. "You should take me over there sometime."

"We can all go!" Lydia says.

"Now, now, honey," Al says. "Franklin is working."

"I am working," Franklin says. "Believe me, there's nothing I'd rather do than have the three of you join me for a leisurely day on Cuttyhunk, but it isn't really feasible with the project I'm involved in."

"Of course not," Al says.

Sadie stares at him.

Franklin leaves his parents' house that evening with his secret intact. But how much longer can he hope to keep it that way?

Not much longer, we all suspect. Because who has ever successfully kept a secret on this island?

It's three days later when Tad Morrissey is backing up in the parking lot of Cottle's lumberyard in Edgartown and gets T-boned from the right by Roger Door, who had parked in the Cottle's lot but spent nearly an hour over at Coop's Bait & Tackle talking about where the stripers are running—and, apparently, nipping from the flask of Bushmills he takes with him everywhere.

Tad recognizes Roger Door but doesn't properly know him, and the accident has brought out Tad's infrequently seen Irish temper.

"What the hell?" he shouts. "You just rammed right into me!"

Roger Door tucks the flask under the passenger seat and climbs out of his truck to inspect the damage he did to the vehicle of the angry young man. His wife, Cecily, is going to clobber him. Roger has retired as a general contractor and now works solely as an odd-jobs man, but he is selective with his clients and therefore spends most of his time either fishing in his thirteen-foot Whaler or golfing with Smitty at Farm Neck. And drinking, of course—but only during the day. Roger Door is routinely in bed by eight thirty.

Tad also gets out to inspect the damage and finds a dent the size of Quitsa Pond in the side panel of his F-250. He feels heat rising from the soles of his feet, and his hands start to itch. He wants to punch the old man right in the face—break his nose, bust open his lip. Tad feels about his truck the way most people feel about their children.

"Sorry about that," Roger says. He steps closer to Tad and lowers his voice. "Think we can work something out without getting insurance involved?"

"Like hell," Tad says. He has lived on the island for seven years and has seen the likes of Roger Door way too often—old salts who think they can say anything and do anything because one of their ancestors was banging the original Martha-who-owned-the-vineyard. "I'm calling the police."

Roger Door's shoulders slump. Cecily will have his head on a platter.

A little while later, Sergeant Drew Truman is on the scene, filing an accident report. He knows Roger Door from the Rotary Club, which is a point in Roger's favor, although it seems like Roger might be at fault.

"Give him a Breathalyzer!" Tad says. "He's been drinking."

"I beg your pardon, young man," Roger says.

"I have to get back to work!" Tad says, pointing to the back of his pickup, which is filled with two-by-fours and sheets of plywood. "I'm on a deadline."

Is it possible that Roger Door has been drinking? Drew wonders. It's only eleven o'clock in the morning. The younger gentleman is calling for a Breathalyzer, but it comes across as though he's telling Drew how to do his job, at which Drew takes umbrage. He decides just to give Roger Door a moving violation and puts him at fault for the accident. Their insurance companies can battle it out.

In an attempt to make nice with the hotheaded Irish guy—Drew realizes he's met him once before, at the bar at Sharky's, where he was watching soccer and screaming at the TV—he says, "Where are you working?"

"Daggett Avenue," Tad says. He pulls his phone out of his back pocket and checks the time. "This bleeder cost me forty-five minutes I don't have, and now I'm looking at trying to get back to Tisbury in lunchtime traffic."

Drew nods sympathetically. *Traffic* is every Vineyarder's favorite thing to complain about, followed closely by mopeds and taxi drivers, which are really just subcategories of traffic.

"Daggett Avenue?" Roger Door says. Despite enjoying half a flask (at least) of Bushmills, he experiences a moment of lucidity. "Are you the one working on Billy Frost's house?"

Tad stares at the old man.

"Billy Frost's house?" Just hearing the name Frost causes Sergeant Drew Truman to suffer chest pain. He had fallen for Harper Frost, but what a fool he had been! Just last week, Drew had pulled over a Rooster Express truck for making an illegal U-turn on Meetinghouse Road. Drew had entertained the faintest hope that he would find Harper driving, but it had been Rooster himself. He told Drew that he had fired Harper and that she had left island.

Drew studies Tad. "*Are* you working on Billy Frost's house?"

Tad shrugs. "Does it matter? Or can I go?"

"Just answer the question, please, sir," Drew says, though he knows the question is out of bounds. "Are you working on Billy Frost's house?"

Tad has promised Franklin that he will keep his mouth shut about the job, but he isn't about to lie to an officer of the law, and this guy, he knows, is a hometown hero and a member of one of the most prominent families in Oak Bluffs. He probably has the power to make Tad's life miserable in ways Tad can't even imagine. Besides, he needs to get out of there. His poor truck!

"Yeah," Tad says.

"And who is it you work for?" Drew asks, though suddenly he knows the answer because they talked about it at the bar at Sharky's. He works for . . . for . . .

Tad knows this is it—the end of Franklin's fantasy that he could work on Billy Frost's house and have a wild-ass love affair with Harper Frost's twin sister, Tabitha, without anyone finding out about it. *Oh, well,* Tad thinks.

"Franklin Phelps," Tad says.

Since Drew broke up with Harper, he has only one confidant: Chief Oberg. The chief has been very patient and nurturing with his sergeant because Drew Truman is a straight arrow with unimpeachable character and integrity, and with the current troubling atmosphere surrounding law enforcement, Chief Oberg has devoted himself to focusing on the cops he considers his shining stars. When Drew gets back to the station, he finds Chief Oberg in the break room eating kale salad out of a Tupperware container. He tells the chief about the accident, then he reveals that Franklin Phelps is working on Billy Frost's house.

"That's weird, right? Because Harper was having an affair with Dr. Zimmer, and Dr. Zimmer is married to Sadie, who is Franklin Phelps's sister. That's a conflict of interest, right?"

Chief Oberg stabs a piece of kale. His wife, JoAnn, is on a diet, and when JoAnn is on a diet, the whole house is on a diet. After his shift, he's going to stop at Shiretown Meats for an Italian sub with extra hot peppers. "It's the Vineyard, Drew," the chief says. "Everything here is a conflict of interest."

He says this to placate his young colleague, and Drew thanks him dutifully and wanders away. But the person who does agree with Drew that it's a conflict of interest is Shirley Sparks, Chief Oberg's administrative assistant, whose desk is right outside the break room. Shirley is in the Excellent Point book group with Franklin and Sadie's mother, Lydia Phelps, and she finds it interesting—indeed, startling—that Franklin is working on the house of the father of the woman who betrayed his sister. She wonders if Lydia knows about this. If she does know about it, she must need someone to talk to. And if she doesn't know about it, she should.

Shirley calls Lydia.

AINSLEY

What started out as the Worst Summer of Her Life has gotten better. First Ainsley succeeded in recapturing Teddy's interest. Since bumping into him at 21 Broad, he has texted her every day, asking when he can see her, when they can hang out. Both

Caylee and Harper counsel Ainsley to be slow and measured in her responses. Ainsley does love Teddy, but he hurt her—emotionally for certain but also physically that afternoon in the cubby—and Ainsley isn't sure that getting back together with Teddy is what she wants. It's nice to have him in pursuit, however. A lot nicer than pining away for him.

Caylee catches Emma shoplifting two pairs of Hanky Panky low-rise thongs from the store, and she calls the police. Dutch shows up to get Emma off the hook, but his appearance only makes things worse because it turns out that Dutch Marlowe was the one who got Caylee fired from the Straight Wharf. Ainsley's head spins at this news. On the one hand she thinks, *Of course it was dirty, disgusting Dutch Marlowe who grabbed Caylee's ass.* And then somehow Dutch managed to turn the tables so that Caylee was the one who got fired. On the other hand, Ainsley is grateful to Dutch because if Caylee hadn't gotten fired she wouldn't be working at the ERF boutique and they wouldn't now be friends. Caylee has taught Ainsley so much—about grace and kindness and the power of pure intentions. She leads by example. After breaking up with Ramsay, she has chosen not to date anyone else for a while; she wants to spend time with herself, she says. Ainsley loves this idea. She decides that she may get back together with Teddy down the road, but for the rest of the summer and the beginning of her junior year, she is going to spend time with herself. She has gone beyond her summer reading assignments and is devouring all of Edith Wharton, book by book. She has started getting up earlier so she can jog down the Cliff Road bike path—to the water tower and back, two miles round-trip—before work. She has signed up for a class at the Corner Table called Cooking Basics because one of the things she loves about Aunt Harper is her home-cooked meals. Ainsley imagines her mother returning to find her daughter well read, in shape, and accomplished in the kitchen.

A text arrives from Teddy a few days after Ainsley told him about the shoplifting that says: *Did you hear the latest about Emma?*

Ainsley's insides turn cold. Has Emma been hurt? Has Emma been in an accident? Has Emma *died?* The thought is, frankly, horrifying—which also shows how much Ainsley has evolved. A few weeks earlier, Emma's untimely demise seemed like the only answer to ending Ainsley's agony.

What? she texts back.

Dutch is sending her to boarding school, Teddy says. *In Pennsylvania. The George School.*

Ainsley shrieks. Emma is going to boarding school! In Pennsylvania! Ainsley can't believe how ecstatic this news makes her. The prospect of finishing high school without having to deal with either Emma-the-enemy or even Emma-the-friend is like a golden sunrise. Ainsley can start fresh; she can reinvent herself. She can be good.

I wish her well, she texts.

It's a Tuesday, and Ainsley is working with Caylee when Candace Beasley walks into the boutique. Ainsley gasps. Candace has cut off her hair; her long, shiny strawberry-blond locks have been hacked into a blunt bob that barely clears the back of her neck. She still wears the grosgrain headband, however. Today's is black with tiny white polka dots, and it matches her simple outfit of white Current/Elliott boyfriend shorts and a scoop-neck black T-shirt. Once Ainsley recovers from the surprise of Candace's haircut, she grows wary about why Candace is here. Maybe she has come to finish what Emma started. Maybe there's a snub-nosed revolver in Candace's straw clutch.

Caylee reaches out to touch Ainsley's shoulder. She must recognize Candace. "Can I help you?" Caylee says.

"Oh," Candace says. "I came to talk to Ainsley."

There are three other women browsing. One is a woman named Lisa Hochwarter, who has spent more than five thousand dollars in the boutique so far this summer. She religiously follows Caylee's Facebook posts and nearly always comes in to try on and then buy the outfit of the day. She also bought a vintage men's watch because she loves the way Harper wears Billy's watch. Ainsley, Caylee, and Harper all fawn over Lisa—not just because she's their best customer but also because she's irreverent and funny. She's a reading specialist in Pawtucket, Rhode Island, and she has a rottweiler/black Lab mix named Potter who has become best friends with Fish.

Ainsley says, "You can help Lisa. I'm okay."

"You sure?" Caylee says.

Ainsley steps out from behind the register to help Candace. "Your hair."

"My mother forced me to donate fourteen inches to Locks of Love," Candace says.

"Forced you?" Ainsley says.

"I had to make amends," Candace says. "I've gone way off the rails this summer, according to my parents."

Ainsley shrugs. "You hang out with Emma. Emma invented off the rails."

"Did you hear she's going to boarding school?"

"I did," Ainsley says. "Teddy told me." She says this as a jab, but Candace remains unfazed.

"Teddy and I broke up," Candace says. "It was never that serious."

"Well," Ainsley says. "It seriously hurt my feelings."

"I know," Candace says. She wanders over to a rack holding several Roxie dresses in a rainbow of colors and fingers the obi of the one in peach. "I came in to apologize to you. I should never have gotten mixed up with Teddy or with Emma. I guess..." Her voice trails off, and Ainsley sees her eyes shining with tears. "I was hurt back when you... when we stopped being friends. I didn't understand it. You dropped me because I wasn't cool enough. And now I understand that I *wasn't* cool enough. I matured more slowly than you did. I couldn't have kept up with you and Emma."

Ainsley blinks. "I was cruel to you. I'm the one who should be apologizing."

"No," Candace says. She shakes her head, and her short hair shimmies. "Let me finish. I wanted to be friends with Emma, and I wanted to date Teddy... not because they were suited for me but because you had them."

"It's okay, Candace."

"I egged your house with Emma."

"I know."

"I get sick when I think about it," Candace says.

Ainsley gives her a sad smile. "Me, too."

"Part of me believes that with Emma leaving, you and I can be friends again."

Ainsley thinks about this. "Maybe we can," she says. "But I'm holding off on having a boyfriend for a while, and I'm also holding off on having a best friend."

"Fair enough," Candace says. She stuffs her hands into the front pockets of her shorts and tilts her head. "Is it true that your mother left for a while and her twin sister came to take her place?"

"Yeah," Ainsley says. "But that's not as crazy as it sounds."

Or maybe it *is* as crazy as it sounds, Ainsley thinks later. When she's finished at work, she checks her phone. She has been so absorbed in her own drama that she's lost track of her mother. The last time Tabitha called was…five days earlier. Is that possible?

Ainsley sits on a bench on Main Street near the place where she has chained her bike and does the unthinkable: she voluntarily calls her mother.

"Darling!" Tabitha says. She sounds happy—giddy, even—and Ainsley reels for a second. Xanax, maybe?

"Hi, Mama," she says.

"I was just thinking about you," Tabitha says. "You should see what we're doing to Gramps's house. It was a total disaster area, but we're redoing everything, and it's going to be gorgeous, like one of the houses in *Domino*."

Who is *we?* Ainsley wonders. She says, "I thought you and Aunt Harper had agreed to tear it down."

"Harper wanted to tear it down. She didn't see the potential. Do you know what we found under the wall-to-wall carpeting?"

Ainsley tries to guess what would be exciting to someone like her mother. "Savings bonds?" she says.

"Basically," Tabitha says. "There are random-width heart-pine floors under the carpet."

"Sick," Ainsley says, then she remembers that her mother dislikes this response.

"So tell me," Tabitha says. "How's the store?"

"The store is good," Ainsley says. She isn't sure what Harper has told Tabitha about the changes they've made at the boutique. "It's really busy all the time. Meghan says sales are way up."

"Mmm-hmm," Tabitha says. "I heard you had a party."

Ainsley is caught off guard by this. "A party?"

"Meghan told me," Tabitha says. "I heard all about the punch and the popcorn—"

"I didn't drink any of the punch," Ainsley says.

"—and the avocado toasts . . . and the music . . ."

"The thing is, Mama, since the party? The reputation of the store has totally changed."

"Oh, I'm sure it has," Tabitha says.

"No, for the better. It's become a place where people want to shop. It's hip now, it's cool."

"Your grandmother doesn't want a hip shop or a cool shop," Tabitha says. "Your grandmother wants a dignified shop, a classic, timeless shop. That has always been the idea. That has always been the guiding principle."

"But her designs aren't timeless," Ainsley says. "That's why her Newbury Street store closed, isn't it? The only people who want to buy the ERF label are, like, a hundred years old."

"Your aunt is cheapening the brand," Tabitha says. "She has always sullied everything she touches, and this is no different."

"Mama—" Ainsley says.

"But I've washed my hands of it for the summer," Tabitha says. "And I haven't said a word to your grandmother because she's trying to heal, but I assure you she will be very unhappy, and it's entirely Harper's fault."

"Why do you hate Aunt Harper so much?" Ainsley asks.

Tabitha ignores the question. "I am curious about one thing," she says. "Meghan says you hired a new sales associate."

"Um . . . yes," Ainsley says. She wonders how bad it would be if she hung up right now and later claimed the call dropped.

"Who is it? I meant to call the boutique and find out, but I've been consumed with this renovation."

"Um . . ."

"Ainsley."

Ainsley considers lying and making up a name—Carrie Bradshaw, or no, that won't work, so something else—but she will be found out. And what is her new pledge? To be a good person. To tell the truth.

"Caylee Keohane," she says.

There is silence. Ainsley cringes.

Then Tabitha says, "Caylee, the little girl Ramsay dates?"

"Dated," Ainsley squeaks. "They broke up. They broke up before we hired her." Ainsley wants to speak up in Caylee's defense and explain the Facebook posts and the outfit of the day and how successful this campaign has been and why Caylee is such a good person and a team player and what a kind, supportive friend she's been to Ainsley. And she's not a little girl: she's twenty-two years old, an adult. But Ainsley is afraid that if she defends Caylee, her mother will only get angrier, so she says nothing.

"Huh," Tabitha says, and she hangs up.

* * *

Ainsley rides her bike home as fast as she can.

When she reaches the carriage house, she runs upstairs. For the first time all summer, the central air is on, and Aunt Harper is wrapped in the mohair blanket from Nantucket Looms, which cost as much as a new car; Tabitha doesn't like Ainsley to use it. The blinds have been pulled, and the upstairs is as dark as a cave. Ainsley stares at her aunt. Is she sick?

"Hey," Ainsley says. She nudges her aunt. "Are you okay, Aunt Harper?" It's not like her aunt to sleep in the middle of the day. On her other days off, she is a regular Vasco da Gama, out exploring parts of the island Ainsley didn't even know existed.

Harper's eyes flutter open. "Yes," she says. "I'm just really, really tired. I'm sorry."

"You don't have to be sorry," Ainsley says. "But I need to tell you something."

Harper sits up—gingerly, it seems—with her arm bracing her midsection as though her stomach hurts, and she brings her feet to the floor. "What is it?"

"I talked to Tabitha," Ainsley says. "My mother, I mean."

"Okay..."

"She found out about the party. She says we're sullying the ERF brand. Making it less distinctive or distinguished or whatever."

Harper scoffs. "Of course she said that. She must not care about actual money."

"But that's not what I'm worried about," Ainsley says.

"What are you worried about?"

"She asked who we hired to work in the boutique, and I told her it was Caylee, and she hung up on me."

"She'll get over it," Harper says. "Caylee is a stellar employee. Tabitha is just bitter."

"But what if she comes back here and fires Caylee?" Ainsley says. "What if she shows up and undoes all the changes we've made?"

Harper stands up to give Ainsley a hug. "You don't have to worry about this. This is old, old stuff between me and your mom coming to the surface. We disagree on... well, just about everything. I don't want you getting caught in the middle."

"I just want things to stay like they are right now," Ainsley says. "If Tabitha... if my mother comes home, everything will go back to the way it was. But I think maybe she's too busy renovating Gramps's house to come back here."

"We're tearing Gramps's house down," Harper says.

"No," Ainsley says. "Mama is renovating it, she said. I guess she found some kind of special wood under the carpet."

"What?" Harper says. Her voice is suddenly loud and sharp, and Ainsley takes a step backwards. She congratulates herself for somehow managing to make things worse. "Does she not understand I need money? I can't wait six months or a year to see the sale proceeds! I can't spend a hundred and fifty thousand dollars on a *chair rail* and *Berber rugs* and a *clawfoot tub* and whatever else she thinks that house needs. I need money! I need security! I need a nest egg!" Harper grabs her phone. "I'm putting an end to this."

No! Ainsley thinks.

Harper goes down to her bedroom. Ainsley hears her shout, "Tabitha, what have you done? We agreed to tear the house down! Put the land on the market! And sell it!"

Ainsley collapses on the sofa and holds her head in her

hands. She had thought the experiment of her mother and aunt switching places was working.

"You don't know what the Vineyard Haven real estate market is like!" Harper screams. "It could be a year—or longer—until we see any money." She pauses, and Ainsley assumes her mother is talking. "It's *not* tit for tat! I threw that party because I was trying to help the store! I was trying to improve sales and make some money to pay the rent—and I did! You're renovating Billy's house because... because you want a vanity project! I should file a cease-and-desist order! Well, fine, maybe I will! We'll see how little you care when the sheriff comes to visit!"

Ainsley groans. The experiment is not working.

The following afternoon when Ainsley enters the carriage house, she hears Fish barking, and she knows there's trouble.

Her mother is here, she thinks, and her stomach drops to her feet. The FJ40 wasn't in the driveway, but that doesn't mean anything. It's high summer; maybe she couldn't get it across on the ferry. Maybe it's parked over in front of Seamless. Ainsley didn't think to look.

Ainsley takes the stairs two at a time and finds Aunt Harper kneeling on the living-room floor, her phone in one hand, her eyes squeezed shut, her mouth open but no sound coming out.

"Aunt Harper!" Ainsley says. "What is it? What happened?" She immediately thinks this is her mother's fault. Or her grandmother's. Maybe they're the ones who have called the sheriff or filed legal action.

Her aunt rocks back on her heels and lets out a strangled cry.

Ainsley instinctively knows that something big has happened, something bigger than a disagreement about store policy or Vineyard real estate.

Someone is dead. But who? Who?

It takes a few minutes for Ainsley to get Harper calmed down enough to piece together the story. It's not her mother, and it's not Eleanor. It's a friend of Aunt Harper's, a close friend, a boyfriend, maybe. A man named Brendan. He killed himself, overdosed intentionally on pills.

Ainsley's stomach sours. Suicide combines the awful shock of an unexpected death with something even more sinister. To kill yourself means to experience the ultimate blackness; it means inhabiting a room with no air, no light, no hope. It terrifies Ainsley.

"His mother told me he wasn't doing well," Harper says through her tears. "But I didn't go back. I thought if I went back, I would make things worse. And look—I've made things worse. He's gone, and it's my fault."

"No," Ainsley says. She doesn't know anything about this person Brendan or his relationship with her aunt, but calling his suicide her fault feels wrong. Her aunt is a loving soul, kind all the way to her core. She has confessed to Ainsley that she has made a bunch of poor choices in her life. She didn't make the most of her potential; she got mixed up with some bad people, and she knowingly betrayed some good people. She hasn't gone into much detail about any of this, nor has she explained why Tabitha hates her so much. She has been too busy tending to Ainsley and the store and Ramsay and Caylee and Meghan and Fish. But now Harper is the one who needs tending to. "No, not your fault. Don't say that again." Ainsley tries to think what Harper needs most right that second: ice water, arms around her, then action, a plan. They will go to the Vineyard: Harper, Ainsley, and Fish. Ainsley will book the ferry. She will ask Meghan to cover their shifts at work. She will help Harper get back home.

TABITHA

When Franklin gets home from his parents' house, it's late, and he's drunk.

"How was it?" Tabitha asks carefully. She expected him hours ago: she finished the first coat of paint in the powder room by seven thirty, then decided to see what all the hype was about, so she drove to Menemsha and waited forty minutes for a lobster roll from Larsen's Fish Market. She couldn't get over how mobbed Menemsha was with people waiting for the sunset. It was like a day plucked from the 1970s—happy people with sandy feet lining the wall overlooking the water, drinking wine from waxy paper cups. A guy with a guitar played "Hotel California," then segued into "I'd Like to Teach the World to Sing," then transitioned into "Beth" by Kiss while people sang along. Nantucket didn't have a nightly community gathering like this. The best place to watch the sunset on Nantucket was at Galley Beach restaurant. When the sun set, the patrons clapped, then they got back to their vintage Veuve Clicquot and forty-three-dollar Dover sole. And that, Tabitha supposed, was the difference between the two islands.

Well, one of the differences.

The lobster roll was delicious, although Tabitha was so hungry by the time she finally got it that she stuffed it unceremoniously into her face, then wished she'd gotten two of them.

She expected Franklin to be home by the time she got back, but he wasn't. She tamped down the anger and resentment that arose. They had been together such a short time; she hardly owned him.

Now here he is, smelling like he dove into a swimming pool filled with Jameson.

"It was..." Franklin says. "It was..."

Tabitha waits.

"I stopped by the Wharf on my way home," he says. "Wharf Pub."

"Okay," Tabitha says. She tries to keep her voice neutral. Something is bothering him. Or maybe he just needed to blow off steam. Maybe he had friends to see. Maybe going to the Wharf Pub is something he always does after having dinner at his parents' house.

"You said something earlier that made me wonder," he says. "You said Wyatt was your *children's* father. But I've only heard you talk about Ainsley. Do you...do you have a child I don't know about?"

Tabitha grows rigid. Here it is, then. It's her chance. And yet she doesn't like having it forced upon her. Her first instinct is to deflect the question, or even lie. Then she can backpedal later. She doesn't want to lie to Franklin; she takes a deep breath. It's dark and late, and Franklin is drunk; somehow this all serves to make saying the words easier.

"Had," she says. "I had a son named Julian."

"Tabitha."

"He died," Tabitha says. Incredibly, she remains dry-eyed. She speaks like she's reading words off a page. "He was born at twenty-eight weeks. That's very premature. His lungs... well, it's always the lungs with preemies. He stayed in the NICU for ten weeks, up in Boston, and I stayed with him. And then, finally, they let him come home. He still wasn't completely healthy, we knew that, so we rented a cottage across the street from the hospital here." Tabitha swallows. "It was hell. I didn't sleep. It's probably fair to say I didn't sleep the entire time he was alive."

"That must have been so..." But his voice trails off as if he doesn't know what word to choose, as if he doesn't know what it must have been like, and he's right. He doesn't know.

"I was half out of my mind," Tabitha says. "That's an expression, but in my case, it was true. I was certifiably insane. All that mattered was my baby. I wanted him back in the hospital, but our insurance had run out, and Wyatt refused to let me take money from Eleanor. Plus, I mean, the baby was fine—not thriving, maybe, not fat or bouncing, but he was fine." The tears start as Tabitha remembers Julian focusing his eyes and holding up his head. He had grabbed her finger. He never cried, not in the robust way of a newborn, anyway, and that had bothered Tabitha. He made a weak bleating noise when he was hungry or wet; that was all his little lungs—the size of eggs—could produce.

But the doctors had said he was *out of the woods.* How many times had that phrase been uttered? *Out of the woods,* like a child in a fairy tale, safe from bears, snakes, evil witches living in crooked houses. The doctors had also made it clear that there were no guarantees; every premature baby was at risk. And Julian had been slow to gain weight. At times he had been listless and difficult to feed. Tabitha had pumped breast milk night and day, believing that would keep him alive, even though Wyatt pointed out that he ate more when they gave him formula.

Wyatt had tried; Tabitha had to admit that. He had wanted to help both Julian and Tabitha. That was why, in the second week of August, when Julian seemed better and Tabitha was most definitely showing signs of a frayed psyche—crying all the time, dropping dishes, pulling her hair out in clumps—Wyatt had called Harper on the Vineyard, finally taking her up on her offer to help.

Wildflowers, champagne on the edge of the dock, their feet skimming the top of the water, dancing at the Chicken Box. *I can't live... with or without you.*

Tabitha can't go any further.

"He died," she says. "August fifteenth, 2003. He was two months, two weeks, and five days old."

Franklin lies down next to Tabitha but promptly passes out on top of the covers. For the first time, he snores, and she can't fall asleep.

They don't speak of it again. Tabitha wonders if Franklin remembers the conversation, but it isn't anything she wants to revisit, especially not in the bright sunlight while they're trying to renovate Billy's house.

Even hungover, Franklin installs the new kitchen cabinets the next day and sets in the porcelain farmhouse sink. There are two Portuguese guys from Fall River—both named Paulo—sanding down the floors in the living and dining rooms, and a plumbing crew from Mashpee is upstairs redoing the master and second bathrooms. Tad is going to tile the master bath, but for right now he's tearing out the carpet upstairs. As soon as the carpet is out, Tabitha will paint. She also goes out to get sandwiches for everyone from Lucky Hank's, which costs her a hundred and ten dollars and takes ninety minutes because of traffic. But still, everything is good, she tells herself. Everything is fine.

That afternoon, Ainsley calls, and Tabitha is heartened. This is the first unsolicited phone call from her daughter since she's left. Tabitha has no intention of bringing up the party at the store, but somehow the topic pops out of her, and once Tabitha gets started, she can't stop. It's almost as if she's trying to sabotage her own happiness—because she makes Ainsley tell her whom Harper hired to replace Mary Jo.

Caylee. Harper hired Caylee.

No sooner has Tabitha had time to digest this fact—and, yes, a part of her is incensed, but part of her is thinking Caylee *would* be an asset to the store; even Eleanor might agree with that—than Harper calls, screaming like her head is on fire. She has found out that Tabitha is renovating instead of tearing the house down. She's upset that Tabitha is turning Billy's house into a civilized place where some family might live a life of happy refinement.

"Who's working on it for you?" Harper asks after she's gone on her rampage. "Who are you using as a contractor?"

Tabitha will not tell her. There is no way she's going to let Harper interfere with what's going on here. She hangs up.

Tomorrow a landscaping crew from Billerica is coming. They are going to mow the lawn and tear out all the overgrowth, the ugly bushes, the crooked pines, the vines, the weeds, and the sad little vegetable garden. They will sod and mulch, cut beds, plant hydrangeas and perennials. It will be Tabitha's job to water, water, water. The landscaper grew up on the Vineyard and is a good friend of Franklin's. His name is Richie Grennan, and he will be staying at Franklin's house for the two days it will take to do the work.

"Richie and I played football together. He's like a brother to me. I trust him with my life," Franklin says.

Tabitha expects to like Richie, and she expects Richie to like her back. After all, they both love Franklin. Or if Richie doesn't believe that Tabitha loves Franklin—their relationship being too new—she at least expects him to like her because she's paying fifteen thousand dollars for him to do the work on the yard.

Richie is short and fair with a sunburn that ends at the collar and sleeves of his grass-stained T-shirt. He has bright blue eyes and no lips. He nods at Tabitha and says, "Howahyah?" His hands remain on his hips. He's wearing khaki cargo shorts with a leather belt and work boots.

Tabitha smiles. "How are *you?*" she says with a touch of flirtatiousness. "I really appreciate your coming to do this—" She is interrupted by Franklin, who bounds past her and picks Richie up clear off the ground. Richie finally smiles, then Franklin asks if he wants to see the yard, and the three of them head back, with Tabitha trailing behind.

Maybe Richie doesn't relate well to women, Tabitha thinks. Fine: she won't get offended. She listens to Franklin explain to Richie exactly what they want. She doesn't interject because Franklin is on point; he mentions everything they talked about in a logical order. He is her general contractor, so that's his job. He is also her lover, but what does that matter to Richie?

Richie and his crew get to work. Tabitha goes to Skinny's for sandwiches because Franklin mentioned that it used to be Richie's favorite place. He likes the chicken Philly; Tabitha gets him two of them.

After lunch, Tabitha paints the small third bedroom a placid color called Saint Giles Green. Tad is tiling the master bath in honey-colored marble. Franklin is working with the stone guy in the kitchen. The countertops are oiled soapstone except for one section, which is butcher block. The plumbers from Mashpee have hooked up the Sub-Zero fridge and the stand-alone ice machine, and they have installed the fixtures over the farmhouse sink. The gas guy is due that afternoon to hook up the Wolf range—six burners and a griddle.

Out back, Richie is driving a front-end loader and directing his crew of five. He already has half the yard cleared; Tabitha can't get over how much better it looks.

She is thrilled at the transformation of the house, but something feels off. Maybe it's Richie, she thinks. Franklin and

Richie ate their sandwiches out back, sitting side by side on the bumper of Franklin's truck. Tabitha decided to let them have time alone to catch up, and Franklin either noticed and didn't say anything or didn't notice. His attitude toward her is one degree cooler than usual, she thinks. She worries that the story about Julian has changed things. Franklin sees her differently—and not for the better. He must see her now as a person who failed at the most basic task that we, as humans, are given: to keep our children alive.

Tabitha closes herself in the powder room—which, at the moment, is the only functioning bathroom—and splashes water on her face. She needs to get a grip! There is no way someone as evolved as Franklin would think less of her because she lost a child. He went through so much with his girlfriend Patti; surely of all the men Tabitha knows, Franklin is the most equipped to handle the story of Julian.

So then what's wrong?

Probably he's just tired. And Tabitha is tired and upset about Harper. And it's hot. She needs to stop imagining things.

That night, Franklin announces that he and Richie are going to dinner at Offshore Ale and then, most likely, they're going night fishing.

"Oh," Tabitha says. "Okay." She feels stung but tries not to let it show.

Franklin kisses her good-bye on the nose. The nose, as though she's five years old! Richie is already outside climbing into Franklin's truck, so Tabitha grabs Franklin by the shirt buttons and says, "Hey."

"Hey what?"

"Is something wrong?"

"No," Franklin says.

"Then kiss me like you mean it, please."

Franklin looks at her a second, then he places his hands on either side of her face and delivers the sexiest kiss she has ever received. It's not too much; if anything, it's just shy of enough. She wants—needs—deeper, longer, harder. Her legs have turned to sawdust, dandelion fluff, something that can be blown away.

"Was that what you wanted?" he asks.

She can't speak.

"Okay, then," he says. He turns and walks out the door.

Tabitha puts a second coat of Paul Revere's Ride on the powder-room walls—then, since she's on a roll, she starts on the lavender room with an oil-based primer called Kilz. She bids the lavender adieu. There is zen in painting, she finds, but her mind keeps turning over the slight changes in Franklin's behavior. They went from a full-on sex-and-love binge to… well, they'd had sex early that morning before Tad and Richie arrived, but sex isn't exactly what Tabitha is craving. She misses tenderness: hand-holding, Franklin's finger running along her cheekbone, his mouth on the back of her neck.

Tabitha imagines Franklin and Richie out at Offshore Ale, flirting with the young waitresses in tight T-shirts and short shorts; Franklin probably knows them all by name. As the walls of the lavender bedroom become white, Tabitha writes a story across them. Franklin follows one of the young waitresses into the kitchen; they find a dark corner—a pantry, maybe, or the room where the kegs are stored—and Franklin kisses the waitress the way he has just kissed Tabitha. The waitress slides her hand down the front of Franklin's jeans.

Tabitha wonders what he meant by "night fishing." Will they actually go fishing at night, or is it a euphemism for something else?

Stop! she tells herself. The door to the bedroom is closed; possibly the fumes are getting to her. She has no reason to doubt Franklin. But he is a single man out with one of his single friends; they are drinking. And who's to say this relationship is exclusive? They haven't defined it; they haven't set any boundaries or parameters. They've basically been living together for two weeks, but Franklin hasn't called her his girlfriend. He didn't take her to meet his parents. She hasn't been back to his house since that first night; she never learned the address, and she isn't confident she could find it again, although she's pretty sure it's somewhere in Oak Bluffs.

What does Tabitha know about him, really? He picked her up at a bar. Who's to say he won't pick up someone else tonight? She should go somewhere—to dinner or the movies. She overheard someone at Skinny's today talking about eating at Alchemy. Tabitha could easily take a shower, put on a dress, and go find trouble of her own.

Instead she pulls a beer out of the cooler that Franklin keeps on the back deck, then she fishes one of the Ambien she stole from Eleanor's stash out of her purse. She is so agitated that she takes a second Ambien and wanders up to the master bedroom because it's now the only place to sleep. She lies facedown on her father's bed and thinks that she would like to cry. Except that she's suddenly too tired to summon the effort.

* * *

She hears footsteps on the stairs and opens her eyes to see Tad in his Carhartts, carrying his tiling trowel. He walks past her into the master bathroom. Tabitha's mouth is cottony. She wants to sit up, but she can't. She succumbs.

She opens her eyes. Where is she? It takes her a minute: *Nantucket,* she thinks. No—the Vineyard. Billy's house, Billy's room. She turns her head; her neck is stiff.

There's an old-fashioned clock radio on the nightstand. The glowing blue numbers say it's one thirteen. Billy's clock is wrong, which is not surprising. Everything about this house is wrong! Tabitha reaches her arms out to her sides so that her body is in the shape of a cross. No Franklin. She eyes the door to the master bathroom. It's closed tight, and there doesn't seem to be any activity on the other side. But wasn't Tad just there? Or did she dream that?

When she checks her phone, she sees that it *is* quarter after one. In the afternoon! She is appalled at herself. The Ambien knocked her out for fifteen hours, and she still feels woozy. There are no texts and no missed calls from Franklin, which is a good thing. He must be downstairs, working. She can't imagine how she'll explain sleeping the morning away.

She slinks downstairs and is met with the powerful smell of polyurethane. The Portuguese Paulos are varnishing the floors. They look gorgeous, honey-toned and silky. And they were there all along, smothered underneath the hideous carpeting.

"Franklin?" she calls out.

"No here," one of the Paulos says.

"No?" Tabitha says. She tries to remember what was on the docket for today. Kitchen, she thought. Getting to the kitchen can only be done by walking the far perimeter of the living room past the powder room and into the dining area. Through the skinny dining-room windows, Tabitha sees Richie on a spade digging a hole for the mature hydrangeas, whose roots are wrapped in burlap. Richie is here—that's good, she supposes. He and Franklin didn't get lost down the rabbit hole.

Tabitha finds Tad in the kitchen, tiling the backsplash behind the range.

"Hey," she says. "Sorry I slept for so long."

Tad barely looks up. "You're not on my payroll."

"No, I know," she says. "It's just . . . well, I like to get up and at 'em." She watches Tad place the smoky glass tile row by row. This kitchen is going to be spectacular. She can't believe the difference. She clears her throat. She could use a glass of ice water, some Motrin, some strong coffee. "Do you know where Franklin is?"

"No," Tad says. He doesn't offer anything else, and Tabitha listens to the rasping noise of the trowel against the wall.

Tabitha grabs her bag and heads to her car, which has been baking in the midday sun and is now an oven, the seats too hot to sit on. She puts down the windows and waits a few seconds before climbing in. She cranks the AC and backs out of the driveway.

Did Franklin even come home? Were her paranoid scenarios not so paranoid after all? Has he taken some little chickie up to Cedar Tree Neck to skinny-dip in the bay? Would he *do* that? Tabitha's gut says no. Is she being naive? She doesn't think so. She wonders if Harper somehow found out that Franklin was doing the work on the house. Does she still have connections here, someone willing to swing by and check on the house? Did Harper call Franklin? Did she threaten him, or did one of her drug buddies threaten him? Is that why he's staying away? She can't decide if this theory is spot-on or completely ridiculous.

Tabitha tries to go to Mocha Mott's, but there's no parking, then she gets stuck in traffic at Five Corners. She calls Franklin's cell. It rings six times, then goes to his voice mail.

"Hey," she says. She's at a loss. Where *is* he? And what right does she have to know? It feels like the whole world has changed, and she's the last to find out. "It's me."

She hangs up.

Franklin isn't back at the house when she finally returns—she had to go all the way to Tony's Market, in OB, to get coffee, water, and painkillers—and now she's starting to panic. Something is *wrong.* She charges up the porch stairs into the kitchen, where Tad is still working.

"Have you heard from Franklin?" she asks.

"No, ma'am," he says.

"What the hell?" she says. She is angry now, angry and worried. She wants to take it out on whoever is available, but Tad is having none of it. He ignores her.

"You know him far better than I," Tabitha says. "Does he pull these little disappearing acts often?"

"No," Tad says. "He doesn't." He sets the trowel down in the tray and faces her. "Have you called him?"

"Yes," she says. "Voice mail."

Tad nods. "I'm sure he'll turn up."

Tabitha doesn't like anything about that statement, so she storms out to the yard. She approaches Richie from behind and gives him a vicious poke on the shoulder. He's behind this change in Franklin somehow; she just knows it.

"Where's Franklin?" she asks.

"Whoa!" Richie says. He turns on her with a venom that Tabitha doesn't understand. What has she ever done to *him?* Why couldn't he be nicer? Why couldn't he be happy that Franklin has found someone? "I don't appreciate being touched like that."

"Sorry," Tabitha says. But she's not sorry! She is so frustrated and so *confused* that she would like to take Richie's shovel and hit him over the head with it. "Do you know where Franklin is?"

"I haven't seen him since last night," Richie says. "He got a phone call and left in the middle of dinner."

"What?" Tabitha says. This isn't what she expected to hear. Phone call from whom? From Harper? Or someone else? "Is everything okay?"

"You're asking the wrong guy the wrong questions," Richie says. He checks his watch. "We're finishing up now and heading back to America on the five o'clock boat. I'd really like that check."

Tabitha glares at him for a second. He wants his check, and Tabitha wants answers. Who called Franklin? What happened? Where is he? *You're asking the wrong guy the wrong questions.* She would like to take Richie's spade and use it to bury him alive.

She should be counting her blessings, however. Richie is leaving.

"The check will be on the counter," she says.

Richie leaves, the Paulos leave—and finally Tad packs up to leave. Tabitha forces herself to put a coat of Made in the Suede on the walls of the formerly lavender room, but after that she is wiped out, so she sits on the back steps and watches the sprinkler water Billy's newly landscaped backyard. There has been no word from Franklin. He's gone. Tabitha thinks about sending an angry text or leaving an infuriated voice mail; he is, after all, her general contractor, and he simply skipped a day of work without notice. But Tabitha doesn't care about him as her contractor. She cares about Franklin, her lover. She wants to blame Richie for this mess, but she knows, somehow, that it's her own fault. She should never have told him about Julian. Their new relationship was too fragile to hold the heavy weight of that story.

"I'm going," Tad says. He gets to the bottom step then turns around. "Will you be okay?"

Tabitha laughs, although nothing is funny. "Will I be okay?"

"I noticed you didn't eat today," Tad says. "I'm going to the Wolf's Den for pizza. Why don't you come with me?"

It's nice of him to offer, but Tabitha is in no shape to socialize or venture out in public. Her stomach is in knots; she can't imagine eating ever again.

"Where is he?" she asks Tad. "Richie said he got a phone call last night and just up and left. And no one has seen him since."

Tad nods. "If I had to guess..." He lets out a stream of air.

"What?" Tabitha says. She doesn't know Franklin well enough to even venture a guess. What would she guess? That Franklin is married, his wife has been away, and she returned earlier than expected, possibly with their four children in tow?

"I would say it's a family matter," Tad says.

Tabitha gasps, even as her suspicions are confirmed. "Is it my sister?"

"No," Tad says. "I'm talking about Franklin's family. His parents, *his* sister."

"His parents?" Tabitha asks. "His sister?"

Tad raises a hand. "I've said more than I should have already," he says. "Have a good night."

Tabitha sits on the steps until dark, then she wanders inside. Will Franklin stay away another night? Apparently he will. She takes another Ambien, only one.

She wakes up at one thirty-five in the morning with an idea. The phone book is back on the mantel next to the urn containing Billy's ashes. The Vineyard and Nantucket are probably the only communities left in America where phone books are indispensable—boat schedules, restaurant menus, addresses.

Addresses.

A check of *Phelps* offers the following:

Phelps, Albert and Lydia, 35 Edgartown Bay Road, ET
Phelps, Franklin, 10 Grovedale Road, OB
Phelps, Sadie, the Upper Crust, 9111 Edgartown–West Tisbury Road, VH

Sadie is the sister, Tabitha realizes. Sadie, not Charlotte. But what is the Upper Crust? She feels like she should know, but she's drawing a blank. She really only cares about Franklin. She plugs 10 Grovedale Road into her phone. A blue dot appears in Maps, and she climbs into her car.

There is no traffic in the middle of the night, so Tabitha finds herself sitting in front of Franklin's house ten minutes later. The windows are dark, but Franklin's truck is in the driveway, and seeing his truck makes Tabitha thrum with nervous energy. He's here. Isn't it enough just to know where he is, finally?

No. Tabitha gets out of her car and strides up the walk. She rings the doorbell.

She hears him stirring inside, and her nerves shriek. She wants to run. The door opens.

Franklin sees her. Immediately his mouth is on hers, and he's pulling her inside, slamming the door shut. He picks her up and carries her over to the moss-green velvet sofa, where he had been sleeping. He lays Tabitha down on the sofa, then tears her ninety-dollar T-shirt in half, cups her breast, and feeds it to himself as though it's food and he's starving.

Afterward, Tabitha cries. She bleats and howls—no holding back. Every bad thought, every worry, every jealousy, every insecurity comes pouring out. Franklin wipes her tears away with his hands first, then with the napkins that are next to the uneaten take-out dinner from Sharky's on the coffee table.

"Why?" she says. "Did my sister call you and tell you to stop? Did Harper call?"

"No," he says. "The problem is my sister. Sadie."

Franklin's sister, Sadie, is the wife of Dr. Reed Zimmer. Franklin's sister, Sadie, is the woman who slapped Tabitha and threw champagne in her face. These are the extenuating circumstances.

Franklin sits on the edge of the sofa, holding his head in his hands. "I can't work for you anymore," he says. "And I can't see you."

"What?" Tabitha says.

"She's my sister," Franklin says. "And Harper is your sister. Your twin sister."

"Exactly," Tabitha says. "Harper is my *sister.* She's not me. We aren't the same, Franklin. You know this. I'm not Harper."

"I do know that," Franklin says. "And I like Harper, regardless of what she's done. But my sister is a mess. She can't handle this development. She... and my parents... my parents..."

"You're a grown man," Tabitha says. "Surely you don't still cater to what your *parents* think?" As soon as the words are out of her mouth, Tabitha pictures Eleanor. Eleanor has ruled Tabitha's every thought and deed for the past thirty-nine years, short of the last few weeks.

"I'm sorry, Tabitha," Franklin says. "It's just bad luck. And

I wasn't honest. I should have explained who I was the night I met you at the Ritz. But back then, I didn't think it would matter."

"You thought I was a one-night stand," Tabitha says. "A throwaway."

"Isn't that what *you* thought?" Franklin says. "Be honest. I barely knew you. It was for fun."

"A drunken fling," Tabitha says. *Isn't* that what she thought? She certainly hadn't intended to end up this emotionally vested.

"I didn't know I was going to fall in love with you," Franklin says.

"Are you?" Tabitha says. "In love with me?"

Franklin nods into his hands. "I think I am," he whispers. Then he raises his head and gazes into her eyes to deliver the parting blow. "But it doesn't matter. Sadie is my family."

HARPER

They take the inter-island ferry: Harper, Ainsley, and Fish. Caylee and Meghan will mind the shop. This is going to be a short trip, one night, which they will spend in Harper's duplex.

Harper says to Ainsley, "I'm sure you're anxious to see your mother, but I don't think I'll be able to control my temper around her."

Ainsley says, "That's okay. I'll see Tabitha—I mean, my mother—when she comes back to Nantucket, whenever that is."

"Thank you," Harper says. She places a protective hand on her abdomen. She is *verklempt* about Tabitha renovating the house. She understands exactly what happened: Tabitha heard about the party at the store from Meghan, and she figured that then gave her the right to do whatever she wanted. There was no way the opportunity to avenge was going to get past Tabitha; she has never let an affront go unanswered. Never! In many ways, Harper and Tabitha are like the Hayley Mills characters in *The Parent Trap*—one cuts the other's dress during the dance; the other sets an elaborate trap of honey and string. But what Tabitha did is more than a prank. It concerns Harper's livelihood, her survival. Harper needs the money from the proceeds of the sale. Tabitha has no idea how badly Harper needs it.

It's disorienting to visit the Vineyard in the manner of the lowliest of tourists: the day-tripper. The ferry pulls into Oak Bluffs, and Harper is presented with a vista that is as familiar to her as her own kneecaps, yet she sees it with new eyes: the green expanse of Ocean Park, the jaunty colors of the gingerbread houses in the Methodist campground. Harper could take Ainsley on the Flying Horses carousel right now; they could have dinner at the Red Cat. But those things wouldn't make the Vineyard feel like home.

What makes the Vineyard feel like home for Harper is the people. First of all, obviously, Billy. But Billy is dead.

From there it gets even more difficult: Drew, Reed, Brendan.

Five of the gingerbread cottages in front of them are owned by the Truman-Snyder family—Drew's mother and his aunties, who made Harper the pot of lobster stew. Right now, Drew will be in his cruiser—maybe on Main Street in Edgartown, maybe issuing a parking ticket out in Katama, maybe sitting with his radar gun in the elementary school parking lot. He is so handsome, so well built, so well intentioned. He must hate Harper's guts, and for good reason. She used him as a distraction from Reed.

Reed is…well, if he's on the Vineyard, he's doing a good job of hiding. Harper might be able to ask people she knows—Rooster? Franklin Phelps? Greenie?—if they've seen him or heard from him, if they know where he is. *I need to talk to him,* Harper would say. *It's important.* But she will leave it at that.

Brendan Donegal. Brendan should be sitting by the koi pond at Mytoi or walking on East Beach skipping stones, but now Brendan, too, is dead. Harper takes a deep breath, then winds Fish's leash around her wrist as she disembarks from the ferry. Fish pulls her along; he knows they're home. Ainsley is right behind them. Ainsley has aged about fifteen years in the last twenty-four hours, Harper figures. That's what handling a tragedy does to a person.

They are renting a car from A-A Island Auto Rental, on the wharf. It's a short trip, but Harper can't be dependent on cabdrivers who may or may not know their way around by now. They pile into a generic gunmetal-gray Jeep. Nobody will recognize her.

"Are you hungry?" Harper asks Ainsley.

"No," Ainsley says.

"Me, either," she says. She hasn't been able to eat since Edie's call. "Let's go do this, then."

Ainsley nods. She gazes out the window. "It's so pretty here," she says.

"That it is," Harper says.

* * *

It's one of those clear blue days that seem to have been made for the Vineyard. The heat and humidity are gone: everything has a crisp edge. How many days like this has Harper taken for granted? Someday she, too, will die. Fish will die, Ainsley will die, the baby inside Harper will die. It's a grim train of thought, but it's not nearly as daunting as what lies ahead. Harper has to see Edie and, in her own way, say good-bye to Brendan.

In Edgartown, Harper obeys every traffic law and speed limit; she lets a driver from Tisbury Taxi go in front of her at the triangle. There is, she thinks, a first time for everything. She can't have Drew or anyone else from the Edgartown police pulling her over. She drives down Main Street, Ainsley oohing and aahing over the Old Whaling Church and the Daniel Fisher house, then Harper pulls in line for the *On Time III,* even though the line is longer by two cars than the one for the *On Time II.* But Harper is avoiding everyone she knows, including Indira Mayhew, the ferry master on the *On Time II.*

She puts down the window to buy a ticket.

"Long time, no see, my friend."

Harper turns. Indira is here, working on the *III.*

"Hi," Harper says. "Yes, I've been away."

"Anywhere good?" Indira asks.

"Nantucket," Harper says.

"You poor child," Indira says, then she smiles. "I'm kidding. My father used to love taking our boat over to Tuckernuck. And on rare occasions we went to the big island. I remember Cokes and oyster crackers at the Anglers' Club."

"It's good to see you," Harper says. When the light turns green, she drives onto the ferry.

"Are you okay?" Ainsley asks.

"No," Harper says.

Chappaquiddick has changed. It used to bring Harper a sense of peace and love—now she feels sadness and regret. *Brendan!* she cries out in her mind.

She feels it's her fault.

When she passes the entrance to Mytoi, her heart keens. She continues down Chappaquiddick Road until she reaches the Donegal residence.

Edie is expecting her. She is sitting on the old-fashioned bench swing on her front porch, and when Harper pulls in, she stands.

Harper gets out of the car. Ainsley follows, bringing Fish on a leash.

"Edie," Harper says. "I'm so sorry." She embraces the tiny woman at the top of the porch stairs, then she turns to introduce Ainsley.

"My niece, Ainsley," she says. "And this is Fish."

"Fish," Edie says, and she bends down to stroke Fish under the chin. "Brendan used to talk about Fish all the time. I admit it took me a while to figure out that Fish was a dog." Edie smiles sadly at Ainsley. "My son got things mixed up at times."

"I'm sorry for your loss," Ainsley says.

Edie nods, lips pressed together so tightly they look bloodless. "Would you like to take Fish for a walk on our beach?" she asks her. "I'd love to spend a few minutes with your aunt alone."

"Absolutely," Ainsley says.

"You can just follow the path around the house," Edie says.

Ainsley leads Fish down the porch steps and around a robust pink hydrangea bush—the Strawberry Sundae variety, Harper notes, because she still has a landscaper's sensibility.

"Shall we walk to Mytoi?" Edie asks.

Harper nods, then holds Edie's arm as they descend the stairs.

"This is no one's fault," Edie says. "Not mine and certainly not yours, so if you're harboring any guilt, I want you to let it go."

"I should have been here," Harper says. "I should have come when you called."

"It wouldn't have made a difference," Edie says. "Brendan's accident left him damaged, but that wasn't the problem. The problem was that he was still intact enough to realize how damaged he was. He knew he was limited, and he hated it. He said it was like his mind was in a straitjacket. He would look at his feet and know what movements he needed to make to tie his shoes, but he couldn't get his hands to cooperate. We were lucky he lasted as long as he did."

"Where did he get the pills?" Harper asks.

"One of his friends," Edie says. "Or former friends. They all did drugs, those surf boys."

Harper nods. True enough. "I didn't know that Brendan still talked to any of those guys."

"Every once in a while, one of them would check in," Edie says. "Spyder and Doobie, mostly. They would call after I'd bumped into them at Cronig's. Seeing me made them feel guilty."

"They loved Brendan," Harper says. "We all loved Brendan. Worshipped him, back in the day. He was so much better than anyone else. He was a demigod. I remember being so flattered that he even knew my name, years and years ago, back when I worked at Mad Martha's. And then..." Here Harper censors herself. She wants to be honest with Edie, but not so honest that she ruins the moment. "And then after his accident...I mean, I knew he wasn't the same, but I was still...I don't know...I guess you'd say *starstruck* at first. Here was Brendan Donegal, who had won so many titles and traveled to so many countries, who had surfed with Kelly Slater and John John Florence, and he was suddenly accessible to me." Harper swallows. Does this sound awful? Does it sound like she was somehow happy that Brendan had his accident because it gave her a chance to be close to him? "I soon came to love and appreciate the person Brendan had become. After a while, I forgot that Brendan the surfer even existed. His past didn't matter. My past didn't matter. That was the gift of being with Brendan. He kept you in the moment." Harper closes her eyes. *It's hot; the pond is still; the coffee is strong; your eyes are sad.* Every Wednesday afternoon and every Sunday morning were theirs, together.

Come back. Please.

They are at the entrance to Mytoi now, and both of them hesitate.

"I donated money here in his name," Edie says. "There will be a bench or a sculpture—I haven't decided what exactly. But I wanted something here on Chappy that would honor him, that I can visit, that you can visit."

"That's a beautiful idea," Harper says. "Have you changed your mind about a service?"

"No," Edie says. "I had the body cremated. I'll bury the ashes in the family plot, next to his father. The priest will come, but no service."

Harper nods. They have entered the garden, and they automatically fall quiet. It's the blessing of Mytoi—the possibility of silence, of stillness, of contemplation. They cross the footbridge. Harper gazes down at the koi swimming, then she and Edie sit down side by side on the red bench. Harper's pain will never be greater than it is right now. She had never imagined coming to Mytoi without Brendan. The place and the man and their relationship were three strands, braided together. She knows she should feel grateful. After all, what if she had never found him? His friendship was such a gift. He appeared to her when everyone else on the island had forsaken her; when she felt wicked and cheap, he arrived to make her feel valued and worthwhile.

Suddenly the tears fall. She is crying, and there is no stopping her; she wishes she had the stiff upper lip of Edie and Eleanor's generation, but oh, well. Possibly Edie isn't too reserved to cry—simply too sad, her grief so deep and embedded that it won't break loose.

Edie pulls a handkerchief out of the pocket of her pants and hands it to Harper, who accepts it gratefully and blows her nose.

"I'm pregnant," Harper says.

Edie, who is already sitting ramrod straight, seems to grow an inch. "Is the child . . . Brendan's?"

"No," Harper says. "It's not. Brendan and I never . . ."

"Oh," Edie says. "I wasn't sure."

"I wish it were his," Harper says, then realizes this is the utter truth. But of course the baby is Reed's, conceived that fateful night at Lucy Vincent, when Reed recklessly made love to her without protection. "More than anything, I wish it were."

* * *

Edie stands on the porch and waves as Harper backs out of the driveway.

"Was it as bad as you thought?" Ainsley asks, once they are back on Chappy Road, headed for the ferry.

"No," Harper says.

Walking back from Mytoi, Edie had said, "If you need a place to stay, before or after the baby is born... I don't want to assume anything... but if you need a place, the cottage, Brendan's cottage, is yours free of charge for as long as you want it."

"Edie, thank you," Harper said. Tears had threatened again—tears of fear and confusion, because Harper wasn't at all sure what her future held. Would she be with Reed or go it alone? Would she be able to find a job? Or would she have to rely on the eventual proceeds from the sale of Billy's house? She tries to picture living on Chappy through the fall and winter. Would that be the worst thing? "I'm not sure what my plans include, but that offer means a lot. And who knows? I might take you up on it."

"I hope you do," Edie said. She had squeezed Harper's arm. "Imagine. A baby."

Harper drives to Tisbury, to her duplex, which is stuffy and hot. Harper runs around, opening windows, apologizing to

Ainsley. Compared to the carriage house, her duplex is as underwhelming and anonymous as a suite at the Residence Inn.

"It's fine," Ainsley says. "I really just want to walk around, shop a little, see Vineyard Haven. Can I walk to town from here?"

"You *can,*" Harper says. "But it's far. I'll drop you off, then you can call me when you're ready to come home. How does that sound?"

"Great," Ainsley says. "Thank you."

Harper lets Ainsley out at Five Corners. One thing she has not missed is the traffic. It's insane, worse than Harper remembers—and it's not even August! While she's sitting in an endless line of cars waiting to turn, Fish asleep across the backseat, Harper eyes the road that will take her past Billy's house. Should she do a drive-by? See what the place looks like and figure out exactly whom Tabitha found to do the work? Harper is freshly incredulous that Tabitha made such an enormous unilateral decision. Harper needs money, and she needs it soon! She has a baby on the way!

But Tabitha, of course, doesn't know that.

Harper fights the urge to drive past Billy's. In her fragile emotional state, she wants to avoid an in-person confrontation—because that is, undoubtedly, what it will become. This trip had one purpose; that purpose has been served. Harper will pick Ainsley up at seven thirty, take her to the Red Cat for dinner, and afterward go home to bed. Then maybe—*maybe*—in the morning, Harper will swing by Morning Glory Farm for a couple of muffins, just so Ainsley can experience one. Then back to Nantucket on the noon boat.

Harper pulls up in front of the duplex. There is nothing to do inside. Coming back to the Vineyard like this was a mistake: temptation is everywhere. Harper thinks about trying to find Drew so she can apologize. Will he appreciate that or find it patronizing?

And then there's Reed. Reed. Reed. Reed. Reed. Harper visualizes herself driving past the hospital, past his house, past Sadie's pie shop. She can drive out to Aquinnah on State Road and come back on South Road in the hope that maybe he's riding his bike. Does he have a favorite beach? Lobsterville? Great Rock Bight? Harper has never asked him. He's a doctor—maybe he doesn't go to the beach.

She *will* drive past Billy's house, she decides. It's the safest thing she can do.

She loops in the back way, hoping and praying that Tabitha is out so she can sneak in and get a better look. As she approaches, she sees a green truck pulling out of the backyard. It's Tad, the Irish carpenter. Harper knows him from around. He used to date one of the other landscapers who worked for Jude, a girl named Cory, but Harper is pretty sure they broke up. She has seen Tad out at the Ritz and the Trampost but always alone. Is *he* working on the house? How did Tabitha find him? Tad is friends with Franklin Phelps, but maybe that connection didn't come up or didn't matter. Maybe in the weeks since Harper has been away, everyone has forgotten about Harper and Reed Zimmer; maybe it wasn't that big a deal to begin with. Now that Harper has been away, it seems possible. After all, summer is in full swing. There are ninety thousand people on this island—*ninety thousand!*—and surely there are more exciting things to talk about.

Harper waits across the street until Tad's truck turns the corner, then she creeps along until she has a clear line of vision into the backyard.

Oh, my! she thinks. The backyard has been completely transformed. The lawn is now carpeted with green grass. There are beds of perennials and hydrangeas. All the scrub has been removed, and the vegetable garden is gone. *How* did Tabitha find anyone willing to do this? Harper didn't think there was a landscaper on the island who was willing to work on a Frost house.

The house seems quiet. Curiosity overwhelms Harper. This is Billy's house, and for her first ten years on the Vineyard, it was also her house. It's her house once again, half of it willed to her. She doesn't have to feel like a prowler or an intruder. She has every right to go inside—more than every right!

She marches up the back steps. The door into the kitchen is unlocked.

Astonished doesn't begin to explain how Harper feels when she walks inside. She can't—cannot—believe the transformation. Her mouth drops open as she runs her hand over the stone countertops and as she opens the cabinets, which are the color of burned honey. The hinges are like butter. The wood feels solid and true. The floor is still plywood, but the appliances are in—Sub-Zero fridge, Wolf range, Bosch dishwasher. There's a separate ice maker! And a wine fridge! She blinks and turns in a circle. This *is* Billy's kitchen, right? This is his house?

Harper steps into the living and dining area. The walls have been painted the color of custard, and the floors are random-width heart pine. Was *this* what was hiding under the carpeting all these years? The floors are sumptuous, and the overall effect of the room is bright, clean, elegant. Harper peeks in the powder room. Gone is the *Jaws* poster and the unspeakably smelly toilet. The walls are pewter, and there is a sleek white glass column for a sink. Harper didn't even realize sinks like this existed except in the pages of magazines.

She did it, Harper thinks. Instead of tearing down Billy's house and turning it into a pile of rubble, Tabitha saved it. Harper feels simultaneously proud of her sister and ashamed of herself for being so shortsighted. Harper tries not to guess how much money Tabitha spent to make this happen. It's not like she plunked the money down on a craps table in Vegas, though. They *will* sell this house; Harper can see that now. They will see a sizable payday. Harper isn't sure why she's surprised that Tabitha was right about this. Tabitha is always right.

Harper approaches the stairs. The crappy mustard-yellow Aztec-print carpet has been removed. The wooden treads are exposed and now feature a navy-blue wool runner with a white diamond pattern. Classic. Harper looks up. The world's ugliest chandelier has been replaced by a simple blown-glass globe surrounding an Edison bulb. Gorgeous. A staircase that used to be merely a means to an end is now a work of art in and of itself.

As Harper climbs the stairs, she hears a noise.

"Tabitha?" she says.

Harper peers in the lavender room, which used to be her room. It has been painted a creamy beige; the little bedroom is now sage green. The bathroom between the two has a new pedestal sink and a glass shower stall; it's in the process of being retiled.

The noise is coming from Billy's room. It sounds like crying, but that can't be right. Harper fears walking in on something.

"Tabitha?" she says a little louder.

The noise becomes clearer. Crying. It's her sister, crying.

Harper pokes her head in the room. The floors are now a deep, rich cherry. Unlike all the other rooms, in which the furniture has been removed, Billy's king-size bed remains, along with the stacked milk crates that he saw fit to use as a nightstand. Maybe Tabitha is crying because it's so ugly, Harper thinks, and this makes her smile, although obviously something serious is going on, and Harper mentally prepares herself for the news that Eleanor's condition has worsened.

"Tabitha?" Harper says, too loudly to be ignored now. "It's Harper. I'm here. What's wrong?"

Tabitha lifts her head out of the nest of pillows. Her face is contorted in anguish, her eyes are swollen, her face splotched, her hair tangled. She's wearing a man's Hot Tin Roof T-shirt and a pair of denim shorts. The shorts are Current/Elliott and retail for a hundred and fifty dollars at the ERF boutique. Harper congratulates herself for recognizing this, and it reassures her that this is, in fact, her sister before her.

Tabitha in a Hot Tin Roof T-shirt, though—wow. There is a first time for everything.

"What's *wrong?*" Tabitha says. She plucks a tissue from a box on the milk crates and wipes at her face. "What's wrong is that you ruined my life. Again."

"I did...what?" Harper says. "How did I ruin your life this time?" She takes a deep breath and tries to think what she might possibly have done. "I've been following your instructions. I take care of Ainsley. She hasn't had a drink all summer. Hasn't gone to a single party. Hasn't gotten in any trouble. And the store—okay, maybe things at the store aren't exactly the way that you and Mommy want them. But sales are up five hundred percent!"

"I don't care about the store!" Tabitha says. "I could care less about the store or Mommy. I care about me. For the first time ever in my life, practically, I care about myself."

"What?" Harper says. "I'm lost."

"I fell in love," Tabitha says.

"Whoa," Harper says. "With whom?" Try as she might, she can't imagine Tabitha falling in love with anyone on the Vineyard. Except for maybe Ken Doll. Has Tabitha fallen in love with Ken Doll?

"Franklin Phelps," Tabitha says.

With Franklin Phelps? Harper thinks. It takes her a moment to connect the dots. Then she sucks in her breath. Tabitha has fallen in love with Franklin Phelps. Sadie's brother.

"I met him at the Ritz," Tabitha says. "He was singing. And while he was singing, some jackass started hitting on me at the bar."

"Jackass?" Harper says. She knows many, many people who fit this description.

"Franklin saved me. He brought me home."

"When was this?" Harper asks.

"My first night here," Tabitha says. "And then Franklin took on this job. He's the general contractor."

"He *is?*" Harper says. "I saw Tad leaving, but I didn't think... I mean, forgive my asking, but you knew he was Sadie's brother, right?"

"How would I know that?" Tabitha says. "I had no idea, and he didn't tell me. But then when I found out he was a contractor and I asked him to work on the house, he said he couldn't. He said there were extenuating circumstances, but he wouldn't tell me what they were. Then he changed his mind and agreed to work on the house. I mean, have you even seen this place? It's incredible."

"Incredible," Harper says. Her heart is constricting. The house is incredible, and the idea of Tabitha and Franklin working together to make it so is crazy and wonderful—two people Harper would never have put together in her mind, but she can see it now.

"Then he had dinner with his parents, and Sadie was there, and I guess she isn't doing well, but it was still okay, sort of, until Sadie found out that Franklin is working here and dating me. She can't handle it. She asked him to stay away from me."

"And he listened to her?" Harper says. "He's a grown man, first of all, and second of all, you're not me."

"You don't get it," Tabitha says. She manages to rise from the bed, but she seems smaller, waiflike; heartbreak has diminished her. "Sadie is his sister. And you are my sister."

"And I ruin everything," Harper says.

"You ruin *everything,*" Tabitha says. "I've basically lived in fear of people spitting on me since I've been here. Random strangers are bad enough, Harper. But this. This!"

"You should have told me you were seeing Franklin," Harper says. "I would have warned you."

"Warned me you were screwing his sister's husband?"

"Yes," Harper says.

"You are incredibly selfish," Tabitha says. "And you always have been. You went with Billy. You left me and never looked back."

Harper stares. Tabitha is hurting, she reminds herself. She is venomous like this because she hurts. But now that Tabitha has brought it up, Harper is being given something she has never had before: a chance to defend herself. "That's not true. What we did was fair. We shot for it. I even gave you best out of three, Pony, and you still lost. And no one was more surprised than I was. Getting to go with Billy was the only time I ever beat you at anything. And you've made me feel awful about it for my entire adult life."

"After Julian died, I promised myself—"

"What happened with Julian wasn't my fault," Harper says. "And it wasn't your fault. It was *nobody's* fault, Tabitha." It feels wonderful to state her case after all these years of silence. "Julian was sick. He died. It was tragic, Tabitha, and I can't pretend to know what it feels like to lose a child, but I assume it's the worst pain I've ever felt times a thousand, or times a hundred thousand. I never understood why you blamed me, why you ordered me out of the house, forbade me from coming to the funeral, and banished me from your life, but you are *always right* and I am *always wrong,* so I didn't even question it. I accepted the blame! For fourteen years, Tabitha, I thought I was evil. That's probably why I got messed up with Joey Bowen. I thought so little of myself: what did it matter if I delivered a package for him? What did it matter if I went to jail? What did it matter if I ended up floating facedown in Edgartown harbor? You had already made me feel despicable. And come to think of it, maybe that's why I've had such trouble with men. Because I was waiting for one of them to assure me I had value. Reed Zimmer was the person who finally did that. He loved me, which made me feel like I was better than I had believed myself to be since Julian died. I knew he was married, and I knew what I was doing was wrong. But I was powerless in the face of how much I loved him and how much I needed him to love me. Maybe now that you're in love with Franklin, you can understand that."

"Forgive me if I don't equate destroying someone's marriage with love," Tabitha says. "You are selfish and reckless and—"

"And I'm always wrong," Harper says.

"You were wrong in stealing another woman's husband," Tabitha says. "And you were wrong the night that Julian died. Admit it."

"If it helps to hear me say it, I'll say it. I'll scream it. *I was wrong.* The night that Julian died, I was wrong. I made a decision for both of us. I was pushy. But even if I hadn't been pushy, even if I had *never come to Nantucket at all,* he would still be dead. You know that. In your heart, I believe you know that."

"Get out," Tabitha says.

"Tabitha."

"Get *out,*" Tabitha says.

Back at her duplex, Harper throws her bag and Ainsley's bag into the rented Jeep. She is still shaking when she goes to pick Ainsley up at Five Corners.

"Change of plans," she says with false cheer. "We're taking the ferry home tonight."

"Aww," Ainsley says. "How come we can't stay?"

"Because," Harper says. "We can't."

TABITHA

She watches Harper screech out of the driveway. After feeling a vengeful sense of triumph, she collapses on the bed and cries fresh tears. She goes all the way back to the original hurt: it's not fair that Tabitha got paired up with Eleanor and has spent her adult life being held to impossible standards while Harper got to go with Billy and do whatever the hell she felt like doing. Running drugs! Sleeping with Billy's married doctor!

What happened the night Julian died *was* Harper's fault! Who else's fault would it have been?

And yet, with Harper gone, Tabitha feels an absence way down in her core. Harper is, for better or worse, her twin. They aren't the same person, not at all, but Tabitha knows Harper, knows her down to her bone marrow, her tiniest cells. Does she love her sister? Yes, she acknowledges this. But the anger is all-consuming. Tabitha needs to even the score. She needs to exact revenge so that she and Harper are on equal footing. Tonight is her chance. Right now.

She gets into the FJ40 and drives to Our Market, in Oak Bluffs, where she buys a very cold bottle of Domaines Ott rosé and a basic corkscrew—and, while she's at it, a couple of nips of Jägermeister. The cashier looks at her strangely and says, "Harper? I thought you left island."

Tabitha smiles brightly. "I'm back!" she says.

She drives up island on South Road. She turns off on a dirt road because she needs a quiet place to drink and think. The road dead-ends at some trees, but beyond the trees, Tabitha sees water. She carries her purchases out to a small beach, where she is instantly attacked by mosquitoes and no-see-ums. She doesn't care. This place has what she needs: solitude.

She has forgotten to bring a cup; she will have to drink the cold rosé from the bottle, like a Provençal hobo. Oh, well. Since she is pretending to be Harper, she might as well start acting like Harper.

She takes long draughts of the wine, then sucks back both nips. Her head spins. She hasn't eaten in... days. Since lunch the day that Franklin first vanished. The wine loosens Tabitha up; she's able, finally, to breathe all the way in and all the way out, to loll her head on her neck, to stretch out her arms. Another few sips, and she will be on her way.

Back in the car, she regroups. She collects her hair in a ponytail and smiles into the rearview mirror. In her own mind she looks as different from Harper as anyone could, but the rest of the world sees them as identicals. Even Eleanor and Billy used to have trouble telling them apart. One year, Eleanor mislabeled the twins in the photo she sent with the Christmas card, and she never noticed. Tabitha and Harper had debated pointing it out, but they ultimately decided it wasn't worth the uproar. Eleanor would either have thrown the batch of cards away and made them sit for the photographer again—or, worse, she would have stated that no one would know the difference and *so what does it matter?*

In Tabitha's memory, Harper had been more upset about the mistake than Tabitha was. She had lobbied to tell Eleanor, but Tabitha silenced her. Tabitha remembers feeling indignant about Harper's discontent. Why wouldn't Harper feel *grateful* about being mistaken for Tabitha? Why did she so vehemently want to establish her own identity?

Back in the days of growing up, Tabitha had loved Harper more than Harper loved her. Is that possible? The year Tabitha had become a pony, Harper was the only person allowed to ride on her back, although friends and younger neighborhood children had asked. And throughout the entirety of their childhoods, Harper was the only person Tabitha would let brush her hair or scratch her back or apply her suntan lotion. Harper had been born with a thicker skin. She didn't care how she looked; she didn't care about grades or activities in school. She put in just enough effort to meet Eleanor's impossibly high standards, although she didn't much care about Eleanor's or Billy's approval.

That indifference, of course, would catch up with her later.

Tabitha drives out South Road toward Aquinnah, keeping her eyes peeled for the simple wooden sign. She can't remember where it is exactly, but she's sure she'll recognize it when she sees it.

Maybe she was distracted and missed it, or maybe it was closer to Chilmark than she thought. When she crosses the bridge, she knows she's gone too far, so she turns around and heads back. She will find it. She has to. But she hopes it will be soon, because she's losing daylight.

Good old Sheep Crossing... the first cottage after the turn is where my brother-in-law is hiding out.

Did he say the first cottage after the turn? Left or right? That night at the Outermost Inn seems like a long time ago.

Then, just as Tabitha begins to wonder if she and Franklin even took South Road—maybe it was State Road?—she sees the sign: SHEEP XING. Yes! This is it. She hits the brakes. Doubts gather in her mind like gawkers hovering around the site of an impending disaster. What is she doing? What does she hope to achieve? Tabitha drives past the first driveway on the left very slowly so that she can get a good look at the house. It's a simple saltbox with gray shutters and white trim; it looks like any one of a hundred homes on Nantucket. There's a black Lexus in the driveway and a racing bike leaning up against the porch railing. Black Lexus = doctor car? Does Reed Zimmer ride a racing bike? Tabitha knows nothing about the man. She doesn't even recall what he looks like; she barely glimpsed him after being slapped and doused by his wife. All Tabitha registered was a male presence on the other side of Sadie, trying to control her.

Tabitha drives past. The road becomes a dead end, but there is enough privacy for Tabitha to feel like she can pull over and rest a second.

She swigs from the bottle of wine. And that, as it turns out, is the swallow that unlocks the vault in her mind.

It's mid-August of 2003. Julian is not yet three months old. Tabitha looks like a woman who has been lost in the wilderness and given up for dead. She hasn't eaten a full meal or slept more than a few hours at a time since Julian was born. She and Julian are at home with Wyatt and Ainsley now; they have been permitted to leave the hospital, which makes things both better and worse. Better, because who wants to live in a hospital? Worse, because in the hospital, Julian was monitored all day every day.

Now that they're home, Wyatt has gone back to work, and Tabitha has been left with both Ainsley and Julian. Tabitha is frazzled, but that word is too cute to describe how on edge she is. At the end of their first full week at home, she snaps at Ainsley. When Ainsley cries, Tabitha shakes her, hard. Not hard enough to hurt her, but hard enough to scare herself. Tabitha calls Wyatt at work, sobbing. She can't do it, she says. She can't do it alone. He needs to come home and help her.

And then we'll do what *for money?* he asks. He flat-out refuses to accept financial help from Eleanor. It's almost like he's daring Tabitha to suggest it so he can leave her.

Never mind, Tabitha says.

The next day, Harper walks in the door.

"I'm here," she announces triumphantly, as though she is the answer to all Tabitha's problems. "I took four days off work. I don't have to go back until Sunday." From her bag, she produces a bottle of Billecart-Salmon brut rosé champagne, which, she says, is ambrosial; she lifted this bottle from the restaurant where she waitresses, Dahlia's.

"But you paid for it, right?" Tabitha says.

"Right," Harper says with a wink. "With my hard work and exemplary attitude."

Tabitha can't bring herself to care that Harper stole a bottle of champagne from her workplace. What does it matter?

"We won't get a chance to drink it anyway," Tabitha says. "I'm nursing."

"So pump and dump," Harper says. "I'm sure you have enough breast milk stored in the freezer to feed the Gosselin kids. This bottle has our names on it."

"Whatever, Harper," Tabitha says. She feels teary again for

no reason; maybe because she desperately wants to drink champagne, but she just can't. Julian starts to cry, and Harper says, "There's my baby." She points at Tabitha. "You sit. Or, better still, go take a nap. I'll handle the kids, then get started on dinner. You look like Flat Stanley."

Tabitha wants to protest. She wants to remind Harper that she has no idea how to take care of a toddler or a sick infant; it's not something she can bluff her way through. But Tabitha is too tired to state her objections. The idea of a nap, an *uninterrupted* nap, followed by a home-cooked meal is too seductive to turn down.

As it turns out, Harper is a competent nursemaid and an excellent cook. She makes a bouillabaisse filled with scallops, mussels, and chunks of lobster. Tabitha eats three bowls with salad and crusty bread to sop up the juices, and then, amazingly, she feels like a human again.

Harper's arrival on Nantucket is, in fact, an answer of sorts. Ainsley is two years old and newly verbal; she asks questions nonstop, the most frequent of which is *Why?* To which Harper chooses among three answers:

Because there is pie in the sky.

Because there's a sty in my eye.

Because the guy makes me sigh.

Ainsley accepts all three responses with a solemn nod, as though she is being handed valuable pieces of wisdom.

Harper is also terrific with Julian. She doesn't mention how pallid he looks; she doesn't compare his feeble crying to the sound of a windup toy that is running out of windup. She treats him as though he were a normal baby. She calls him stud and stallion. And when he's inconsolable and won't settle or nurse, Harper dances him around the room, singing "If I Had $1000000," by the Barenaked Ladies, which puts him instantly to sleep.

Wyatt is impressed. "She's good with him."

Tabitha nods. Half of her is resentful that Harper has proved so skillful with the children, but half of her is relieved. She has slept more since Harper has been here than she has in the three months prior.

On her last full day, Harper gets up early and rides Tabitha's bike into town. She comes home with a bouquet of wildflowers that she bought from one of the farm trucks on Main Street.

"Something to remember me by," she says, putting the flowers in water and leaving them on the kitchen counter. "And by the way, we're going out tonight."

"No, we're not," Tabitha says.

"Yes, we are," Harper says. "Wyatt okayed it. He'll stay home with the kids. He thinks it's a good idea."

"He does *not* think it's a good idea," Tabitha says. Wyatt is terrified of being left alone with the children, which is one reason for Tabitha's exhaustion.

"Well, I talked him into it," Harper says. "We are going to drink the champagne I brought, we are going out to dinner, and we are going to dance at the Chicken Box."

At this, Tabitha laughs. There is no way they're dancing at the Chicken Box. Tabitha hasn't been to the Chicken Box since her first summer on Nantucket. "I don't think you get it," she says, "because you live a life free of responsibility. But I have two children, Harper. I'm a *mother.* I can't just go out on a wild bender."

"Who's talking about a wild bender?" Harper says. "We'll put the kids down, then go out. We have an eight thirty reservation at 21 Federal. Then to the Box for the first set. Home by midnight. It's all arranged. You're not allowed to back out. You *need* this, Tabitha. I'm afraid if you don't let some steam off, I'll be back here next month to commit you to Sapphire Farms."

Only now that so much time has passed can Tabitha effectively analyze why she let Harper talk her into going out. Was it the mention of Sapphire Farms—the mental institution for genteel Boston ladies who suffer mental breakdowns? Eleanor had several friends who had gone to Sapphire Farms, ostensibly because they needed "a break from the city," though the twins knew a trip to Sapphire Farms meant that these ladies were either batshit crazy or at least unable to cope with daily survival. Was it that Tabitha was afraid of Harper, unable to stand up for herself and say no? Was it that being set free from her life—even for a matter or four or five hours—was too tempting to resist?

Yes. Harper had presented an irresistible opportunity. She was the serpent offering an apple from the forbidden tree. And Tabitha, being a vulnerable and weak mortal, had taken a big, juicy bite.

Tabitha doesn't remember being nervous or worried. She doesn't remember asking Wyatt whether he was *really* okay with letting her go out; she doesn't remember going back to give Ainsley and then Julian one more kiss. She *does* remember putting on a gauzy white sundress. She remembers letting Harper braid her hair. She remembers plucking a marguerite daisy from the bouquet of wildflowers and sticking it behind her ear.

They decide to carry the bottle of Billecart-Salmon down to the end of Old South Wharf, where Harper pops the cork off into the harbor and they sit on the edge of the dock with their feet skimming the surface of the water as they pass the bottle back and forth between them, swigging and swilling and delighting in the lawlessness of it.

Or at least Tabitha is delighting in it. She feels like a new person—or, rather, like an old person, the person she was before she became a mother at twenty-two.

They put on their sandals and walk to 21 Federal, Tabitha's favorite restaurant. Tabitha thinks about calling to check in with Wyatt, but she doesn't. If she hears the baby crying, her night will be ruined.

They are seated at a two-top in the front room of the restaurant. They split a starter of portobello mushroom over Parmesan pudding, then they split the pan-roasted halibut and a bottle of very cold Sancerre. They split a crème brûlée. Everyone in the restaurant is looking at them, doing double takes. *Twins. Identicals.* There are men at the bar who offer to buy them an after-dinner drink. The men are well-dressed, older. They look wealthy. They look married.

"Ignore them," Harper says. "They're just into the twin thing."

But Tabitha doesn't want to ignore them. She never imagined she would feel desirable again, and these men seem so self-assured, so worldly. This was the kind of man Eleanor meant her to marry, she is certain. Eleanor did not mean for her to spend her life with a housepainter who doesn't even have halfway decent health insurance. Tabitha winks at the men, then flutters her fingers in a wave.

"No," Harper says, pulling Tabitha up by the arm. "We are not going down that road tonight, Pony."

Outside, Harper flags down a taxi, and they proceed to the Chicken Box. Harper buys them two beers apiece, then they wend and weave their way up to the front row, where they can see the band.

They dance with abandon, hands in the air. The band plays "With or Without You," by U2, and Harper throws her arm around Tabitha's neck and the two of them belt out the truest words ever written in a song. For them, at least.

I can't live... with or without you.

They stumble home sometime after one in the morning. The hem of Tabitha's dress has been trampled; the braid is falling out of her hair. But she is happy. For the first time in months, she is happy.

The house is quiet, and Tabitha shushes Harper, who is giggling and rummaging through the fridge for something to eat.

"Can I make popcorn?" Harper asks.

"Too loud," Tabitha says.

She tiptoes into the baby's room, and immediately her milk comes in. She groans at the prospect of pumping and dumping and heating up a bottle. She bends over to kiss her son. Because she is so drunk, so delirious with wine, music, and freedom, it takes her a moment to realize that something is wrong.

Tabitha doesn't want to go any further in her memories, but the door to the vault is heavy, and now that it is hanging open, she can't slam it shut.

Tabitha picks up Julian and presses his chest to her ear. Suddenly she is screaming, screaming, *screaming!* Harper appears first, holding a spoon smeared thick with peanut butter. Tabitha hands the baby to Harper, who drops the spoon.

Save him! Tabitha cries. As if Harper might be able to do this.

They run across the street to the hospital and burst into the emergency room. Harper is crying now, too, which scares Tabitha. Harper thrusts Julian into the arms of a nurse.

Save him! she shrieks.

The doctor on call performs CPR and mouth-to-mouth resuscitation, but Julian doesn't respond. The doctor doesn't announce a time of death because the baby was dead on arrival. Sometime during the night, he simply stopped breathing.

Where was Wyatt in all this? Tabitha wonders now. He was at the hospital: he must have been. Or did he stay home with

Ainsley? Yes, that was it—Wyatt was at home, asleep in Ainsley's twin bed, a copy of *Curious George Goes to the Zoo* open on his chest, Ainsley fast asleep next to him. It would have made sense for Tabitha to blame Wyatt. The one and only night he was left home to care for the children ends in tragedy. But Tabitha had never blamed Wyatt for what happened. He was, at the time, as heartbroken and sick as Tabitha was, if not more so.

No, the person Tabitha blamed was Harper. Harper had brought a bouquet of wildflowers into the house; quite possibly it was the pollen from the Queen Anne's lace or the foxglove that overtook Julian's delicate lungs. Harper was the one who had *insisted* Tabitha go out. She led Tabitha astray. If Tabitha had stayed home, this wouldn't have happened.

Harper's fault.

Harper's fault.

Harper's fault.

Tabitha turns the car around and drives back to the cottage where the Lexus and the racing bike are. This is where Dr. Zimmer is living; Tabitha feels sure of it now. She swings into the driveway and kills the ignition. She strides up the walk and knocks on the front door, then waits. Her eyes burn; her tongue thickens. What is she *doing* here? What is she going to say? She's not sure, but she can't seem to stop herself.

The door opens. It's the doctor. She recognizes him instantly, from just that one glimpse of him at the reception. It's more than that, though. It's that Dr. Reed Zimmer recognizes *her*. His eyes fill with...well, the only word that comes to mind is *wonder*. And love.

"Harper?" he whispers. There is a catch in his voice. He can barely speak.

This, Tabitha thinks, is how she wants Franklin to look at her. This, she realizes, is how Franklin *does* look at her. But that doesn't matter anymore.

"Hi," Tabitha says. And she steps inside.

NANTUCKET

The Hy-Line ferry accommodates wheelchairs, and so this is how Eleanor Roxie-Frost travels back to Nantucket, accompanied by her sister, Flossie, and her longtime housekeeper, Felipa Ramirez. Eleanor doesn't love everyone on the boat treating her like an invalid, but—although she can now take several steps by herself—she isn't able to make it up the ramp unassisted, so a wheelchair is a necessary evil. Her consternation about her disability is overshadowed by her relief at getting home to Nantucket.

Boston has been her home all her life, but in the summertime, there is no place like this island.

How many of us remember the summer of 1968, when Eleanor first set foot on Nantucket? She was on her honeymoon with Billy Frost. The two of them were cruising Nantucket Sound in a fifty-foot Hatteras captained by a retired Cape Verdean fisherman named Barker. Barker had taken them to the Vineyard for three days, where Eleanor and Billy had stayed at the Katama Shores Motor Inn. Billy had rented a CJ-7 and driven them out to the nude beach. He had gone into the water without his trunks, but Eleanor kept her suit on, despite the other beachgoers looking at her like *she* was the odd duck. They had danced until the wee hours at the Dunes a Go Go, and it was quite fun, but Eleanor had felt altogether more at home once they got to Nantucket, where things were a bit more staid. They had a suite at Roberts House, amid the cobblestone streets; they walked two blocks each night to dine at the Opera House. They rented bicycles and rode to 'Sconset, where they lunched on oysters and vichyssoise at the Chanticleer. As they were leaving that lunch, they spied Paul Newman playing tennis across the street at the Casino.

"Shall we go introduce ourselves?" Eleanor had asked.

"Absolutely not, darling," Billy had said.

Eleanor had been keen to buy property on Nantucket, but Billy favored the Vineyard, where, admittedly, prices were more reasonable. They quarreled about it for twenty years until they divorced—and then they both got what they wanted, Eleanor supposed, although she had certainly had moments when she'd wished she'd been more flexible.

Eleanor has heard from Tabitha a handful of times—and from Harper twice—although conversations with both twins have been decidedly one-sided. Eleanor talks about how she's doing, how she's feeling, her progress with physical therapy, and her struggle to get off the painkillers. One morning she realizes that neither twin has said a word about herself, but then Eleanor realizes that if she asks how they're doing, they'll candy-coat the truth. To figure out what's going on, Eleanor will have to get home and see for herself.

* * *

She is met at the ferry by her usual cabdriver, Chet Holland. Chet's sister is a transgender woman in Toronto named Desirée, and Desirée Holland loves to wear the ERF label, a fact that secretly thrills Eleanor. Eleanor beams at Chet and introduces him to Flossie. "My baby sister, Flossie."

"Oh, yeah?" Chet says. The sister is a younger, perkier version of Eleanor with platinum-blond instead of silver hair. And fake breasts, if Chet had to guess. "You happy to be back on the rock?"

Flossie rolls her eyes. "You can keep your Boston baked beans and foggy gray islands. I'm a Florida girl."

Hell, yeah! Chet thinks. He fills his own idle time daydreaming about Florida himself. He checks out the left hand of Eleanor's baby sister, Flossie, thinking he might like to take her out and show her what Nantucket has to offer. But Flossie sports a rock the size of the *Titanic* iceberg on her ring finger. Never mind.

Chet pulls into Eleanor's driveway, on Cliff Road.

"Wait a minute," Eleanor says. "Is this the right house?

"Sure is," Chet says. True, he hasn't driven Eleanor anywhere all summer, but this *is* her house, of that he is certain. He hits the brakes and waits for Eleanor to orient herself. She's getting older, plus she's a creative genius (at least according to his brother/sister Dave/Desirée), so maybe her brain is too crammed with new designs to recall what her house looks like. Einstein had a problem like that—he didn't know his own phone number!

"I haven't been here since Slick Willie was president," Flossie says. "But it's just as I remember it, Ellie. Prettier, even."

The housekeeper says something in Spanish that sounds urgent. She's pointing to the house.

"Wait a minute," Eleanor says. She's confused. It *is* her house, but something is off. She curses herself for taking the extra oxycodone that morning. She felt she needed it to get through the ordeal of traveling, but it has left her addled. She snaps her fingers. "I know what threw me," she says. "I do *not* recognize that car." Here she points to the navy-blue Bronco in the driveway of the carriage house. Whose car is that? It looks like something a spoiled teenage boy would drive, or a man going through a certain kind of midlife crisis. Maybe it belongs to a boyfriend of Ainsley's. Or possibly a boyfriend of Tabitha's. Someone new? Eleanor does not at all understand why Tabitha broke things off with Ramsay Striker. Eleanor didn't convey to Tabitha how heartbroken she was about the split. She dealt with it the same way she handled all unpleasant topics: by ignoring it.

Eleanor studies the car another second. She has seen that car before, she realizes. She has *ridden* in it—but when? Then she remembers: she rode in it on the way to Billy's memorial reception. It's Harper's car! But why is Harper's car here on Nantucket? Eleanor rummages around in her mind; she can't think of any reason.

"Of course this is my house," Eleanor says. "I don't know what's wrong with me." To Chet she says, "Carry on."

Felipa and Flossie make up the bedroom on the first floor while Eleanor rests in an armchair on the glassed-in porch that overlooks Nantucket Sound. From the house phone, she tries Tabitha's number, but she gets no answer, and Eleanor doesn't believe in leaving messages. Eleanor is too exhausted to call the store. Honestly, that store is the bane of her existence. Tabitha has done a terrible job managing it in recent years, and the thing has become a financial albatross. Eleanor has given serious thought to closing it, but if she does that, what will Tabitha do for work? And this summer, Ainsley is working at the store as well, although Eleanor hasn't heard word one about how she likes it. Probably she sits around and plays on her blasted phone.

Phones have become the scourge of modern society, if you ask Eleanor. Possibly the best thing about Boston was how out of touch she was.

Still, she has missed her water views, her Simon Pearce candlesticks displayed on the table in front of her, the smell of this house, and the chiming of these clocks. There are certain culinary delights particular to Nantucket that Eleanor has missed as well—the lobster bisque from the Sea Grille, the cheeseburger from Le Languedoc, the truffle-Asiago frites from Fifty-Six Union. Would it be cruel of Eleanor to send Flossie out on a gastronomic scavenger hunt so that they might have all three items for dinner tonight? Eleanor can arrange for Chet to drive Flossie; he had seemed to take a shine to her. Yes, Eleanor will do exactly that. Flossie is headed back to Palm Beach the day after tomorrow. Eleanor needs to enjoy Flossie's companionship while she still has it. And she needs to find Tabitha.

When Flossie comes out onto the porch carrying two giant Mount Gay and tonics—it must be five o'clock, Eleanor thinks; Flossie is always right on the nose with happy hour, and the drinks are always ice cold and very strong—Eleanor gives her the instructions for dinner.

Flossie rolls her eyes. "Can't we just get everything at the same restaurant?"

"No," Eleanor says. "We can't. Chet will chauffeur you around. You'll like that."

"*He'll* like that," Flossie says, and she trills her musical laughter.

"Also," Eleanor says, "would you mind terribly going over to the carriage house to fetch Tabitha?"

"Happy to," Flossie says. She raises her glass in a cheers. "I'm not going to lie. I can't wait to get home. But I'm really going to miss you, Ellie."

Eleanor feels color rising to her cheeks. It's true—the silver lining in the cloud of breaking her damn hip has been spending the past few weeks with Flossie.

Sisters, she thinks. There's nothing like them.

Flossie comes back a scant ten minutes later. "There's no one at the carriage house," she says.

"No one?"

"No one," Flossie says. "I left a note on the counter, telling them we were home."

"Good," Eleanor says. "I'm sure Tabitha and Ainsley are at the store."

But by eight o'clock that night—after the bisque, burger, and truffled fries are consumed and cleared away—there is still no word from Tabitha. Eleanor tries Tabitha's cell phone—voice mail. She sends Flossie back over to the carriage house.

"Nobody home," Flossie says.

Eleanor purses her lips. *What is going on here, exactly?* she wonders.

In the morning, Eleanor is awakened by the doorbell. She's disoriented at first, and the Ambien she takes each night to get to sleep leaves her voice as dry as crackers. She hears Flossie's light, quick steps on the stairs, then she hears voices. There is a tap on Eleanor's door.

"Come in," Eleanor croaks.

The door opens, and Tabitha steps in. Eleanor blinks. "Where in God's name have you been?"

"Mommy?" Tabitha says. "I'm Harper."

"What?" Eleanor says. This is *Harper?* Well, it's first thing in the morning. The way Eleanor always used to tell the twins apart was that Tabitha's eyes were more almond-shaped, and Harper's were rounder, as though she were in a constant state of amazement—but that distinction is only useful when the twins are standing side by side, and how long has it been since *that's* happened?

"I'm Harper," Tabitha says again.

"You're Harper," Eleanor says. She decides to be thrilled with this development. She has missed Harper! Harper went to live with Billy. But now Billy is dead.

Billy is dead, and Eleanor is broken. It's a distressing state of affairs. They had been such a striking couple in their day.

Eleanor notices something in Harper's face, something she hasn't seen in years and years but that she recognizes nonetheless. Her daughter is upset. Her daughter needs her. Somehow Eleanor knows exactly what to do.

She holds out her arms. "Come," she says. "Come to Mommy."

The story tumbles out: Harper and Tabitha have switched places, just like the little minxes in that movie they used to love. Harper has been here on Nantucket taking care of Ainsley and minding the store, and Tabitha has been on the Vineyard, renovating Billy's house so the girls can sell it and realize a profit. Speaking of profit, Harper—with the help of some poor soul named Caylee (that can't be her *real* name, can it? Eleanor wonders)—has made some deeply unorthodox changes at the store (involving *social media,* Eleanor thinks with a shudder), but sales are up by 500 percent over last year.

Eleanor accepts news of these "changes" with equanimity, surprising even herself. Probably she is not fully awake.

But then Harper starts to weep. Eleanor hears about Tabitha's love affair with the builder and that the builder's sister is the woman Harper betrayed with Billy's doctor. The builder can't see Tabitha anymore, and Tabitha is heartbroken. Tabitha blames Harper.

"She hates me, Mommy," Harper says. Eleanor loves that Harper still calls her Mommy, whereas Tabitha switched to "Mother" when she was ten years old. "She hated me for so long, then after Billy died, we patched things up, at least to the point where we were speaking. But now it's over for good."

"Nonsense," Eleanor says. She dispatches Felipa to fetch the house phone, and not only does Eleanor call Tabitha, she also leaves a message. "Tabitha, this is your mother. I want you back on Nantucket immediately. No excuses. I expect to see you in a matter of hours. At the most!" She disconnects the call and brushes the hair off Harper's shoulders. "You've gotten sun on your face," she says. She nearly launches into a lecture about wrinkles and premature aging, but because this morning seems to be unusual in its every aspect, she refrains. "A little color suits you."

MARTHA'S VINEYARD

It's common knowledge that Dr. Reed Zimmer has taken a leave of absence from the hospital because of "personal reasons." Most of us know that Dr. Zimmer admitted to having an affair with a patient's daughter. This was not cause enough to fire Dr. Zimmer, but it was cause enough for the hospital board president, Adam Greenfield, a.k.a. Greenie, to suggest he take a break until the brouhaha blew over.

"We have the reputation of the hospital to consider," Greenie said.

Dr. Zimmer reportedly accepted the censure without argument. He then moved out of the house he shared with his wife, Sadie.

Sadie placed a sign in the door of her pie shop that read: CLOSED UFN. This was a huge disappointment to the hundreds of summer visitors who counted Sadie's pies as a seminal part of their summertime experience.

Some of us wondered whether Reed and Sadie had left the island together in an attempt to mend their marriage. Perhaps they headed to a place where nobody knows them. Their house, right next to the Field Gallery, would have rented for a pretty penny—at least that's what Realtor Polly Childs thought when she drove by in her LR3. She was curious enough to pull up in front of the house and bold enough to knock on the front door. Polly was no stranger to island scandal and rumors, having once been ensnared in their vicious tentacles herself.

Sadie Zimmer had answered the door. She knew who Polly Childs was, of course, though they had never officially met. "Yes?"

"Just wondering," Polly said, "if you're planning on renting your home this summer. I have clients who would pay ten thousand dollars a week for it in August."

Sadie had given Polly a tired, barely tolerant smile. "Not renting," she said, and she closed the door in Polly's face.

Later people reported sightings of Sadie Zimmer at Alley's General Store and the up-island Cronig's. Christine Velman saw Sadie driving out to her parents' house in Katama—and in conversation a few days later during the meeting of the Excellent Point book group, Lydia Phelps confirmed that Sadie was remaining on the Vineyard for the summer, although she was taking a break from the pie business. Reed had moved out, Lydia told Christine, although whether he was off island or still on the Vineyard was unknown. Most of us guessed he was off island—and, as we know, off island is a *very* big place.

But then, late on the evening of the Fourth of July, Ken Doll nearly ran over a bicyclist on South Road. Thankfully Ken Doll caught a flash of reflective gear and swerved out of the way. But the incident flustered Ken Doll. Who goes biking at eleven o'clock at night? he wondered. He was only on the road himself because he had to retrieve his teenage daughter, Justine, from a party at Lucy Vincent. He put the window down to shout a warning at the biker—but when he saw it was *Dr. Reed Zimmer* he was so surprised that he hit the gas instead. He had heard that Dr. Zimmer had left the island for good.

But no. Reed Zimmer was still on the Vineyard, living in nearly hermetic seclusion at Sheep Crossing in a house owned by his medical-school roommate's elderly aunt Dot, who let the house sit vacant except on the rare occasions when the medical-school roommate used it himself. The medical-school roommate, Dr. Carter Mayne, worked as the head of the infectious diseases department at the Cleveland Clinic, a demanding job that left him precious little vacation time, so when Reed called saying he had marital problems and asking whether he could use the house for the summer, Carter said, *Of course, man, it's yours. The key is under the mat. I'll let the caretaker know.* Carter refused Reed's offer of fair-market rent, because if anyone understood marital problems it was Dr. Carter Mayne. He was on wife number 3, and he was about to leave *her* for a nurse in the burn unit.

Carter's aunt's cottage is nothing special, but Reed doesn't want, nor does he deserve, anything special. Every minute of every day since Sadie caught him at Lucy Vincent with Harper has been excruciating.

Reed fell out of love with Sadie all at once, a year and a half earlier: it was as if someone had thrown a switch from IN LOVE to NOT IN LOVE. This had happened in the dark days of January during a blizzard. Reed and Sadie had been trapped at home as the snow piled up outside. Sadie had built a fire and put a short-rib-and-onion pot pie in the oven; she had opened a bottle of red wine and turned up Harry Connick Jr. on the stereo. She patted the seat next to her on the sofa and said, "Come sit with me." Reed dutifully sat, and she handed him a wineglass, which he accepted, despite the fact that he rarely drank, and when he did—that is, if there was no chance he would be called into work—he preferred beer or a Scotch. They had clinked glasses, and Sadie said, "Kiss me."

Reed could remember feeling repulsed. He had not wanted to kiss his wife. He had not been charmed or lulled by the cozy wintertime domesticity. He could see where things were headed: Sadie would want him to make love to her, and he simply didn't want to. He took a sip of his wine, hoping alcohol might work its magic, might make him feel something for the woman next to him. It was nothing short of deliverance when, a second later, the house phone rang: Reed was needed at the hospital.

Reed had thought of himself as saved. Spared.

But Reed wasn't a quitter. He was thoughtful and methodical by nature. He figured that if the switch could be turned off, then it could also be turned back on.

The night of the blizzard he had been called upon to deliver a baby—Dr. Vandermeer, the OB, was stuck in Woods Hole—and Reed, who had not been in a delivery room since his ob-gyn rotation in medical school, found the experience enormously gratifying. The patient was a first-time mother, Alison, who had been determined to give birth without drugs, but the baby was big, and it was a struggle. Alison was swearing and screaming; the agony on her face troubled Reed, and he almost encouraged her to give in—at least take some Nubain—but in the end he was glad he didn't. Alison handled each contraction like a mountain she had to summit, and Reed and the two labor-and-delivery nurses cheered the way they might have for an elite athlete—Michael Phelps or Lindsey Vonn. After four hours of fight and nearly fifty minutes of pushing, Spencer Douglas entered the world weighing nearly nine pounds, a beautiful, healthy baby boy.

When Reed and Sadie reunited post-blizzard, nearly thirty-six hours later, Reed described the birth to Sadie. He detailed Alison's determination, the focus in her eyes, the strength of her will, the raw power of a female when she was in the midst of her most profound and fascinating function: giving birth. Reed had been a doctor for more than twenty years by that point, but he had still been struck by the nobility of it.

He had grasped Sadie by the shoulders. "We should have a baby."

"What?" she said.

"Why not?" Reed said. Since the birth of Spencer Douglas, Reed had cottoned to the idea of having a child. Children, as Reed understood it, often saved marriages.

But at the mere suggestion of having a child, it seemed that Sadie's own switch had flipped to the off position. It wasn't just that she dismissed the idea, it was that she was viscerally offended by it. She had believed them to be of a single, childless mind. Reed's change of heart was a betrayal. Sadie slept in the guest room that night. But then, a few days later, Reed found her back in their bed, and he thought she had come to her senses. However, when he tried to crawl in, she'd stopped him.

"I shouldn't be the one sleeping down the hall," she said. "You should."

And so for the year and a half that followed, Reed had been sleeping alone. Not only did Sadie not sleep alongside him, she also wouldn't touch him at all. She avoided his hands when he passed over the car keys or the newspaper; she steered clear of him in tight spaces. At certain junctures, Reed wondered how long she was planning on keeping up the embargo. Of the two of them, Sadie had been the more physical—the first to initiate sex, the first to offer a back rub when Reed had had a bad day at work, the one who insisted on holding hands at the movies. One night Reed said, "You can't get pregnant with your IUD in, you know, Sadie. No matter what I may or may not want."

"I know," Sadie had said. Her resistance to him seemed to have nothing to do with any actual fear of getting pregnant. Rather it was an act of hostility, of power, of torture.

Reed relieved his urges in the shower. He went for long bike rides. He stayed overnight at the hospital; the nurses commented on his devotion to the patients.

It was back in October, after nearly ten months of living without touch, kiss, or caress, when Reed bumped into Harper Frost at Morning Glory Farm. He had noticed the woman standing in line in front of him because of the pleasing way her ass filled out her jeans. When she turned around and he saw it was Harper Frost, the daughter of his patient Billy Frost, he was pleasantly surprised. Reed liked Harper for a couple of reasons. She was down-to-earth; she was concerned about Billy's treatment but not uptight. She and Billy had a charming, irreverent repartee; Reed enjoyed listening to the two of them parry. Harper teased her father about his smoking, his drinking, and his legion of female admirers, and Billy teased Harper right back about her nagging him as though she were his wife or mother. He called her "my old lady." The two of them seemed very close—they talked about scalloping, fishing, Dustin Pedroia and the future of the Red Sox, Billy's handicap at Farm Neck (Billy claimed it was a three, but Harper said it was a hundred and eleven), and a restaurant in the North End that made a crab-and-artichoke ravioli they loved. Listening to them, Reed once again felt a pang for a child of his own. Who, he wondered, would take care of him in his old age?

Sadie? Not likely.

At the farm, he bought Harper a cup of coffee, and they sat and talked, and it was the happiest hour Reed had passed in some time. Two weeks later, when Reed asked Harper to go for a drink, it was a spur-of-the-moment decision but also one he'd been considering since they parted ways at Morning Glory Farm. Reed knew it was a risk—going for drinks (which turned out to be dinner as well) with a patient's daughter—but until they walked out of Atria that night, Reed was still able to tell himself they were only friends. Reed had a populated life—his patients, his colleagues at the hospital, his wife's family—but he hadn't had a friend since medical school except for Sadie. And now, it was safe to say, Sadie was no longer his friend.

Reed had started kissing Harper—why? Because the night air was finally crisp after such a hot summer? Because he was high from the wine, the food, the companionship? Because at dinner Harper had unwittingly brushed his shoulder and knocked her knee against his? The circumstances demanded it, Reed thought later, when he tried to rationalize his actions. But that was cowardly. The decision hadn't been foisted upon him by outside "circumstances." The decision had been consciously made. By him.

Once Reed had kissed Harper, once he had made love to her in the backseat of his car—well, the genie could not be put back into the bottle. He thought about her nonstop. At first it was only sexual. His brain was engulfed in a fug of overwhelming desire for an act that he had been so long denied. A few weeks in, however, there were intimate conversations and the inevitable sharing of histories, and Reed realized that Harper was an extremely complex human being. He heard about her upbringing, her parents, her identical twin, her elite private school, her rarefied life in a town house on Beacon Hill. But then that particular storybook ended. Her parents divorced, Harper attended Tulane, then moved to Martha's Vineyard to live with Billy. Reed heard about her series of jobs: scooping ice cream, selling carousel tickets, landscaping for Jude Hogan—and one or two nights a week, serving drinks at Dahlia's. Reed was both proud and ashamed to say that he had never set foot in that particular establishment; it was rumored to be a hotbed of cocaine, infidelity, and summer money. Harper had fallen prey to the scene; she had agreed, on one occasion, to deliver a package for Joey Bowen. She had not known there would be any danger, but she had ended up handcuffed and lying facedown on a client's lawn. There was a fair amount of public shame, she told him. Reed pointed out that it might have been worse; she could have ended up in jail. Harper said she would rather have served her time. Instead the citizens of the island seemed determined to make her pay in other ways.

Reed and Harper saw each other once a week at first, then more often. But when the weather started to warm up, Harper became less available. Reed then discovered that she had started dating an Edgartown policeman, the young, charismatic, well-connected Drew Truman. Reed couldn't believe the way this discovery pierced him. He had never in his life felt so jealous. He realized he had no right; they had made no promises. But he didn't care. He couldn't stand the thought of Harper with anyone else. He left the hospital midshift and showed up at her duplex and demanded that she break things off with Drew.

She had laughed in his face.

Dr. Reed Zimmer, a pillar of the hospital, if not the community, found himself caught in a conundrum commonly experienced by lesser men. He was in love with someone other than his wife but unsure if he had the gumption to leave his marriage. To leave would bring pain, shame, scrutiny. He didn't think he could stand it; he *liked* being held in high regard—which was, he realized, a character flaw in itself.

Reed had allowed himself to believe that he was invincible. Unlike every other unfaithful man in the history of the world, he would not get caught. He would stay with Harper until Sadie left of her own accord, and surely that would be soon. Sadie was as miserable in the marriage as he was. In the spring, she started talking a lot about Tad Morrissey, the Irish carpenter who worked with Franklin. Tad was wonderful, Sadie said. Tad had come to the pie shop to build some new shelves, and he had shimmed the back door, which Sadie always had a hard time closing in the summer.

Reed convinced himself that Sadie was having her own affair—with Tad Morrissey. Was there anything wrong with that? Reed wondered. He and Sadie were both being discreet, keeping up appearances. They went together to the start-of-summer barbecue at Lambert's Cove with Sadie's family. Reed liked Sadie's family: her parents, Al and Lydia; her brother, Franklin. Lo and behold, Franklin brought Tad Morrissey with him to the barbecue as his "date," he joked—but really, Reed suspected, Tad was Sadie's date. Possibly Franklin knew about Sadie, and Tad was in on the deceit. Certainly no one batted an eye when Sadie sat next to Tad by the fire or when Sadie jumped up to fetch Tad more potato salad.

"While you're up, I'll have a little more as well," Reed had said. But Sadie had pretended not to hear him.

Sadie only paid attention to him that night when he was checking his text messages—and when he stepped away from the fire to call Harper back.

"Where are you going?" Sadie asked. "You're not on call tonight."

"I had a patient die unexpectedly," Reed said. Lydia heard this and crossed herself. Sadie rolled her eyes, which only showed how much her contempt for him was spoiling her soul. She turned away, asked Tad if he wanted another beer, and Reed was free to talk to Harper.

He should never have met her at Lucy Vincent. In retrospect, that much was obvious. But Billy had *died,* and Reed was taken as much by surprise as she had been. Billy had congestive heart failure and myriad other ailments, but Reed had thought he would last weeks longer, maybe even the entire summer. Some people had a dogged survival instinct, and Billy Frost was one of them. He had seemed like the kind of man who could live forever, despite his terminal condition.

Reed had thought Sadie was asleep when he left the house. She had been in their bedroom with the door closed, the lights out. Reed no longer kept any clothes or belongings in that room, so there would be no reason for him to open the door and check on Sadie; if she was awake, she would think he was coming after her for sex. They had both had a lot to drink at the barbecue, and whereas this sometimes led to a fight, on the ride home Sadie had been benign, nearly kind—the result, Reed assumed, of spending an evening in close proximity to her beloved.

He eased the Lexus out of the driveway, feeling like a teenager sneaking out from a house ruled by overbearing parents. Once he hit South Road, he experienced a heady sense of freedom. He was alive. How many moments of how many days had he failed to realize that? If someone had asked him then if he had any intention of going back to Sadie that night or ever again, he might have shrugged and said, *What for?*

Sadie had trailed him. She had heard the car pull out—or perhaps she had sensed something, overheard part of his conversation with Harper, read some impending deception on his face—and jumped out of bed. Possibly she had been waiting for *him* to go to bed so she could sneak out to meet Tad. However it had happened, he had been caught with Harper in the parking lot of Lucy Vincent.

Caught.

At first he thought he could talk his way out of it, using a measured voice and reasonable calm. Sadie had been quite drunk; her eyesight wasn't reliable. It had been dark, and she was without her glasses.

But Sadie had embarked on a full-blown investigation, which Reed, unfortunately, didn't discover until after Sadie made the abhorrent scene at Farm Neck. In the days that followed Billy Frost's memorial reception, the affair between Harper Frost and Dr. Reed Zimmer was all anyone talked about. It made Reed queasy to think about how lurid and trashy his private life must seem, that he had been revealed to be just one more faithless slug. A cheater.

Sadie forced Reed to go to his in-laws' house, in Katama, to confess. Al Phelps had cast his eyes to the floor, uncomfortable and embarrassed at hearing Reed's admission of guilt. Lydia had cried as though she were the one Reed had betrayed.

"Shame on you," she'd whispered.

Reed would have liked to explain how bad things were at home, that Sadie wouldn't sleep with him, wouldn't accept a cup of coffee from his hands, wouldn't kiss him good-bye when he left for work. But what did that matter? There were two kinds of people: the faithful and the unfaithful. He was unfaithful. And he had blithely chosen to believe that his wife was also unfaithful. He had created a whole fantasy relationship between her and Tad Morrissey, which, he realized now, was only for the benefit of his aching conscience.

Greenie, Adam Greenfield, the president of the hospital board of directors, had asked him to take a leave of absence for the summer.

"Go away," he said. "By September, this will be old news."

Reed had, initially, considered leaving. He could go to California, Oregon, Washington State, Alaska. He could return to

Cincinnati, where he had grown up. He could spend a nostalgic summer driving past the house where his parents had raised him with tall, cold glasses of milk placed at the one o'clock position above his dinner plate, where he had conducted open-heart surgery on a frog he found floating in his mother's koi pond, where he had learned how to mow a lawn in contrasting diagonal stripes, and where he had played third base in summer-league baseball. Third base had been the perfect home for him, a lefty. He would eat chili from Skyline and ice cream from Graeter's. He would track down Tracy Sweeten, the girl with blond feathered hair whom he had loved in seventh grade. When Reed bumped into Tracy or other people he'd known growing up, they would say they'd heard he was a doctor back East. A few might remember that he lived on an island, although he doubted anyone would be able to imagine the Vineyard. Cincinnati was flat, midwestern: it was cornfields and trout ponds, as far from the cliffs of Aquinnah, the surging Atlantic, and East Coast elitism as one could get, aesthetically and philosophically.

Reed had chosen to stay because when it had come time to drive his Lexus onto the steamship, second thoughts had taken him hostage. He didn't want to run away. He turned the car back toward Oak Bluffs and checked into a new hotel called Summercamp; it was so new that the receptionist didn't display any recognition when he gave his name.

And then, out of desperation, he'd called Carter Mayne.

Aunt Dot's house was on a road that few people knew about. The first thing Reed did when he got to the cottage—after stocking up on groceries at the Stop & Shop in Edgartown, which was so overrun with tourists that again he went unrecognized—was to shut off his cell phone. And then, because he feared that shutting it off wouldn't be enough, he threw it into the woods behind the house. He was tempted every minute of every hour to call Harper. Greenie had, somehow, heard that Harper had lost her job and left the island, although even Greenie admitted that this was merely the "word on the street." Reed had driven by her duplex and had not seen her Bronco out front, but that didn't mean anything. Was Harper gone? Where would she go? She had never expressed any desire to be anywhere but Martha's Vineyard. In this they were alike.

Reed's summer had been quiet—indeed, silent—until Sadie had somehow discovered where he was. She was the one who had wanted him out of the house, wanted him gone—she didn't care where, just gone—and yet apparently she had called Carter and bullied him into telling her the truth: Reed was staying at Aunt Dot's house. Or maybe bullying hadn't been required; Carter had always been weak when it came to women.

Sadie had stopped by the house only once, ostensibly to see if he was "okay," but she had ended up calling him names, calling Harper names, hurling insults, and then, finally, tear-stained and hiccupy, she had asked, "Do you love her?" She had not been brave enough to ask before, and Reed had been grateful.

He said, "You left a vacuum. And as I'm sure you recall from reading Aristotle, nature abhors a vacuum."

"That's not an answer to my question," Sadie said.

The answer to Sadie's question was yes: he loved Harper. To say so seemed cruel, but Sadie must have read it on his face, because she turned and left before he could say anything.

* * *

Reed lived a quiet, deliberate life in the manner of Thoreau. Being without a phone, without any way to communicate, was rather like ceasing to exist except in the present moment. He rose at four thirty (a benefit of living at the far eastern edge of the time zone, light this early) and biked to Great Rock Bight to swim, returning along North Road by six or six fifteen, before the rest of the island—most of them on their summer vacation—thought to stir. He hermited himself most of the day, reading paperback novels from Aunt Dot's shelves. He read Elmore Leonard's *Get Shorty* and Louisa May Alcott's *Little Women*. He read *Jaws* and *The Caine Mutiny* and *This Side of Paradise,* which put him to sleep four days in a row until finally he gave up on it.

He biked again at night, after dark. He fixed himself a simple supper at ten or eleven and slept fitfully, dreaming of Harper.

His neighbor two doors down was an executive with Coca-Cola from Atlanta named Dick Davenport (Reed wondered whether this was a made-up name) who stopped by to ask if Reed would mind picking up his newspaper while he was away; he had daily delivery of the *Vineyard Gazette.* Reed didn't love agreeing to a regular obligation, but no sooner did Dick Davenport ask than Reed realized Dick must have mistaken him for Carter, so Reed felt he had to say yes. He then took to reading the *Gazette* every day—and this was how Reed discovered that Brendan Donegal had died.

Reed's heart broke for Harper. Brendan had been Harper's friend; he was a person she had steadfastly visited on Chappy twice a week, no excuses. The obituary in the paper detailed Brendan's early life on the Vineyard and his surfing successes—major competitions won, endorsements. Then it described the accident on South Beach, drugs the likely culprit. He convalesced from the accident with his mother, in her home on East Beach. And a couple of days earlier, he had suffered an "accidental" pharmaceuticals overdose.

Reed feels certain that wherever Harper has been hiding, she has heard the news of Brendan's death and will return to the Vineyard, even though the newspaper explicitly mentions that there is *no service planned.* Reed awakens the day after he reads the obituary and feels Harper drawing closer to the island. She's on the ferry. She's with Fish. She's wearing her white denim shorts and Billy's light-blue golf shirt; her hair, which normally hangs heavy and long, is in a ponytail, a concession to the heat.

Reed has half a mind to drive to the Vineyard Haven ferry dock to pick her up. But then he realizes he has completely abandoned all reason. He isn't picking up Harper's aura or her energy. Reed is a scientist. He doesn't have a mystical bone in his body. He only pictures Harper in the white shorts and blue shirt because that was the last outfit he saw her in. It was a day or two after Billy's reception. Reed had chanced a drive past Harper's duplex because he had been powerless against his desire to see her and talk with her in person about what happened. He had sent her a text message asking her not to contact him, which was curt and cruel. He wanted to remedy that. But when he was on approach, he saw Harper coming out of the house. She climbed into the Bronco and drove off in haste. She was going to meet someone, Reed had thought. Probably Drew Truman. Reed had carried on to the hospital.

And as for him envisioning Harper with Fish, well, that

was a given. If Harper returned to the island, she would have Fish with her.

But still, the feeling lingers—insistent, pervasive. Harper is coming home.

It's no real surprise, then, when Reed hears the knock on his front door. It's ten past eight at night; the sun has descended past the tree line on Sheep Crossing. It's dusk, but not dark.

Reed tries not to anticipate. It might be the goofy neighbor or a Jehovah's Witness, although the hour is a little late for both.

He opens the door, and there she is. She is not as he imagined her. She's wearing jeans shorts and a Hot Tin Roof T-shirt, neither of which he's seen before. There is something off about her face that he can't quite pinpoint. But then again, he thinks, he isn't the same, either. He must look like a different person to her as well.

"Harper?" he says.

She goes to him.

TABITHA

He kisses her, long and deep. It's a skillful kiss, she thinks, but she feels nothing except a sharp stab of longing for Franklin. Chemistry between two people is a slippery, elusive thing. Love is not transferable.

Still, she participates. The thrill here is in the deceit. She tries to imagine what Harper would do, and decides to run her hands through the doctor's hair. Yes, this appears to be right. The doctor kisses her more deeply, pulls her closer. Tabitha feels him stiffening against her leg, and she hesitates. Kissing is one thing, but how far is she willing to go? When she knocked on the door, she had assumed: all the way. Anything less would be shy of revenge.

The doctor's hand travels up the inside of Tabitha's shirt. He is clearly fooled, even though Tabitha is, as Eleanor so kindly pointed out, heavier than Harper, a little thicker in the midsection. The doctor reaches up to unfasten her bra.

Whoa. She pulls away, casts her eyes down.

"Hey," the doctor says. "I love you, Harper. You need to know that. I love you."

Tabitha nods as tears fill her eyes. The doctor loves Harper, and no doubt Harper loves the doctor. But because of this, Tabitha is doomed to be alone.

"I love you, too," she whispers to the floor.

She allows the doctor to lead her by the hand to the back bedroom. With each step, she considers turning around. She had intended to betray Harper, but with each passing moment, she becomes more aware that she's betraying Franklin. If he could see her right now *with his brother-in-law,* he would... what? Tabitha is also betraying the doctor, which bothers her as well, though less. The doctor is hardly an innocent in all this.

As the doctor shuts the door behind them, Tabitha reluctantly sits on the bed. The doctor lifts her shirt up over her head, removes her bra, gently encourages her to lie back. He starts kissing her stomach.

It's then Tabitha realizes that the person she is ultimately betraying is herself.

"Stop," she says.

The doctor, obedient, looks up. He sees something in her face—or he doesn't see something.

"Harper?" he says.

"No," she says. "I'm not Harper."

AINSLEY

She is summoned to her grandmother's house after she gets home from work. Getting to the boutique and seeing Caylee that morning had been a relief; it felt like she had been away forever. Something had happened with Harper, although Ainsley wasn't sure what. She had been fine after seeing Mrs. Donegal, but when Harper picked up Ainsley in Vineyard Haven, she was trembling, teary, weird.

Adults remain a mystery to Ainsley.

Harper's mood improved when they got back to Nantucket, even once they learned that Eleanor was in residence at Seamless.

"I should probably go say hello," Harper said when they saw the note from Aunt Flossie on the kitchen counter. "I haven't seen Flossie in eons."

"Me, either," Ainsley said. She had last seen Aunt Flossie on spring break in Florida when she was in sixth grade. Flossie was a younger, much more fun version of her grandmother.

"But can we wait until morning?" Ainsley wasn't quite ready for things to go back to the way they'd been. "Grammie is probably asleep anyway." It was nine thirty at night.

"You're right," Harper said. "Let's wait until morning."

Harper had headed over to Seamless the next morning, but Ainsley had to get to work at the boutique. She thought perhaps she had dodged a bullet at least for another day, but as soon as she gets home, Harper says, "Your grandmother would like to see you."

"Oh," Ainsley says. "Are you coming, too?"

"No," Harper says. "She wants to speak to you alone."

Ainsley dreads the mandatory solo audience with her grandmother; she expects a lecture. Even the sound of the doorbell when Ainsley rings it—she and Tabitha are required to ring the bell when Eleanor is in residence so they don't catch her "indisposed"—sounds ominous.

Felipa answers. Ainsley hasn't seen Felipa in weeks, but there is no cheerful reunion. Felipa nods at Ainsley as though she's the exterminator. "Senorita."

"Hey, Flippah!" Ainsley says. "Qué pasa?"

Felipa leads Ainsley to the glassed-in porch, where her grandmother is sitting on the divan, wearing a silk kimono—black with white lilies. There's a cane hooked over the arm of the divan. Eleanor's hair is more white than silver now. She looks about a hundred years old.

"Hi, Grammie," Ainsley says. She senses that her grandmother can't stand up to greet her, so she bends over to kiss Eleanor's powdered cheek. She smells Evening in Paris. She wonders if Grammie has heard about the pilfered Bombay Sapphire and her in-school suspension. But the girl Ainsley was back then isn't the girl Ainsley is now.

Eleanor pats the divan. "Sit, sweetie," she says. "I've missed you."

Ainsley sits. The view over Nantucket Sound is pretty, and Ainsley tries to relax. Her grandmother doesn't sound at all angry—but then why the formal summons? "Where's Aunt Flossie?" Ainsley asks.

"She's out for the night," Eleanor says. "She has a date with Chet, my taxi driver."

"She does?" Ainsley says. "I thought she was married."

"She is," Eleanor says. "Her husband is eighty-five years old, however. She wanted to enjoy the company of a younger man tonight. It's perfectly harmless, I assure you. Besides, I needed Flossie out of the house. We're having an intervention."

Suddenly Ainsley wants to puke. An *intervention?* She hasn't had a drink all summer, hasn't smoked any dope, not one cigarette. Doesn't her grandmother know this? Ainsley needs to explain. Just when things are finally straightening out for her, she's getting shipped off to rehab? Well, she won't go. She won't! "Grammie, I don't think an intervention is necessary."

"But it is," Eleanor says. "I've let this feud between your mother and your aunt go on for too long. I should have set things straight fourteen years ago."

"What?" Ainsley says.

"Julian's death was my fault," Eleanor says. "I'm the one your mother should be blaming, not your aunt."

"What?" Ainsley says. She has never once heard her grandmother speak Julian's name. But the shock of this is overridden by her relief that the intervention is not meant for her.

Eleanor says, "I want you to know, my darling, that there are many things in my life I regret. I have made horrible mistakes. I've treated the people I love most in abominable ways. Billy, for one. I loved him, but I shat all over the man. At some point I decided I had outgrown him or that he had never been good enough for me in the first place. That wasn't true, of course. Your grandfather was the most handsome, gracious man in the city of Boston. But I made him feel small. I insulted him, I called him names, I drove him away. He hated me for years. And your mother! I can't even begin to enumerate my transgressions against your mother." Eleanor's voice wavers, and Ainsley shifts uncomfortably. On the cigar table next to the divan, her grandmother has a drink, probably her usual Mount Gay and tonic. She brings the glass to her mouth, but her hand is shaking.

"Grammie," Ainsley says. She would like to say something comforting to Eleanor, but what can one say to a seventy-one-year-old woman that won't sound patronizing? Her grandmother *has* been awful to the people closest to her. She's a battle-ax, a dragon lady. She prefers that people fear her rather than love her. And yet Ainsley is impressed that her grandmother has reached this moment of self-awareness. Probably it's a result of breaking her hip. Ainsley supposes that being so incapacitated is humbling and painful and reminds one of one's own mortality.

Ainsley is saved from having to speak because a second later the doorbell rings, and shortly thereafter Harper walks in. She smiles sympathetically at Ainsley. "Did Mommy fill you in, then?"

"Kind of," Ainsley says. But not really. Eleanor brought up Julian but never finished the thought.

There is no time to pursue this idea, because the doorbell rings again, and Ainsley thinks, *FedEx? Or Flossie?* Would Eleanor make Flossie use the doorbell while she was *staying* here? Quite possibly.

"What's the big emergency?" a voice says.

Ainsley's head swivels. Her mother walks onto the porch.

"Sit down, Tabitha," Eleanor says.

Tabitha takes a head count. She stares hard at Harper, then her eyes rest on Ainsley, and there's a glimmer of a smile. "Hello, darling," she says. She holds out her arms, and Ainsley can't help herself—she rushes into them. It's her mother.

"Mama," Ainsley says.

Tabitha squeezes her, kisses the top of her head. Ainsley inhales, hoping for the familiar Mom scent, but her mother smells like she has been living with a litter of feral cats at the bottom of a laundry hamper.

"I need you girls to sit," Eleanor says.

Ainsley reclaims her place on the divan. Harper perches on the arm of an overstuffed chair, and Tabitha dutifully sinks into the matching chair. Ainsley looks back and forth between her mother and her aunt. After spending so much time with Harper, Ainsley thought she would be able to easily distinguish between the two, but they are eerily identical. If Ainsley closed her eyes, and they switched places or didn't, changed clothes or didn't, would she be able to tell them apart?

"What is it, Mother?" Tabitha says.

"She wants to broker a peace treaty," Harper says. "I'll help her out. I'm sorry, Tabitha. I'm sorry for everything. I'm sorry about the party at the boutique, I'm sorry I hired Caylee, and... I'm sorry about Julian."

"Julian!" Tabitha says. She casts an eye at Ainsley. "We aren't talking about this in front of my daughter."

"We most certainly are," Eleanor says. "Ainsley is more than old enough to know what happened." Eleanor lifts her drink to her lips, then slowly, carefully sets her glass down. She looks at Ainsley. "Your brother was born prematurely. It's a miracle he lived at all, frankly. But his lungs never caught up to the rest of him."

Ainsley nods. This much she knows, or thinks she knows. She can count on one hand the number of times Julian's name has come up in conversation, but his ghost is always hovering around, haunting them. His death is the foundation of her mother's personality—her sorrow, her impatience, her indifference.

"Please stop, Mother," Tabitha says softly.

"Your mother blames your aunt for Julian's death," Eleanor says without taking her eyes off Ainsley. "That's why they didn't speak for so many years."

"Blames her why?" Ainsley says. "If he just stopped breathing?"

"She—" Tabitha says.

"I—" Harper says.

"Your aunt came to Nantucket to help," Eleanor says. "And on her last night here, she persuaded your mother to go out to dinner, to go out dancing. And that was the night that Julian died."

"I wasn't home," Tabitha says. "If I had been home, it wouldn't have happened!"

"Nonsense!" Eleanor says. "That is complete nonsense,

Tabitha Frost, and you know it!" Eleanor's voice is louder and sharper than Ainsley has ever heard it. Eleanor's anger is usually expressed by her choice of words, not by the volume at which she speaks them. "Your father and I could never figure it out," Eleanor says. "We used to puzzle over it. What had happened? Why the discord? Billy thought one thing, I thought another."

"I'm afraid to ask," Harper says.

"That was between Billy and me, and I'm certainly not going to share our private conversations with you now," Eleanor says. "I brought you here so I could apologize. I need to say I'm sorry."

"For what, Mother?" Tabitha says.

"I blame myself for Julian's death," Eleanor says. "First off, I should have insisted on paying for a longer stay in the hospital—"

"Wyatt would never have accepted your charity," Tabitha says.

"Will you *please* let me finish?" Eleanor says.

They're all quiet, and Eleanor takes the opportunity to enjoy a dramatic pause. She takes a prolonged sip of her drink. They all watch as her hands tremble, and the ice does a nervous dance in the glass.

"We opened the boutique at the Candle Street location that summer," Eleanor says. "Remember?"

"Yes," Tabitha says.

"I was desperate to have it ready for Memorial Day weekend," Eleanor says. "And we had that unseasonably warm weather." She looks at Tabitha, and her eyes brim with tears. "I worked you to the bone. There you were, six and a half months pregnant, and I was asking you to carry boxes and move racks of dresses down sidewalks and up and down curbs in the sweltering sun. I barely let you sit down, and when you did, do you remember what I gave you to drink? Do you remember, Tabitha?"

"An espresso," Tabitha says.

"I gave you espresso," Eleanor says. "I thought it would pep you up." She shakes her head, and one tear drops. "I had such a trial carrying the two of you that as far as I was concerned, being pregnant with one baby was no big deal. Part of me, I'm sure, thought you were getting off easy." Eleanor stares at her hands in her lap. "I was monstrous. You started complaining of pains, and the next thing I knew you were in full-blown labor at twenty-eight weeks." She takes another sip of her drink. "I'm responsible for Julian's premature birth. And therefore I'm responsible for his dying. Why you've been blaming your sister is beyond me."

Everyone is quiet for a while, processing Eleanor's confession. Ainsley is in awe of the many ways that parents are able to screw up their children's lives. She had thought she was nearly out of Tabitha's grip—in a couple of years she will be eighteen, an adult—but now she realizes a mother's rule can last one's entire life.

"I'm confused about this so-called puzzling you and Daddy used to do," Harper says. "These private conversations. You and Daddy never even spoke, did you?"

"Don't change the subject," Tabitha says. She turns on Eleanor. "You're only taking the blame now to protect Harper."

At that moment, Eleanor drops her glass. It glances off the edge of the cigar table, hits the floor, and shatters. There are glass shards and ice everywhere. The drink splashes all over the Tabriz rug and the bottom of Eleanor's kimono. But Eleanor barely bats an eye, making Ainsley think her grandmother dropped it on purpose.

"Just let it be my fault!" Eleanor says. "I want the two of you to kiss and make up! I want you to do what siblings are supposed to do—hate your parents but love each other! Flossie and I both despised my mother; even now, sixty years later, we talk about how awful she was. I don't know what I would have done if I didn't have Flossie to commiserate with. She's my sister. But you, Tabitha Winford Frost, and you, Harper Vivian Frost, are *more* than sisters."

Ainsley scoots over so she can take her grandmother's hand. "You heard Grammie," Ainsley says to her mother and her aunt. "Since we're talking about Julian, we might as well acknowledge that I lost him, too. I saw the pictures of him that you hid in the bookshelves. I was never allowed to claim him *or* mourn him. All my friends think I was always an only child. But you two have each other. You're so lucky." Ainsley turns her gaze to her mother. "Please, Mama, forgive Aunt Harper. For me."

"It was never just Julian," Tabitha says. "I've been angry since Harper left with Billy. She won, and I hated her for it."

"Won?" Eleanor says. "I would hardly describe going with Billy as winning. Or am I dreadfully mistaken?" She looks up at Tabitha. "I always figured you came to your senses and decided you would be happier with me."

"The point is, Mother, we *shouldn't have had to choose!*" Tabitha says. "It was cruel of you—and of Daddy, too—for agreeing to it, for breaking the two of us apart like that. We were inseparable, you knew that, but you thought nothing of snipping us apart like we were paper dolls. One minute we were a duo, a team, a party of two—and the next minute I'd lost the game, and Harper was leaving."

"What game?" Eleanor says.

"We shot rock, paper, scissors," Harper says. "The winner got to go with Billy."

"Oh, for heaven's sake!" Eleanor says.

"What's rock, paper, scissors?" Ainsley asks. It sounds like something an early English settler would play.

"It's a game Billy taught the twins because that's how he and his schoolyard chums used to settle disputes at Boston Latin." Eleanor looks into her lap. "The winner got to go with Billy. The *winner?* And the loser had to stay with me. Was I really *that bad?*" Tears shine in Eleanor's eyes, and Ainsley feels a lump presenting in her throat. Her poor grandmother! She built a career, she made money, she owns houses and fancy things... but she had not been the girls' favorite. Ainsley knows how she feels. She's an only child, but there have been plenty of times recently when she has felt like nobody's favorite.

"We were kids, Mother," Tabitha says. "We were sheltered seventeen-year-old girls."

"I suppose your father would have been far more appealing," Eleanor says. "Billy Frost was as charming as the devil himself. Women of all ages loved him. And you two girls... well, you both adored him blindly. You always fought to be the one he carried around on his shoulders. Both of you Daddy's girls, through and through. Just like Flossie and me." She turns to Ainsley. "Be warned, darling, you come from a long line of strong, disagreeable women!"

Tabitha says, "Harper asked a valid question, Mother. When did you and Daddy have these chats about us? You never called him, and when he came to Nantucket, you refused to see him."

Eleanor wipes her eyes and laughs. "That shows how little

you pay attention. Billy came over every night of his stay, after you were asleep."

"He did?" Tabitha says. "And you... what?"

"What do you think?" Eleanor says. "Like I told you, I loved Billy Frost with all my heart. I was never able to resist him. Nor was he able to resist me, I suppose." A smile crosses her face, and she sits up a little straighter in her chair. "I would like you girls to give each other a hug, a real hug. And then I'd like you both to clean up this mess I've made."

Ainsley knows her mother and aunt are nearly forty, too old to be ordered around, but they comply with Eleanor's wishes. Harper holds out her arms and, incredibly, Ainsley watches her mother take a step toward her. Soon they're embracing. It's surreal to see two people so alike clinging to each other that way. Ainsley imagines them four decades earlier, floating side by side in the womb. They have been together since the moment of conception. It's a miraculous thing, when she thinks about it.

When they separate, Tabitha bends down to pick up the shards of glass, and Harper cups her hand to accept them. Ainsley, figuring she'd better not just sit around like a lap dog, hurries into the kitchen for a sponge and a towel. She tries to imagine herself explaining what transpired here today to Caylee. *My grandmother took responsibility for my brother's premature birth... my mother and aunt played a game with rocks, paper, and scissors that determined their futures... my grandmother confessed that she had been secretly rendezvousing with my grandfather for all these years, even though they're both really old.*

She sees Caylee's smile.

And why not? Despite the drama, when Ainsley bends to

mop up the sticky mess of rum and tonic she feels . . . good. It'll probably only last a couple of minutes, but for now she's going to enjoy being part of a happy family. Or if not a happy family, then at least a family without any secrets.

No sooner has Ainsley formulated this thought than Harper clears her throat.

"I'm pregnant," she says.

TABITHA

This summer, she and Harper have agreed on very little, but they both agree—once they are out of Seamless and back in the carriage house—that it's time for Harper to return to the Vineyard for good. Tabitha will go back with her, but only for a day or two. She needs to pack up her things and settle up with the subcontractors. She needs to write up a punch list of things for Harper to take care of before they put Billy's house on the market.

"So you're *both* going to the Vineyard?" Ainsley says. "You're going together?"

"In Harper's car," Tabitha says. "And I'm bringing our car back." She feels heinously guilty leaving her daughter again, but she has to tie up loose ends.

Franklin, she thinks. She will try to find Franklin to say good-bye. She owes him that. She owes herself that.

Eleanor isn't happy that Tabitha and Harper are leaving, but she has Flossie for one more day, and she has Ainsley.

Besides, she was the one who orchestrated the reunion. She really has no right to complain.

As the ferry pulls into Oak Bluffs, Harper and Tabitha sit side by side in the front seat of Harper's Bronco, and Fish is asleep in the back.

"Are you nervous?" Tabitha asks her sister. She told Harper that she had gone to see Reed. She admitted that it had been her plan to pull a secret twister and seduce the doctor under false pretenses, but she hadn't been able to go through with it. She also told Harper how in love Reed had seemed—with the person he believed to be Harper. She then gave Harper the address.

You need to go see him, she said. *Especially now.*

"Nervous doesn't begin to cover it," Harper says. "How about you?"

"Why would I be nervous?" Tabitha asks.

Harper shrugs. A little while later, she says, "Was it real between you and Franklin? I mean, it happened really fast."

"Harper," Tabitha says. "It was real."

They don't say much on the ride to the house. Tabitha has been gone less than a full day, but she's relieved to be back on the same island as Franklin. She wants so badly to believe that he'll come to his senses and live his life for himself.

She and Harper walk in the back door of Billy's house into the kitchen. Tad is on his hands and knees in front of the refrigerator.

He's putting in the last of the new floorboards. When he looks up, his eyes dart back and forth between the twins.

"Whoa," he says.

"Hi, Tad," Harper says. "Freaked out by the twin thing?"

Tabitha doesn't care if he is or isn't. "Is Franklin here?" she asks. "Have you seen him?"

Tad gets to his feet and wipes his hands off on his Carhartts. "He was here earlier today, actually."

Tabitha's heart feels like a bird smacking against a window. "He was?"

"He was. He asked for you. I told him you left."

"You told him . . . did you tell him where I went?"

"I didn't know where you went," Tad says. "You bolted out of here without a word. He could see, obviously, that you'd left your car behind."

"So then what happened?"

"Then he left," Tad says.

"How long ago was that?" Tabitha asks.

"Hours ago," Tad says. "And no, he didn't tell me where he was going or when he'd be back." He turns his attention to Harper. "How have you been?" he asks.

"I wouldn't know where to begin," Harper says.

HARPER

She has a harder time leaving Nantucket than she thought she would. It doesn't take her long to pack, and with one hour in town, she's able to say her good-byes. At the boutique she hugged Meghan and gave baby David Wayne a kiss on the forehead.

Then she held out her arms to Caylee. "Thank you," she whispered. "You saved the store."

"Don't be dramatic," Caylee said.

"Tabitha was angry when she found out you were working at the store," Harper said. "But even she can't argue with a five-hundred-percent increase in sales."

"Is she going to let me stay?" Caylee asked.

"Absolutely," Harper said. "I bet you'll even grow to like her."

"You think?" Caylee said.

"But not as much as you like me, of course," Harper said.

Harper walked up Main Street to the offices of Striker & McClain. The receptionist, Bonnie, narrowed her eyes at Harper.

"Which one are you?" she asked.

"Harper," Harper said.

"I only ask because I heard Tabitha is coming back," Bonnie said.

Wow, Harper thought. Nantucket gossip moves even faster than Vineyard gossip. That must be because it has a shorter distance to travel...and less traffic to deal with.

"That's right," Harper said.

At that moment, Ramsay appeared to save her.

"If you're leaving, then I assume your sister is coming back," Ramsay said.

"She is," Harper said. She considered informing Ramsay

that Tabitha had fallen in love over on the other island, but she bit her tongue. For all she knew, Tabitha was planning to get back together with Ramsay—and wouldn't it be just like Harper to ruin that, too? Harper gave Ramsay a hug. "The Vineyard is only eleven miles away, you know. You're welcome anytime."

"I'll come in the fall," Ramsay said. "How about that?"

"Great," Harper said. She figured he was just being polite. People on the Vineyard always vow to do things "in the fall," when the hectic pace of summer is over, but then the fall becomes busier than anyone could have predicted, and the holidays loom on the horizon. Harper had offered the Vineyard up to Meghan and her husband as well, but she doubted they'd ever come. Those eleven miles might as well be eleven hundred; the Vineyard might as well be Vegas or Venus.

If Ramsay does come in the fall, he will learn that Harper is pregnant. She imagines meeting him at the ferry with her rounded belly—*surprise!*

It had been hardest, of course, to say good-bye to Ainsley. There were so many things Harper wanted to tell her niece: *Be a good girl, be kind to your mother, be patient with your grandmother, don't drink until your twenty-first birthday, then you and I will drink together, good champagne. Don't smoke, ever. Never fall in love, fall in love with abandon, things will make sense when you're older, things will never make sense. Life isn't fair, make good decisions, don't beat yourself up when you make bad decisions, value yourself the way I value you. Travel. Listen. Question. Wear sunscreen, use birth control, don't buy tomatoes out of season. I will miss you. You are a wonderful, talented child, Ainsley, and I'm only ever a boat ride away.* And then, last but not least: *Scissors cut paper, rock smashes scissors, paper covers rock.*

Ainsley said, "Next summer can I come live with you on the Vineyard and be your nanny?"

Nanny? Harper hadn't yet thought of herself as a person who would need a nanny. But for Ainsley's sake, she smiled and said without hesitation, "Absolutely."

She leaves Tabitha at Billy's house to take a shower and pack, and she drops Fish and her belongings off at the duplex. Fish collapses on his Orvis bed and closes his blue eyes and Harper is glad. She feared he would want to go with her when she left, but she needs to do this alone.

"I'll be back in a little while, bud," she says.

Fish doesn't even lift his head.

Sheep Crossing: she knows the road, although as a delivery person she has overshot it half a dozen times at least. It's nothing more than a slender dirt-and-sand path, really, with a tiny wooden sign half hidden by overgrown brush. Harper turns onto the road, blood rushing in her ears, anxiety coursing through her in a way that can't be good for the baby.

We're going to meet your father, she thinks.

She pulls into the first driveway on the left, as Tabitha said to do, and there is the Lexus and there is Reed's bike. Harper is sweating now, and her breathing is shallow; her nerves are in control. She turns off the car and sits, then thinks, *Well, this is it.* She walks up to the door and knocks.

"Hello?"

Harper turns at the voice. A man—not Reed—is strolling across the lawn holding a bottle of Scotch. The man has a handlebar mustache waxed into curlicues, and despite the heat, Harper shivers. She can handle just about any variation on a man's appearance—after all, for three years she lived with Rooster's cockscomb, and before that she lived with Joey Bowen's mullet—but she cannot tolerate a handlebar mustache.

The man offers his hand, and Harper shakes it expediently.

"I'm Dick Davenport, the neighbor," he says. "Would you be looking for Dr. Zimmer?"

Dick Davenport? she thinks. The name fits him perfectly: he's half barbershop quartet, half 1970s porn star. "I would be," she says, wishing she had paid attention at Winsor when they were learning about tense in English class. *Would be* is the conditional? Past conditional?

"He's not home," Dick says. "I took him to the ferry around lunchtime. I was just stopping by to drop off this Laphroaig as a thank you. Reed collected my newspapers while I was home in Atlanta."

"Oh," Harper says. Dick looks like he wants to hand her the Scotch. "You took him to the ferry? Was he going somewhere?"

"Yes," Dick says. He gives Harper a conspicuous once-over.

"You're very, very pretty. You aren't single by any chance, are you? I would love to take you to dinner. How about tonight? I happen to know the new reservationist at the Covington."

Harper is completely blindsided. The neighbor of the house where Reed is hiding—or *was* hiding, as he has apparently left on the ferry for parts unknown—is asking her on a date. "Thank you, but I can't. I'm having dinner with my sister tonight."

"I'll take you both out," Dick says. "Is she as pretty as you?"

"Maybe another time," Harper says. She takes a few steps backwards until she is an arm's length away from the Bronco, and she watches as Dick sets the Scotch inside the screen door. She slips into the driver's seat, doesn't bother with the seat belt. She can't get out of there fast enough.

Dick waves. Harper throws the car in reverse.

When she gets back to Billy's house, Tabitha is sitting on one of the brand-new kitchen stools, drinking a glass of champagne. The bottle is on the counter next to her, and Harper blinks, thinking she's seeing things. It's Billecart-Salmon rosé, the same champagne that Harper brought to Nantucket fourteen years earlier, the champagne they drank together on the end of the dock while skimming their feet against the water's surface. Does Tabitha realize this? Did she choose this champagne on purpose? She must have: very little escapes her sister. So is this a sign, then? Tabitha has forgiven Harper? She's ready to move on? For real?

Harper is unconvinced.

"Get a glass from the cabinet," Tabitha says. "I'll pour you a teensy bit."

"Did you find Franklin?" Harper asks.

"Called him, went straight to voice mail. Went to his house. His truck is there, but he's not home. I peeked in the windows."

"Reed is gone, too," Harper says. "His neighbor said he drove him to the ferry but didn't say where he was going."

"When I saw your car pull in, I figured something like that," Tabitha says.

Harper pulls a champagne flute from the new glass-front cabinets. The kitchen bears no resemblance to the unsanitary stinkhole it used to be. Harper sees that Tabitha bought new stemware from Tiffany—the champagne flute still has the blue-circle sticker on the base.

"These seem pretty fancy," Harper says. "Are we going to make any profit after all this work?"

"Huge profit," Tabitha says. "The glasses are for show. We'll take them with us when we sell."

Now that the house is such a showpiece, Harper doesn't want to sell; she would like to live here herself in Billy's new old house. But that isn't the deal, and she can't argue with the phrase *huge profit.*

Tabitha lifts the bottle and pours a token amount of champagne into Harper's flute. She raises her own glass. "There's a man still left in this house," she says.

"There is?" Harper says. "Is Tad still here?"

"No," Tabitha says. "Billy. His ashes are on the mantel. What do you say we give him a proper scattering?"

Billy, Harper thinks. She closes her eyes and sees her father in the hospital bed. How many hours did she spend playing spades with him on the little Formica table attached to his bed? Harper remembers all the way back...to the phone calls that used to come for her father in the middle of the night when they lived on Pinckney Street. Apparently there were emergencies in the city of Boston that only Billy Frost could fix: half the rooms at the Park Plaza had lost power; the walk-in fridge was on the fritz at Locke-Ober; there had been an electrical fire in the boiler room of the public library. Billy was the electrician of choice among Boston's elite in those days. His career wasn't as glamorous as Eleanor's, but he had held his own. He was popular with union bosses and local politicians; nearly everywhere they went—Southie, Chinatown, Fenway—Billy bumped into someone who owed him a drink.

When Eleanor asked him for a divorce, he had been more resigned than angry, as if he'd figured that day would come sooner or later. And in many ways—most ways, even—he had been happier in his life on the Vineyard. Harper can see him on the beach at Cape Poge, patiently pulling the hooks from the mouths of every fish they caught, his motions competent and assured. Billy was a man who always knew what he was doing. She pictures him in his usual seat at the Lookout, turning to see her walk in, grinning, signaling the bartender, Sopp, and calling out, "A beer and a dozen Malpeques for my old lady, please!"

Harper tries to imagine Billy as a young man, setting eyes on Eleanor Roxie for the first time. They met at the Country Club in Brookline, at a Christmas party Eleanor's parents threw every year. Billy had come to the party as the date of Eleanor's first cousin, Rhonda Fiorello, but Eleanor didn't care for Rhonda and had no qualms about stealing her date away. Eleanor was twenty-one, a senior at Pine Manor, and

Billy, an older man at twenty-three, had done two years at UMass, Boston, in electrical engineering before switching to trade school. Harper had seen pictures of her parents in their beautiful youth, and she marvels that the attraction they felt for each other in 1967 had endured fifty years... *if* Eleanor was telling the truth about Billy sneaking over to her house in the middle of the night.

Harper has been so caught up in her own drama that she hasn't been able to mourn Billy's passing. She hadn't planned on scattering Billy's ashes at all, mostly because she couldn't bear to do it alone. But now that Tabitha is here, the decision seems appropriate.

"Let's do it," Harper says. She and Tabitha touch glasses and drink.

Harper drives, because the Vineyard is still, technically, "her" island, and Billy was "her" parent.

"You knew him better than I did," Tabitha says. "And I never knew him here. Where would he want his ashes to be scattered?"

Harper has been wondering the exact same thing. She decides that part of Billy should rejoin the land, and part of him should rejoin the water surrounding it. Part of him should stay with Harper, and part of him should go to Nantucket with Tabitha. It's hard to know how to feel about the ashes. They aren't *Billy,* but they aren't nothing, either.

"We'll scatter a quarter at the harbor in Oak Bluffs and a quarter at Farm Neck," Harper says.

"The golf club?" Tabitha asks.

Harper nods. If there's one thing Harper is sure of, it's that Billy would want to have his remains fertilizing the tee at the third hole.

"I never wanted to go back there again," Tabitha says.

"Oh, well," Harper says.

Farm Neck has closed for the day, and Harper worries that they will be denied access to the course. She asks at the front desk for Ken Doll, who appears within seconds looking as dapper as ever—tie, matching pocket square, shiny buckled shoes. He smiles when he sees the twins, which Harper supposes is nothing short of a miracle, seeing as how Harper invited disgrace right in the front door of this private club.

"Harper," he says. "And Tabitha!"

He's excited to see Tabitha, Harper realizes, and she feels the ancient hurt of people always preferring her sister. But in this instance, she knows she should be grateful.

"We have a favor to ask," Harper says.

"Wow," Tabitha says as they stand at the tee of the third hole. "Look at that view."

Harper nods. The third hole has the finest vista, possibly, on the entire island—across Sengy Pond over the beach with the tip of Chappy visible in the distance. If there is a heaven and Billy has anything to say about it, Harper thinks, it probably looks something like this.

They proceed to the harbor in Oak Bluffs next. Harper finds a parking spot right near the ferry dock—a miracle in itself—and now Tabitha carries the urn. There are tourists *everywhere,* and Harper adjusts her expectations for this venture. It's not going to be a peaceful, profound moment; they should each toss a handful and try not to attract anyone's notice. There are families shopping and eating ice cream, trying to enjoy summer. Nobody wants to be witness to an ersatz funeral.

Harper leads Tabitha down the dock but stops dead in her tracks. There is a motor yacht as white and sculptured as a wedding cake right in front of them, and on the back of the yacht, all dressed up, is Drew Truman amid a gaggle of elegant-looking older black women. *His mother,* Harper thinks, *and the aunties.*

"What's wrong?" Tabitha says. She follows Harper's gaze. "Do you know those ladies? Girlfriends of Billy's? Think they want to join us?"

"No. Keep walking," Harper says, without opening her mouth.

"Why?" Tabitha says. "Look, one of those women is wearing Mother's dress!"

Harper turns. One of the aunties—or maybe it's Yvonne, because she's the one who is standing closest to Drew—is wearing the Roxie in ivory. The dress accentuates Yvonne's waist but still presents a classic silhouette. Harper feels an unexpected surge of pride. Her mother designed something that will last generations beyond her death. How many people can say that?

As they head down the dock, Harper with her head down, there's a sharp whistle, and involuntarily Harper looks up. Drew is waving at her, and... Polly Childs, the Realtor, has suddenly materialized at Drew's side. Polly drapes an arm over Drew's shoulder and gives Harper a finger wave.

"Hey, Harper," Drew says. "Hello, Tabitha!"

"Do I know that guy?" Tabitha asks.

"You met him at Billy's reception," Harper says. "He's the policeman I was sort of dating."

"Looks like he's sort of dating someone else now," Tabitha says. "Sorry, Sis." She grabs Harper's hand, and they walk purposefully down the dock. Tabitha removes the top from the urn, and they reach in for a handful of their father's remains.

"Ready?" Tabitha says. "One, two... three!"

Together they throw the ashes into the air. The powder sparkles like mica.

"We love you, Daddy," Harper says. If the baby is a boy, she decides then, she will name him William.

"If the baby is a boy, you should name him William," Tabitha says.

Harper whips her head around to look at her sister. *You can read my mind?* she nearly asks. *Is this a talent you've had all along?* But she notices that there are tears standing in Tabitha's eyes. Poor Pony.

Harper throws an arm around Tabitha's shoulders. She marvels at how everything in the world is bearable now, with her sister at her side.

MARTHA'S VINEYARD

The most underrated force at work in the universe is that of coincidence. And yet who among us hasn't been at its mercy?

Sadie Zimmer has left the house only when necessary since Reed moved out. She closed the pie shop, has turned down invitations to barbecues and cocktail parties with friends, and has repeatedly said no to joining the Excellent Point book group even though her mother has been relentless in trying to get Sadie to think about something other than her pathetic life circumstances.

"That's the wonderful thing about books," Lydia said. "You get to read about other people's trials and tribulations. Spend an afternoon with Kafka, and you'll be counting your blessings you didn't wake up to find yourself turned into a cockroach."

Sadie doesn't want to read Kafka; she doesn't even want to read Nicholas Sparks or Maria Semple. Sadie wants to wallow in self-pity. It feels good: poring over Reed's cell-phone bills and detailing the number of calls he made to Harper and how long those calls lasted. Stalking Harper on Facebook, although admittedly the offerings there are sparse. Harper hasn't posted anything since she put up a photo of her and her father landing a forty-inch striped bass in 2014 with the caption: *Size matters! Forty inches!* In that photo, Harper is squinting under the brim of a Farm Neck Golf Club visor. She's wearing white cutoff shorts and a man's fishing shirt turned back at the cuffs. Is she pretty? Sadie supposes so, but she has a reputation for trouble—Joey Bowen and all that—and as a doctor, Reed has professional and personal standards to uphold. If he started up with Harper Frost, he must have been desperate. He *was* desperate, Sadie knows, because she froze him out as a husband and as a man. What did she expect—that he was going to live out his adult life without sex? Sadie had had no intention of letting him back into their marital bed. She had been the one who fantasized about leaving Reed. She had an agonizing crush on Tad Morrissey, but she would never have had the courage to act on it—out of fear of rejection and, she supposes, because she worried what her parents would think and how the rest of the island would talk about her.

They are talking about her now, but at least she's cast as the sympathetic victim.

Sadie scrutinizes the photo on Facebook a little while longer. She shifts her focus from Harper to Billy. Sadie had always liked Billy Frost. He had come over to replace some fixtures at the shop way back when. But thinking about this leads to thinking about Harper coming into the store to buy her father a lobster pot pie. Harper had *come into the store!* Had she been sleeping with Reed then? Yes, she had. By his own account, their affair had started in October, and Harper had come into the store in March or April. She had been screwing Sadie's husband for six months, but she had seen nothing wrong with stopping in to get Billy a pie. Probably she had been checking Sadie out.

And what, Sadie wonders, had she thought?

But then one day Sadie wakes up, and she doesn't feel wretched. She actually feels pretty good. It's a beautiful day.

She can walk right across the street to Grange Hall, where they hold the farmer's market. She finds herself craving egg rolls from Khen's. And while she's at it, she'll grab some gladiolus, a bottle of Nicky's olive oil, and some lemon ginger honey from the Martha's Vineyard Honey Company.

The first person Sadie bumps into inside the Ag Hall is Dorrit Prescott, Patti Prescott's mother. Dorrit's face lights up in direct proportion to Sadie's spirits sinking. It's not that Sadie doesn't like Dorrit; Dorrit is a wonderful person. It's just that since Patti's death, however many years ago it was, Dorrit has become intense; she doesn't believe in small talk. She likes to get heavy, deep, and real, even while standing in front of the jelly table at the farmer's market.

"Sadie!" Dorrit cries.

"Hi, Dorrit," Sadie says. She grabs a jar of hot pepper jelly from the table. She suddenly finds herself ravenous after not having had an appetite for weeks. The delicacies of the farmer's market have been within a softball's throw of her house, but she has had no interest in them until today. Now she wants a little of everything—a popover with raspberry butter from Kitchen Porch, a mango lassi from Mermaid Farm, Eidolon cheese from Grey Barn, Vineyard Sunshine granola from Little Rock Farm, rugelach from Beth's Bakery. She doesn't have time for a therapy session with Dorrit Prescott.

Dorrit grasps Sadie's forearm. *Here it comes,* Sadie thinks. She's going to ask about the affair and about Reed leaving. She's going to ask how Sadie is "doing."

"How's Franklin?" Dorrit says. "I heard through the grapevine that he was dating someone from Nantucket. Is that true?"

Franklin? Sadie isn't prepared for a question about Franklin, although it makes sense that Dorrit would ask, since Patti was Franklin's girlfriend and he hasn't dated anyone seriously since Patti killed herself. Sadie can't *believe* that the one person he does have feelings for is Harper's twin sister. It's the most insidious of ironies, the most nefarious of plot twists.

"I hope you tell me it's true," Dorrit says. "All Turk and I want is for Franklin to find someone he loves. He's been through so much. He deserves it."

Sadie nods her agreement. Franklin does deserve it. Back when Patti died, Sadie worried that he would never recover. And then plenty of times in the intervening years Sadie wondered if he would ever fall in love again.

"I'm not sure what's going on with Franklin's love life," Sadie says. This is a bold-faced lie. Sadie does know what's going on with Franklin's love life: nothing. Sadie told Franklin he had to choose between her and Tabitha, and he dutifully chose her, his sister, his family, because that is the kind of solid, loyal person he is.

I am a bitter, miserable ogress, Sadie thinks. Franklin deserves love just like anybody else. More than anybody else.

"It was good seeing you, Dorrit," Sadie says. "I'm going to get some rugelach."

"You need it," Dorrit says. "You're too thin."

Sadie gets the rugelach and a fresh-squeezed OJ from Good Tastes, then she steps into the sun. She'll sit outside and enjoy this feast, then she'll go back in for a popover and a big box of sea-salt caramels from Enchanted Chocolates to take home. Why not? She *is* too thin.

At that instant, she sees Tad Morrissey sitting in the grass by himself with what she recognizes as a nitro cold brew from Chilmark Coffee. He waves her over.

"Come sit with me," he says.

Later, after Sadie puts a dozen gladiolus in water and takes a shower—she's meeting Tad for pizza that night—she sends Franklin a text. It says: *Go be with Tabitha. You have my blessing.*

Reed Zimmer sees Franklin Phelps standing in line at the snack bar on the inter-island ferry, and he wonders if Sadie has sent Franklin to follow him. Why else...honestly, for *what other possible reason* would his brother-in-law, Franklin Phelps, be heading to *Nantucket?*

Reed waits until Franklin is engaged with the girl behind the counter, then he hurries up the stairs and finds a seat in the sun on the upper deck. He leans his head back against the molded plastic chair and promptly falls asleep.

Franklin has brought nothing with him for his trip to Nantucket except his wallet and his guitar.

The wallet provides money with which to buy two beers; he'll have no more than three, he decides. Traveling by ferry to the other island to track down the woman you love is only a grand romantic gesture if you're clear of eye and pure of heart.

The guitar provides Franklin with friends. No sooner has he sat down than he has a trio of teenage girls asking if he knows the song "Here" by Alessia Cara.

"No," he says. "But I do know 'Sunshine' by Jonathan Edwards."

"Never heard of it," says a girl with pink braces. "Do you know any Meghan Trainor?"

"Negative," Franklin says. "I know 'Free Bird' by Lynyrd Skynyrd."

"How about Justin Bieber?" a girl with a pierced eyebrow asks. " 'Love Yourself'?"

"Nope," Franklin says proudly.

They compromise on "Killing Me Softly"—Franklin knows the Roberta Flack version, and the girls know the Fugees' version, and it's fun. The girls are good singers. From there, requests start rolling in. Franklin plays some James Taylor, some Bob Dylan, some Cat Stevens. Soon everyone in his section of the boat is singing, and some guy even offers him a ten-dollar tip. Franklin smiles as he waves the money away. He needs help, all right, but not that kind.

Reed wakes up to a round of applause coming from inside the boat. He blinks his eyes and sits up straight as Nantucket comes into focus. Lighthouse, jetty, big houses along the harbor—it's not so different from the Vineyard, he thinks. He should be fine.

When they dock, he hangs back to let everyone else get off first. If Franklin hangs back as well, then Reed will know he's only there to keep tabs on him. And how will Reed explain this trip? It's folly, really. He received a visit from Harper's twin sister, Tabitha, which almost ended disastrously—but Tabitha admitted her identity in the nick of time and ran from the house. Reed thought that if Tabitha is on the Vineyard, then Harper might be on Nantucket, with their mother.

Reed had scoured the woods behind Aunt Dot's house for his phone. He found it, but it was cold and dead, ruined by moisture. He rode his bike to the library to use a computer and found one Frost listed in the white pages on Nantucket—an Eleanor Roxie-Frost. Is that Harper's mother's name? Yes, he thinks so.

Franklin is lucky enough to get a taxi right away. It's actually offered to him by the parents of one of the teenyboppers in his audience. It's only when Franklin gets into the taxi that he realizes he has no idea where he's going. He checks his phone and sees he has a missed call from Tabitha. It must have come in while he was playing. He nearly calls her back, but then he thinks *how much better* it will be if he just shows up to surprise her.

He leans over the seat. The cabdriver is a middle-aged guy wearing a "Free Brady" T-shirt.

"Do you by any chance know where the Frosts live?" Franklin asks.

The driver nods. "Sure do."

NANTUCKET

Eleanor and Flossie are enjoying their last happy hour together, with Ainsley for company. Eleanor sent Felipa to 167 to get the bluefish paté, the guacamole, and two pounds of shrimp cocktail. Eleanor wants to send Flossie off in style. They're ordering in from the Lobster Trap tonight—surf and turf!

Eleanor raises a glass. "Flossie, I don't know what I ever would have done without you."

Flossie clinks her glass against Eleanor's. "Probably inspired Felipa to murder you in your sleep."

The doorbell rings. Eleanor looks at Ainsley. "Maybe it's your mother, back already. Go see, please, darling."

Ainsley rises, and Flossie says, "I can't believe you make your own daughters ring the bell. Honestly, Ellie, you need to loosen up."

Eleanor disagrees. She's about to inform Flossie that she is loose enough as it is, thank you very much, when Ainsley walks onto the porch escorting a very handsome gentleman holding a guitar.

He bows in front of Eleanor as though she's a queen. Eleanor loves this man already! But who is he? And why the guitar? Eleanor fears this is a singing telegram or a male stripper, something orchestrated by Flossie on her last day in order to loosen Eleanor up.

"I'm Franklin Phelps," the gentleman says. "I've come in search of Tabitha."

"Tabitha?" Eleanor says. Here is the suitor, then! The brother of the woman married to Billy's doctor. Eleanor remembers herself and holds out her hand. "Franklin, I'm Eleanor Roxie-Frost, Tabitha's mother."

"And I'm Flossie," Flossie says, offering her hand. She wants right in on the action, Eleanor sees. Typical Flossie! She can't leave a good-looking male alone. "I'm Tabitha's aunt."

"Nice to meet you both," Franklin says.

"I told him Mom's not here," Ainsley says. "She's on the Vineyard."

"Comedy of errors," Franklin says. "I just came from the Vineyard."

"She'll be right back," Eleanor says. "By morning, anyway. You might as well sit tight right here. I'll have Felipa make up the guest room."

"I couldn't impose," Franklin says.

"I want you to impose!" Eleanor says.

"Me, too!" Flossie says.

Eleanor turns to Flossie, trying not to let her impatience with her flirtatious younger sister show. "Can we offer Franklin a drink, Flossie?"

"We can!" Flossie says. "What's your poison, Franklin?"

"A beer would be wonderful," Franklin says. "Or a whiskey, if you don't have beer."

"Whiskey it is," Eleanor says. She waves Flossie away to fetch the drink. "Please sit, Franklin. And then tell us what it is you do for a living. Are you a professional musician?"

"I play the guitar for fun," Franklin says. He settles in the armchair opposite Eleanor and places the guitar case at his feet. "By trade I'm a carpenter. I have my own construction business. I'm helping Tabitha and Harper renovate Billy's house."

Eleanor claps her hands. "Well, when you're finished with

that, you can renovate *my* house," she says. She casts her eyes around. What could use a spruce-up? Surely there must be something.

Flossie returns with Franklin's drink. "The house is perfect as it is, Ellie," Flossie says. She winks at Franklin. "That's just Eleanor's way of saying she likes you."

Eleanor is embarrassed by this statement, although she does indeed like this gentleman—he's adorable! Eleanor didn't think she would ever like anyone as much as she liked Ramsay Striker, but she's pleased to see she was wrong about that.

The doorbell rings again.

"Grand Central Station," Flossie mutters.

Ainsley stands up. "Maybe that's Mom."

But the person Ainsley brings into the glassed-in porch next is another gentleman caller. This one is bespectacled and a bit more buttoned-up: khaki pants, custom-tailored shirt (Eleanor knows bespoke when she sees it), and suede Gucci loafers. Ainsley looks like she's popped a whole habanero pepper unwittingly into her mouth. She's pink, and her eyes are bulging.

Cute Franklin gets to his feet. "Reed?"

The new caller turns to Eleanor. "Hello, ma'am. I'm Dr. Reed Zimmer. I'm looking for Harper."

"Harper?" Eleanor says. She gasps. "Are you the father, then?"

"Father?" Franklin says.

The doctor blanches. *"Father?"* he says.

"The father," Flossie says in clarification. "Of Harper's baby. She's pregnant, you know."

It's clear from the misty look that comes over the doctor's

face that he *doesn't* know. Leave it to Flossie to let the cat out of the bag, Eleanor thinks. The moment of everyone's speechless shock gives Eleanor a chance to compare and contrast the two gentlemen before her. Franklin, with his darling mussed hair and his flip-flops, seems like he would be more Harper's type. And this Dr. Zimmer, with his glasses and his bespoke shirt, seems like he would be more Tabitha's type. But apparently it's the other way around.

There is nothing more mysterious, confounding, and unknowable, Eleanor thinks, than the desires of the human heart.

"Flossie," she says. "Can't you see the man needs a drink?" To the doctor, Eleanor says, "Please sit down. And try the bluefish paté. It's wonderful."

EPILOGUE: FISH

His is a life of the senses, but over the course of his twelve and a half years—or eighty-seven and a half years, depending on who's counting—he has also developed other intelligences. He has become savvy with places—both new and familiar—and with the circadian rhythms of day, night, and season, but mostly he has become adept at reading human emotion. If he were ever granted the ability to speak, he would spend half his time asking questions—*Why wear clothes? Why use utensils? Why litter?*—and the other half explaining people to themselves.

When the weather cools down and the days grow shorter, Harper's shape starts to change, then her scent starts to change. Harper packs up their things—again—and Fish wonders if they're going back to the other island for good. But instead they take the barge to Chappy. Harper moves them into a cottage that smells strongly of the Surfer. Fish races around the house looking for the Surfer but finds nothing except a sock under the bed. He brings the sock to Harper, and she lets out a soft cry.

The Surfer is replaced by the Doctor. The Doctor is around

a little bit at first, then more often, then all the time. He becomes the one who lets Fish out in the morning and before bed. Harper, however, still takes Fish for long walks—now on East Beach. Fish loves East Beach. It's replete with dead crabs and seaweed, snails, mermaid's purses, scraps of picnic. As Harper walks him she says things like, "What am I *doing,* Fish? What am I *doing?* I don't know anything about being a mother."

If Fish could talk, he would tell Harper she's wrong. She has been the kindest, most steadfast mother he could have dreamed of.

Sometimes when Harper, Fish, and the Doctor are together lounging on the sofa or watching TV and Harper falls asleep, the doctor will take Fish's head in his hands and stare him straight in the eyes. "I'm telling you, man-to-man," he says. "I will take care of her. I will take care of her and you, and I will take care of that baby."

Fish supposes he should register surprise at the news of a baby, but his is a life of the senses, so he has already figured out there is a baby coming. He's already felt a second heartbeat thrumming in his ear as he lays his head on Harper's belly. And then, only a day or two ago, he felt a kick. Instead of being affronted, Fish was flattered. The baby was reaching out. The baby, he guesses, will be his friend, possibly the most excellent friend he has ever known.

A day arrives that seems important. There are balloons, presents, a cake delivered from someone named the Tiny Baker, who is, in fact, tiny and who brings a pug named Lucy Bean with her. Lucy Bean barks at Fish and bares her teeth as Tiny Baker hands over the cake. Fish merely shakes his head; pugs are difficult to take seriously.

It's not Baby Day, he doesn't think. He soon learns it's Harper's birthday, her fortieth birthday. She and the Doctor and Fish and Edie, the Surfer's mother, will celebrate—light the candles, sing, eat cake—but there is something Harper must do first. She and Fish drive out to Cape Poge alone. Fish is confused. Harper has forgotten to bring her fishing pole.

"I know this may seem crazy," Harper says. "But I'm going to wish Tabitha a happy birthday. She's standing on the beach at Ram Pasture, on Nantucket, and she is going to wish me a happy birthday."

Fish stares off into the distance. All he sees is water.

"With me on Cape Poge and Tabitha at Ram Pasture, we are as physically close as we can get while still remaining on our respective islands," Harper says. She touches her protruding midsection. "She and Franklin are coming over on Friday so that we can close on Billy's house, but that isn't our actual birthday. It's imperative we do this today." She checks Billy's watch on her wrist. "I call out to her at three twelve, because that's when Pony was born. Pony will call out to me at three fourteen, because that's when I was born."

Harper cups her hands around her mouth and shouts, "Happy birthday, Tabitha!"

Fish stares off into the distance. Water and more water. People are nuts, he thinks. Even Harper.

But then, just about ninety seconds later, Fish cocks his head. It's faint—possibly he's projecting. But no, it's real—a voice nearly identical to the one he hears every day, but just a little bit different. It's a nuance only a very perceptive dog would notice.

"Happy birthday, Harper! Happy, happy birthday!"

Fish barks.

ACKNOWLEDGMENTS

I am a twin. I am not, however, an "identical"; I'm a "fraternal." I have a twin brother named Eric Hilderbrand. Our mother named me Elin (pronounced "Ellen") but spelled it in this unusual way, causing forty-seven years of confusion, because of our Swedish ancestry...and because she wanted my name to be perfectly symmetrical with my twin brother's name. Eric and I have always been very close, but I have chosen to dedicate this novel to all of my siblings. We are a blended family of five, together since 1976. After Eric and me in the order comes my stepbrother, Randall Osteen ("Randy," "Rand," "the Bean"), who is absolutely one of the greatest guys in the world, despite early-warning signs that he would be troubled (he was a fan of the Quebec Nordiques, he refused to eat cranberry sauce with "can indentations," and don't get me started on the galoshes he chose to wear during the infamous Hilderbrand family Easter egg hunt). Rand is my usual partner in crime at Jazzfest in New Orleans, so we have secrets from the rest of the family. After Randy comes my stepsister, Heather Osteen Thorpe. Heather is my biggest champion, my loudest cheerleader, my everyday best friend. Did we dress up as ducks and perform roller-skating shows in the basement? Yes. Did I take her to fraternity parties at Johns Hopkins when she was fifteen years old and the standing president of SADD? Yes. No matter how low I get, I know I will never sink, because I have Heather. She is my buoy and my light. At the end of the line is my brother Douglas Hilderbrand, the youngest and most sensitive of us all. Doug reads all my novels and will nearly always call me crying when he finishes because the emotional terrain I choose to write about resonates profoundly within him. He has also been known to cry over certain Dan Fogelberg songs.

I could not have handpicked four finer human beings to have shared my childhood memories with: digging the hermit crab pools, badminton games, collecting beach glass and scallop shells, fighting for the outdoor shower, executing the old "round the apple tree" play in family games of football, home movies, writing letters to Santa, orchestrating elaborate ploys to get out of church, watching *The Love Boat,* blaring Foreigner's "Hot Blooded" in the car—and years later, throwing our first parents-aren't-home party (the details of which will remain in the vault for at least another decade, but I'll say this: it involves cigars ground up in the garbage disposal). As adults, my siblings are not only exemplary citizens and my closest friends, they are also remarkable parents—collectively, of ten children. We lost our captain—my father—when all of us were in the midst of adolescence, but not one of us veered off course. Our relationship with one another set a solid, even foundation that we were able to build our respective lives upon.

I could never have written this novel without the generosity and open-mindedness of the people of Martha's Vineyard.

Of special note is the police chief of Oak Bluffs, Erik Blake. Erik answered hundreds of questions for me over the course of fifteen months; my debt of gratitude to him is enormous and eternal. I want to also thank Erica McCarron a.k.a. the "Tiny Baker," Steve Caillhane, Mark and Gwenn Snider, Liza May Cowan, and all of the members of the Facebook group "Islanders Talk." I had thought that as a Nantucket novelist writing about the Vineyard, I might be looked at askance—but nothing could have been further from the truth. Over the course of the past year and a half, I have a brand-new love, understanding, and appreciation of Martha's Vineyard and all the wonderful, generous, thoughtful people who live there.

A third location in this novel—one more deeply explored in the extra chapter entitled "The Country Club," about Billy Frost meeting Eleanor Roxie in 1967 (available in certain editions of this book)—is Beacon Hill in Boston. I spend six weeks each fall living on Beacon Hill, and I would like to thank the people who make it feel like home: Paul Kosak and Anouk van der Boor, Julie Girschek, Michael Farina, Nina Castellion of E. R. Butler, Tom Kershaw of the Hampshire House, my barre buddy Liz King, Jennifer Hill from Blackstone's, and Rebecca, Laura, and Brie of Crush. (I revise… and I also do a fair amount of shopping.)

As I've told you countless times before, my editor, Reagan Arthur, is an actual genius. She runs the company, Little, Brown, that publishes me, and she still finds time to be the editor of my dreams and take nature photos for Instagram. My agents, Michael Carlisle and David Forrer, are devoted to the happiness and well-being of Elin Hilderbrand the novelist and of Elin Hilderbrand the person—for this, I could not love them more; they are the finest gentlemen in the business. Special kudos to my killer publicity team of Katharine Myers and Alyssa Persons, as well as other super important people at Hachette: Peggy Freudenthal, Terry Adams, Craig Young, Matt Carlini, Andy LeCount, and the legendary Michael Pietsch.

And then there's my home team. I feel silly repeating the names year after year, but I can't live, write, or smile without the following people: Rebecca Bartlett, Debbie Briggs, Wendy Hudson, Wendy Rouillard, Margie and Chuck Marino, Anne and Whitney Gifford, Richard Congdon, Elizabeth and Beau Almodobar, Evelyn and Matthew MacEachern, Heidi and Fred Holdgate, Norm and Jen Frazee, Jen and Steve Laredo, John and Martha Sargent, Dave and Laura Lombardi, Manda Riggs, David Rattner and Andrew Law, Shelly and Roy Weedon, Helaina Jones, MKF, the Timothy Fields, big and small, and Ginna, Paul, and Christian Kogler. Also, the entire staff of the Nantucket Hotel deserves mention because it is, without doubt, my home away from home, and large portions of this novel were written by the pool there.

Beth Boucher, you get your own few lines: I've had superlative nannies in the past (Za, AV, Steph, Sarah, Erin), but you took on a job more daunting than theirs because of the incendiary ages of my children last summer (sixteen, fourteen, ten). Who wants to keep track of a sixteen-year-old boy? Nobody! A fourteen-year-old boy? Absolutely nobody! Thank you, Beth. You kept them alive, you kept them content, you kept them engaged. They preferred you to me—which is, of course, the whole point of hiring a nanny.

Lu Machiavelli: You are a flower-box maven! I don't even know what those flowers are in Eleanor's windows, but they sound outrageous!

Finally to my children, Maxwell, Dawson, and Shelby: This is both a thank-you and an apology. Writing two novels a year requires discipline and solitude, neither of which is optimal for parenting three busy kids. This past year there were balls dropped, games missed, tempers lost, and meals repeated week after week (as Dawson likes to say, *You always make the same three things!*). But please know that with every word I write, I honor the three of you as well as the incredibly beautiful island on which you are growing up. I am lucky for so many reasons—but mostly I am lucky to have three smart, talented, healthy, and thriving children like you.

ELIN HILDERBRAND

Here's to Us

Laurel Thorpe, Belinda Rowe and Scarlett Oliver share only two things in common: a love for the man they all married, celebrity chef Deacon Thorpe, and a passionate dislike of one another.

When Deacon shockingly takes his own life, the women must come together in order to see out his final wish: to have his whole dysfunctional family – wives, children and all – return to his favourite place on earth, the idyllic eastern bluff of Nantucket.

But with everyone under one roof, putting differences aside will be no simple feat. Each wants to claim a special place in Deacon's life. And yet, as certain secrets are revealed and confidences shared, improbable bonds will begin to form, as this unlikely family says goodbye to the man they loved.

Out now

HODDER

ELIN HILDERBRAND

The Rumour

Nantucket writer Madeline King has a new novel coming out and it's got bestseller potential. But Madeline is terrified, because in her desperation to revive her career, she's done something reckless: revealed the truth behind an actual affair involving her best friend, Grace.

And that's not the only strain on Madeline and Grace's friendship; one fateful night, the two women argue, voicing jealousies and resentments that have built for twenty years. Bereft of each other, they get caught in the snares of a mysterious and destructive stranger.

THE RUMOUR is an irresistible novel about the power of gossip to change the course of events, and the desire of people to find their way back to what really matters.

Out now